LIPSTICK ON HIS COLLAR

'I'd give my right arm to be in your place. I mean knowing all the right people, having all the right doors open for you.'

'But that's the problem. I'll never know if I was good enough to get there on my own.'

Olivia leaned back in her chair and looked at Hallie over her wine glass. 'Screw getting there on your own, honey. Getting there is all that counts.'

Elizabeth Villars is a fulltime writer whose six previous novels include *Wars of the Heart* and *The Normandie Affair*. She has also worked in the publicity department of a major American publishing house — an experience that proved invaluable in the writing of *Lipstick On His Collar*. She lives in New York City.

Lipstick On His Collar

Elizabeth Villars

HEADLINE

Copyright © 1990 Elizabeth Villars

The right of Elizabeth Villars to be identified as the author
of the work has been asserted by her in accordance with the
Copyright, Designs and Patents Act 1988

First published in Great Britain in 1990
by Simon and Schuster UK Ltd

First published in paperback in 1990
by HEADLINE BOOK PUBLISHING PLC

10 9 8 7 6 5 4 3 2 1

Grateful acknowledgements to the publishers of
'Thanks for the Memory' by Leo Robin and Ralph Rainger
for permission to reprint lyrics. 'Thanks for the Memory' –
Copyright © 1937 by Paramount Music Corporation.
Copyright renewed 1964 by Paramount Music Corporation.

ISBN 0 7472 3463 9

Typeset by Avocet Robinson, Buckingham
Printed and bound in Great Britain by
Collins, Glasgow

HEADLINE BOOK PUBLISHING PLC
Headline House
79 Great Titchfield Street
London W1P 7FN

for Lewis
and, of course, for Stephen

BOOK
ONE

I

The week Hallie Porter made the cover of *Time* magazine, she found out her husband was sleeping with her best friend. It was funny she hadn't figured it out sooner. The affair had been going on for three months. Maybe she'd been too distracted to notice. Or maybe they'd suddenly become careless because she'd been so distracted.

Actually, they'd been less careless than downright dumb, at least for two intelligent people. Jake had a mind like an IBM mainframe. Behind clear blue eyes, innocent as a morning sky, Olivia's worked more like a calculator. Yet those two whiz kids had been setting up an assignation on an extension that rang a few feet from Hallie's office. Both of them should have known better. Both of them should have known Hallie better.

The firm's stationery, *Literary Market Place*, and the cover of *Time* all identified Hallie as publisher, but despite the title, she was still incapable of doing what any secretary at Rutherford and Styles carried off with ease. Hallie couldn't walk past a ringing phone without picking it up. That night in September she picked up the phone ringing on the secretary's desk outside the office of Olivia Collins, her editor in chief and, until then, best friend. Olivia picked it up in her office at the same time.

Hallie recognized Jake's voice immediately. 'I'm going to be a little late tonight,' he said.

Hallie started to answer. It was a reflex. She'd forgotten she was talking on someone else's phone. Olivia beat her to it.

'Oh, honey,' she wailed.

Improbable as it seemed later, Hallie still wasn't worried. Olivia had a thick Southern drawl that Jake loved to mimic and a habit of calling everyone from her manicurist to agents, which Jake happened to be, 'honey.' Besides, there were a dozen legitimate reasons for them to be getting together for a drink after work.

'I should be able to make it by seven,' Jake said.

'I'll leave the door open,' Olivia answered.

Hallie put her hand over the mouthpiece of the phone. She was sure they could hear her breathing.

'Where will you be?' Jake asked.

'In bed,' Olivia said. 'Waiting.'

'In that case, I'll definitely be there by seven.'

'You'd better be, honey.' Olivia's laugh, like her voice, was pitched low and quiet. Men often had to lean closer to hear her. 'Or I'll start without you.'

Hallie knew it was a cliché – not only Olivia's line but the whole mess. Precedent, however, didn't apply. At that moment, Hallie was sure no one in the world had ever hurt the way she was hurting. What Hallie did next was a cliché, too. She went into the ladies room and threw up her expensive expense-account lunch.

Afterward she was sorry she hadn't brought the toothbrush she kept in the lower drawer of her desk. She rinsed her mouth out with cold water, but it didn't help. The bitter taste lingered.

Back in her office, she closed the door and sat behind the desk. Nothing in the room had changed in the past five minutes. The line of recent best sellers still marched across one shelf of the overflowing bookcases. Two manuscripts still sat on one side of her desk. Several ads still lay on the conference table, waiting for her approval. The out box was still full of printouts and papers. The in box still overflowed with problems awaiting her decisions. The Chrysler Building was still glowing in the streak of late-afternoon sunshine beyond her window. Nothing had changed, except that now it all seemed to be at a tilt. Or maybe that was Hallie, because suddenly she felt so dizzy she had to clutch the arms of her swivel chair to keep from falling out of it.

There was a knock at the door. A voice that sounded strange in Hallie's ears said, 'Come in.'

Olivia opened the door and looked around the room in surprise. It was an informal company. They closed office doors only for meetings.

'You working late or hiding?' Olivia drawled and pushed the mass of blond ringlets that was always tumbling over her forehead out of her eyes.

Hallie did something then that surprised her. She acted as if nothing had happened.

5

'I swore I was going to break the back of this manuscript tonight.' She put her hand on top of one of the boxes on her desk. She wondered if Olivia had seen it shaking.

Olivia hefted her new T. Anthony briefcase. It was overflowing with work, and Hallie knew it wasn't just for show. Jake would leave her bed by nine, ten at the latest. That would give Olivia plenty of time to look at a manuscript or two. She took her work seriously.

'Me too. Only I'm going to take them to bed.' She gave Hallie a mock salute with her free hand and started down the hall. 'It's where I do my best work, honey.'

Hallie sat absolutely still while Olivia's footsteps disappeared down the hall. She should have confronted her. She should have fired her. For a moment she even thought of calling her back. But she didn't, because she knew that if she started out accusing Olivia, she'd end up disgracing herself with tears and screams and the whole wronged-wife tirade. It would be like undressing in public. Everyone would see the flaws.

She continued to sit silently in the empty office until she heard the elevator doors open and close. Finally she stood, walked to her office door, and closed it. Only then, only when she was sure she was alone, did she begin to cry.

The door to the bathroom, like every other door and wall in the jerry-built postwar building, was paper thin. From the kitchen, Olivia often heard the baby in 8A crying. Sometimes it went on for hours and made her wonder why people had kids. From the bedroom, she frequently heard the two men in 8C making love. James was a screamer. Now, lying in bed and listening to Jake singing in the shower, she thought about Hallie's apartment. All those prewar Park Avenue buildings had walls like the Rock of Gibraltar. The brass canopies sparkled like gold and the concierges and doormen wore dark green livery the color of money. Olivia's gum-chewing doorman wore a threadbare gray jacket and called her 'babe.'

On the other side of the bathroom door, Jake switched tunes. At least, Olivia thought he did. It was hard to tell, because he wasn't so much singing as humming offkey. It sounded like someone keening, and it drove her crazy. But not as crazy as what she knew she was going to see when he came out of the shower and back into the bedroom.

He did it every time. He'd get out of the shower, grab a towel, and come into the room, still humming in that maddening way or talking to her about some book deal. The water would be streaming down his long beautiful body onto the cheap carpet, but his thick dark hair would be bone dry. Because he was going home to Hallie. Every time Olivia saw that dry hair she wanted to slap him.

She got out of bed and crossed the small, cluttered bedroom to the bathroom. The door squeaked a little, but Jake couldn't hear it above the sound of the water and his damn keening. She pulled aside the shower curtain and stepped into the tub.

His back was to her. She put her arms around his

waist. He stopped humming and laughed. Her hands trailed south. His conscience might be thinking about getting home to Hallie, but his body had other intentions. He turned toward her. His skin was smooth and slippery. He smelled of soap. He tasted of Scotch. He never lost his balance for a minute.

When it was over they lathered each other again. Olivia looked up at Jake. He had a sweet, satiated smile on his face. And his hair – goddamn him! – his hair was still dry.

II

Hallie let herself into the apartment. She'd known it would be empty. A true Southerner, Olivia was the languid type. And Jake was not a man given to quickies. The idea made her stomach flip over again. She went into the bathroom and threw up the rest of her lunch. This time she brushed her teeth afterward, but it didn't help. Her stomach ached, her throat was raw, and the acrid taste of her own bile remained.

Her shoes clicked down the long parquet hall. The sound made her think of her father's typewriter echoing through the enforced silences of her childhood. Everything in that household – conversation, laughter, even anger – had stopped dead when the great writer had sat down to work. Hallie had learned the art of self-control at an early and impressionable age.

She stood in the doorway to the living room. She'd taken such pride in this room, their home. Now she saw it for what it was. The two sofas facing each other in front of the fireplace looked overstuffed, the gleaming surfaces overpolished, the massive

9

sprays of flowers in the huge Chinese vases overdone. The room could have stepped out of the pages of *Architectural Digest*. It was that unlived in.

She sank into the sofa. It was so deep she thought she'd drown. She picked up the copy of *Times* he'd tossed onto the coffee table. Her own picture stared back at her from the cover. She tried to look at it objectively, but she knew you could never be objective about something like that. She told herself the pale skin wasn't washed out against the dark eyes and thick eyebrows, merely dramatic. Though the black hair was hopelessly straight, it was thick. But there were no excuses for the sharp nose and wide mouth. At some publication party or awards dinner, she'd once overheard two agents talking about her in the ladies' room. One had called her a barracuda. Hallie hadn't minded the reference to her business acumen, but after the other two women had left the room, she'd come out of the stall and sat staring at her reflection for a long time.

Hallie opened the magazine to the article on 'The New Breed of Publisher.' She'd already read the piece when it first arrived in her office, but that had been before she'd picked up Olivia's phone. Hallie had loved the article then, and it had loved her back.

There were several pictures. 'Putting the style back in Rutherford and Styles' read a caption under a photograph of Hallie in her office. 'To the manner born'. was the line under the picture of a chubby seven-year-old Hallie playing croquet with her father, Amos, at the farm in Connecticut. 'A pride of literary lions' ran under a photograph of Quentin

Styles. A picture of Will Sawyer, taken from the dust jacket of his most recent best seller, crested another caption. 'Holding hands and a blue pencil simultaneously.' The handholding was strictly metaphorical. A sultry Olivia smiled out over the words 'Sharing the rewards.' Elsewhere in the article Olivia was quoted as saying there was no truth to the rumors. It wasn't like working for Lucrezia Borgia. Hallie Porter was demanding but fair.

Then there were the pictures of Hallie and Jake. One had been taken at an opera benefit. Jake was devoted to a lot of good causes. He liked to put on his Paul Stuart tuxedo for the New York City Ballet and the Metropolitan Museum and the Globe Theater in London. He was wearing the tuxedo in the picture and, of course, he looked sensational in it. That was Jake's secret weapon. Not that he was handsome, but that he was so handsome everyone took him for a lightweight. By the time they found out he wasn't, it was too late. He was smiling that white, shark's-teeth smile, but the way his eyes crinkled made it look okay, even genuine. One beautiful, long hand was resting on her bare shoulder. Hallie wondered now how she'd ever let Jake talk her into that dress. Women with big breasts – even bony, angular women with big breasts – shouldn't wear strapless sheaths. 'Couple clout' the caption said. Hallie felt her stomach heave, though she knew there was nothing left in it. She turned the page.

It was even worse. A picture taken at the farm showed her and Jake stretched out at opposite ends of a chintz-covered sofa, their eyes on the

11

manuscripts on their laps and their feet touching. There was snow outside the windows, and you knew there had to be a fire in the hearth even though you couldn't see the fireplace. It was that kind of picture. 'A working marriage' the caption said.

She heard Jake's key in the lock, heard the door open and close, but from where she was sitting in the living room she couldn't see into the foyer. There was the sound of a briefcase hitting the floor, then a few seconds of silence. It was late September, too early for him to be wearing a coat to take off. Maybe he was checking himself in the hall mirror, though she knew he would have done that before he left Olivia's. Hallie pictured him snapping those damn hand-painted suspenders into place, checking his collar for lipstick, his dark pin-stripe suit for blond hairs. She wondered what he did about showering. He was too fastidious to come home without it, too smart to walk in with that thick dark hair slicked down with water.

Hallie watched him enter the living room. He gave her one of those big shark smiles. Only a guilty man could smile that way. He bent to kiss her. She turned her cheek.

'You're awfully dour . . .' he said.

When she'd met Jake, he'd pronounced the word to rhyme with *sour*. He'd had trouble pronouncing a lot of words in those days, because he'd learned them from books rather than conversation.

He picked the magazine up off her lap. '. . . for a woman who just made the cover of *Time*.'

He studied the picture. 'It's good.' He looked from

12

the magazine to Hallie and laughed. 'Serious but sexy.'

He started to flip through the magazine. 'Christ!' he said when he got to the picture of the two of them at the opera. 'Would you buy a used car from that man?'

She saw his eye move to the facing page. 'It's a good picture of Olivia,' she said.

'It's okay.'

'You mean you think she's even better looking than that?'

He didn't answer, just turned another page. 'I like this one,' he said when he got to the picture of the two of them in the library at the farm.

'Did she start without you?' Hallie asked.

He looked up from the magazine. He wasn't smiling anymore, but his eyes were clear and level. Hallie thought they looked just the way they did when he was trying to get an editor to raise a bid on a book he was auctioning off.

'What do you mean?'

'I mean, did Olivia start without you? You said you were going to be late, and she warned you not to be too late or she'd start without you. It's a pretty old line. I thought she could do better.'

He sat on the sofa opposite Hallie and put the magazine on the table between them.

'Do you want to tell me what you're talking about?'

'You mean, how much do I know?'

She didn't tell him how much she knew. She threw the magazine at him.

*   *   *

Jake followed her into the bedroom. There was a faint red mark on his cheek where the magazine had hit him.

Hallie went back out to the hall. He followed her there. She went into the kitchen. Her hands were shaking so badly she dropped the ice tray. He picked it up. And all the time he kept talking. She was jumping to conclusions. He'd met Olivia for a drink. That line had been a joke. They'd gone over the contract for that diet book. The more he talked, the more certain Hallie was. She'd learned a long time ago that one lie was better than a dozen.

She took her drink into the bedroom. He followed her there. She sat on her side of the bed and put her glass on the night table. That was when she saw it. She put her head in her hands and began to cry. Again.

Jake moved from the door to the bed and put his arm around her. She jumped up and jostled the night table. A pile of books tumbled to the floor. Her drink sloshed over onto the wood. But the thermometer and the chart with all the numbers carefully filled in just lay there, reminding her of everything she'd lost.

That morning's reading had been higher than the others. She'd been fertile. The timing had been right. They'd taken good advantage of it. It had been after ten by the time Hallie reached her office. She wondered now if he'd been thinking of Olivia all that time.

'Leave me alone!' Hallie screamed.

'No,' Jake said quietly.

14

She threw the chart to their unborn child at him. 'Maybe that was the problem,' she shouted. 'You were servicing too many accounts!'

He bent to pick up the chart from the floor. He couldn't face her on that one, because he knew how much she wanted that baby. Maybe he had hurt their chances, but then she'd hurt their chances, too.

He put the chart back on the night table. 'Servicing is right,' he said quietly. 'Like a printer or an advertising agency. But if you could have done it without me – if Superwoman could have had Superkid on her own – there's no way I could have kept you in bed till ten o'clock on a weekday morning.'

'Get out.'

'And that's another thing.' His voice was rising now. He was losing the battle to control his own anger. 'Don't ever tell Superwoman she isn't perfect.'

'I wasn't the one who was screwing around!'

They stood staring at each other, and for the first time they felt a terrible stillness between them.

Hallie broke it with another shout. 'Get out!'

'Hallie.' His voice was hoarse. It had sounded the same way in bed that morning. She wondered suddenly if he'd had to concentrate to keep from slipping and calling her Olivia.

'All right,' she screamed, 'if you won't go, I will.'

She started down the hall to the front door. Her heel caught on the runner. She stumbled, steadied herself against the wall, raced ahead. She yanked

15

open the front door. He pushed it closed. They stood staring at each other. The stillness had become a deadness.

'All right,' he said. 'I'll go.'

It had started to rain. The automobile tires racing down Park Avenue made a sizzling sound on the pavement.

'Taxi, Mr Fox?'

Jake stared at the doorman for a moment, as if he couldn't understand the words. 'No,' he said finally. 'No, Louie, I think I'll walk.'

He started down Park. He felt the doorman staring after him. Louie knew he was a practical man, not the kind who walked in the rain without a trench coat or umbrella. But Jake wasn't that practical. He wasn't the kind of man who stopped for personal effects when his wife threw him out.

Olivia's apartment was only a few blocks away. She'd take him in, pour him a drink, open her arms, take off her clothes, and his. The thought should have made him feel better. It made him feel rotten. He wondered what Hallie was doing back in the empty apartment.

'Hell!'

He didn't realize he'd spoken aloud until a woman with an umbrella walking a Lhasa apso in a raincoat turned to stare.

Jake kept walking. The rain ran down his neck. He thought of Hallie curled up in bed, a manuscript on her knees, a wall of them beside her.

He stopped at a telephone on the corner of

Seventy-ninth and Park and dialed Olivia's number.

'Hi, honey,' she said as soon as she heard his voice. Jake recognized the pleasure in hers and knew it wasn't only from the fact that he was calling her, but from the misconception that he was calling her from home.

Jake didn't kid himself. He'd slid into this affair backwards. The prevailing passion had been anger rather than love. He'd been furious at Hallie. Olivia had simply turned up at the right time. At first, he'd been besotted. It had been a long time – seven years of marriage and four before that, to be exact – since he'd slept with another woman. And in the other-woman department, Olivia was no slouch. Gradually his vision had cleared. He even tried to break the affair off. Jake hated all the illicit trappings, but Olivia thrived on them. She got a kick out of meeting him with Hallie and pretending that they hadn't separated only minutes before. She liked making him tell her things in front of Hallie that he'd already told her when they were alone. She couldn't resist brushing against him accidentally in front of other people and pressing her leg to his under a table. She loved all the clandestine cruelty. Maybe it was because she still felt like an outsider. Maybe it was because she was jealous of Hallie. Jake wasn't sure why. All he knew was that Olivia took to those tiny deceptions like a veteran spy in a Le Carré novel.

She heard the street traffic before he could explain anything. 'You're not calling from home.' He recognized the disappointment in her voice.

He told her everything. Well, not everything. Just

17

that Hallie had overheard their conversation and thrown him out.

'You poor baby,' Olivia said, but her mind was clicking ahead. She wondered if she was winning Jake and losing her job at the same time. It wasn't fair. She'd worked hard for that job. She'd worked hard to make something of herself. And now Hallie, who'd never had to lift a finger for anything, was going to take it all away.

Not without a fight, Olivia swore. She needed a strategy. And for that she need more information. 'Come on up,' she said.

He'd been right. Hallie didn't want him, but Olivia did. Only right now Olivia was the last thing he wanted. He couldn't tell her that.

'I don't think it would be wise.'

'Wise? Honey, when have we ever been wise?'

'Maybe we ought to start now.' He said something about ugly divorces. He mentioned the words *settlement* and *alimony*. And she believed him.

Why shouldn't she, Jake thought as he began walking south again. Jake Fox was known to be a smart operator, a wily negotiator, a man who knew that the only place for sentiment was on the flap describing some steamy romantic novel.

Olivia hung up the phone, went into the kitchen to pour herself a glass of wine, and carried it back to the bedroom. The sheets were tangled, and a pillow lay on the floor.

She wished Jake had come back. He'd been elusive on the phone. It made her nervous. Olivia had the

18

feeling they were building a sacrificial fire. She'd be damned if she was going to be the offering.

There was a thumping sound, then a shriek on the other side of the wall. James and Brian were at it again.

On second thought, it might be better that Jake wasn't spending the night. She knew what she had to do in the morning, and she had to do it early.

BOOK
TWO

III

Hallie Porter's first meeting with Olivia Collins was prophetic. Hallie caught Olivia red handed. They were at a publication party for a self-help book that promised a happier life through thinner thighs. At that time neither of them needed the book, but both of them were determined to make the most of the party. They were fresh out of college and working as editorial assistants. That meant that each evening, when they finished their secretarial duties for their respective editors, they got to take manuscripts home to read and evaluate. Hallie was putting in her overtime for Slater House, a venerable publisher where her father, Amos, and her godfather, Quentin Styles, had agreed she should learn the ropes before coming over to Rutherford and Styles. Olivia had landed a job at Apogee Books, a brash young hardcover house that had grown out of a flashy paperback operation.

The party was winding down, and Hallie was on her way out of the room when she noticed a woman with blond curls she would have killed for stuffing something into her handbag. It was a Hermes handbag that, Hallie learned later, Olivia had received the previous Christmas from a man overcome with guilt for having left Olivia alone during the holidays while he took his wife and children south. Even the props were prophetic that night.

Olivia didn't notice Hallie at first. She was too busy stuffing another napkin full of hors d'oeuvres into her handbag. Then she must have felt someone staring at her, because she looked up. Their eyes met. Olivia didn't even blush. She clicked the bag closed and held out her hand.

'Hi, I'm Olivia Collins, Apogee.'

Hallie took her hand. 'Hallie Porter, Slater House.'

Olivia went on staring at Hallie. 'You're Amos Porter's daughter.'

Hallie stared back at her. She'd never learned how to avoid the anger, but she'd learned how to camouflage it. That early training in self-discipline had paid off. 'And you must be Mr Collins's little girl.' She turned and started toward the door again.

'Hey!' Olivia caught up with her. 'I didn't mean anything by it.'

Hallie kept walking. 'Neither did I.'

Olivia stopped walking. 'I heard you were a bitch. They didn't say you were a snob, too.'

Hallie turned and walked the few steps to Olivia. 'I'm sorry.'

'No sweat. Look, you want to go someplace and get something to eat?'

Hallie pointed to the Hermes bag. 'I thought you'd already taken care of dinner.'

'That'll keep till tomorrow night. I'd rather talk, compare notes. I don't know anyone at Slater.' Olivia frowned. 'Oops, I forgot. I can't go out. Tomorrow's payday, and I've got exactly a dollar seventy-five and two subway tokens to my name. I'd ask you to come to my place and share my ill-gotten goods' – she hefted the handbag – 'but my place, such as it is, is in Hoboken.'

Hallie would never have considered it if her parents had been in town – they cast a long enough shadow without trucking people home to meet them – but Cecelia and Amos were in Barbados with Amos's portable typewriter.

'Why don't you come to my place? There's bound to be something in the fridge.'

Olivia followed Hallie into the entrance hall of the townhouse and glanced around at the Queen Anne chairs, the Sheraton table, and the Mary Cassatt painting hanging over it. Her eyes finally came to rest on Hallie.

'It's my parents' house,' Hallie explained. 'I'm just staying here till I can afford a place of my own.'

'Sure.'

Hallie didn't bother to answer. There was nothing she could say. It wasn't hard to exist on an editorial assistant's salary when you lived in your father's house and had a mother who couldn't walk into Bergdorf's or Saks without picking up something for you. It was damn near impossible to survive on that salary if you really had to live on it. That was one of the many things they discussed over the cold chicken they found in the fridge. Cecelia and Amos were away, but Mae, the housekeeper, had stayed on to take care of the house, and Hallie.

'Thank God for men,' Olivia said.

Hallie held up her glass of wine. 'I'll drink to that.'

'Without them and publishing parties, I would have starved to death. I've been in New York for a year and a half and I haven't had to pay for my own dinner once.'

Hallie reared up on her feminist haunches. She had no patience with women who screamed equality – until the check came.

'You let men pay for you when you go out!'

Olivia glanced around the kitchen that covered most of the ground floor of the townhouse. With the terra-cotta floor tiles and huge window overlooking a small yard, it might have been a Tuscan garden.

'I guess it's different from letting them pay when you stay home.'

For a minute Hallie looked exactly the way she had when Olivia had asked if she was Amos Porter's daughter. Olivia knew she'd gone too far. She had to back up quickly.

'Listen, I don't know what you're in such a snit about. I'd give my right arm to be in your place. I don't mean only living here. I mean knowing all the right people, having all the right doors open for you.'

'But that's the problem. I'll never know if I was good enough to get there on my own.'

Olivia leaned back in her chair and looked at Hallie over her wine glass. 'Screw getting there on your own, honey. Getting there is all that counts.'

*   *   *

Hallie and Olivia began lunching together. Olivia was usually the one who called. Hallie was frequently the one who paid. Olivia never asked her to. She never even hesitated when the check came, but once or twice, when Olivia said she'd just have a cup of soup or a small salad because it was one or two or four days till payday and she didn't know how she was going to make it, Hallie began picking up the check. It would have been unconscionable not to. All payday meant for Hallie was that she could treat herself to a taxi home from work or a facial.

The balance of those lunches was continually shifting. Olivia knew the latest gossip. Hallie had met the people Olivia gossiped about. Hallie knew the customs of the country. Olivia had an instinct for the reality behind them. They had an argument about it once. Olivia was reporting on the latest scandal at Apogee. One of their most respected authors, a great woman of letters, had been accused of plagiarizing from a little-known biography. Hallie was shocked. More than that, she was skeptical. Surely the woman who'd given Hallie her first set of *Winnie the Pooh* couldn't be guilty of plagiarism.

'I've seen her book,' Olivia said. 'And I've seen the one she filched from. She might as well have Xeroxed the material.'

'It was a mistake,' Hallie insisted. 'Haven't you ever done that? You know, used a sentence or a phrase and then realized you'd just heard someone else use it. It may be theft, but it's inadvertent.'

'Sure,' Olivia admitted and took a bite of her

cheeseburger deluxe. Hallie was treating that day. 'But I never inadvertently quoted three full pages.'

When the scandal turned into a lawsuit and the woman of letters had to pay close to a hundred thousand in damages, Olivia didn't gloat. She just told Hallie, sweetly really, that she oughtn't to be so gullible in the future. Hallie swore to herself she wouldn't be.

A few months later, Olivia found an apartment on Avenue A. The building was deteriorating, but the mostly young tenants – artists and writers, the vaguely creative and the merely hopeful – were on their way up. Olivia asked Hallie if she'd like to share the place. Hallie weighed the assorted cons against the pro of being on her own and said sure.

It was a long way from the townhouse on Seventy-third Street, but it was all Hallie could afford if she wasn't going to take money from her parents, and she wasn't. It was an even longer way, at least geographically, from the room Olivia had rented in Hoboken, and you didn't have to use a bridge or tunnel to get there.

Hallie said it wasn't much. Olivia said it was a dump. Neither of them minded much. Hallie was finally on her own. Olivia was finally in Manhattan.

They were well suited as roommates. Neither was excessively sloppy or compulsively neat. Each was understanding of the other's idiosyncrasies, or maybe both were merely too driven at work to care much about what went on at home.

They began sharing things. The designer clothes Cecelia bought for Hallie, which always managed to fit Olivia, though she was two inches shorter and consisted entirely of curves while Hallie was mostly angles. Inside information about what was happening at which houses. Invitations to publishing parties. That was how Hallie and Olivia ended up at the National Book Awards that year. And that was how they managed to meet Jake Fox at exactly the same time.

They were standing, drinks in hand, intentionally bored expressions on their faces, in the lobby of Alice Tully Hall while the reception bubbled around them.

'Think of it. One well-placed bomb and you could wipe out the entire book business.'

Olivia and Hallie turned at the words. They were facing a tall man with a big white smile that spilled over them like a floodlight.

Olivia responded first. Maybe her reflexes were faster. Or maybe the heat of that smile had slowed Hallie's reaction time.

'Olivia Collins.' She held out her hand.

Jake transferred his drink to his left hand and took it. 'Hello, Olivia Collins. I'm Jake Fox.'

Olivia looked up at Jake from under that fringe of lashes. He looked down at her from under a fringe that was even darker and thicker. Just as Hallie was beginning to think they'd forgotten she was there, Jake turned to her. They introduced themselves. Hallie couldn't decide whether she was relieved that the big shark's smile didn't change or annoyed.

It took another thirty seconds for them to list credentials. Apogee. Slater House. Artists' Management Inc.

Hallie and Olivia interpreted the information. Both of them knew the AMI Agency wasn't a big pond in the business. It was an ocean. Neither of them had ever heard of Jake Fox, which meant he was a tiny fish. Hallie decided that with those eyes and that smile, she wouldn't care if he were a minnow. She had a feeling, from the way Olivia was still smiling up at him, that Olivia had decided the same thing.

Hallie felt a hand on her shoulder and turned to find a man in an impeccably tailored, double-breasted suit that couldn't quite hide the effects of too many publishing lunches.

'It's been a long time.' Henry Grainer was talking to Hallie, but the pale eyes that almost disappeared into the folds of his round shiny face were focused on Olivia. And Olivia's were focused on Henry Grainer. She was looking at him exactly the way she'd been looking at Jake a minute ago, only more so.

Olivia had recognized the face from the photographs. She'd known the name even before Hallie introduced them. Henry Grainer ran one of the most powerful publishing houses in the business. He ran it by will and by whim. People who worked at Campbell and Grainer – the name remained, though Winston Campbell had been driven into premature retirement several years earlier – said it made surviving in the imperial court of Byzantium look easy.

Olivia turned to face Grainer and, in doing so, managed to turn her back on Jake Fox completely. Twenty minutes later, Olivia left the party. Henry

Grainer left with her. Or maybe it was the other way around.

Hallie didn't know whether to thank Olivia or murder her. On one hand, she was left with Jake Fox. On the other, Jake Fox probably thought he was stuck with her.

He stood looking after Olivia and Grainer as they passed out of the crowded lobby into the dark city beyond, then turned back to Hallie. She cast around for conversation. Her mind went absolutely blank. He didn't help. He stood looking down at her. He was probably trying to figure out how to get away.

She decided to make it easy for him. She wasn't an altruist, but she wasn't a masochist, either, and she didn't want to be ditched.

She held up her half-empty glass. 'Well . . . I guess I'll . . . uh . . . freshen this.'

'I'll do it.' He took her glass and disappeared into the crowd.

That was the end of that. She just wished he hadn't taken her glass. She didn't particularly want another drink, but she couldn't stand around without a glass in her hand. She started toward one of the other bars. She was standing at the edge of the crowd, inching her way in, when she heard the voice behind her.

'I couldn't find you.'

She turned and was face to face with Jake again.

He handed her a drink. 'If you're trying to shake me, you'll have to do better than that.'

A man took a step back and crushed Hallie's foot.

31

A woman reached for a cigarette and jostled Jake's drink with her elbow.

'This is a zoo,' Jake said, 'but I make it a practice never to turn down free food and booze.'

'I know what you mean.' She didn't, of course, but she had no intention of getting into that with him.

'I have a fantasy.' He stopped and smiled at her. 'Actually I have several, but there's one I can tell you about. Someday I'm going to be so successful that I'll never have to stand in a crush, drinking cheap generic vodka, eating greasy hors d'oeuvres, and making polite conversation again.'

'Your conversation isn't so polite.'

'Hey, don't get defensive. That was meant as a compliment. You know, like we're in this thing together.'

Hallie was debating what to say to that when one of the award winners passed. Hallie congratulated him. He thanked her and asked how she was. After he had moved on, Hallie turned back to Jake. He wasn't smiling anymore. And he didn't look quite so sure of himself.

'How do you know him?'

Hallie shrugged. 'I've been working in publishing for a while. When I was in school, I had summer jobs and stuff,' she added before he could push it.

The crowd was starting to thin. Jake put his glass down on a table. 'Listen, I don't have Henry Grainer's expense account . . .' he began, but before he could go on, an editor who'd presented one of the awards stopped at their side. She took Hallie's hand, kissed her on the cheek, and asked how she was.

Hallie said she was fine and introduced Jake.

The editor managed to shake his hand and dismiss him at the same time. 'Give my love to your folks,' she said as she moved off.

Jake stood looking after the editor, then turned back to Hallie. 'Is there anyone in this business you don't know?'

'Hundreds.'

'Who're your folks?'

She figured she might as well get it out of the way. 'I guess you didn't recognize my name.'

'Hallie?'

She couldn't decide whether or not he was putting her on.

'Listen,' he went on again, before she could make up her mind, 'what I was about to say was, how about dinner? Providing it's cheap. I haven't got Henry Grainer's expense account.'

'That's okay,' Hallie said. 'I haven't got my roommate's tastes.'

'Are you coming back to my apartment?' Jake asked as they were leaving the restaurant.

Hallie hesitated – not because she was indecisive but because she was scared. All through dinner she'd been terrified that he wouldn't want her to.

'I thought you'd never ask,' she said.

Jake's apartment building made Hallie's look upscale. He opened the downstairs door with two keys. Once inside, he leaned against the peeling wall and pulled her to him. His mouth was soft and his chest was hard, and something in the back of her mind said kissing Jake Fox was about the nicest experience she'd ever had.

He unbuttoned her coat and put his hands inside. It was even better that way. 'I have a confession.'

She'd been leaning against him, and now she stiffened a little. She should have known. There was a woman. He was already committed. A man. He had eclectic tendencies.

He felt her tense and laughed. 'I live on the fifth floor.'

She could have collapsed with relief. Instead she hung on to him in the gloomy hallway. They went on kissing for a while. He unzipped the back of her dress. His hands were warm on her skin. She loosened his tie and began unbuttoning his shirt.

He put his hands on her shoulders and held her a little away. 'If we keep this up, we're going to scandalize the neighbors. And in this dump that isn't easy.' He was smiling, but his voice was hoarse.

He took her hand and they started up the stairs. She hung back a little, partly because the stairs were narrow but mostly because she wanted to watch him. He was wearing a trench coat, but she could sense the body beneath. He moved beautifully.

On the third landing, he stopped and kissed her again. 'Still with me?'

She nodded. Her nose rubbed against his cheek. She couldn't place the aroma, but she knew she liked it.

'One more,' he said when they reached the next landing, and this time he didn't stop.

There were four locks on his door. He started at the top and worked his way down. She stood hugging herself. She was suddenly trembling. For some reason she assumed it was from the cold.

He pushed the door open, let her go in ahead of him, then kicked it closed behind them. There was a desk lamp on the floor. He bent and turned it on. Hallie had a quick impression of a tiny room with a lot of books and a mattress on the floor.

They stared at each other. A small tic pulled at the side of his mouth. Hallie thought she'd never seen anything so beautiful.

'Do you want a drink?'

She'd had a couple of drinks at the party, and they'd had wine with their burgers. A drink was the last thing she wanted. She shook her head no.

They went on staring at each other. She felt hopelessly awkward. She crossed to the window and began reading the spines of the books piled on the ledge. When she turned back to him, she saw he'd stripped down to his trousers. His body was like that tremulous tic that pulled at the side of his mouth. Absolutely beautiful. His shoulders were wide. He was so lean she could see the outline of his ribs beneath the smooth, dark skin. There was a light dusting of dark hair across his chest. It narrowed into a fine line that ran down his stomach and disappeared into his trousers. Her own stomach tightened.

He crossed the room and put his arms around her. He'd already unzipped her dress halfway. Now he finished the job. She took her dress off and dropped it over a chair. They were both half clothed. Not yet naked but already defenseless.

He kissed her, and she wound her arms around his neck and moved and turned her body against his as if he were a hearth.

He unhooked her bra. She opened his belt. They went on kissing. They didn't even stop as they sank to the mattress and fumbled out of the rest of their clothing. It was even better without anything between them.

They were moving faster now. Hungry mouths. Desperate hands. Hot flesh. Then suddenly, at exactly the same moment, as if some signal had been given, they stopped moving and drew apart and looked at each other. Though neither of them knew it at the time, it was a moment neither would ever forget. There was silence in that moment and something so serious it frightened them both. The moment seemed to go on for a long time. Then they came together and began again, slowly now, so slowly that the anticipation was almost agony.

His hands were maddening and his mouth was, too. She felt his tongue in the hollow of her neck, teasing at one breast, then the other, tracing the line of her ribs, down her stomach, between her legs. Her body was a field of tender, exposed nerves. She writhed and moaned and begged yes and please and God and Jake.

And still it went on. He worked his way up till his face was on a level with hers again, and he kissed her, and now it was her turn to explore, and her hands and her mouth discovered his body, smooth skin and hard muscle and beautiful tendon. She loved the touch of him and the taste of him, loved it so much she wanted it to go on forever, so she was careful with her hands and her mouth, slow and careful and gentle.

Then when she thought that neither of them could stand it any longer, he entered her, and she cried out again in pleasure, and he did too, and it went on that way, on and on and on, until her body shocked her in a shuddering, howling convulsion, and his did too, and they clung together in the sheer terror of it.

He lay on his side, his head propped up on one hand, his other tracing aimless patterns over her body. Across one breast, around the other, down her stomach. His eyes followed his hand. There was only a single dim lamp on in the room, but Hallie felt as if she were lying in a spotlight. The rational part of her mind started working again. She wondered if he was comparing her to Olivia. After all, he'd talked to Olivia first. Olivia didn't have shoulders that were too wide and ribs and pelvic bones that stuck out and breasts that were too large. Olivia said men liked women with big breasts, but Olivia came from a world where people still thought the test of a man was how much bourbon he could drink and the test of a lady – not a *woman,* but a *lady* – was how many men she could drive wild with desire and still remain a virgin. All the men Hallie had ever known had a thing about Twiggy or old Audrey Hepburn movies. Not that Olivia fit that bill, either. Olivia was perfectly proportioned. Tiny waist, nicely rounded hips and behind, the kind of breasts that made a statement rather than a scandal when she didn't wear a bra.

She wondered if he wanted her to leave. She wasn't cut out for one-night stands. What if he couldn't wait to get rid of her? Hallie knew that she wasn't supposed to care, but she wasn't that independent. At least not when it came to this. The idea of lying naked and unwanted in a strange bed made her cringe.

She sat up. 'I'd better get going.'

He pulled her down again. 'Why?'

'It's late.'

His hand was making patterns on her breast again, only now they didn't seem so aimless. 'If you hang around, it'll be early before you know it.'

'Are you sure –'

He rolled over on top of her. 'Shut up,' he murmured against her mouth. He kissed her for a long time. 'Shut up and screw.'

Hallie thought they were the four most romantic words she'd ever heard.

IV

Hallie and Olivia passed in the hall of the railroad flat on Avenue A the next morning. Olivia was still wearing clothes from the night before. Hallie had just changed out of them.

'How'd it go?' Hallie asked.

'You're looking,' Olivia called over her shoulder as she headed for the shower, 'at Campbell and Grainer's newest editor.'

Hallie followed her to the bathroom. 'You're kidding!' Olivia began pulling off her clothes. 'Would I kid you about something like that, honey? I got the job this morning over coffee in his *pied-à-terre*. Mrs Grainer's at their country place. At least, that's when he made the offer. Actually, I think I got the job sometime during the night.'

'Congratulations.'

'Thanks. It couldn't happen to a more deserving woman. I worked my ass off.' Olivia stepped into the shower. 'What happened at the party after I left?'

'Not much,' Hallie said, but her smile in the mirror was so wide she couldn't put on her lipstick.

'You shouldn't have wasted your time with that

baby agent from AMI,' Olivia called over the sound of the shower. 'Not with a room full of A-list people.'

'I didn't waste my time,' Hallie said.

Olivia turned off the water and opened the shower curtain. 'Why, honey, from that smile on your face, I'd say them colored lights Tennessee Williams is always talking about must have gone off.'

Hallie's cheeks turned a deeper pink than the blusher. 'Hurry up and get dressed, Olivia. You're going to be late for work.'

Olivia began toweling herself. 'I'm not going to work. I have an appointment with Hank.'

'Hank! You call him Hank!'

'Among other terms of endearment.' Olivia frowned past Hallie at her own reflection in the steamy mirror. 'But unfortunately, there were no colored lights. Why do the ones with power always look like skinned rabbits when they take their clothes off? He was so . . . *pink*.'

'You don't have to go to bed with them to get ahead.'

'Correction,' Olivia said through a cloud of Chloe dusting powder, '*you* don't have to go to bed with them to get ahead. Some might even say – ' She stopped.

Hallie turned from the mirror where she'd been trying to finish her makeup. 'Some might even say what?'

'Nothing.' Olivia started down the hall.

'What were you going to say?'

'I'm late.'

Hallie followed Olivia into her room. 'You were

implying that Jake Fox was using me to get to my father.'

'I wasn't. Honestly. Damn!' Olivia peeled off a torn stocking found another in the pile on the floor, and began pulling it on.

Hallie sat on the side of the bed. She'd managed to put the thought out of her head for a while. Now Olivia had brought it back.

'I'm not even sure he knows who my father is.'

'You're right,' Olivia said. 'He asked me if you were Amos Porter's daughter – when that agent came over to talk to you and Hank – but then the agent left before I even had a chance to answer.' She smiled at Hallie. 'I'm sure he doesn't know, honey.'

Half a dozen times that day Hallie picked up the phone and started to dial Jake's number. Each time she put it down again before she finished. To hell with him. She wasn't going to break the date. She just wasn't going to show up for it. She'd never done that in her life. Just stood someone up. But then no one had ever made a fool of her like this. She remembered the smile on Olivia's face. 'I'm sure he doesn't know, honey,' she'd said. 'I'm sure he's crazy about you for yourself.'

Hallie sensed him at the door to her office before he said anything. She looked up from the manuscript she was trying to read. He wasn't smiling now. That made two of them.

'I was under the impression we were going to have

dinner. I've been stooging around in the lobby under that impression for the last half hour.'

'Were we?'

'You know we were.' He moved to the chair on the other side of her desk. She wished he hadn't. There was something about the way he draped his long lean frame over that chair that made her remember the night before.

'Do you want to tell me what this is about?'

'Maybe you got your days wrong. Or your people. Maybe it was Amos Porter you wanted to see.'

He winced. 'I'm sorry. I guess I should have let on right away that I knew who you were.'

'It's okay. You probably got a good laugh out of it.'

'Listen,' he began, then stopped. He sat up, put his elbows on the desk, and leaned toward her. She shrank back.

'You don't have to do that,' he said. 'You don't have to act as if I'm Jake the Ripper.'

'It's not that. It's . . .'

When she didn't finish the sentence, he went on. 'What I was trying to say was that I didn't get a laugh out of it. I was trying to be . . .' He hesitated, made a self-deprecating face at her, and pretended to shoot his cuffs. 'Cool. Laid back. All that stuff. Hell, Hallie, you knew everyone who was anyone at that party. I knew a handful of people, strictly lower level. I didn't want to make a big deal about it. Like your roommate.'

'What about my roommate?'

'When you introduced her to Henry Grainer, she practically genuflected.'

'She's going to work for him.'

He smiled that impossible smile at her. 'I guess while she was down on her knees, she figured she might as well do more than genuflect.' He caught himself. 'I'm sorry. I barely met her. For all I know she's the most brilliant editor since Max Perkins. Or wildly in love with Henry Grainer.'

'She says he reminds her of a skinned rabbit.'

'She's got a point. But I'm not interested in her.'

'Even now that she's a full-fledged editor at C and G? She'll be buying a lot of books.'

He closed his eyes for a minute, as if he were losing patience. 'Listen, I didn't mean to insult her. She's your roommate, and I'm sure she's a perfectly nice person. Exemplary. Goes to church every Sunday and sends money home to her invalid mother. But can we stick to the point?'

'Which is?'

'I wasn't trying to put anything over on you last night, Hallie. I was just trying to protect myself.'

'Against me?' She was incredulous.

'You think you're harmless?' He stood, started moving around the desk to her, then thought better of it and stopped. He retraced his steps to her door, closed it, and threw the lock. Until then Hallie hadn't even realized her office had a lock. He started toward her again. She got up as he came around her desk. She wasn't sure if she meant to meet him or ward him off.

'I'll show you how harmless you are.' He opened his jacket and began unbuttoning his shirt. 'This is from your fingernails.' He reached for her. She didn't step back. 'And look at this.' He turned to show her one earlobe. 'When I came in this morning, my secretary –'

She laughed. Finally.

'All right. I don't have a secretary. The receptionist said I had this – well, bite on my ear.'

She reached up and touched his ear. 'What's the receptionist doing looking at your ear anyway?'

'I asked her to.' He was unbuttoning her blouse now. 'I told her I was wounded.' His hands on her skin were warm. 'Mortally.' He took her hand and put it inside his shirt on his chest. 'Shot straight through the heart, babe.'

V

A few months after Olivia had gone to work at Campbell and Grainer, Hallie came home with the news that the current managing editor of Slater House was leaving.

'Who're you up against?' Olivia asked.

'Up against? I don't even know if I'm in the running.'

Olivia shook her head and increased her speed on the stationary bicycle that Amos had bought ten months earlier and used twice. Hallie had told her mother she didn't know where they'd put it in the railroad flat, but Olivia had said they'd find room.

'We're going to put you in the running, honey.'

'But I don't know anything about production.'

'That's why you want the job.' Her breath was coming in short gasps now. 'To . . . learn . . . a . . . bout . . . pro . . . duc . . . tion.' She stopped pedaling. 'How are you going to run a house someday if you don't know anything about production?'

Hallie knew Olivia was right. She also knew that Scott Westin, the editor who was definitely in the running for the job, knew a great deal about production. Hallie wanted the job. Westin was qualified for it.

'We've got to work out a strategy.' Olivia began pedaling again. 'The publisher chooses the managing editor, right?'

Hallie said that was right.

'It's a shame Templeton's gay.'

'What makes you think that?'

'I just assumed. I mean, the way he looks. That chiseled face. And the way he dresses. Oscar Wilde hits Barney's. I know he's married, but since when does that mean anything?'

Hallie laughed. 'If Tom Templeton's gay, he puts up a good front.'

Olivia stopped pedaling again. 'What do you mean?'

'The last sales conference. On Long Boat Key.'

'Don't rub it in, honey. You get white sand and the Gulf of Mexico. I get a plastic conference room at the Forty-second Street Hyatt. Thank God I'm out of Apogee. But what happened at the sales conference?'

'Nothing much. There was a party in someone's suite one night. Everyone had a lot to drink. Templeton left when I did. He said he'd walk me to my room. Since his was just down the hall from it. I couldn't very well say no.'

'Not if you had any sense.'

'So there we were. Tom Templeton, the legendary publisher of Slater House, and Hallie Porter, associate editor.'

'Not for long, if you played your cards right. I can't believe you never told me this.'

'It was pretty tawdry.'

'The plot sickens. Go on.'

'There isn't all that much to tell. One minute we were walking along talking about books, and the next he had one hand on my ass and the other up my blouse. He kept saying he'd had his eye on me for a long time. At least he kept saying it when his tongue wasn't in my mouth.'

'Not exactly the subtle type.'

'Are you kidding? I've had more subtle approaches from undergraduates.'

'Did it get better in bed?'

'It didn't get to bed.'

'Don't tell me he's one of those nature freaks. Sex *sur la plage*.'

'I didn't sleep with him, Olivia.'

Olivia's shoulders sagged. Either the exercise or Hallie had done her in. 'Let me get this straight. Tom Templeton, the man who just happens to run Slater House, tells you he has the hots for you, and you say thanks, but if it's all the same to you, I'd rather go to bed with a good manuscript?'

'He's old, he's married, and that night he smelled like a distillery. Besides, even before I met Jake, I knew Tom Templeton wasn't my type.'

'He doesn't have to be your type!' Olivia screamed. 'He's your boss!'

'Another good reason not to go to bed with him.'

Olivia sat on the bike seat, staring at her roommate. 'You realize that if you had, you'd already be the new managing editor of Slater House?'

'Maybe, but who wants to get the job that way?' Hallie stopped. 'I'm sorry. You would have got the job even if you hadn't slept with Hank.'

Olivia laughed. 'Listen, honey, there wasn't any job until I slept with Hank. But don't worry. My skin isn't that thin. On the other hand, your head is as thick as they come. You're hopeless. Absolutely hopeless.'

Nonetheless, Olivia continued to hope and to scheme.

'Okay,' Olivia said a few nights later, when they were sitting around the chipped Formica table in the kitchen. 'Scott Westin's your main competition. What do we have on him?'

'What do you mean?'

'I mean, what's his dirty little secret?'

'He cheats on his expense account.'

'Give me a break, honey. Everyone cheats on expense accounts, and if you don't, I don't want to know about it. I don't think I can live with anymore virtue.

'Isn't there anything else?' Olivia asked when Hallie came back from paying the pizza-delivery boy.

'He took a kickback from a printer once. At least once.'

'All right! Now you're talking. Tell.'

'It was about six months ago. When Jill – you know, the current managing editor – was in the hospital. Scott filled in. That's why he knows so much more than I do about production. Anyway, I saw him having lunch with a printer one day. That afternoon, he came to my office and asked me not to say anything about the envelope. The funny thing was, if he hadn't mentioned it, I never would have thought there was anything strange. I mean, I'd walked by just as the printer was handing him an envelope, but I assumed it was some production forms or something.'

'You would. Well, that takes care of old Scott Westin.'

'You don't really expect me to go to Tom Templeton and tell him?'

Olivia looped a piece of melted cheese around her finger and licked it. 'You're right. That would look vindictive. You'll have to write an anonymous letter.'

'No way.'

'Do you or do you not want to be managing editor?'

'Not that much.'

'You're not at Harvard anymore, honey. This is the real world, and the real world doesn't run on the honor system.'

Hallie picked a piece of pepperoni up between her thumb and forefinger, but instead of putting it in her mouth she stared at it. 'I don't believe you have to be a bitch to get ahead.'

Olivia tossed a crust into the box and took another slice. 'Maybe not, but it sure helps.'

A week later, Tom Templeton called Hallie into his office. He asked her how she'd like to be the new managing editor. She said she'd like it fine. She couldn't wait to tell Olivia. She was vindicated. She'd won the job by hard work and ability.

'I thought about this decision carefully,' Templeton went on. 'I suppose you know it was between you and Westin.' Hallie nodded. 'It was a close race. Would you like to know what convinced me you were right for the job?'

Hallie said she would and prayed it had nothing to do with the next sales conference in Florida, which was only a month away.

'A few days ago I got a call from a printer. He just wanted to tell me what a terrific guy Scott Westin was. Responsible. Hardworking. Knew production backward and forward.' Templeton hesitated. 'It made me think, Hallie. Can you guess what it made me think?'

She hoped the question was rhetorical, but Tom Templeton sat behind his big desk, waiting for her to answer.

'That maybe this printer had some reason for wanting Scott to be managing editor?'

'Give the little lady a great big hand. We use the best printer for the job at this house, Hallie. And we don't take kickbacks. Understand?'

She said she did.

'Fine.' Templeton stood. 'Now all you have to do is learn production.'

So much for getting the job by hard work and ability.

Hallie learned production. By the time she left Slater House for Rutherford and Styles two years later, she knew everything there was to know about the physical production of that commodity called a book.

Olivia learned some lessons of her own during that time. Once the emperor had withdrawn his favor, it wasn't easy surviving in a Byzantine court. At first, Olivia had been relieved the affair was over. She'd met him at an A-list party, but, as she'd confessed to Hallie, his performance in bed had been no better than C-plus. Then, as another year passed, Olivia realized the implications of the breakup. Henry Grainer didn't fire her. He just made her position untenable. She couldn't sign books. She was left out of meetings. One day the editor in chief called her into his office and raked her over the coals about some minor entry on her expense account. Olivia told Hallie she had to get out.

Hallie agreed and was careful not to point out that when you lay down with the boss, you didn't necessarily get up with job security.

'Do you think you could put in a word with Quentin Styles for me?' Olivia asked.

Hallie could, of course, and not only because Quentin was her godfather. She was doing well at R and S. A few smirky rumors lingered. With Hallie Porter's connections, an occasional detractor still murmured, an illiterate could do well. But at that point another editor would cite her list, which was pretty impressive or an agent would talk about negotiating with her, which was pretty grueling; or a writer would tell about working with her, which was pretty wonderful. Then two first novels she'd acquired won PEN awards, and all but the bitchiest rumors stopped.

Hallie said she'd speak to Quentin.

'You realize you'd be bringing in someone at your own level?' Quentin pointed out, and Hallie wasn't sure whether he was speaking as her publisher or her godfather. 'You'd be competing for the same books.'

'My strength's fiction. Olivia Collins has a nose for commercial nonfiction. Some model's makeup tips, an actress's favorite recipes, the latest pop psychologist's guide for finding a marriageable male.'

'Nonbooks.'

'We'd make a good team. You're always telling me I'm too literary.'

'I'm not *always* telling you that.' Quentin's long patrician face grew longer when he frowned. 'I mentioned it once when you wanted to turn down that multigenerational saga.'

'From slave ship to supermodel in four generations. Olivia would have loved it. She can smell a miniseries a mile away.'

Quentin told Hallie he'd interview Olivia.

'And speaking of marriageable males,' he said when Hallie reached the door of his office, 'I hear things are getting serious with Jake Fox. People are beginning to ask me when you're going to post the banns.'

'It's none of their business. We're not. I mean, why are people talking about Jake and me anyway?'

'Because you're an editor at Rutherford and Styles

and Jake is the goddamn wunderkind of the agency business.'

It was true. Jake had left AMI and started his own agency. Everyone had said he was crazy. It was too soon. He didn't know enough. He didn't have enough clients. Everyone was at least partially right. He had only a handful of clients, but they were respectable clients. He began negotiating more than respectable advances for them. Then he got two hundred thousand for a first novel by a Nebraska farmer with literary leanings, and the book climbed to the top of the bestseller lists and stayed there for several months. Word got out among writers. Jake Fox made you money. More important, Jake Fox made you a name. Writers began to flock to him. Editors followed. They had no choice if they wanted to buy the hot manuscripts by the promising writers.

It riled Quentin. He didn't like Jake's brash style. Except for the moments when he envied it. That and his youth.

'He's a good agent,' Hallie said.

'Just be careful.'

Hallie wasn't exactly angry at the warning. She knew Quentin was just making noises like a godfather. But she still didn't like the implications.

'Of what?'

Qentin peered at her through his rimless glasses. 'What have you got that he wants?'

Hallie started to laugh. 'My irresistible body?'

'A bit more than that.'

Hallie was stung. 'In other words, he couldn't possibly be interested in me alone.'

'I didn't mean that, and you know it.'

But she didn't know it. That afternoon on the porch with her parents came back to her. If her own father thought she was undesirable, what did a man like Quentin think?

'I just don't trust him,' Quentin said.

'He's all right.'

Quentin stared at her for a moment. 'Maybe he is, but you deserve better than "all right," Hallie.'

'I hear you and this agent Jake Fox are a serious item,' Cecelia said.

'Did Quentin send out a press release or use the phone?' Hallie asked.

'Quent's your godfather. He's interested in your welfare. Why don't you bring him for dinner?'

Hallie knew she couldn't avoid it any longer, but she went on stalling. 'Quentin?'

'Very funny, Hallie. This Jake Fox.'

'*This* Jake Fox?'

'Why don't you bring Jake Fox to dinner? So far you haven't let us have more than two sentences with him at parties. Next Wednesday?'

'I'm not sure we're free.'

'So it's "we"?'

'I'm not sure Jake's free.'

Jake said he was free, and even if he weren't, he would have rearranged things. He was eager to get to know Hallie's parents.

Hallie thought of her conversation with Quentin. *What is he after? What have you got that he wants?*

'Especially my father,' Hallie said to Jake.

'Both of them. Your mother seems like quite a woman.'

Hallie read the subtext. She's not like you, or, more to the point, you're not like her.

There were only the four of them for dinner. Hallie was of two minds about that. She didn't like the idea of her parents scrutinizing Jake, but at least Quentin, Cecelia's perpetual extra man, wasn't there to judge as well. Cecelia couldn't have been more correct with Jake, which wasn't necessarily a good sign. With Cecelia, correct meant anything from 'I like him a lot, but after all we just met' to 'I think he's awful, but he is, after all, a guest in my home.'

'Well?' Hallie asked her mother after dinner when Amos had taken Jake off to show him some first editions.

Cecelia hesitated for only a moment. 'He's charming.'

'You say that as if charm were a slightly disreputable quality.'

'Let's just say I'm reserving judgment.'

'What's wrong with him?' Hallie demanded.

'I didn't say anything was wrong with him, baby. I said I was reserving judgment.'

'You think he's using me.'

Cecelia stared at her daughter for a moment. 'Not necessarily, but you seem to.'

Hallie dropped the subject.

Amos and Jake returned. Mae, the housekeeper, served coffee in the living room. Jake led off with a comment about one of Amos's books. Hallie had the feeling he'd been working up to it. Jake was playing the evening like a publishing lunch. You made small talk over the drinks, traded gossip over the meal, and got down to business when the coffee came.

The book he mentioned happened to be one of Amos's less critically acclaimed novels. Amos regarded it pretty much the way a mother would the least attractive but sweetest tempered of her brood. Hallie couldn't remember whether she'd ever discussed that particular novel with Jake, but he wouldn't have needed her to know how Amos would feel about it. The way Jake talked about the book, he must have been boning up on it ever since Cecelia had issued her invitation to dinner. Maybe even before.

They moved from that novel to Amos's other work. As the evening wore on, Amos segued into personal anecdotes. He might have been doing a talk show. He didn't ask Jake a single question about himself.

Nonetheless, Jake volunteered information. He mentioned a few of his clients. Hallie winced inwardly. To Jake those authors were stars. To Amos they were small potatoes, if he recognized the names at all.

Cecelia asked Jake how he'd got started in publishing.

'I was a traveler – a salesman,' Jake explained, though Cecelia had been of, if not in, the business for long enough to know what a 'traveler' was. 'For Wigdons.'

'Oh!' Cecelia said, and then, because she realized

her surprise had been rude, she went on. 'I always thought Wigdons was such a stuffy house.'

'It was,' Jake said. 'Is. But they were trying to avoid lawsuits. So they hired me as the house ethnic.'

'House ethnic?' Amos's bushy brows, diabolically black against the mane of white hair, lifted.

'House Jew, sir. Wigdons still wasn't ready for Blacks or Hispanics.'

The gothic arches of Amos's eyebrows rose higher. Cecelia dropped her eyes. They seemed embarrassed for Jake, or maybe only by him.

'Well,' Jake said, 'I wouldn't call it the worst fiasco of the decade. Maybe only of the year.'

They were walking across Seventy-ninth Street toward Hallie's apartment. She and Jake and Olivia had fanned out to separate apartments in more upscale neighborhoods. Jake took Hallie's hand and put it in the pocket of his trench coat.

'Didn't you like them?' Hallie asked.

'I'd say it was the other way around.'

Hallie remembered the way her mother had looked when she'd said Jake was charming. 'But they were perfectly polite.'

Jake laughed. She heard the undercurrent of bitterness. 'Perfectly polite is right. I bet they don't hang up on insurance salesmen or guys peddling stocks and bonds either.'

They covered another block in silence. In the pocket of his trench coat, her hand still nested in his. His skin gave off a lot of warmth.

'Does it bother you?'

He laughed again. 'Sure it bothers me. No one likes to be disliked. Or at least distrusted. Me more than most people probably. But I'm not all bent out of shape.'

'Good.'

He turned to look at her. 'Is that all you have to say? Don't you want to know why?'

A reason had occurred to her, and she didn't much like it. Jake wasn't worried about her parents because he wasn't serious about her.

'Okay. Why?'

His fingers tangled with hers in his pocket. 'Because for one thing, they're not the members of the family I'm interested in.'

Hallie's stomach did a small backflip. The rest of her kept its cool. 'And for another?'

'Because you've got this funny love-hate thing going with your parents. One minute you're crazy about both of them, the next you're acting like some rebellious kid. Given that scenario, I figure I stand as much of a chance if they're against me as if they're for me.'

As if he had anything to worry about.

Hallie and Jake were spending a lot of time together. They were also spending a lot of time with Olivia. They worked together. They played together. They went away for weekends together. Olivia usually brought a man along. Some were older and filthy rich and some were younger and sexy, most were smart or at least witty, and a few were nothing more than hunks. Hallie and Jake took the minor variations in stride. Olivia went through men the way she did manuscripts, at breakneck speed. Hallie and Jake teased her and occasionally worried about her, and, though they never came out and said it, even felt a little sorry for her. But those were the halcyon days, when none of them could do any wrong and even the quarrels had happy endings. The worst quarrel, the one in the Italian restaurant, had the happiest ending of all.

It happened several weeks after the night that Hallie had returned from seeing an author in Santa Fe and Jake had surprised her at the airport with a limo. In fact, according to her calculations, it had to do with that night he'd surprised her at the airport. They'd both been reckless in the back seat of the limo.

'Are you sure?' Jake asked. He was turning the stem of his wine glass with his fingers, and his eyes were on the glass rather than Hallie. She figured it was just as well. The lighting in the restaurant was dim, but not dim enough to hide the bruised-looking smudges under her eyes.

'No, I'm not sure,' she snapped. 'I'm late, but I'm not sure. Even that damn take-home test isn't sure yet.'

He went on staring at his glass.

'Of course, marriage is out of the question,' she said and waited for him to contradict her.

He still didn't say anything.

'Pregnancy isn't a good reason to get married,' she insisted.

'It's not a reason *not* to get married,' he said, but

she could tell from his voice that he had other reasons up his sleeve.

'How do you feel about an abortion?' he asked.

'Lousy.'

'Me too.'

They didn't speak for a while. When he finally broke the silence, his voice was hard, harder than she'd ever heard it, he still wasn't looking at her.

'You're right, though. Marriage is out of the question.'

The words knocked her back in her chair. She realized suddenly that she'd been fooling herself. She didn't really think marriage was out of the question, and she hadn't expected him to, either. She'd expected him to say, that's fine, that's terrific, we were going to get married anyway, so we'll just do it a little sooner and have the baby. Our baby.

'Then that's that,' she said.

They sat staring at each other.

'Is that all you have to say?'

She had a lot more to say, but the words were the kind that left you exposed and vulnerable. She closed her mouth and smiled.

Jake registered the smile. It was well below thirty-two degrees Fahrenheit.

'What else is there to say?' she asked through the icy grin. 'We're in perfect agreement. We both know marriage is out of the question. We both don't want an abortion. We both know I'm going to have one.'

His fist came down on the table. The people next to them glanced over, but Jake didn't even notice.

'Damn your father!'

The smile felt frozen on her face, but she wasn't going to drop the facade, 'I don't think we can blame this on my father.'

Jake was immune to irony that night. 'I can make it on my own, Hallie. Goddamnit, I *am* making it on my own. But no one will ever believe that. I mean, what would you think about an agent who just happened to marry Amos Porter's daughter? What do you think? Admit it. You'd never trust me.'

He was wrong. Suddenly she trusted him completely.

A week later she got her period. A month after that they moved in together.

Cecelia was pleased. She'd stopped reserving judgment even before Hallie had told her about the conversation in the Italian restaurant. She suggested they go shopping for the new apartment.

'What kind of mother are you, anyway?'

'An interested one. That's why I want to go shopping with you.'

'I mean, why aren't you incensed or at least offended? You're supposed to want me to get married, not live in sin.'

'What I want,' Cecelia said, 'is for you to be happy. You seem happier with Jake than I've ever seen you.'

Amos agreed with only half the sentiment. He said he wanted Hallie to be happy. He only wondered if she'd be happy with Jake. He didn't say she wouldn't, merely wondered if she would.

'Just the other day you said he was one of the best agents in town.'

'He is. Jake's aggressive and smart and hungry as they come. Everything I want in an agent but not necessarily what I'm looking for in a man for my daughter.'

'You've been talking to Quentin.'

'I admit I've been listening to Quentin. He doesn't trust Jake.'

'In other words,' Hallie said, hearing her voice begin to rise, 'you think he couldn't possibly be interested in me for myself.'

'In this world, baby, we all come packaged a certain way.'

Hallie thought of Olivia. She glanced across the room at her mother. She remembered that incident on the porch again.

She couldn't have been more than twelve or thirteen, because she hadn't yet lost what Cecelia blithely called her baby fat. They were at the farm. Cecelia and Amos were in the kitchen, and they hadn't realized that their daughter was outside the window. Hallie could still remember what she was reading. It was 'Winter's Dream' from a collection of short stories, and at the time she'd wanted more than anything in the world to be a willowy, reckless Fitzgerald heroine.

'Maybe you should put her on a diet,' she heard her father say and stopped reading. 'I can't abide fat women.'

Something fell out of Hallie then, or maybe she fell out of something. A moment before she'd been lying in the hammock, happily lost in Scott Fitzgerald. Now she'd come crashing out of that safe escapist cocoon, through the safety net of the hammock, through the strong whitewashed floorboards of the porch, down to the crawl space beneath. That was where she belonged. In the dark, dirty space beneath the house where the spiders and snakes and slimy, loathsome things lived. There was no place for her in the big, bright house, illuminated by her father's brilliant words and her mother's shining beauty.

'For God's sake, Amos, she isn't a fat woman, she's a chubby little girl.'

'That's exactly my point. I'm concerned about what she's going to grow up to look like.'

'She's going to grow up to look just fine!'

Hallie wished her mother hadn't shouted. Cecelia only raised her voice when she knew she was wrong.

'If only she had a little more of you and a little less of me,' Amos said.

'She's going to be lovely. Just wait. In a year or two she'll slim down and get those braces off . . .' Cecelia let her voice trail off, as if she weren't quite sure how to end the sentence.

'I hope so,' Amos said. 'But if she doesn't, I suppose it's lucky she's so much like me, after all. If she's not going to have the looks, at least she'll have the brains and talent.'

Cecelia had been right. By the time Hallie was fifteen, her body, except for her breasts, was made up entirely of angles, while her newly revealed teeth were perfectly straight. As far as Hallie could see, it was an improvement, but it wasn't a miracle.

'You mean I'm not attractive enough for Jake,' she said to her father now.

'That isn't the kind of packaging I meant. I was talking about me. You might as well face it. You come packaged as Amos Porter's daughter.'

She didn't need Amos to tell her that. And she didn't bother telling him about the fight in the Italian restaurant. He'd just sigh at her naïveté and say Jake was even smarter than he'd thought.

The night they moved into their new apartment, Olivia turned up with a bottle of champagne and a pizza with the works. It was a sweet gesture, and Hallie felt sorry for Olivia when she went home alone. She looked so forlorn. That was the way Hallie described her to Cecelia on the phone the next day.

'I wouldn't worry too much about Olivia,' Cecelia said. 'She can take care of herself.'

'I know that, but I still felt sorry for her. I mean, there Jake and I were in our new apartment together, and there she was alone.'

'But that's just the point. She wasn't alone. She was horning in on the two of you on your first night together.'

'She wasn't horning in.'

'Had you invited her?'

'She brought champagne and pizza.'

'So do delivery boys, and all they're looking for is a tip.'

VI

A year after Hallie and Jake began living together, Amos Porter's agent keeled over in the locker room of the New York Athletic Club. By that time no one even raised an eyebrow when Amos chose Jake Fox to represent him. Jake had made that much of a reputation. Six months after that, Hallie and Jake were married.

Two hundred guests filled the townhouse on Seventy-third Street. If the wedding wasn't small, it was unpretentious. Hallie had only three attendants. Her two Harvard roommates served as bridesmaids. Olivia was her maid of honor.

Hallie felt sorry for Olivia that day too, at least for a moment. It occurred just before the ceremony.

Olivia had finished fastening the long line of buttons that ran down the back of Hallie's embroidered silk gown, and Hallie had gone to the landing under the fanlight to pose for stills. When the photographer was finished, Hallie went back to her room to put on her veil and get her bouquet. It never occurred to her to knock, though it should have. She'd caught Olivia at things before. Once, in the old apartment on Avenue A, she'd walked in on Olivia and a juvenile editor – or, rather, an editor of juvenile books. Hallie had stood in the open doorway to Olivia's room too embarrassed to move, but Olivia had just laughed, waved to Hallie over the editor's naked shoulder, and kicked the bedroom door shut. So that afternoon Hallie should have known enough to knock. But she didn't. She just opened the door to her bedroom. After all, it was her room.

Olivia was standing in front of the full-length mirror in her maid-of-honor's dress and Hallie's bridal veil.

Hallie didn't mind Olivia trying on her veil. In the office the secretaries were always trying on each other's engagement rings. Hallie chalked it up to harmless curiosity and a little wishful thinking on Olivia's part. Until Olivia turned and saw Hallie in the doorway. Olivia hadn't even blushed when Hallie had walked in on her and that juvenile editor. Now she went dead white. From the look on her face, she might have been stealing the veil with the crown of tiny seed pearls rather than trying it on. Her lipstick-red mouth opened into a black hole. She began to explain. The explanations turned to apologies. The more she talked, the more flustered she became.

'Forget it,' Hallie said.

It never occurred to Hallie that in Olivia's mind she'd been trying on more than Hallie's veil.

By the time Hallie and Jake were in his little Austin Healy, driving to Maine, she'd forgotten the incident herself.

Olivia had been appalled when they'd announced they were going sailing in Maine on their honeymoon.

'What do you suggest?' Hallie had asked. 'Niagara Falls?'

'Paris, honey. The Georges Cinq or the Ritz. Room service round the clock. Four-star restaurants. Shopping. Chanel. St Laurent. Cartier.' Her voice had fallen to a religious hush on the last word.

'Too crowded,' Hallie had said. 'Too many people.'

Jake, who'd been stretched out on the couch next to Hallie, had started to laugh. 'You don't understand the haute-WASP mentality, Olivia. The only thing they haven't had is hardship. So what do they do for fun? They rough it. Hallie wanted to go to the South Pole by dog sled but I put my foot down.'

Hallie had shot a elbow into his ribs. 'Jake's the one who came up with the sailing idea.'

Jake had put an arm around her neck in a hammerlock. 'That's only because I'm upwardly mobile.'

They'd chartered a Hinckley, all sleek lines and varnished wood. As soon as they saw the boat, Hallie said it reminded her of one Amos had owned when she was young. Jake said it reminded him of the boats that used to come into the yacht club where he'd worked during high-school summers. They were always skippered by arrogant old men in faded red trousers, and there was always a daughter running up and down the gleaming teak decks on long tan legs, tossing him lines and secret smiles that invited and dismissed at the same time.

'I never thought I'd end up married to one of

them,' he said as they set sail.

Hallie tossed him a line. 'The hell you didn't. You always knew we were pushovers for you.'

The first night out they anchored in a deserted cove. There were no other boats, not even a house on the island, only stands of towering pines that made the air smell like Christmas and a watermelon-colored sun that turned the bay into an Impressionist patchwork of pink and lavender and blue. They both knew the water was too icy, but they also knew the opportunity was too good to waste. They didn't even have to speak. Standing there in the cockpit, just after they'd set the anchor, they looked at each other. Then they laughed and began tearing off their clothes.

Hallie squealed as she hit the water. Jake followed her. His body described a shining bronze arc through the air. There was a flash of white where the sun hadn't touched him. He howled as he hit the water.

They splashed wildly, then clung together for warmth in the icy water, half lovers, half children. He dunked her. She shot great cascades of spray at him with the heel of her hand. They swam toward each other again and wound icy arms and legs around each other. They gasped at the cold.

She went up the ladder first. He followed. They raced below to the cabin for towels. Jake wrapped her in one, then wound another around himself. He said her lips were blue and kissed them. She wound her arms around his neck. The towel fell to the cabin floor, but the warmth coming from his body enveloped her.

They tumbled into the forward bunk, wet hair and hungry mouths and long, tangling arms and legs. His skin tasted salty and smelled as clean as the pines. They moved slowly at first if the gentle bobbing of the boat were teaching them how to make love. But gradually their skin grew warmer, and their hunger built, and their urgency overtook them like a sudden storm. The force of it reverberated through her body like thunder, and she thrashed and shuddered and clung to him like a drowning woman.

Afterward they lay tangled together in the forward bunk whispering to each other, though no one except the gulls and the pines and wind could hear them. Finally another kind of hunger roused them, and they tugged jeans and sweaters over their naked bodies and steamed some lobsters on the primitive alcohol stove. They tore through the shells and feasted on the meat, and their mouths and chins grew shiny with butter, so that when they tumbled back into the forward bunk, they could still taste dinner on each other's mouth.

They fell asleep locked together for warmth. During the night Hallie awakened to the boat's rocking and realized they'd been making love in their sleep. She opened her eyes and saw that Jake's were open too, but neither of them spoke. There was no need to.

The next day they sailed up a fiord. They didn't talk much then either, not even to give each other tacking directions. As they beat their way between the sheer rocky cliffs, their movements were perfectly tuned to each other and the boat.

At the head of the fiord was a small town. They took the dink ashore and were momentarily startled by a resort in the throes of a Fourth of July celebration, but they caught their balance and wandered down the main street, holding hands and eating old-fashioned strawberry shortcake and picking their way through yard sales made up of the shards of other people's lives.

Inevitably, they stumbled into a second-hand bookstore. There was a first edition, though not in good shape, of Hemingway. When the laconic old man who ran the store saw Jake point it out to Hallie, he grew suddenly talkative and began bringing out his treasures. There were two more Hemingways, both in mint condition, a Faulkner, and an Edith Wharton. The old man slid them lovingly from the plastic kitchen bags he kept them in and spread them out on the table like so many jewels. Hallie reached for the Wharton, but he snatched it back. 'I'll turn the pages for you,' he said.

He kept rooting around in open boxes and on out-of-the-way shelves and coming up with more. Finally he produced a first edition of *Voyage Out*.

'This was Amos Porter's first novel,' he explained.

Jake and Hallie smiled at each other, but neither said a word to the man. To identify themselves would be to break the spell. It was as if they were in disguise that weekend, masquerading as the people they really were rather than the sum of things they were already becoming.

BOOK
THREE

VII

Quentin Styles liked to breakfast alone in the library of his twelve-room duplex on Fifth Avenue. There had been times over the years when he'd had to put up a battle to enjoy such a simple but solitary pleasure. His first wife, who'd waited for him through the war and whom he'd married in the wave of weddings that had swamped his generation immediately after it, found her husband's habit subversive. She believed in the prevailing American religion of the day, Togetherness. By the time Quentin came down to breakfast every morning, the first Mrs Styles was sitting at one end of the long Queen Anne table, fully dressed, impeccably made up, pouring his coffee, buttering his toast, and doing all those annoying little things the magazines, which were written by women, told her men wanted done for them. When they finally divorced, it was over other matters – the girl who'd waited for him to come home from the war had grown into the woman who'd grown tired of waiting for him to come home from the office and found Togetherness with someone else – but Quentin had learned his lesson.

His second wife, a photojournalist, subscribed to neither the doctrine of Togetherness nor the magazines that touted it. Nonetheless, on the mornings she was in the apartment on Fifth Avenue rather than in Korea photographing GIs, in Kenya snapping Mau Maus, or in India immortalizing starving children, she had a tendency to burst into the library spewing ideas for photography books Quentin had to publish.

The third Mrs Styles was more lethargic. In fact, when it was over – and it was over quickly – Quentin realized that his third wife had spent most of her time in bed. Before he'd married her, he'd found the arrangement convenient. Later it became merely annoying. On the rare occasions when she was awake before Quentin left the apartment, she was careful to give no sign of it. Quentin had loved his last wife least of the three, but he'd appreciated her breakfast habits most. Since she'd left the apartment – though she'd taken the house in Palm Beach – he'd gone on breakfasting alone in his library each morning.

It wasn't a particularly cheerful room at that time of day. For one thing, it faced west. For another, the dark wood paneling and somber carpet and draperies had come down intact from Quentin's father. The only sparks of color in the room were the dust jackets of the books Quentin had published over the years. Shelf after shelf, wall after wall attested to Quentin's colorful past. There were dozens of books he'd bought cheaply from unknown writers and turned into best sellers. There were several novels that the

US postal service had once deemed pornography and the critics now hailed as classics. Quentin Styles was a smart businessman. He also had a passion for literature. That was how he and Amos Porter had found each other during the war. That was how he and his late partner, Timothy Rutherford had come to publish Amos's first novel about it afterward.

George, the houseman who had been with Quentin longer than any of his wives, knocked on the library door and opened it without waiting for an answer. He said a Ms Collins wanted to know if she could see Mr Styles.

Quentin put down his copy of the *Wall Street Journal*. Editors, even editors in chief, didn't turn up at the apartment of the president of the company uninvited unless something was up. He told George to show her in.

Olivia heard the man's footsteps just in time. She turned away from the foyer mirror quickly. She didn't want the butler to catch her checking her hair and lipstick. He was arrogant enough without that. The butler had thrown her, but only for a minute.

She followed him down a long hall. On one side she glimpsed a living room. It had a fireplace and a baby grand and a lot of what the interior-design books called conversational groupings. In Olivia's living room there was space for one conversational grouping – the sofa and a chair. In the house where she'd grown up the only conversational grouping had been an old davenport facing the television.

On the other side of the hall there was a dining room the size of a small restaurant. Olivia ran her tongue over her teeth again to make sure there were no lipstick smudges, then over her lips.

The butler opened a door and stood to one side. Olivia stepped into the room. Quentin was sitting beside a small table in front of the windows. Olivia had a quick impression of an awful lot of silver and china for one man's coffee and toast. She thought of the pottery mug that perched on the side of her sink while she put on makeup in the morning.

Quentin stood. He never did that for her in the office.

Olivia kept her eyes on him as she crossed the long library. Central Casting might as well have sent someone to play the Grand Old Man of Publishing. Unlike many tall, gaunt men, he didn't stoop but carried himself erect, like a man who was ashamed of nothing, which is not the same as having nothing to be ashamed of. He had a mane of gray hair and a long face with a prominent Roman nose. His eyes, behind rimless glasses, were pale gray. His suit was gray too and without style. Olivia was willing to bet the same tailor at Tripler had been making it to the same specifications for longer than she'd been alive. A thin gold watch chain ending in an old-fashioned pocket watch stretched across his vest. No woman in her right mind would call Quentin Styles a sex symbol. Still, there were stories, and there were all those wives. There was also something about the patrician air that intrigued Olivia. She supposed it was the contrast between the appearance of propriety and the reality of the man. Sometimes she sat in meetings and wondered what was going on beneath that stuffy gray flannel.

He led her to a chair, offered her coffee and asked what brought her there. She sensed the wariness neath his correctness.

'I've come to ask your help,' she said.

He was sitting across from her in a big wing chair, his long sepulchral fingers splayed on each arm. How many times had she seen those hands resting on Hallie's shoulder as they walked the halls of Rutherford and Styles? He was Hallie's godfather. Olivia had barely had a father, let alone one with a deifying prefix.

'My help?'

His voice hadn't been exactly warm to start with. Now it cooled several degrees. He knew if Olivia came asking his help, it had to be help against Hallie.

She told him the whole story. She made no effort to spare herself, but she didn't try to put Jake in a good light either. She had a feeling Quentin was not one of Jake's biggest fans.

'I'm not trying to excuse what I did,' she went on. 'And I'm certainly not asking you to excuse me. I'm just saying that my personal mistakes have nothing to do with my professional abilities.' There was no telling what was going on behind those flat gray eyes. 'I have two books on the bestseller list.'

His smile, like his voice, held little warmth. 'One, actually. I've already seen next Sunday's "Book Review".'

'I'm a good editor.'

'So I've heard.'

'Just look at some of the properties I've acquired for R and S.' She rattled off a string of titles and authors. If they offended Quentin's literary sensibilities, they gratified his business instincts.

He sat staring at her for a while. The pale gray eyes unsettled her.

'Are you sure you wouldn't like some coffee?' he asked finally.

'Perhaps I will after all.'

Olivia was out of her chair before Quentin could stand. She might not be a Southern lady, but she had grown up in the South. 'I'll pour.'

She liked the heft of the silver coffeepot in one hand, the fragility of the china cup and saucer in the other. She carried two cups across the room and held one out to Quentin. He took both from her and put them on the end table beside his chair. He stared up at her. Her gaze down at him was steady. They both smiled.

She put her hands on his shoulders. The cloth of that drab gray suit was surprisingly soft, Quentin's shoulders surprisingly hard. He put his hands on her hips. She moved between his legs. His hands moved down her skirt and up under it to her thighs. She saw the look of surprise on his face, then pleasure. Olivia knew the convenience of pantyhose, she preferred the advantages of a garter belt and stockings.

'I'm an old-fashioned girl,' she murmured.

His hand moved beneath her bikinis.

She bent to kiss him, removed his rimless glasses, and kissed him again. Then she went to work on his belt.

There was something to be said for older men, and it was called patience. He didn't tug at her bikinis, just slid them smoothly down her legs. She stepped out of them the same way. Her skirt was narrow, but he managed to hike it up around her hips. He leaned forward. She felt the slight chafe of his beard against her thigh. His tongue was as clever as his fingers. She decided there was something else to be said for older men, and it was called experience.

He started to ease her onto his lap. 'Wait a minute,' she said. She reached for her handbag, unzipped an inner pocket, and took out a small foil packet.

'*Semper paratus*,' Quentin said.

Olivia moved onto his lap. Her arms were around his neck, her knees locked around his waist. Her tongue licked at his mouth.

'I like a man who knows his Latin,' she murmured and opened his mouth with her own. It was even better this time. Olivia always like the taste of herself on a man's tongue.

He moved slowly, his eyes fastened on her like small silvery dimes. He was gauging her pleasure and measuring his own to it. Like the old-fashioned gentleman he was, he politely allowed her to go first.

Quentin watched her finish the repairs, retrieve underwear, tuck in her blouse, smooth her skirt. She didn't bother with her makeup. She probably knew she didn't need it. She was a very knowing young woman. She was, in fact, a little too calculating for Quentin's taste. At least she would have been a while before. But one thing Olivia didn't know was that she had time on her side. Or timing. Quentin, a man who'd been known to forget birthdays, anniversaries, and other significant dates, knew the time to the minute. Seven months, two weeks, three days ago.

The widow of a politician had given an elaborate dinner party. There had been ten, perhaps twelve around the table, but she'd arranged it all for Quentin. She'd been after him. And Quentin had been interested. She was a handsome woman, if a little too painstakingly cared for. She was an intelligent woman. She had some wit. Quentin had gone to the dinner willingly. He'd stayed after the other guests eagerly. His spirit had been willing and eager, but his body had let him down.

Impotent.

The word still made him shiver.

Afterward, he'd tried to figure out why. He'd spent the last seven months, two weeks, and three days trying to figure out why. It wasn't the woman. At least it wasn't her appearance. That fifty-some-year-old face and body had been stitched and tucked to a semblance of thirty-year-old perfection. It wasn't that he didn't like her. Over the years, especially when he was young, he'd made love to women he'd liked less. He'd told himself it was simply one of those accidents of time. It happened to all men after a certain age. It would pass.

Only it hadn't passed. For seven months, two weeks, and three days he'd felt no desire. That wasn't normal. At least it wasn't normal for him.

Until this morning. Before Olivia had even

touched him, he'd felt a familiar stirring, a need he'd been terrified he'd never feel again. And now, watching her move around the room, he knew why. That night with the politician's widow had reeked of desperation. She was a nice woman, turned frantic by the need to be held, to be loved, to be wanted again. The panic, like passion under the same circumstances, had been contagious. And deadly. Within minutes it had killed all desire, though they'd gone on for God knows how long trying to revive it. That had been the worst part. The memory of that agonized, futile thrashing still shamed him. He'd sworn he'd never humiliate himself that way again. That was why he hadn't dared touch a woman since. Until this morning. Until Olivia.

When she'd first walked into the room, she'd been nervous, even diffident. She was worried about her job. And she was intimidated by Quentin, or at least what he stood for. He'd seen the way she looked around the room. He'd picked up on her reaction to George. But once they were alone, once Olivia had begun to talk, she regained her confidence. And her daring.

She'd crossed the room to him, put her hands on his shoulders, and moved between his legs. She hadn't even considered the possibility that he wouldn't respond to her. She hadn't been desperate. She hadn't even been hungry. She'd just been willful and curious and astonishingly ready. The combination had worked on him like a miracle drug. For that he was grateful. The irony was that she was asking so little in return. He would have discouraged Hallie from firing her for the house's good, as well as for Hallie's own. The only change was that now he had a third reason.

'You know,' he said, 'I would have urged Hallie not to fire you even if this hadn't happened.'

She'd been buttoning her jacket, and now she looked up at him with those wide, fearless eyes. He'd be damned if he didn't want her all over again, not that he'd try to do anything about it. He wasn't going to push his luck.

She crossed the room and straightened his tie. 'That's funny, because I would have made this happen even if you hadn't gone to bat for me with Hallie.'

Oddly enough, he believed her.

Every Tuesday Quentin and Hallie lunched together. That was, every Tuesday that Quentin was in town rather than Palm Beach or Palm Springs or some other palmy place pursuing his financial interest and personal pleasures. They lunched at Quentin's club.

Until a few years ago the club hadn't admitted women, not even for a meal. There were still urinals in the ladies' rooms. There were still members who averted their eyes when women walked into the grill, though during the warm months Hallie saw some of those same members sitting in the windows of that granite bastion of male privilege, checking out the women who parade Fifth Avenue in various states of summer undress. Quentin never sat in the window. He wasn't a man for spectator sports.

Quentin was waiting in the grill when she arrived, his long fingers curled around the stem of a martini glass, his eyes focused on a manuscript on the table. No business papers were permitted in the grill, but literary manuscripts were another story, or so Quentin had convinced the club years before. Quentin had gone into publishing when it was a gentleman's profession. Sometimes he pretended it still was.

He stood when Hallie reached the table and kissed her on the cheek. A few recalcitrant members frowned in their direction. That was one of the reasons he'd done it. The other was his genuine fondness for his goddaughter.

The waiter pulled the leather-upholstered chair out for Hallie. It was so heavy she couldn't have moved it herself. Like the urinals, the chair was supposed to remind her she was there on sufferance.

She saw Quentin frown when she ordered a glass of white wine. He'd never quite got over the good old days of publishing that starred the three-martini lunch.

He went on frowning after the waiter left. That was when Hallie realized it had nothing to do with the drink she'd ordered.

'Olivia came to see me this morning.'

'I didn't know you were in the office.'

'She came to the apartment.'

'Cozy.'

'She said she was afraid to go to the office. Thought you'd fire her on sight.'

'I plan to.'

'She has two best sellers on the list.'

'One. I saw next Sunday's "Book Review" before I left the office. She also happens to be screwing my husband. My estranged husband.'

'She told me.' He picked up the pad and pencil. 'What do you want for lunch?'

Hallie had barely managed to keep down the black coffee she'd had that morning, but again she had no intention of undressing in public. 'Anything.'

Quentin scribbled an order on the pad. The waiter came and took it away.

'She wants to stay with R and S.'

'She should have thought of that before she . . .' Hallie couldn't finish the sentence. The shock was beginning to wear off. Reality was sinking in. The crude slang wasn't enough to trivialize it.

'She says that her personal mistakes have nothing to do with her professional abilities.'

'Where does she think she's working, Utopia Press?'

Quentin caught the waiter's eye and pointed to his glass, then turned back to Hallie. 'I agree with her.'

Hallie put her glass down and stared at Quentin. She'd been hearing rumors ever since she was a child. True, they were only rumors, but from where Hallie sat a man was guilty till proven innocent.

'So Little Miss Boy Scout got to you too,' she said.

'Little Miss Boy Scout?'

'Olivia is always sexually prepared.'

Quentin took the fresh drink out of the waiter's hand before he could put it on the table and swallowed deeply.

'I'm not interested in Olivia's sexual predilections,' he said dryly, 'but I do care about your future. If you fire her, Hallie, you're the one who's going to look foolish.'

'You mean I don't already?'

'So far this affair hasn't got around. If it had, I'd have heard something.'

'It will. Jake moved out last night.'

'People will hear you've separated. Not exactly front-page news these days. Half the men I grew up with – at least half of those who're alive – have left their wives.'

The waiter brought lunch. Hallie looked down at her plate. The fish lay like a limp white rag. Her stomach lurched.

'Are you telling me not to fire her?'

'I'm not telling you anything. You're the publisher. As the chairman, president, and CEO, not to mention your godfather and old friend, I'm merely giving you some advice.'

'You expect me to go on working with her?'

Quentin put down his fork and put his hand over Hallie's.

'When that magazine hit the stands yesterday, you became the smartest and most successful publisher in the business. At the age of thirty-six.'

Hallie heard the undercurrent of intensity in his voice and realized suddenly that Quentin had never made the cover of *Time*.

'Don't ruin it with some tawdry scandal that, just for the record, isn't even a scandal in this day and age.' He let go of her hand. 'People are envying you today. Don't give the bastards reason to start laughing at you tomorrow.'

That night Olivia stopped in the door to Hallie's office again. She looked so scared Hallie almost felt sorry for her. The habits of friendship, like those of marriage, die hard. Maybe she would have felt sorry for her if Olivia hadn't looked so good as well. Her hair was a mass of honey-colored ringlets. A year earlier she'd convinced Hallie to perm her own. The resulting disaster had taken months to grow out.

Olivia cleared her throat. Her small pink tongue darted over her lips.

'I guess it won't do any good to say I'm sorry.'

Hallie stared at her. Did this honeyed belle really think she could charm her way out of anything?

'That's right. It won't.'

'I didn't think–'

'What did you think? That I wouldn't mind? That I'd turn Jake over to you like some manuscript I didn't have time for?'

Olivia dropped her eyes. Her lashes lay like a fragile web on her cheeks.

'The trouble with you, Olivia, is that you're too used to dealing with men.'

Olivia lifted her eyes and met Hallie's. 'I suppose Quentin told you I went to see him.'

'It was a smart move.'

That took a moment to sink it. When it did, Olivia couldn't help herself. She smiled. The dimples came out. Hallie wanted to slap her.

'I knew you wouldn't let personal feelings interfere with your professional judgment,' she said.

'Don't you believe it, Olivia. I'm keeping you on for personal reasons.'

Olivia stopped smiling.

'To remind me never to trust anyone again.'

VIII

There was a party – another party – that night. Though publishing is an industry manned by people who pay constant and noisy lip service to solitude, it would grind to a halt without lunches, dinners, and publication parties.

This one was for Lily Hart, an aging actress who had enough celebrity left to sell seventy-five thousand hardcover copies and, eventually, a million or so paperbacks of her life story. She thought the party was for her, and with good reason. Copies of her book were placed strategically around the ballroom of a club that was private, though not so exclusive as Quentin's. All night long the publicity director would bring people over to meet Lily Hart, and the publicity assistant would get her drinks, and men and women who hadn't yet opened her book and had no intention of doing so would tell her how marvelous it was. Lily Hart would think a lot of business was being transacted for her book. A lot of business would be transacted, but it would have nothing to do with Lily Hart's book. In quiet corners of the room an agent would mention a hot property to an editor, the head of a paperback house would whisper a figure to a subsidiary-rights director, someone in movie development would con an editorial assistant into a look at a manuscript, a writer would try to impress a critic, and a publisher would offer Amos Porter an astronomical sum of money to lure him away from Rutherford and Styles. Amos would string the publisher along for a while – he liked to see how high his stock had gone – but he'd never take anyone up on the offer. Amos Porter and Quentin Styles had been through thirteen books together. Even Hallie couldn't come between them. Amos was the only writer Quentin still edited. Quentin was the only editor Amos trusted.

When Hallie arrived at the party, neither her father nor Quentin was there, but her mother was standing alone in front of one of the French windows overlooking Fifth Avenue. Cecelia was wearing what *Vogue* used to call 'the little black dress,' wearing it with the kind of style found only in the pages of *Vogue*.

Cecelia was sixty-two. She looked fifty. A knockout fifty. An eye and chin tuck had helped, but good bones, a proud bearing, and constant vigilance had done most of the job. Hallie crumpled a little. Cecelia wasn't the kind of woman who'd pick up the phone and discover she'd lost her husband.

It had been the same all Hallie's life. No matter how hard she tried to put herself together, no matter how successful she thought she'd been, the minute she saw her mother, she knew she was a failure. Tonight it was just further corroboration.

And it wasn't only Cecelia's appearance. It was her presence. She was standing alone at the edge of a swirling party, but she didn't look unhappy or even uneasy, only vaguely bored.

Hallie said hello to several people on her way across the room.

'Why do you still come to these things?' she asked her mother.

Cecelia seemed surprised by the question. 'Why not?'

Hallie didn't press it. Her mother came to these things because her father, despite his insistence that he hated parties, came to them. Besides, what else did Cecelia have to do? That's why she was early and Amos was late. Cecelia lunched. She shopped. She kept up with people. She read voraciously. She did an incalculable amount of good for the sick and the poor, the underprivileged and the arts, but there was still something missing. Hallie had recognized it even as a child, when Amos used to disappear into his study to work and Cecelia, in the vacuum he left behind, just used to disappear a little.

'Besides, Lily called and asked us to be sure to come.'

'I didn't know you knew Lily Hart.' Hallie hadn't known, but she might have guessed. There weren't many celebrities her parents didn't know.

'Amos wrote the screenplay for one of her movies. About a hundred years ago.'

About a hundred years ago, Hallie knew, was 1951, when Amos had ridden the crest of his newfound fame as a novelist out to Hollywood. At the time, Amos had said he knew what he was getting into. He'd heard the cautionary tales. But Amos Porter was different. The moguls weren't going to chew him up and spit him out as they had Fitzgerald and Faulkner and West. Several months and one broken contract later, he and Cecelia had returned east. Hallie never found out what had happened, but eighteen months after that Amos's new novel was proclaimed the most scathing indictment of Hollywood since *The Day of the Locust*. Amos hadn't been different, but he had been revenged.

Cecelia looked at her daughter closely. 'You could use a touch more blusher.'

Hallie laughed. She realized it was the first time in twenty-four hours she had. She was a grown woman, head of one of the major publishing houses in the country, a celebrity who'd just made the cover of *Time*, but to her mother she was still a recalcitrant teenager who was alternately a little too bookish or a little too willful. Hallie had the feeling her father was going to up at any minute and ask what she was reading in school.

That was what it had been like growing up as the only child of her famous father and beautiful mother. There were plenty of messages, only sometimes they were more mixed than one might expect. Hallie had never forgotten that incident during her senior year when Amos had come to Cambridge to deliver a lecture. Afterward, he'd wanted to discuss his talk with Hallie over dinner – he valued her opinion, he'd insisted – but not until she'd gone back to her room and put on something more feminine than Jeans and a sweater.

'Feminine!' Hallie had protested. 'Is a chastity belt feminine enough?' But she'd gone to her room to change into a skirt.

That was about the time Cecelia had started sending her daughter all those letters asking what she planned to do with her life after graduation. 'A woman,' Cecelia had written, 'should have something of her own.' Hallie had agreed, but she wasn't sure what her mother thought that something ought to be, since there was another letter about how Cecelia had been cleaning out the attic at the farm and found Hallie's old doll, Guinevere. 'What a good little mother you were,' she'd written. 'You bathed and diapered and fed her that tiny plastic bottle with such somber love.'

Hallie hadn't bothered to write back that she'd been an only child. Her parents had loved her, but they'd had each other. She'd had Guinevere. It wasn't like having someone to love her the way her parents loved each other, but it was having someone all to herself to love.

Hallie told her mother a drink would have the same effect as blusher, and they pressed through the throng to the bar, then surfaced from it with drinks. Amos had somehow managed to enter the room with a glass in his hand. Hallie suspected he'd sent a secretary or reader, who was overwhelmed by the party in general and the presence of the great Amos Porter in particular, to get it. Amos's wife and daughter always chided him about the way he turned people into servants, but he just pointed out that the sweet young thing would dine out for months and probably end up telling her grandchildren about the time she'd brought Amos Porter a drink. And he was right.

He kissed Cecelia, then Hallie. At least he didn't mention her lack of color, but then Amos expected less of his daughter, at least in the beauty department.

'I have to talk to you both,' Hallie said, though she wasn't looking forward to the conversation. She wondered if Amos would say I told you so. She knew Cecelia would think she'd failed.

Even in that din, there was no missing her tone. The fine lines around Cecelia's eyes that she'd gone to considerable pain and expense to erase were suddenly visible. Amos's heavy black brows rose like twin steeples.

'What's wrong?' he asked, but before Hallie could answer, Vera Cantrell, who'd just paid a small fortune to run part of Amos's next book in *View* closed in on them.

Vera was as smooth and glossy as the stock her magazine was printed on. Amos said she had the mind of a sponge, the tongue of a viper, and the moral sense of an avocado, but from the way he turned to her now they might have been Siamese twins separated at birth. He put his hands on her waist, she put crimson talons on his shoulders, and they embraced. Hallie didn't blame her father. For one thing, he knew the importance of oiling the wheels. For another, he had always been a pushover for adoration, and *View* habitually referred to him as 'the greatest American writer working today.'

'Amos,' Vera breathed.

'Vera,' he replied.

This was a man, Hallie thought, celebrated for his quick wit.

Vera turned to Cecelia, and Cecelia turned on the charm. As an artist's wife, she knew as much or more than Amos about the importance of oiling the wheels.

When Vera turned back to Amos, Cecelia caught her daughter's eye. 'Dinner,' she mouthed to Hallie, then swiveled her perfect smile back to Vera.

Hallie moved off to congratulate Lily Hart on the publication of her book. That was when she saw Jake.

Hallie hadn't expected him to show up. Even Olivia had had the sense or the taste not to come. But he was working his way across the room, smiling that big white smile, shaking hands, doing business as usual. For the first time in her life, Hallie realized what a bastard she'd married.

Over the head of the guest of honor, she watched him moving to the corner where Cecelia was standing. It wasn't an accident. Hallie knew how Jake worked a room. He sized it up the minute he walked into it, then navigated accordingly. He always managed to get to the people he wanted to and elude those he didn't. If he ended up face to face with Cecelia, he'd meant to.

Cecelia let him take her hand. She even let him kiss

her cheek. The Quisling! Then Hallie remembered. Her mother didn't know.

The room was growing more crowded. Hallie heard herself saying all the ordinary things. This writer was up for grabs. That editor wanted to change houses. An agent was looking for a six-figure advance. A house had just taken a bath on a hard-and-soft deal. Books, money, gossip. Movies, miniseries, magazines. Affairs and break-ups. Hallie wondered how long it would be before she made that list.

She glanced across the room. Her mother and Jake were still talking. Cecelia's face was perfectly composed, but the twin furrows between her eyes had grown deeper. Jake must be telling her the whole story, his whole story. Hallie wondered what Jake's story could be. How could he justify to his wife's mother the fact that he'd been cheating on his wife. Then she remembered an old joke between Jake and her. Caught red-handed in Eden, he would have mumbled through a mouthful of Granny Smith, 'Apple? What apple?'

There were three bars. Hallie started toward the one farthest from her mother and Jake. Quentin stopped her on the way and said there was someone he wanted her to meet. He introduced Jonathan Graham. Hallie recognized the name immediately. It didn't match the appearance.

Jonathan Graham had hair like corn silk and a smile that was straight out of *Huckleberry Finn*. He also had a reputation for running Allied Entertainment Corporation as if it were an automobile assembly line. Hallie had heard that 'bottom line' were the two most imaginative words he knew. She wondered what he was doing here, then remembered Lily Hart had made most of her movies for World Pictures. A couple of years earlier, Allied had acquired World. The takeover had been, to say the least, hostile. The financial pages had been filled with battle reports for months.

Hallie indicated her glass, which she made a practice of keeping half empty for just such getaways, and told Graham it had been nice meeting him. On her way to the bar, another hand reached out and stopped her.

'Now that her face is in every doctor's waiting room she's forgotten her old authors,' Will Sawyer said to the man beside him. 'Not to mention her old friends.'

Will Sawyer was Hallie's favorite chèvre and chardonnay liberal. He was also one of her most successful authors and had been since she'd published his first book more than a decade before.

'Just remember, Hallie, I knew you when,' Will said. He touched her cheek with his. So did Carter Bolton. The fact that Hallie knew and liked Will and barely knew and didn't particularly like Carter had nothing to do with the cheek touching. It was that kind of party.

'I was just telling Will,' Carter said, 'that the next time you quote one of my reviews of one of his cockamamie books in an ad, you'd better use my name as well as the name of the paper. You don't think I heap all that praise just for the fun of it, do you?'

Carter smiled at Hallie, and she remembered what she didn't like about him. He was a friend of Olivia's. They'd met when she was in college and he was the writer in residence. Olivia had taken a course in creative writing. He'd taken her to bed. Her and every other female undergraduate in the seminar. Olivia had found out about the others at the end of the year, when they'd critiqued each other's work.

'You haven't lived, honey, till you've read half a dozen thinly fictionalized adolescent accounts of a torrid affair with the great writer in residence.'

'It must have been agony for you,' Hallie had said.

'Not so terrible. I got an A. And Carter helped me get my first job in publishing.'

'What about the other five women?'

'I guess they just weren't as talented.'

Hallie hadn't asked about the men in the class.

Will told Hallie he'd give her a call the next day. He wanted to deliver the rest of his next book. She promised to take him to lunch to celebrate.

'How about dinner?' he asked, as he always did. It was a long-standing joke between them that she never took Will for dinner because Jake didn't trust the two of them together after dark. Will always pointed out that since he wasn't a vampire, he was perfectly capable of doing anything he or she or both of them wanted to do in daylight.

'Dinner,' she agreed. He looked surprised. 'Call tomorrow, and we'll set it up.'

Hallie moved off to another bar, though she didn't need a fresh drink. She glanced around the room. The crowd was still thick and the traffic at the bar still heavy, though the hors d'oeuvres had begun to thin. She'd done her job. Now she wanted out. She glanced across the room. Her parents were talking to the guest of honor. Cecelia was wearing her formal face, the one that smiled out from the pages of *W* at least once a week. Amos looked uncomfortable or perhaps merely bored. He didn't have much patience with movie people.

Hallie started across the room. She could save her father and make her getaway at the same time. That was when she ran into Jake. Like Jake's running into Cecelia, Hallie knew it was no accident.

He maneuvered her into a corner. She had to let him in front of that crowd.

'How are you?' he asked.

'Fine,' she lied.

'I called you a couple of times this afternoon.'

'I wasn't in my office.'

'Sure.'

He stood looking down at her. There wasn't any shark's smile now. Hallie knew he was too smart for that. There were dark smudges under his eyes. She wondered if Olivia had kept him up all night.

'We ought to talk,' he said.

'That's what lawyers are for.'

It was the first time in all the years Hallie had known Jake that she'd caught him off guard.

'Have you seen one already?'

'Where do you think I was all afternoon?' she lied again.

'You mean that? One transgression, and it's all over?'

'One transgression?' she repeated. 'Oh, I get it. Last night was the first time.'

'Hallie.' Her name came out as a plea.

She felt the stinging behind her eyes again and turned away. She barely made it to the ladies' room before she started to cry.

Sheila Dent, the publicity director, came in a moment later. She stopped dead when she saw Hallie. 'What's wrong?'

Hallie caught Sheila's eyes in the mirror. Sheila was a good PR woman. She had a direct line to every major talk show and all the metropolitan dailies. If there was one thing Sheila knew, it was how to get the word out.

Hallie turned from the mirror. The tears were streaming down her cheeks now, but that was all right.

'I must be crazy,' Hallie said, 'trying to break in contacts at a cocktail party where people still smoke.'

IX

They never did get out to dinner that night. Hallie had the feeling her mother didn't trust her not to make another scene like the one in the ladies' room. Hallie didn't mind. Her jaw muscles ached from being clenched into a smile.

They went back to the townhouse. While Amos fumbled for the key and Cecelia produced one from her handbag – it was Mae's night out – Hallie stood in the vestibule, remembering the stories she'd grown up on. Her parents loved to reminisce about the good-old, bad-old days when they were young and poor. Hallie knew all the stories. She also knew that only a month before a real-estate developer had offered six and a half million for the house. From that vantage point, poverty was bound to look romantic.

Amos said he was going up to his study. Just for a moment, he insisted. Something had come to him at the party, and he wanted to get it down before he lost it.

'I'll be back in a flash,' he said as he started up the stairs to the fourth floor. Normally he would have taken the elevator, especially after a party, but not after this particular party. He hadn't seen Lily Hart in years. She looked old. It made him feel ancient. He told himself he wasn't ancient. Besides, men aged more gracefully than women, and once-beautiful movie stars aged least gracefully of all. Lily Hart was old. Amos Porter was a mature writer at the height of his powers. His big feet pounded up the stairs. Toward the top of the first flight, he took the steps two at a time. He wondered if Cecelia was watching.

Cecelia and Hallie went down the hall to the library. This was the show library where they read and entertained and watched the evening news. Nonetheless, Amos's presence dominated this room as well as his working library upstairs. Thirteen novels, translated into twenty-eight languages, filled the shelves between the widows. Hallie's eye ran over the familiar rainbow of book spines, foot after foot, yard after yard of Amos Porter, Amos Porter, Amos Porter. Cecelia called it the Great Wall. They settled at opposite ends of the long leather sofa.

'I suppose Jake told you the whole story,' Hallie said.

'He told me his story. I'm waiting to hear yours.'

Hallie told her. Cecelia didn't speak until her daughter was finished. Then she asked what Hallie was going to do.

'Divorce him.'

'Tonight, presumably.'

'It's not a joke.'

'I know it's not, baby.'

Hallie thought that it had been years since her mother had called her 'baby.'

102

Cecelia thought it had been years since she'd dared call her daughter 'baby.'

'But I'm trying to help you keep your sense of humor, because you're going to need it.' She reached out and took Hallie's hand. 'I'm also trying to keep you from doing something you'll regret.'

'Are you telling me to forget the affair?'

'If only you could. But, of course, that's the one thing you'll never be able to do. Do you love him?'

'I did.'

Cecelia looked at her daughter for a long minute. Hallie thought, not for the first time, that her mother's eyes were as dark and unintelligible as camera shutters. They recorded everything and gave away nothing.

'Can you really turn it on and off that easily?'

Hallie pulled her hand out of her mother's grasp. 'For God's sake, he's been screwing my best friend!'

'I never thought of Olivia as your best friend, but that's not the point. Jake is. And he isn't unique.'

'You mean it's the nature of men? They screw around?'

'Men. Women. Didn't you have a best seller on the subject a few months ago? Rather sordid, I thought. Full of steamy case histories and questionable statistics.'

'I don't want to be one of those statistics. You aren't.'

Cecelia laughed. 'Your father belongs to an exclusive club. Shakespeare, Proust, Amos Porter, and God.'

The familiar joke hit Hallie with new force. Cecelia

put up a good front. She joked about Amos's pomposities and teased him about his foibles, but she was the keeper of the flame. She was the one who'd built the Great Wall of his books. She was the one who kept the friends and groupies away from his study so he could work, just as she'd kept Hallie quiet as a child because Daddy was writing. And even before that, she was the one who'd married a returning World War II vet with no future except his own dreams, and who'd believed in them and him so strongly that she'd given up her own writing to support his. Hallie knew that her mother's jokes about her father were the armor that protected the soft core. And Cecelia's soft core was her fierce adoration of and – this was the part that frightened Hallie – total dependence on Amos.

'Did you ever think,' Cecelia asked, 'that maybe that was all he was doing? "Screwing her," as you so eloquently put it?'

'Isn't that enough ?'

'You never used to take sex so seriously'. 'You're part of the post-pill, pre-AIDS generation. Sex was something between a birthright and a pastime. All I'm saying is that it may not have meant anything to Jake.'

'Then why did he do it ?'

'You tell me. He's your husband.'

'I thought we were happy.'

'Apparently one of you wasn't.'

Hallie jumped up off the sofa. 'I won't buy it!'

'What?'

'Your generation's party line. If a husband has an

affair it must be the wife's fault.' Hallie stood staring down at her mother. 'I'll tell you why Jake was screwing around. Because when he sees something he wants, he has to have it.'

'That's the way he got you, baby.'

Hallie wished her mother hadn't said that. It brought it all back. She collapsed on the sofa and started to cry. Again.

Cecelia pulled her daughter to her and held her and rocked her as if she really were a baby. But there was a difference. Now Cecelia didn't tell her daughter that everything was going to be all right.

Amos came back, and they went down to the kitchen and rehashed it all over again. Hallie had the feeling she'd be doing that for the rest of her life. Finally, Cecelia walked her daughter to the door. Hallie picked up her briefcase. Cecelia looked from it to her daughter's face.

'A husband isn't like a briefcase or a pair of running shoes.'

Hallie stood staring at her mother. No mascara streaked her cheeks. Her eyes looked clear as a baby's, or an ad for Visine.

'What's that supposed to mean?'

'You don't trade him in that easily.'

Hallie turned away from the image of perfection and started out of the townhouse. 'You do if he's defective.'

X

Every Wednesday morning the editorial board of Rutherford and Styles met to decide which proposals and manuscripts the house would buy. Twelve people attended the meeting, which was not to say that twelve people made the decisions. The senior editors presented their books and those of their underlings. The directors of subsidiary rights, marketing, and publicity shot them down. Hallie had the final say. Quentin hadn't attended an editorial meeting in years.

Hallie was the last one to get to the conference room that morning. It seemed to her that everyone stopped talking when she entered. She told herself it was only her imagination. She took her place at the head of the table and noticed that Olivia had taken her usual seat on her right. You had to hand it to Olivia. Thirty-six hours earlier she'd been caught in bed, or at least promising to be there, with Hallie's husband. Twenty-four, she'd been almost out of a job. Now she was back in her old place as if nothing had happened, as if she and Hallie were still the most successful female buddy story in the history of publishing.

Olivia presented two books that morning. Hallie wasn't particularly high on either of them, but she ended up giving the go-ahead to one. She was damned if she'd have the whole house, or anyone who knew, think she was spiteful.

By the time she got back to her office, there was a stack of pink phone slips waiting. None was unusual, but a few were unexpected. Editors she hadn't seen in months and agents she no longer dealt with were suddenly calling. Publishing was, as this business with Jake and Olivia proved, an incestuous business. As in any close family, news traveled fast. Nobody was so crass as to call and say, what's this I hear about you and Jake splitting up? But everyone would be eager to suggest lunch or dinner or a drink. Everyone wanted the dirt. Hallie and Jake had, as *Time* had pointed out, 'couple clout.' Correction, Hallie thought. They had had it.

She figured she'd be safer returning writers' calls. The working ones were usually more plugged in to their word processors than the grapevine. She should have known Will Sawyer, with his parties and causes, talk shows and interviews, would be an exception to that rule, but then her mind wasn't functioning at full speed that morning.

She dialed Will's number. She'd managed to call the one person who would come out and ask about Jake and her. Will hated hypocrisy.

'Is it true or just a rumor?'

'It's true.'

'I'm sorry.'

The funny thing, Hallie thought, was that he

sounded that way. He sounded curious but he sounded sorry too.

'Want a shoulder to cry on?'

Hallie felt the need welling up, as powerful as sexual hunger. An arm around her shoulder, a strong voice murmuring reassurances, a male presence convincing her she wasn't ugly, undesirable, a failure. It was tempting. She opened her mouth. She could feel the words forming. But even before she spoke them, she knew the pathetic, self-pitying sound of them. It reminded her of the pity in Amos's voice that afternoon on the porch, and the disgust. She wouldn't give anyone the satisfaction.

'Nothing to cry about,' she said brightly, too brightly, she thought. 'How about that manuscript?'

'It's brilliant. But don't take my word for it. I'll swap you the last five chapters of *American at the Crossroads* for an expense-account dinner. Remember, you promised it would be dinner this time.'

They got out their calendars. Will was going to Washington to chastise a cabinet member. Hallie was going to Cambridge to see a Nobel-Prize-winning writer. He had a party. She had a dinner. They found an evening ten days away.

The week went on that way. A few people said they were sorry. Hallie said thanks. On the lunch circuit admirers said she was taking it well. Others insisted they'd always known she had printer's ink for blood and a profit-and-loss statement where her heart ought to be.

She called Wendell Tyson, Amos's attorney, and

left a message with his secretary that she wanted the name of a good divorce lawyer. Wendell called back and gave her the name of a man who was, he insisted, the best 'matrimonial attorney' in town. Hallie thought it was an odd euphemism. 'Matrimonial' applied to the judge who'd married her and Jake. The lawyers who would take care of the break-up ought to be called 'divorce,' but she didn't mention the distinction. Wendell was a busy man without much interest in semantics.

Hallie put the name down on her Rolodex. She was late for a meeting.

Jake telephoned several times. She finally took the call. He wanted to know if she was planning to use the country house for the weekend. A few years before they'd bought an eighteenth-century wreck near her parents' farm in Connecticut. Since then it had taken too much of both their money and their time. She told him she wasn't planning to use it that weekend.

'Do you mind if I do?'

'I thought you'd want to stay in town. To get your books out of the apartment.'

'I don't have any place to put them,' he said.

Hallie knew there wasn't an inch of unused space in Olivia's apartment.

She wondered if he was planning to take Olivia to the country for the weekend but refused to ask. Jake's life was his own now, and the house was half his. She remembered a magazine editor she'd lunched with a few months earlier. The woman's face had turned ugly with rage and her voice had rasped with bitterness. 'I'll burn the house down before I'll let him take that bitch there,' the woman had said. Hallie had pitied the editor, but she'd been a little contemptuous of her, too. That lunch had only reinforced what Hallie had learned at an early age. It was safer to keep the pain to yourself.

'Don't forget to turn the heater down when you leave on Sunday night,' Hallie said.

'Sure,' Jake answered and wondered what he'd expected. That she'd break down and tell him she couldn't stand the idea of his going to their place without her? That she'd suggest going with him? Not Hallie. She'd think of the practical side. She'd remind him to turn down the furnace.

Jake had no intention of taking Olivia to the farm that weekend. For one thing, he wanted to be alone. He had to sort things out. For another, it seemed too tacky, kind of like sleeping with one woman in another woman's bed. At least he'd never done that.

He put his hand over his eyes and leaned on his desk. Christ, was that what he passed off as scruples now? For the hundredth time in the last few days he tried to figure out how he'd got where he was.

Olivia liked to think of herself as a survivor. Not because she was so good looking, which she happened to be, or so good in bed, which she also was, but because she was smart. Olivia had a built-in seismograph that measured what was going on in a man's mind while the rest of her concentrated on what was going on with his body. She could distinguish a one-night stand from a full-scale affair before they were even in bed. She could spot the difference between the voice of a man who meant what he was saying and one who only thought he did before they were out of it. It was a God-given talent. Some women could play the piano. Others could cook. Olivia could take care of herself. At least she'd been able to until now.

Damn Jake and his Jewish guilt! She'd seen it before. She'd had to fight through it that first night at his and Hallie's apartment. But she'd had the ammunition. For one thing, Jake loved sex. He wasn't a womanizer. He didn't want to rack up notches on his belt. He just loved sex. For another, he'd been furious at Hallie. It had been as easy as pushing buttons.

But now Hallie had found out, and if Jake was still furious, he was even more guilty. He was trying to cool Olivia. Only she had no intention of being cooled. When she'd read the words 'couple clout' in that article on Hallie, her mouth had watered. She had no intention of being cooled.

'Oh' was all she said when Jake announced he was going to the country for the weekend and made no mention of taking her. She managed to get a lot of suffering into that one syllable.

Jake picked up on the sound. 'Don't you have plans?'

'Well, actually . . .' She let her voice trail off.

'Actually what?'

'I've kind of got out of the habit of making plans with other people. I mean, you never knew when

112

you could get away from Hallie, and when you could, well . . . Oh, hell, honey, there's no point in playing hard to get. I stopped making plans with other people because I wanted to be with you whenever I could. And that's always been whenever you could.'

Jake asked her what time on Friday she'd be ready to leave for the country.

The weather forecasters predicted a perfect Indian-summer weekend.

'Come up to the farm,' Cecelia urged her daughter. 'It'll be good for you to get away.'

'I have too much work.'

'Bring your manuscripts. You can work up there.'

'It's more than manuscripts,' Hallie snapped. 'I'm trying to run a publishing house here, and some goddamn agent has set an auction for Friday afternoon. We can't all drop everything and go to the country just because we feel like it.'

There was silence on the other end of the line.

'I'm sorry,' Hallie said. 'It's not your fault.'

Cecelia still didn't answer. She was thinking that in some way it might be. She'd been determined to keep Hallie from repeating her own mistakes, desperate to teach her daughter the lessons it had taken her a lifetime to learn and to spare her the pain of learning them. Cecelia had thought she'd been successful. Now she wondered if she'd been too successful.

Hallie told her mother she'd take the train up on Saturday.

Cecelia and Amos were waiting at the station. Hallie saw them as soon as she swung down from the train. Amos was leaning against the racing-green Jaguar, Cecelia was standing beside it. She still looked better in men's trousers than any woman Hallie knew.

'Are you two posing for *Town & Country* or waiting for your daughter?' Hallie asked.

Amos took the overnight bag from her. 'What makes you think the two pursuits are mutually exclusive?' he said through teeth clenched around a carved English pipe.

They all climbed into the car.

'How did the auction go?' Cecelia asked.

'I dropped out at three hundred and seventy-five thou.'

Amos honked at the car in front of them, which had actually come to a full stop at a stop sign. 'What was the book?'

'A first novel.'

He gunned the motor. 'You know how much of an advance I got for my first novel?'

Hallie and Cecelia both knew, but they waited for him to tell them again.

'Twelve hundred dollars.'

'That was in 1947,' Cecelia said. 'And in the last forty years you've made more than a million in royalties on it, darling.'

'What was the first novel?' Cecelia half turned in the front seat to ask her daughter.

'That's the best part,' Hallie said. 'An autobiographical novel by an eighty-four-year-old

114

woman. She wrote it years ago but whipped it into shape in a nursing home.'

Amos reached over and patted Cecelia's thigh. 'There you go, sweetheart. Why don't you write a novel? Then I can retire.'

That afternoon Cecelia and Hallie drove back into the village. There'd be ten for dinner that night – an intimate evening by her parents' standard – and Cecelia wanted to pick up a few things. She pulled the Jaguar into the big parking lot behind the galleria. When Amos and Cecelia had bought the farm, there'd been no parking lot and no galleria of shops. If you wanted to pick up a few things, you drove down to the general store left your car, with the keys in it, in front; and settled for whatever dusty packages were left on the shelves. The general store was long gone, replaced by a maze of achingly cute shops selling crème fraîche, early American quilts, and designer ice-cream cones. Main Street was a war zone. On one side were the refugees from the city dressed in Ralph Lauren's dreamy vision of English country life or the fading American frontier; on the other were natives in polyester and nondesigner denim. Hallie read the mutual hostility in the faces of both factions, though a few of the locals said hello to her mother. The Porters had been around for a long time, and Mrs Porter was known to be a nice woman.

Cecelia had to stop in the hardware store. Hallie said she'd check out the boutique windows. They'd meet in the Cheshire Cheese.

Later, Hallie couldn't figure out why she'd drifted into the lingerie store. She wasn't an aimless shopper. There'd been nothing in the window that attracted her. And it wasn't as if she needed anything. The way her life was going, she could walk around in torn bras and old-fashioned cotton briefs and no one would be the wiser. If she were a more superstitious woman, she would have said it was a sixth sense or some supernatural force or vibes. Cecelia said it was probably just the end-of-summer sale sign.

Hallie was standing there going through some marked-down robes – if you spent every night reading into the early hours of the morning, you never had enough robes – when she heard the voice from behind the dressing-room curtain. She'd know that voice anywhere, even without the Southern accent.

'Just putting it on makes me feel positively immoral,' the voice drawled.

The saleswoman stuck her head inside the fitting room. 'Wow!' she said. 'You put that on, and I guarantee your boyfriend will tear it right off.'

Hallie told herself to run. Get out of the store. Get out of town. Go back to the farm. But she stood there, unable to move. Then the saleswoman pushed the curtain open a little more, and it was too late to run.

Hallie and Olivia stood staring at each other. Olivia was the one who was half undressed, but somehow Hallie felt exposed. 'Hello, Olivia.' Hallie was shocked at the sound of her own voice. It was so dispassionate, she might have been calling a meeting to order.

'Hallie.' Olivia's voice was faint, as if she weren't sure of her ground. 'I didn't know you were out there.'

They stood staring at each other for another minute. Hallie could feel the sweat running down her sides. In the three-way mirror the images of a half-naked Olivia went on into an eternity of perfection.

'It's a nice nightgown,' Hallie said finally in that same cool voice.

' "Nice" is putting it mildly,' the saleswoman said. 'I told her, the minute she puts that on, her boyfriend – '

'We heard you!' Olivia's voice cut her off. The saleswoman looked stunned, but neither of them was paying attention to the saleswoman.

'Look, Hallie,' Olivia began, but Hallie mumbled something about being late. She never did remember how she got out of the store.

Outside, the sun was hot on her face. It illuminated her shame. She pulled her dark glasses out of her bag and put them on, but it was no good. She couldn't hide. She stumbled into a couple eating ice-cream cones, almost fell over a child in a stroller, and finally collapsed onto one of the benches on the town green.

She was going to have to get used to it. Jake and Olivia. She put her head in her hands.

'Hallie! I thought you were going to meet me in the cheese shop.'

Hallie turned at the sound of her mother's voice. Here at least was solace. That was when she saw

117

them. Cecelia and Jake were crossing the green toward her.

'Look who I ran into in the hardware store,' Cecelia said.

Jake smiled, not the big shark's smile but a small, shy one that was turned inside out by a fleeting nervous tic at one side of his mouth. Hallie recognized that tic and fought against it. Damnit, he ought to be embarrassed.

'I'm still trying to fix that faucet in the downstairs bathroom,' he explained.

'You never were any good at fixing things,' Hallie said. Then she turned and crossed the green to the parking lot.

'Was that supposed to be a double entendre?' Cecelia asked when they were back in the car. 'Because marriages can be fixed, you know.'

'Not this one.'

'He seemed eager to see you. When I told him I was meeting you, he walked along with me. I think he was hoping for an invitation to come back to the house.'

'With or without Olivia?'

'There's no reason to assume he brought her out for the weekend.'

'I'm not assuming. I ran into Olivia. Trying on nightgowns. Black and lacy. You know the kind.'

Cecelia had nothing to say to that.

But the conversation wasn't closed. 'Do you have any idea when this affair started?' Cecelia asked later that afternoon, when they were on the wide porch that wrapped around the house. Cecelia and

Amos were in Adirondack chairs, and Hallie was stretched out in the hammock. She could tell from her mother's voice that she'd been thinking about the question for some time.

'I don't know. I don't even want to know.'

Amos nodded approval without looking up from his book.

'My guess is the beginning of the summer,' Cecelia said. 'When you were in London.'

'You mean because I was out of town? Then why not last spring when I went to Boulogne? Jake didn't go to the book fair. Or during any of the other trips, for that matter?'

'Because something bothered him about that trip. We had dinner the night before you came home, and I could tell.'

Amos looked up from his book. 'I didn't notice anything.'

'What were you doing in London anyway?' Cecelia asked.

'The usual. Buying books. Seeing English publishers and a couple of authors. It was pretty hectic. That's why I stayed a few extra days. But it wasn't any different from any of the other trips.'

'It was to Jake.'

Hallie had had enough of her mother's theories. Her mother's excuses. When you were powerless, you found reasons to do what you had no choice not to do. But Hallie wasn't powerless. She had a choice. She'd seen to that. She and Amos and, to be fair, Cecelia. A woman ought to have something of her own, Cecelia had written. And her life, a pale shadow of Amos's, had driven home the lesson.

Hallie had learned it well. She had her own work, her own money, her own life. She swung her legs over the side of the hammock and faced her mother.

'The affair had nothing to do with that trip to London or anything else except the fact that Jake wanted to go to bed with Olivia and he did. Now, can we drop the subject, please?'

Amos closed his book. 'I think Hallie's right. In fact, I think she's behaving admirably.'

'It all depends on how you define "admirably",' Cecelia said.

'Grace under pressure,' Amos answered.

Cecelia looked at her husband. He believed in grace under pressure. She believed in survival.

XI

'What do you have against Quentin Styles?' Olivia went on pushing the bentwood rocker back and forth with her toes while she stared down at Jake. He was stretched out on the hooked rug in front of the hearth where a straw basket overflowed with dried flowers. Everything about the house was perfect, Olivia thought, except the fact that it belonged to Hallie. At least half of it did.

Jake looked up from the book propped on his chest. 'I don't have anything against Quentin. Except that Quentin has something against me.'

Olivia stopped rocking. The motion was equivalent to a hound pricking up its ears.

'What?'

'I wish I knew.' The answer wasn't exactly ingenuous. Jake didn't know for sure what Quentin had against him, but he suspected.

'I get the feeling he didn't want you to marry Hallie.'

Jake put down his book. 'How did you know that?'

Olivia smiled. It wasn't only that she was so smart. Other people were so transparent. 'Just a guess, honey. From watching Quent with Hallie.' From envying Quent with Hallie. Hallie, who had everything and everyone. 'I've done some research on Quentin.'

Jake picked up his book again but Olivia went on.

'There was a file. A few years ago one of the editors was trying to get him to write his memoirs. You should see the women he's had affairs with. Rita Hayworth. Lily Hart. There were rumors about Marilyn Monroe, but, of course, there are always rumors about her. Simone de Beauvoire – in his older-woman period.'

'Everything but the Atlantic cable.'

'What?'

'It's an old saying. Quentin would know it. He – or she – has laid everything but the Atlantic cable.'

'Quentin's not so old. I mean, some women like older men.'

'You'd know more about that than I would.' Jake turned a page.

Olivia caught herself. She was trying to get information, not give it away.

Quentin was still an unfinished story. The sex had been good, but she'd seen him twice in the office since that morning and he'd acted as if nothing had happened. Of course, both times there'd been other people around and Olivia had been equally correct. She made it clear to Quentin that she knew how to play the game. Still, a longer-running contract wasn't out of the question. Their advantages and interests were well matched. Quentin had pots of money, power, and all the right connections. She had youth, looks, and brains. Olivia went on rocking while she calculated the odds. What if he got sick? What if he had a stroke and turned into a vegetable?

Behind his head Jake heard the chair stop rocking. Then it started again.

That was what pots of money and sanatoriums and private nurses were for. What if he had a heart attack? But she was getting morbid. There was nothing wrong with Quentin. The morning in his apartment had proved that. She thought of moving into that apartment, entertaining in that apartment, receiving Hallie in that apartment. Maybe then Hallie would finally stop condescending to her, Hallie and everyone else.

It was something to think about but not get carried away with. Her mouth savored the words 'couple clout.' She'd blown it at that National Book Awards party so many years ago, but she wasn't going to make the same mistake twice. Jake had less money but more of a future. He also had that thick fringe of lashes, that loose-jointed way of moving that was like a whispered promise of sex, and – sorry, Quent – the ability to keep that promise three or four times a night. Besides, a bird in the hand, Olivia's mother always used to say.

Olivia slid to the floor.

'Aren't you tired?' She pushed his book side and stretched out on top of him.

Jake laughed. 'I assume that's a euphemism. I don't think you actually want me tired.'

She opened his belt.

'I'm not worried.'

She unzipped his jeans.

'I took a life-saving course.'

She kissed him.

'I'm good at mouth-to-mouth resuscitation.'

She slid down until she was kneeling between his legs.

'Or mouth-to-anything else you have in mind.'

Later that night they went up to the bedroom with the old four-poster Jake and Hallie had found at a flea market. He hadn't forgotten his fastidiousness, merely recognized its absurdity. There wasn't much point in worrying about a bed when you'd already done pretty much everything you could on the living-room floor.

Hallie lay in the darkness, listening to the voices of the old farmhouse. Creaking eaves, groaning foundations, tree branches sweeping over shingles, the wind rattling windows. If there were human sounds in the house, she couldn't hear them. The walls were thick, and her parents' room was far down the hall. When she was a child, the distance had frightened her. Her mother and father had seemed so far away in the darkness. As an adolescent, she'd welcomed it. By then she'd learned about sex or at least read about it. It was something that happened to beautiful women. Women like her mother. Women like Olivia.

Hallie turned on her side. It didn't help. She thought of her parents down the hall, locked together in lifelong marriage. She thought of Jake and Olivia locked together in the bed she and Jake had bought.

She sat up, turned on the light, and took a manuscript from the night table. At least she still had her work.

XII

On Tuesday morning Quentin's secretary called Hallie's to ask if they could meet at one rather than their usual twelve-thirty. There would be a third for lunch, and one o'clock would be more convenient for him.

Hallie didn't tell her secretary to find out who the third was. If Quentin had wanted her to know, he would have included it in the message. If he didn't want her to find out, he wouldn't have told his secretary.

Hallie put the pieces together. The week before Quentin had played the peacemaker in her professional life. Now he was going to work on her personal life. Hallie thought of Quentin pleading Jake's cause. Infidelity, like politics, made strange bedfellows.

Olivia came into Hallie's office as she was getting ready to leave for lunch. Olivia was wearing an Armani jacket that she'd blown more than two weeks' salary on – Hallie knew, because they'd been together when Olivia had bought it – and carrying a boxed manuscript.

She held it out to Hallie. 'I thought maybe you could take a look at this before tomorrow's meeting. I've already got two good readings on it, but they're asking six figures.'

There was nothing odd about the request. For the small books Hallie relied on the reports of Olivia and the other editors, but she usually took a look at the big ones herself. The terms 'big' and 'small' referred to monetary advances rather than length or literary quality.

Hallie took the box from her. The label read 'The Jackie Kay Agency.' Jackie Kay had split off from one of the big agencies and taken a stable full of young writers with her. The young writers were growing up. Jackie's agency was coming of age. None of this was unusual, except for one thing. Jackie had never submitted anything to Olivia before. When she had something for R and S, especially something big, she'd always sent it straight to Hallie.

Olivia watched Hallie glance at the label, then smiled. The dimples came out. She turned and left the office. Hallie watched her go. Beneath the Armani jacket, she was wearing a short tight skirt and heels so high Hallie couldn't have walked in them. The skirt and shoes were a mistake. Legs were Olivia's one shortcoming. Literally. Her legs were short and thick at the ankles. They weren't grotesque, just a letdown after the rest of her. They were, Hallie thought, the single area in which she had it over Olivia, thanks to Cecelia.

Quentin was alone at the table when Hallie got there.

Gray suit. Watch fob. Martini. He stood when she reached the table and kissed her on the cheek. It was the regulation Tuesday lunch. There was only one difference. The pale gray eyes behind the rimless glasses didn't meet hers.

'Where's the mystery guest?' Hallie asked as she slid into the chair the waiter dragged out for her.

'He'll be along.' Quentin dropped his eyes again. 'I imagine you've guessed who it is.'

She ordered a martini. Quentin looked surprised, then worried.

'I have my suspicions,' Hallie said.

'I thought it would be better to let him explain things himself.'

'I know all about those explanations.'

'You ought to at least give him a chance.'

'Now you sound like Cecelia.'

'What does she have to do with it?'

'Jake got to her, too. He's enlisting a whole damn army of support.'

'You think I'm talking about Jake?'

'Who else?'

That was when Jonathan Graham joined them at the table.

Graham spent the rest of lunch reassuring Hallie. Quentin didn't say much, except that he'd sold out to Allied Entertainment Corporation. Sold out, Hallie thought, was right.

Graham said he wanted Hallie to stay on as publisher. He told her she'd have a free hand. He added that there'd be a nice fat contract. Quentin and Hallie had never bothered with one.

'That'll be the only change, Hallie. A contract to protect you and us. As for the rest, we want you to go on doing exactly what you've been doing.'

The waiter brought a second drink for Quentin, and Hallie pointed to her empty glass. Quentin looked alarmed. If Graham even noticed, he didn't show it.' He was drinking Perrier.

'I don't have a lot of experience with this sort of thing,' Hallie said to Graham, 'but I do know one thing. Nobody acquires a company *not* to change it.'

Hallie had expected Jake at lunch that day. She wasn't expecting him when she walked into the apartment that night. She hadn't bothered to put on lipstick before she'd left the office. Someday, she thought as soon as she saw him, she'd learn to listen to her mother. Or was it her father?

Jake was sitting in the living room with a drink. She'd been walking into the apartment and finding him that way for years, except that now he wasn't reading anything. He was just sitting there, waiting.

'I needed a couple of things the housekeeper forgot to pack.'

'Did you get them?'

'I thought I'd wait around till you got home.'

'What for?'

Jake clenched and unclenched his fist. He wondered if she was trying to make him angry or just acting out of habit.

'Because we ought to talk. We've shouted, and you've threatened, and I've pleaded, but we haven't talked.' He stared at her. 'Not for a long time.'

She sat across from him. 'Fine. We'll talk. I thought I'd keep the apartment. You take the house. Same with the furniture in each. You'll want some of the books that are here, but I want some that are in the country.'

'You're forgetting the computer, the art-deco collection, the Stella litho . . .'

'I don't care –' she began.

'I was joking, Hallie.'

'Maybe I don't think it's funny.'

'And maybe I think there's more to it than dividing up the spoils.'

He put his drink down on the table and his head in his hands. She couldn't see his face, only the thick, dark hair raked by finger marks. She didn't trust him for a minute.

'I don't want a divorce, Hallie.'

'What did you have in mind, a ménage à trois?'

He looked up. 'I thought you didn't think it was funny.'

She didn't tell him that black humor was the only thing that stood between her and breaking down in front of him.

'I don't care about Olivia,' he said.

She stood. He looked up at her. She could tell from his face that he thought he'd pulled it off. Everything was going to be all right again.

'You really are more of a bastard than I thought.'

His face collapsed.

'You screw Olivia and tell me you don't care about her. While you were still screwing me, that is.

Incidentally, how long–' She stopped, suddenly aware of the grating sound of her own voice. 'Forget it.'

He started to say something, but she cut him off. 'We've talked. Now it's up to the lawyers.'

She decided to call the name on her Rolodex the first thing in the morning.

XIII

Hallie never did get to call the lawyer the next morning. The phone was ringing when she walked into her office. It didn't stop all day. Allied Entertainment Corporation had announced its acquisition of Rutherford and Styles. Jonathan Graham, Allied's CEO, had said he had no intention of interfering with R and S's publishing or management style. When the papers called, Hallie told them the same thing. Rutherford and Styles would continue to publish books of literary merit and commercial potential. She called Sheila Dent, the publicity director, into her office and told her to send out a release corroborating the lies they were all telling each other.

Still, the phone kept ringing. There were several feelers to see if Hallie was looking for a job and two outright offers. A few agents called to ask how this would affect contracts under negotiation. A friend in venture capital wanted to warn Hallie about Jonathan Graham.

'He's a shark,' Martha said.

'No kidding.'

Then there were the writers.

'I won't be censored!' Will Sawyer screamed. At least Hallie thought it was Will and that was what he was saying. His voice was garbled, and the words were almost unintelligible.

'Is that you, Will? I can barely hear you.'

'I'm calling from the plane. I said I won't turn my stuff into white bread to conform to some damn corporate policy.'

'Your professional integrity's safe with R and S, Will.'

A novelist whose book had been under option by World Pictures for what felt like a lifetime called.

'Does this mean they're finally going to make it into a movie?' she asked.

'Hope springs eternal,' Hallie told her.

Even Amos got into the act.

'I never thought I'd see the day I'd be published by a bunch of Hollywood moguls and Wall Street tycoons.'

'You're not. You're being published by R and S and edited by Quentin.'

'Didn't Quent tell you?'

'Tell me what?' Hallie was getting tired of Quentin's surprises.

'He's going to be strictly corporate from now on. Won't pick up a blue pencil. Not even for me.'

'We'll work something out,' Hallie said.

'We're going to have to give it serious thought. My first instinct was you, but I'm not so sure. It would be like going to your own child for open-heart surgery.'

Hallie looked at the lights on her telephone. They were flashing like a Christmas tree. 'We'll think of something.'

She pushed the button for the next call. It was Cecelia. There really was some sort of sixth sense between her parents. Amos was calling from his study. Cecelia was downstairs on her own phone. But they'd both called at exactly the same time.

'I won't keep you,' Cecelia said. 'Your phone must be dancing off the hook this morning. Ours are. And Amos is in high dudgeon.'

'I know. I just spoke to him.'

'Do you think you could stop by tonight? I'm sure you have something on. We have that benefit for the film institute. I'll be glad when Lily Hart goes back to the coast. But come by for a quick drink. Maybe the three of us can figure out what all this means.'

The phones kept ringing all day. Every time there was a lull, someone in the house took advantage of it to slip into Hallie's office.

'You think they really mean it?' Sheila asked when she brought the publicity release for Hallie's approval. 'That they're not going to change anything, I mean.'

'Of course,' Hallie lied, but Sheila was no dope. She didn't believe it for a minute.

Bob Sherwood, the head of marketing, came barreling in as Sheila went out. Bob was short and squat, and the only hair on his head was a white beard. He looked like a malevolent Santa Claus, with the emphasis on malevolent. At Hallie's first R and S

Christmas party, Bob had cornered her and told her in graphic detail what he wanted to do to her body. When Hallie said that if it was all the same to him she'd rather skip it, he suggested to her and most of the sales force that she was a 'ball-cutting bull dyke.' Since neither Bob nor Hallie had ever mentioned the incident again and had always worked well together, Hallie assumed that either Bob was so drunk or the incident so commonplace that he didn't remember it.

'Did Graham say anything about marketing?' Bob asked.

'He didn't say anything about anything, except that he wants us to go on doing what we've been doing.'

'I hope you told him to blow it out his ear or some other bodily orifice.'

'I didn't think that would be an auspicious start, Bob.'

'I guess there's always early retirement,' he said on his way out of her office.

'Hallie could almost hear the people dusting off their résumés. On her way to the production department, she passed a group of junior and assistant editors. They were making up a list who would be the first to go. She didn't ask them how high they'd put her name.

Olivia was one of the few people who didn't turn up in Hallie's office that day. She had other sources of information.

Olivia couldn't see the reception area from her office, but her secretary's desk commanded a clear view of it. After the secretary and almost everyone else had left, Olivia found a lot of excuses to putter around the desk that evening. A little after six she saw what she was looking for.

At that hour only one elevator was working, and Quentin had to wait for a few minutes. She grabbed her briefcase and raincoat but left her umbrella behind.

'You certainly dropped a bombshell on us today,' she said as she came up behind Quentin.

He turned and smiled. She noticed that he smiled after he saw who was there.

'People always overreact to these things.'

'Easy to say from your position.'

The elevator came. They stepped into it.

'You have nothing to worry about,' Quentin said. 'I know.'

The doors closed. It was the first time they'd been alone since that day in his library.

'I enjoyed the other morning,' Quentin said and waited for a reaction. He wasn't a jealous man by nature, but he had no intention of competing with Jake Fox, at least not in this area.

'So did I.'

The doors opened. Their footsteps echoed across the marble lobby. Quentin didn't say anything else. Olivia tried to figure out whether his words had been a come-on or a kiss-off.

He held the door to the street for her. She stopped under the overhang of the building.

'Damn,' she said. 'I forgot my umbrella.'

'Can I give you a lift?' Quentin indicated the car

waiting at the curb. It was a vintage Bentley. The ubiquitous George was holding the door for them.

'If it's not out of your way.'

Olivia climbed into the back seat. She took her time doing it. When it came to assets, she knew that particular view of her was as valuable as a bluechip stock.

Inside, the car was unlike anything Olivia had ever seen. The beautiful grained wood made her think of a cathedral. The leather upholstery had become butter soft with use. She vowed she'd never be impressed by one of those block-long chrome and plastic limos again.

Quentin followed her into the car.

'Of course, it's out of my way, but' – he glanced at his watch – 'I have a few minutes.'

Olivia reshuffled her expectations. All she had was a ride uptown. She'd been hoping he'd suggest dinner, or at least a drink. She'd been hoping to make progress. Now the most she could expect was information.

'According to the paper, you won't be exactly hands-on with R and S anymore.' Olivia glanced at his hands, then smiled at him. 'I'm sorry about that.'

He laughed. She was obvious and unscrupulous and greedy but that, after all, was what had attracted him in the first place. Appetites, like fears, were contagious. 'I plan to keep a hand in, Olivia. I just won't be editing anymore.'

Olivia forced herself to sound casual. 'Not even Amos Porter's books?'

'Not even Amos. Let Hallie put up with the scenes

and the tirades and the flying typewriters. Amos Porter is my closest friend and a great writer, but he's also a prima donna. I'll keep the friend, but let Hallie handle the writer. Hallie and Jonathan Graham.'

'And how hands-on does he plan to be?'

'I suspect you'll know more about that tomorrow.'

'Tomorrow?' Olivia asked.

'Graham's coming in. He wants to take a look at his new toy.'

By the time Hallie came out of the building, it was pouring. The traffic was stalled all the way up Madison Avenue. The cabs inched and jostled along as if they were being herded. The only lights she saw said 'off duty.'

She opened her umbrella. The wind blew it inside out. That was when she started to cry, again. She'd managed to keep it together all day, but now she stood there on Madison Avenue with the cold rain slicing down her trench coat and running inside the neck, and sobbed over a broken umbrella and a ruined pair of shoes.

She went back to her office and called the car service. They told her there would be half an hour's wait. It took an hour.

The car had a television, bar, and phone. They almost made her laugh, but she knew that if she started laughing she'd end up crying again. There'd been a time, just a little more than a week before, when she'd got a kick out of all that stuff. Success, even the tacky trappings of success, can be heady.

Maybe that was part of the reason, but only part, she and Jake had gone so crazy behind the smoked glass that night so many years ago when he'd picked her up at the airport in the limo. But when you've lost your husband and stand a good chance of losing your job, a little complimentary Scotch and reruns of 'The Honeymooners' don't offer much solace. She picked up the phone and called Cecelia to tell her she was on the way.

The housekeeper let her in. Mae was a stout woman with a bosom like a shelf. She ran the house with an iron hand. Even Amos was a little afraid of her.

Mae told Hallie that she looked like a drowned rat and stood waiting while Hallie took off her coat and shoes. Mae had no intention of leaving them there to drip on her polished parquet. She said Mrs Porter was in the library with Mr Styles, then disappeared down the hall toward the stairs to the kitchen.

Hallie started toward the library. The argument came down the hall to meet her. Cecelia's voice was uncharacteristically shrill.

'I just don't understand how you could do it!'

'Amos will be all right.'

'I wasn't talking about Amos. I was thinking of Hallie.'

'Amos. Hallie. What about me, Cecelia?'

'All right, what about you? You don't need the money.'

'Maybe I need a change. A new lease on life.'

'Stop talking like a pop psychology book. 'There are no second acts in American lives.'

'Stop quoting great lines in American literature. You sound like Amos.'

Hallie had reached the library now. She stood in the doorway. They turned to her. Cecelia's beautifully cared-for skin was ashen. Quentin's face was the color of a good burgundy, attractive in a decanter but frightening in a man, especially a man of his age.

'This is something I never thought I'd see. The two most civilized people in the world raising their voices.'

'Some things are worth fighting for,' Cecelia said.

'That's exactly my point,' Quentin answered.

Quentin didn't stay long.

'I don't think he feels comfortable with us,' Hallie said after he had left. 'But then why did he come?'

'Absolution,' Cecelia said.

'Tell him to try the church.'

Cecelia sat thinking for a moment. 'He says you have nothing to worry about.'

'He's quoting Jonathan Graham.'

'Do you believe them?'

'I stopped believing in Santa Claus when I was six.'

'Five,' Cecelia said. 'What are you going to do?'

'Nothing, for the moment. But I have a contingency plan. It depends on Amos, Will Sawyer, a couple of other star authors. That couple who wrote the book on extramarital affairs you disapproved of.'

'Are you planning what I think you're planning?'

Hallie was about to answer when Mae came into the room. She announced that Jake was on the phone.

'Tell him I'm not here,' Hallie said.

Mae sniffed. She'd been with the Porters long enough to have her own opinions of all of them. 'He asked for your mother.'

'Tell him I'll call him back,' Cecelia said.

'Whose side are you on, anyway?' Hallie asked after Mae had left. She'd forgot her contingency plan for the moment.

'I'm hoping there won't have to be any sides.'

'There already are.'

Cecelia looked at her daughter for a long time. 'Maybe I did too good a job with you.'

'What do you mean?'

'I always wanted you to be independent. I never thought you'd be unforgiving.'

Hallie jumped up and moved to the bar. 'What would you know about it? All you've ever had to forgive were a couple of typewriters thrown against a couple of walls after a couple of bad reviews.'

'It was only one typewriter against one wall after one bad review a long time ago.'

'Exactly. I'll take a broken typewriter over a broken marriage any day.'

'What makes you think a man who does one isn't likely to do the other? They're both signs of self-indulgence.'

Hallie sat down so suddenly her drink splashed over her skirt. 'Are you trying to tell me Amos had an affair?'

'God, if you could see your face. I wouldn't dare try to tell you your father had feet of clay – even

142

if he did. I'm trying to tell you that everyone makes mistakes. Even you.'

'I wasn't the one who was screwing around.'

'No, Jake was doing that. And now you're going to make him pay. By wrapping him up and handing him over to her.'

'I don't have to hand him over. She already has him.'

'He is, as you insist on putting it, "screwing" her. That doesn't mean he's in love with her. Where do you think Jake went after you threw him out?'

'I guess they're living together. I mean, she was with him at the farm last weekend.'

'That was the weekend. And you guess wrong. Jake's staying at the Princeton Club.'

'What's he doing there? He never even went to Princeton.'

Cecelia started to laugh. She'd always insisted it was lucky someone in the family could at crucial moments. 'It's not like the Harvard Club, darling. You don't have to be a graduate to join. But you're missing the point. He could have gone to Olivia's – if I know Olivia, she did everything she could to get him to move in with her – but he went to the Princeton Club.'

'I didn't even know he was a member.'

'Now,' Cecelia said, 'you're getting the point.'

XIV

The plane landed at JFK twenty minutes early. Fortunately the car was early too, or there would have been hell to pay. Jonathan Graham told the driver to take him straight to the Pierre. Streetlights were going off and apartment lights going on as the limo streaked across the Triborough Bridge and down the FDR Drive. It was Jonathan's favorite time of day. He liked getting the jump on his fellow man.

In his usual room at the hotel, he undressed, showered, and told the desk to hold all calls for the next twenty-five minutes. Then, naked, he climbed between the fresh sheets and fell immediately asleep.

He awoke in exactly twenty minutes. The extra five minutes of silence from the desk were insurance. Jonathan Graham didn't like to take calls in a sleepy voice.

He spent the next hour on the phone to London. It was a little before nine by the time he arrived at the offices of R and S. When he got off the elevator, the receptionist's desk was unattended. He wandered down the hall, past empty desks and dark offices. There were no names on the doors, but Jonathan could figure out who owned which office. Quentin's was the big corner one with the anteroom for his secretary. Hallie's was the corner one at the other end of the hall. There was a light just beyond it. He walked to the office and stood in the doorway.

Olivia forced herself to keep her eyes on the manuscript while she counted to five. Then she looked up.

'Oh!' Her hand went to her chest. 'You startled me.'

'I'm sorry.'

Now she managed to look annoyed. All she had to do was pretend he was an unpublished writer pushing his book. She stood and walked around her desk, as if she were going to ask him to leave. 'Are you looking for someone?'

'Anyone, I guess. I'm Jonathan Graham. Of Allied Entertainment,' he added ingenuously and held out his hand.

'Oh, my God! I should have recognized you.' Olivia took his hand and managed to look embarrassed. 'I'm Olivia Collins.'

'The editor in chief, right?'

'Right.'

'Where is everyone?'

Olivia smiled, dimpled, gave an embarrassed little shrug. 'I guess I just like to get in early. Before the phones start ringing. It's when I do my best work.'

He moved to the chair across from her desk. She offered to get him some coffee. 'That gets to work

146

early,' she explained. 'One of the secretaries sets the timer the night before.'

He watched her walk down the hall. He could tell from the way she walked that she knew, or at least hoped, he was looking. Graham catalogued her. Power fucker. That didn't mean anything to him one way or another, as long as she could do her job.

It took her a moment to find the coffee, because she didn't know where the machine was and had to follow her nose. She hadn't got her own coffee in years.

When she came back to her office, Graham was leafing through a manuscript. She ran a quick tally as she put the two mugs down and moved around to her own side of the desk.

She knew from the real buttonholes on the sleeves that the suit was custom made. It was Savile Row pinstripe, not Italian flash. There was a discreet monogram on his right shirt cuff. He looked up at her and brushed a few strands of cornsilk hair back from his forehead. His face was boyish and long, as if he were still growing into it, but his smile was knowing. She wondered if he'd be clever in bed or merely indefatigable. He picked up the cup of coffee, tipped his chair back, and put his feet on her desk. She could have put on her makeup in the reflection from those shoes.

'Tell me what an editor in chief does.'

She sat in her chair and began to tell him. Every so often he stopped her to ask a question. At the end of half an hour, he stood, thanked her, and left the office. Olivia went back to her desk with a smile. It wasn't a major coup. He hadn't shown any personal interest. She hadn't displayed any brilliance. Merely competence and the diligence of being there when no one else in the house was. Throughout history battles had been won with less.

Hallie stopped in the doorway to her office. Jonathan Graham lounged in one of the two leather chairs across from her desk. His blindingly polished shoes were propped up next to her in box.

He looked up from the manuscript he was rifling through. His smile was as fast and smooth as a professional gunman's draw.

'I hope you don't mind my dropping by,' he said. 'Or taking a look at this. It was on your desk.'

'It's your house,' she said.

'Is the place always this dead in the morning?'

So much for not wanting to change things.

'This is publishing, Jonathan. A lot of editors don't come in till ten. Of course, a lot of those same editors spend every night and weekend reading. So I'd think twice before installing a time clock to have them punch in and out.'

He just went on smiling and tipped his chair back at an even more precarious angle. Hallie decided that if there were any justice in the world, he would have fallen.

'There was one editor around,' he said. 'What was her name? Collins. Olivia Collins.'

Hallie couldn't figure it out. Olivia never got in before ten-thirty. She wasn't lazy, merely a night person who, as she'd said to Hallie, did her best work in bed.

'A real go-getter,' Jonathan said.

'That she is.' Hallie sat behind her desk.

'She's the editor in chief, right?'

'That she is,' Hallie repeated.

Graham stared across the desk at her. How did these two women work together? Olivia made it clear she'd go down for power at the drop of a hat. Hallie made a point of standing up to it. Somehow the tension worked. He wondered if it would go on working, and, if it didn't, which of them would prove more profitable.

He took his feet off her desk, righted the chair so it was resting on all four legs, and leaned toward her. He stopped smiling.

'I told you I don't want a fight, Hallie. But if you keep pushing for one, I'll give it to you.'

She asked him if he wanted coffee. He said he'd already had some with Olivia. They got down to work.

Like most people who don't read, Jonathan Graham had a peculiar combination of reverence and disdain for books. Because he rarely opened one, he thought there was something mysterious and magical between its covers. But he knew that all that mystery and magic weren't quite real, at least not as real as the figures in a financial printout. By the time they'd finished, he still didn't know the first thing about the leaders on R and S's spring list, but he could have spouted off every figure Hallie had given him.

She took him around to meet some of the staff. The mystery editor, a balding woman who was rumored to have contributed to the breakup of Quentin's first marriage – she'd been around that long – practically quaked in her old-fashioned gillies. For a minute Hallie thought Sheila Dent was going to kiss Jonathan's ring. Bob Sherwood tried to tell him a dirty joke. As they were passing, Olivia came out of her office and held out her hand to Jonathan.

'I'm so glad we had a chance to talk.' She smiled up at him. He smiled down at her. They looked like a goddamn toothpaste ad. A few weeks ago Hallie would have laughed and teased Olivia about it. Now she felt too shaky to laugh. Olivia was chipping away at her foundations.

Hallie walked Jonathan to the elevators.

'I'll be glad when you get out of here and go back to the coast,' she said. 'Then maybe everyone will get back to work.'

He laughed. 'Like I said . . .'

The editor in Hallie started to correct his grammar. The employee shut her mouth.

'. . . just keep doing what you've been doing. I didn't take R and S over because it was failing.'

For the first time Hallie almost believed him.

XV

The restaurant was so trendy there was no sign outside. Inside, there was a zinc bar sporting wire racks with hard-boiled eggs, a maitre d' perpetually on the verge of a sneer, and the polyglot babble of Eurotrash. Hallie spotted Will Sawyer sitting alone at a table in a corner. He looked out of place but not uncomfortable. As usual, his prematurely salt-and-pepper hair looked as if he'd combed it with an eggbeater, if at all. In earlier days, a scruffy beard had camouflaged the square face and strong jaw that showed him for the right-thinking, all-American boy he was, but he'd shaved that off after he'd begun watching himself on talk shows. He was wearing one of his interchangeable uniforms intended to proclaim him an honorary Black, Hispanic, migrant worker, homosexual, woman, and member of every other oppressed minority. It consisted of a worn blue workshirt, a sloppily knotted, worn wool tie, a worn tweed jacket, and a pair of worn wrinkled khakis. The entire outfit was straight off the racks at Brooks Brothers, and only an intellectual could think it proclaimed him anything but that.

The first thing he did was hand her the rest of his manuscript and tell her she was going to love it. She told him he was probably right. Will had never written anything she hadn't liked. The second was tell her he'd been thinking about the takeover. He'd decided to stay with R and S.

'With one change,' he said. 'The next book I sign with you, not with the house. If you walk, you take me with you.'

Hallie could have hugged him. Instead, she told him she appreciated his loyalty.

'Loyalty, hell! You think I want to be turned over to some junior editor who doesn't know 'hopefully' needs a verb to modify and that I'm the man who coined the terms 'underclass' and 'postfeminism.'

After they'd ordered, he asked how Amos was taking it.

'Like you, he's decided to stay with the house. Unlike you, he's looking for a new editor. Quent is laying down his blue pencil.'

'Looks as if you've got your work cut out for you.'

They swapped stories and gossiped and caught up on the public part of their personal lives during dinner. Then, when coffee came, Will leaned across the table toward Hallie. His eyes were the same shade of blue as the water at a posh Caribbean resort. Will was the first to admit that the color was entirely too decadent for a left-wing social critic.

'How are you getting along otherwise?' he asked. 'Without Jake, I mean.'

'Okay.'

Will didn't say anything to that. Hallie sipped her

espresso and tried to catch the attention of one of the sullen waiters. Maybe it was because she was thinking about getting the check that Will caught her off guard.

'I like Jake,' he said. 'I really do. But I never could figure your marrying him.'

'Why?'

He shrugged. 'Different styles.'

Hallie wondered whether Will was using 'styles' as a euphemism for 'looks.' He probably hadn't thought someone who looked like Jake would marry anyone who looked like her.

'Or maybe I just assumed you'd end up with a writer.'

'A fate worse than death. Present company excluded.'

'Daughters of lesser men than Amos Porter have done it.'

'Married Daddy, you mean?'

'Or maybe, speaking as a writer, it was only wishful thinking.'

So this was what it meant to be single again. Old friends felt obliged to play new roles.

'That isn't obligatory, Will.'

'Obligatory, hell.' He spotted the waiter and signaled for the check. 'I've been in a moral quandary all night. Is it fair to let the publisher pick up the check if you've got designs on the publisher?'

The waiter brought the check. Hallie beat Will to it.

'That's no protection,' he said.

It came back to Hallie in the cab. Years before, at

a party she could barely remember in a loft she'd long forgotten, she'd kissed Will Sawyer. Or rather he'd kissed her, and she'd kissed him back.

Will kissed the way he wrote. He started slow – not tentatively but thoroughly – and built. It was quite an experience. By Sixty-fifth Street they were tangled up in each other. By the time they got out of the taxi in front of her apartment, they both looked rumpled as a bed. It wasn't easy managing a polite good evening to the doorman in that condition, but Will carried it off.

He reached for her in the elevator. She pointed to the closed-circuit TV monitor. He just laughed.

'I'm used to surveillance, Hallie. My life's an open CIA file.'

Hallie decided it was even better standing up. Will wasn't as tall as Jake, and though she'd deleted the cliché from dozens of manuscripts, she had to admit it applied this time. They really did fit. Underneath that shaggy facade, there was a neat, hard body that made its demands known.

The elevator doors opened on the fifteenth floor. She was sorry she didn't have the penthouse.

Will followed her into the apartment. Everything fell apart. Jake wasn't there, but he might as well have been. His ghost lingered in the shadows.

Hallie switched on the lights. It didn't help. The apartment screamed of all those shared years. Will was looking at her rather than the room, but he must have seen its reflection in her face.

'You're going to tell me, 'It's been fun, Will, but good night.''

She shrugged. She didn't trust herself to speak. She felt suddenly awkward and out of her depth. With a desk between them, or even a table with a manuscript on it, she was on safe ground. Here in her apartment, a suddenly single woman, she was on quicksand.

Will took her hand and led her to the sofa, the one where Jake had sat the other night with his head in his hands, telling her he didn't want a divorce, where he'd sat a few weeks earlier when she'd asked him about Olivia, where they'd made love the night it was delivered because she'd said it looked too new and Jake had said there was only one way to break it in.

Will was still holding her hand in both of his. 'Look, Hallie, there's always been something between us. We just never expressed it with sex. Unless you count the abortive grope in that loft.'

'I didn't think you remembered that.'

'You did. Why shouldn't I?' One hand moved up her arm. He was stroking the inside of her elbow. For an angry prophet, he was awfully tender. 'I always wondered why nothing ever happened. I suppose it was timing. The timing's always been off. Until now.'

She couldn't look at Will, but she couldn't look around the apartment either.

'You're going to end up in bed with someone eventually, Hallie. I'm a damn good candidate. I've never used intravenous drugs. I've never had a homosexual experience. Unless you count a circle jerk behind the garage in sixth grade.'

He knew she'd have to laugh at that.

'That's better,' he said when she did.

He traced the outline of her mouth with his thumb. His touch made her lower lip tremble.

He kissed her. The gentleness was still there, but she could feel something else building behind it. 'I want to make love to you, Hallie. I'm damn near crazy to make love to you.'

She closed her eyes. Maybe if she couldn't see the room. The trouble was that now she heard the words more clearly. He wanted to make love to her. But this wasn't love. Attraction, desire, maybe even affection, but not love.

It was almost as if she'd spoken. 'Listen, Hallie,' he whispered. 'We like each other. We respect each other. We make each other laugh. And we're damn near wild about each other's bodies. What more do you want?'

She opened her eyes. That was the big mistake. Behind his head a small silver-framed snapshot that had been taken on their wedding trip stood forgotten among the books on one of the shelves. In it she and Jake, wearing heavy sailing sweaters and jeans, stood with their arms around each other. Enormous smiles creased their darkly tanned faces.

Hallie forced her eyes back to Will's face. It was a perfectly nice face. In the cab she'd thought it was a wonderful face, but in the cab it hadn't been next to a picture of Jake and her.

'You don't really want me to answer that.'

The Caribbean eyes grew a little darker. He leaned back. He let go of her. He stood. Dozens of women were dying to go to bed with Will Sawyer. He didn't have to waste his time coaxing one who was reluctant.

'Okay,' he said, hunching his shoulders forward. 'Read the manuscript. Give me a call after you do.'

She would have stood in the foyer talking to him while he waited for the elevator, but he didn't give her a chance to. When he walked out of her apartment, he closed the door behind him.

XVI

Hallie didn't know why she'd agreed to it. Maybe it was Cecelia's insistence that you didn't trade in a husband like an old briefcase or a pair of running shoes. Maybe it was the fact that Jake kept calling and asking her to. Maybe it was just the way that night with Will had left her feeling.

She agreed to have dinner with Jake.

He chose a place on the West Side she'd never heard of. She knew that was intentional. He didn't want to be interrupted by anyone they knew. When she got there, she knew the rest was intentional, too. The restaurant was quiet and fairly dark.

He stood when he saw her coming across the room toward him.

'You cut your hair,' he said before she even sat down.

'Only a trim.'

She slipped out of her suit jacket.

'That's a new blouse.'

She wondered if the comment meant he liked it or thought it was unflattering.

'That's a new tie,' she said, to prove that two could play the game.

'Okay, we'll stay impersonal.'

He asked her about the takeover, though he knew almost as much about it as she did. They discussed Amos's new book, which would be out in a few weeks. He mentioned a dual biography of Georgia O'Keeffe and Alfred Stieglitz he was about to auction off.

She knew she should let it go, but she couldn't help herself. Just sitting across the table from him brought it all back.

'Olivia's really high on it,' she said.

He put down his knife and fork and looked at her. Even in the candlelight his eyes were hard as coals. 'I'll make a deal, Hallie. You stay off Olivia, and I won't mention Will Sawyer.'

'Will's one of my authors. I've been publishing him forever.'

'Will's been trying to get into your pants forever.'

'Unlike you, not everyone thinks with his libido.'

'Maybe not, but Will Sawyer does.'

She didn't say anything, and that big slick smile crept across his face.

'If I remember correctly, you used to come home from lunches saying Will Sawyer must have a revolving door in his bedroom. For traffic control.'

Hallie couldn't blame Jake for gloating. He'd managed to put into words what she'd been thinking, and fearing.

Outside the restaurant, he hailed a cab and started to get in after her.

'I'm going crosstown,' Hallie said. 'You're going

downtown. You are going to the Princeton Club, aren't you?'

He stood there holding the door open. 'For God's sake, Hallie, is it really this bad? You won't even let me get into a cab with you?'

She didn't tell him she was afraid to. Everything was too mixed up. Memories of that night in the limo. The play of his beautiful long fingers against the white tablecloth in the restaurant. The dreams she was having almost nightly – wrenching, realistic dreams that made every awakening a fresh loss.

'We're going in different directions,' she insisted.

Before she could stop him, he pushed into the cab and slammed the door.

'I said –' she began.

'I heard what you said. Now I have something to say.'

'Where to?' the driver asked.

'Anywhere,' Jake said.

'Gotta go somewhere.'

'Straight,' Jake yelled.

He turned back to Hallie. He wasn't even trying to hold his temper anymore.

'You asked me once how long it had been going on with Olivia.'

'I don't care.'

'You ought to goddamnit! It started last summer. When you were in London.'

'Is that supposed to be an excuse?'

'I don't suppose you remember anything about that trip. I mean, it was just one of a couple of hundred in the past few years.'

'I bought that biography of Charles and Di everyone was after.'

Jake's fist hit the Plexiglas window between the front seat and the back.

'Hey, watch it!' the driver shouted.

'You stayed two days longer than you were supposed to.'

'Now I get it. Those extra forty-eight hours without me drove you to Olivia.'

Jake's fist started toward the window again, then stopped in midair.

'You were due in on a Tuesday night. I rented a limo and went out to the airport to meet you. Pretty dumb. But you see, I was remembering that time I'd met you at the airport before we were married. That was one hell of a ride back to town. Of course, you were just an editor then. I guess you had more time and fewer inhibitions. You weren't so busy playing Madame Publisher.'

It wasn't fair of him to try to put the blame on her. And it wasn't fair of him to bring up that night in the limo.

'I never asked you to meet me at the airport.'

'No, and you never bothered to telex me you weren't coming, either.'

'So you figured that as long as you had the limo, you might as well get some mileage out of it and called Olivia.'

'No. When you didn't get off that plane and I got back into that damn limo, l didn't feel like seeing Olivia or you or anyone. I was so pissed. I just came back to town.'

162

'Then you had second thoughts.'

'Olivia showed up at the apartment. She said she hated to bother you on your first night back, but she had something you had to take a look at before the next morning. I said she wasn't bothering you. You weren't home.'

'And you weren't pissed anymore.'

Jake knocked on the Plexiglas window with his fist again. 'Let me out here,' he shouted to the driver.

The cab pulled over. Jake got out. 'I'm still pissed!' he shouted at Hallie. Then he slammed the door and walked away.

'Where to now, lady?' the driver asked.

Hallie gave him her address. Then she began to cry.

Jake had got one thing wrong. Olivia hadn't gone to the apartment looking for her that night. Hallie hadn't let Jake know she was delayed, but she'd telexed the office.

The night doorman called upstairs to say there was a guy to see her. Even on the intercom his voice was knowing, as if he were telling Olivia a dirty joke.

'I thought you had a business dinner,' she said when she opened the door and found Jake standing in the hall.

He reached under her T-shirt. It was all she was wearing. 'Finished early.' He kicked the door closed behind him.

She put her arms around his neck. 'Judging from your mood, the book is soft-core porn.'

He took one of her hands and held it against him. 'Not soft.'

He kissed her hard. She bit his lip. He tugged her T-shirt up. His body pressed her to the wall. She writhed against it. They wrestled him out of his trousers.

She pulled him to the floor and tried to climb on top of him, but he rolled over and pinned her to the floor. He entered her suddenly. It would have been violently, if she weren't so ready.

Her arms and legs locked around him. It was like trying to hang on to a wild bucking animal. She heard something crash, then her own voice howling. 'Yes,' and 'Jake,' and Yes,' again. And the animal went on, a wild primitive force that thrust into her again and again. And again and again she howled, not words now, only savage sounds that drove them further and further into that black jungle until finally she screamed, a long piercing sound that went through her like a knife, and he shuddered and groaned and collapsed on top of her. It was over as suddenly as it had begun.

He sat up. She righted the umbrella stand they'd knocked over.

'Now that's what I call a greeting,' she said.

He didn't even smile, just leaned back against the base of the couch and tugged at the tie he hadn't stopped to loosen. 'Is there anything to drink?'

She went into the kitchen. He was still sitting that way when she came back with two glasses. She handed him one and sat on the floor beside him. There was a spot of blood on his lip where she'd bitten him. She leaned over. Her tongue darted out and licked the blood away. He didn't move.

'What happened to you tonight?'

He went on frowning into his drink. 'Nothing,' he said finally.

'That wasn't nothing,' she insisted.

'I just missed you,' he said, but he still hadn't met her eyes.

'Are you okay, Mrs Fox?' the doorman asked as he held the door open for Hallie.

No, she wanted to scream. I'm not all right. I'm an idiot. Jake had tried at dinner. He really had. But she'd headed him off at every turn. She hadn't meant to, but she hadn't been able to stop herself, because she was drowning in memories, revalued memories. She'd sat across from Jake at that table, and everything they'd said and done for the past few months had come back, but had suddenly seen it all in a different light. Every word he'd spoken to her during that time was a lie. Everytime they'd made love was a joke. A bad joke on her.

'I'm fine, Louie,' she said and kept her face turned away. She'd be damned if she was going to make a scene in her own lobby.

She pushed the button on the elevator so hard she broke a nail. What was wrong with her anyway? Her mother said she was unforgiving. Maybe Cecelia was right about her, and about Jake. After all, if he didn't care for her, why did he keep calling and pleading and trying to see her?

The elevator doors opened on her floor. She'd made a mistake, but she knew how to fix it.

* * *

'Don't go back to the Princeton Club,' Olivia said. They were still on the floor, but Jake had finished his drink and Olivia knew he was getting ready to leave. He hadn't said anything. He hadn't even reached for his clothing, but she could tell.

Here we go again, Jake thought. 'I have to go,' he said.

'Why?'

'We've been through this. Because you don't want to be named corespondent in an ugly divorce case.'

'I always thought adultery meant sex. I didn't know the legal definition was a sleep-over.'

What she did know was that Hallie would never do anything as déclassé as drag their collective dirty linen through the courts. She'd take the no-fault high ground. But Olivia wasn't about to admit that to Jake.

She picked up his glass and her own and carried them into the kitchen. Another drink would buy her time to maneuver. She came back into the living room with the glasses, handed him one, and sat beside him again. Then she covered her face with one hand as if she were embarrassed. 'Oh, God, listen to me. I swore I'd never get like this.'

She waited for him to say something. He went on staring into his drink in silence. She decided it was time to bring out the big guns.

'It's just that you can't imagine what it's like after you leave. I feel so . . . abandoned. As if I don't mean anything more to you than a quick . . .' Her voice broke, as if she couldn't bear to put a word to the act, though they both knew there were a number of words for it that she used regularly and casually.

But the thought struck home. Jake's late father had given him exactly two pieces of sexual advice in his life. He'd offered the first just before Jake had gone away to college.

'You know what rubbers are?' Leonard Fox asked his son.

Jake said he did.

'You know how to use them?'

Jake said he did.

'Then use them.'

The advice, strangely enough, was timely. The yacht club where Jake had worked for the past four years had put in two tennis courts. He'd spent his last summer before college improving the serves and backhands of affluent suburban matrons who took their exercise seriously. Jake's experience had been limited to the pill and diaphragms and IUDs. He'd never had to use a condom.

The second piece of advice was of a more delicate nature. It had come one Sunday afternoon while Jake and his father were watching a football game on television. The Giants against the Eagles, Jake remembered. His father had had a bet on the Giants.

'When you fool around . . .' Leonard began during halftime.

'Fool around?' Jake asked.

'You know . . . when you have sex.'

'Oh,' Jake said for lack of anything else to say.

'Never just roll over in bed and go to sleep. It's not good manners.'

Leonard went on staring at the scores of the other

games around the country, but he was obviously thinking about something else. 'Don't tell me times have changed. Some things still apply. Even if it's no big romance, you can't just put on your clothes and go home. Other people have feelings too.'

Jake always thought it was the nicest advice his father had ever given him. And it hadn't been hard to follow. He liked women, after as well as before sex. You never saw them clearly before. Hunger got in the way. But afterward, if things were good, there was a moment when everyone's guard was down. He liked the thick sound of a woman's voice after she'd made love, and the bruised softness of her mouth, and the way some of them, the best of them went on touching. He remembered how Hallie's hands, light as moths, used to trace lazy patterns on his back.

The advice hadn't been hard to follow at all. Until tonight. But tonight was exactly when it applied. He'd used Olivia. He'd taken out his rage and frustration and pain on her. And now he was going to get up, put on his clothes, and go home. It was a lousy thing to do. He thought about his life these days. It was one more lousy thing to do.

'I won't go back to the Princeton Club,' he said.

Olivia stared at herself in the bathroom mirror as she rubbed the makeup remover into her skin in gentle circular motions. She'd got him to stay. It was a small victory but a victory nonetheless. Not that any woman in her right mind would want him around in his present condition. The sex had been okay. The sex had been exciting. Quick and dirty. That wasn't Jake's style. She wondered what was up.

He'd said he missed her. Missed her hell! He'd been angry. Absolutely pissed. At what was the question. She pulled a tissue out of the box and began taking off the cream. Not someone he'd had a business dinner with. Jake didn't lose it over business. Hallie. Something had happened with Hallie.

Olivia heard the phone ringing in the bedroom and made a dash for it.

'Livia, sweetheart. It's James, next door. I have two things to say to you. One, don't you ever call me a screamer again.'

She laughed.

'And two, whenever you get tired of whomever you've got in there, sweetie, I want to meet him.'

'What about Brian?'

'He wants to meet him too.'

'My next-door neighbors,' Olivia said after she'd hung up. 'They want to meet you.'

If Jake had heard her, he gave no sign. He was lying on his back, staring at the ceiling. His eyes were hard black stones, and his mouth was a thin angry line. Olivia went back to the bathroom. The shiny face in the mirror stared back at her. She thought of the last time Jake had been pissed at Hallie. It was the night she hadn't come home from London. He'd been fuming when Olivia got to the apartment. In an absolute rage. That had made it even easier than she'd expected.

Hallie let herself into the darkened apartment.

Without turning on the hall light, she walked down the long corridor to the study. Her heels made that lonely typewriter sound on the parquet again. She switched on the study light, sat on Jake's side of the antique partners' desk, and took the phone book from the bottom drawer.

Her hand was shaking so badly it took her a moment to find the number of the Princeton Club. She made a mistake the first time she dialed and had to call again. One of those official phone voices said Mr Fox wasn't in. Did she want to leave a message.

Hallie considered it. Jake might have walked after he'd got out of the cab. He loved to walk in the city, especially at night. What could she say in a message?

To: Jake Fox.

From: Hallie Porter.

Subject: Broken marriage.

Come home, all is forgiven.

Not bloody likely. At least not bloody likely to a telephone operator at the Princeton Club.

'No,' she said. 'No message.'

She put down the phone, then picked it up again. She'd always hated women who did things like this. Jealous women, spying women, petty women. She'd never thought she'd become one of them. Her whole life had been a struggle against becoming one of them.

This time she didn't have to look up the number. Her fingers flew over the buttons.

She wasn't proving anything. Even if Jake was there, Olivia would be the one to answer. Then Hallie would hang up. She wouldn't feel better, only more ashamed of herself. She tensed her muscles as she listened to the phone ringing. It only made her tremble more.

Olivia heard the phone in the bedroom again. Now she was getting annoyed.

'You get it, honey,' she called to Jake. 'And tell James the first time was funny, the second is just a nuisance.'

Hallie was about to hang up when the ringing stopped. Jake's voice at the other end of the line sounded sleepy and thick as cream.

Hallie put the phone down gently as if the mere rattle of a receiver would give her away. Then she made a promise to herself. She'd weakened for a moment, but she'd never weaken again.

XVII

Fall inched forward. Each night the dusk crept into Hallie's office a little earlier. The view didn't help. There'd been a time when she'd loved watching the lights go on around and below her. Every one of them had held a promise. Now she knew the promises weren't going to be kept.

Hallie's contract arrived. At least the covering letter said it was Hallie's. The party of the first part was Allied Entertainment Corporation. The party of the second was Quentin Styles. Her conscience told her to put it back in the envelope and reroute it to Quentin's office. Her curiosity kept her reading.

Finally she started to laugh. Quentin was inspired. And Jonathan Graham wasn't as smart as he thought. Quentin had negotiated himself an override on R and S. There was nothing unusual about that. What was out of the ordinary was the fact that his override was computed according to the number of books printed. Hallie had to read it again to believe it.

Everyone in publishing knew that bookstores could return unsold copies for full credit within a certain amount of time. When it came to paperbacks, they didn't even have to return the books, only the covers. Profits were computed on books sold after returns. Quentin's deal was predicated on books produced. No wonder he'd increased printings recently.

'What's so funny?' Olivia asked.

Hallie's head snapped up from the contract. Olivia was leaning against the doorjamb. She was wearing a short, snug cashmere dress. Hallie knew how Jake would react to that dress – or, rather, to Olivia in it. But she wasn't going to think of Jake anymore. She assumed the old veneer.

'Secretarial incompetence. Graham's office sent me Quentin's contract by mistake. Poor Quent's probably going to have a stroke when he gets mine. The numbers aren't nearly so impressive.'

'I bet they'll do.'

'Be careful, honey,' Hallie drawled, but it was no good. Jake was the mimic in the family. 'Your green streak is showing.'

Olivia flashed a brilliant smile. 'I never tried to hide it. I don't have your unfathomable good taste. But, then, I couldn't afford it. While you were reading lit-tri-ture at Daddy's knee, I was doing buttons and hems for Mama and scrambling for a college scholarship.'

Hallie steeled herself against the familiar flash of guilt. She could blame Olivia for a lot of things, but she could only pity her for her background. It had been so impoverished compared to Hallie's, and she wasn't thinking only of money. Olivia's father had disappeared when she was six. She'd told Hallie she could remember a single outing with him. He'd taken her to a carnival and got so roaring drunk she'd had to lead him home because he couldn't find the way. Her mother had kept the family together. Then the week before Olivia, the youngest and the first in the family to even finish high school, was to graduate from college, Mrs Collins had slumped forward over her sewing machine with a massive stroke.

'You didn't come in here to tell me your life story,' Hallie said, because the knowledge of it cut through her own armor.

'No. I came for a second reading.'

Olivia crossed the room and put the manuscript on Hallie's desk. Hallie didn't have to look at the box. She knew from the smile on Olivia's face it was going to score a point for Olivia's side.

'I wouldn't even bother asking for a second reading. Not with Carter Bolton's name on the title page. But his agent's asking one-point-two mil.'

Hallie was impressed. She didn't much like Carter Bolton, but the public was crazy about him.

'It's amazing how much mileage you an get out of a little undergraduate roll in the hay if you put your mind to it.'

'Thanks, honey, but I owe this one to you.'

'To me?'

'Sure. I've been after Carter for years. But as he pointed out, if he started publishing with every woman he took to bed, he wouldn't have enough short stories to go around, let alone novels.'

'Where do I come in?'

'Carter was looking for a new publisher anyway.

His good friend Will Sawyer told him to go with R and S. Will thinks you're the hottest thing in books since Gutenberg.'

Hallie remembered that night in her apartment. She was beginning to think she'd made a big mistake.

'I just happened to be there with the offer at the right moment,' Olivia said.

Hallie almost asked where Jake had been at the time but decided it was none of her business.

'It's the best thing Carter's ever done,' Olivia said as she started out of the office.

'How would you know?' The words were out of Hallie's mouth before she realized it.

Olivia turned back. 'You know, honey, you've got a real mind-body problem. What makes you think that just because you use one, you can't use the other?'

Olivia waited till she heard the elevator doors open and close. Then she forced herself to wait another five minutes, in case Hallie had forgotten something and decided to come back.

Finally she walked down the hall to Hallie's office and switched on the light. Her eyes went immediately to the out box. There was an inter-office envelope addressed to Quentin Styles.

Olivia didn't expect to find anything unusual in Quentin's contract. She was just curious.

Jonathan Graham called Hallie two days later. 'We just put your contract in the pouch. At least I hope it's yours this time. What did you think of Quentin's?'

'What makes you think I read it?'

'Terrific. Just who I want running my publishing house. A woman entirely without curiosity.'

'It seemed standard to me.'

'Any suggestions?'

'Suggestions?' Hallie repeated, because she couldn't think of anything else to say while she stalled for time. Maybe Graham wasn't as naïve as she'd thought. Maybe he knew all about return policies, and the contract was a test of her loyalty.

Her mind raced ahead. All that was possible but unlikely. Besides, Hallie knew where her loyalties lay. Rutherford and Styles came first, but now that Quentin wasn't running things, he couldn't go on ordering large printings. Any extra money he made would be from her mistakes, and for years he'd been training her not to make mistakes. After R and S, her loyalty lay with him.

For more reasons than one. It wasn't exactly a secret that she was mentioned in his will, and not just for the few pieces of his late mother's jewelry that his wives had overlooked.

'No suggestions,' she told Graham.

XVIII

I thought we might have a drink,' Olivia said.

Jonathan Graham was intrigued. Olivia Collins had called two days earlier. He hadn't had a chance to get back to her. Now she'd called again. Something was up.

'Your coast or mine?' he asked.

'Yours.'

'That's a long way to fly for a drink.'

'I've got to see some people out there anyway.' It wasn't entirely a lie. She had a couple of west coast authors. And she wanted more movie connections. She had plenty of excuses besides the real one.

Olivia had had her secretary book her into the St James Club. Let Hallie bitch when she saw her expense account – if Hallie was still around to approve her expense account by the time it came through.

The bellboy showed her around the room. It didn't speak of money, it shouted it. The boy pushed a button on an inlaid art-deco sideboard. A bar popped up. He pushed a second button. A television swung out. Olivia was delighted. The only thing she liked better than first-class hotels was first-rate sex in first-class hotels. As she peeled off her clothes and climbed into the shower, she wondered again what Jonathan Graham was going to be like in bed. The editor in her laughed. She'd switched tenses. A few weeks ago she'd wondered what he *might* be like in bed.

She wrapped herself in the oversized terrycloth robe with the hotel's insignia, stretched out on the gondola bed – plenty of room for Jonathan Graham's long, lanky frame – and picked up the phone.

Jonathan answered it himself. Olivia was surprised, then realized that even Jonathan Graham's battery of secretaries wasn't likely to hang around till ten o'clock.

'Your place or mine?' she asked. She figured she could risk it, since he'd made the same joke when she'd called from New York.

'Yours,' he said. 'I'll meet you in the Members Room in half an hour.'

He saw the heads turn as she entered. A Touchstone producer nearly fell off his barstool. An ICM agent actually licked his lips. No one knew who she was. A lot of men wondered.

The eyes followed her across the Members Room and watched her stop in front of Jonathan Graham's table. He stood. Olivia held out her hand. The agent and the producer and half a dozen men went on staring for a moment, then returned to their drinks and dinners and gossip. Let them gossip about that for a while, Jonathan thought. Let the bastards wonder.

Olivia noticed the bottle of Perrier in front of Jonathan. She wished she'd had a drink before she'd left the room. She was dying for a Scotch. She ordered a Perrier.

She watched the waiter pour her drink. She could feel Graham's eyes on her. That was okay. That was good. She was wearing her Armani jacket, but she'd left the crepe blouse under it open a few buttons. She looked up and met his eyes.

Women probably found him attractive. Not that appearances mattered in his case. Jonathan Graham could have looked like Quasimodo, and women still would have fought their way into his bed. But he didn't look like Quasimodo, and Olivia suspected that women went to bed with him as much for his boyish, misleadingly innocent face and that long, raw-boned body that he still seemed to be growing into as for his power. And if the power wasn't enough, the air of inaccessibility made him even more intriguing. There was something fascinating about a man who was so clearly not on the make. At least not sexually.

'I wanted to talk to you about R and S,' she said, when he showed no sign of starting the conversation. He was one of those people who found comfort in the discomfort silence produced in others.

'I didn't think you flew out here to discuss great literature with me.'

'Quentin's contract, to be more specific.'

'Don't tell me it was misrouted to you, too.'

She smiled a helpless smile and shrugged. 'You know what interoffice mail is like.'

'It's lucky you people aren't working on Star Wars

or the Stealth bomber. Okay, what about Quentin's contract?'

'He's taking you.'

Jonathan Graham's expression didn't change. His face remained impassive. The only sign that he'd heard her was a small muscle in his jaw that tightened as if he were clenching his teeth.

'I had some pretty high-priced legal talent draw up that contract.'

'High-priced legal talent doesn't necessarily know the book biz.'

'But you do?'

'I cut my teeth on it.' She smiled to show him those even white teeth.

'All right. How's he taking me?'

Olivia laid it all out in a few sentences. Publishers' return policies. Quentin's print orders, the override Jonathan would have to pay. Jonathan didn't say a word, but she knew he'd heard every one of hers.

'I just thought you'd want to know,' she said. 'I realize it doesn't add up to a lot of money. A couple of hundred thou maybe, small potatoes by your standards. But I still thought I ought to tell you.'

He went on staring at her in silence for a moment. 'What do you have against Quentin Styles?' he asked finally.

For once in her life Olivia could tell the truth. 'Absolutely nothing. In fact, I'm fond of Quentin.' That was one way of putting it. 'But I work for you now. Or at least for Allied Entertainment.'

Jonathan smiled. 'There's nothing like loyalty.'

They raised Perriers to that.

They talked about R and S for a while. It wasn't aimless conversation. In fact, it was closer to a presentation. Olivia catalogued the house's strengths, confided its weaknesses, made suggestions about its future direction. For a moment she thought of mentioning Amos Porter and discussing the importance of finding the right editor for the house's leading literary light, but decided against it. From where Jonathan Graham sat, that was penny-ante internal stuff. She stuck to the big picture, long-range plans for new lines, additional imprints, book-related products like audios and videos and computer software. She never once mentioned Hallie's name, and neither did he.

He signaled the waiter. He signed for the drinks. They stood. He put his hand on the small of her back and guided her toward the door. Olivia practically skipped out of the Members Room. It was all going according to plan.

As they made their way to the elevators, portraits of Liz and Liza and Dudley smiled down on them. They stopped in front of the elevators. Olivia wondered if he just assumed that he was coming up with her, or if she was supposed to invite him. She decided to let him make the move. A man who takes over multimillion-dollar companies isn't likely to be shy.

His hand fell from the small of her back. He turned to face her. He held out his hand. 'Thank you,' he said. 'For the information.' He hesitated for a moment, then smiled again. 'And for the company.'

She stood waiting. Jonathan Graham dropped her hand, turned, and walked away.

Jonathan Graham had forgotten Olivia before he was even out of the lobby of the St James Club. He had to give Quentin credit. Quentin came on like a member in good standing of the Old Boys club. If he'd slipped Jonathan the Bones' handshake, Jonathan wouldn't have been surprised – not that Jonathan knew what the Bones' handshake was. You didn't learn much about Ivy League secret societies at a cow college in the boondocks of Montana. And all the time Quentin had been playing the old-school gentleman, he'd been screwing the new boy. Graham had to give him credit. But he didn't have to give him the override. As soon as he got into the car, he dialed his lawyer's number. He wanted a new contract in the mail to Quentin by nine o'clock the next morning. He only wished he could see Quentin's face when he got it.

That solved one problem, but another was gnawing at him. Hallie had seen that contract. Either she was a lot dumber than he'd thought or she was playing a different game. Jonathan didn't think she was dumb.

XIX

Hallie heard the phone ringing while she was in the shower and decided to ignore it. It was still ringing when she got out, so she made a dash for it. It stopped ringing just as she reached the phone. She retraced her wet footprints to the bathroom. It started ringing again as soon as she got there.

'Where were you?' Cecelia demanded when Hallie picked up the phone.

'In the shower.'

'Why don't you take the cordless phone into the bathroom with you? That's what Jake bought it for.'

'Jake bought it because all the agents on the coast have cordless phones. He wasn't thinking of my convenience.' Hallie stopped. 'Anyway you didn't call at seven in the morning to talk about Jake. Or did you?'

'I called to talk about Amos. About that damn limited edition of his new book.'

'He wanted that limited edition. He drove Quentin and me and all of production crazy over it.'

'I know. That's the problem. Now he can't sign it.'

'His arthritis?'

'I didn't tell you that.'

The official family line was that Amos was ageless. His fingers occasionally got stiff from the frostbite he'd suffered in the Battle of the Bulge. It wasn't that he couldn't hear voices in a certain range, only that he preferred to tune them out because he was thinking of more important things. When he'd had to switch to bifocal contact lenses, he'd sworn the ophthalmologist to secrecy. Cecelia had found out only when he'd lost one and she had to have it replaced.

'But he was supposed to come down to the office and sign them this morning,' Hallie said.

'That's why I'm calling. He won't admit it, but he'll never be able to get through them all. You'll have to call and say they aren't ready or something.'

'And let him chew me out for the inefficiency of my production department?'

'It's a small price to pay for your father's dignity.'

'Easy for you to say,' but Hallie already had another idea. She told Cecelia not to do anything. 'I'll call you from the office as soon as I set things up.'

The solution was simple. Hallie would have used it in the first place, if Amos hadn't been such a stickler for detail.

The machine looked like something out of a Rube Goldberg drawing. There were a couple of dozen arms, each holding a pen, all connected to the master pen.

Amos took the master pen in his hand and scrawled an overblown, illegible signature several times. They had a signed limited edition.

Olivia came into the production department just as they were finishing. She was carrying a copy of Amos's book – not one of the limited editions but a first edition that had reached the office a couple of days earlier.

Hallie looked from Olivia to Amos. Those diabolical eyebrows lifted in two haughty arches. He started to turn away from her. Hallie wanted to hug him. But Olivia was too quick.

She put a hand on his arm to stop him. He looked surprised, but he didn't pull away.

'I hate to bother you, Mr Porter,' Olivia said, and Hallie was surprised, again. Olivia had been calling him Amos for the past few years. 'But I wonder if you'd sign one for me, too.' She held the book out to him. He hesitated. Personal animosities were one thing, professional obligations something else entirely.

She pushed the advantage. 'I just have to have a signed copy of this one. I mean, I cherish the others, but this one . . .' She hesitated as if she were too overcome for words. 'I think "great" is the operative word.'

But Amos – bless his soul, Hallie thought – was no pushover. 'Just what did you think was so good? "Great," as you put it?'

Olivia stopped smiling. Her eyes grew wide and serious. 'Do you have a minute? Because I'd really like to tell you, but it will take a minute. It's the heroine. Your other books are all about men. They have women characters in them, and they're all fully drawn. I doubt you could write a cardboard character if you tried.'

Amos nodded. Hallie knew the motion was inadvertent.

'You care about the women in those other books. You admire them or envy them, pity them or hate them. That's the point. You feel all sorts of things *about* those women, but you never feel the women themselves. In this book you do.'

'In other words, you feel you know Carrie.' There was a touch of irony in Amos's voice, but only a touch.

'Know her! I am Carrie. Carrie is me. That's what you did. You went inside Carrie. Under her skin. Into her mind and heart and gut. I read the galleys months ago, then I reread this last night, and I'm still breathless.'

Amos took the book from her, bent over the desk, and signed it. Hallie watched him as he wrote. From the flourish of that hand, you'd never know he found the gesture painful.

He handed the book back to Olivia. She clutched it to her breast.

'Thank you, Amos. Thank you so much.' She still sounded a little breathless.

He inclined his head slightly. He might have been giving royal dispensation.

'No one can accuse you of being a pushover for a pretty face,' Hallie said to her father when they were back in her office. 'It takes sheer, unadulterated flattery to get around you.'

Amos just laughed. Hallie wanted to cry. She was trying to put up a good front, but she didn't think it was funny.

'She may have been flattering me,' Amos said, 'but she put her finger on something. I don't think there's ever been as deep and subtle a portrait of a woman written by a man.'

'I don't know. Tolstoi didn't do badly with Anna. Flaubert was no slouch with Emma.'

'The trouble with you, Hallie, is you have too much respect for the dead masters. They were living, struggling writers once. Someday critics will be sitting around talking about what Porter did with Carrie. Olivia's right. Her moral development may have been arrested in infancy, but her critical faculties are on target.'

XX

Olivia had given Quentin plenty of time. She didn't want him to think she was some Little Nell from the country. She wanted him to know that she understood how the game was played. No ties, no obligations, no recriminations. Now that she'd proven herself, it was time to move. She chose the night of the publication party for Amos's new book.

Unlike Lily Hart's party, this would be no indiscriminate brawl where secretaries and assistant editors made a makeshift dinner of soggy hors d'oevres and jug wine, while editors and agents did business on other people's books. The setting would be Quentin's and Amos's club, which permitted private parties but no corporate bashes. The vintage wines and beluga had been chosen by Amos himself. The guest list had been honed by him to the bare and exclusive bones of the artistic and publishing worlds. Still, Olivia could have attended. She was no fledgling editor but the editor in chief of the house that published Amos Porter. She was also a *persona* considerably *non grata* to the Porter family. That was what she told Quentin.

She hung around until everyone else had left the office. For a moment she'd been worried, because she'd heard Hallie tell Quent she'd wait for him but Quentin had told her to run along. He'd stop by later. Olivia knew, because she was lurking in the hall when he said it.

'So you're really leaving.'

Olivia stood in the doorway of Quentin's office. Several cartons of books were open on the floor, and white rectangles on the graying walls indicated where pictures of Quentin and an assortment of great, or at least famous, writers had hung.

Quentin looked up at the sound of Olivia's voice and smiled. Once or twice in the past weeks he'd toyed with the idea of calling her, but the thought of Jake had always stopped him. Quentin had regained his appetite for sex but not for sexual competitions.

He looked around the office. 'It's about time.'

She stepped into the room. 'But you can't retire.'

'I'm not. I'm branching out. I'll keep an office at Allied on the coast.'

'I hear you cut quite a deal with them.'

He stared at her for a moment. 'Where did you hear that?'

She smiled. 'The grapevine.'

The grapevine, he thought, was behind on this one. He had cut quite a deal, but at the last minute someone – Quentin wished he knew who – had got to Jonathan Graham. It was still a sweet deal, just not as sweet as it had been a week earlier.

'Can I offer you a drink? I don't think my secretary's packed the whiskey yet.'

'I don't want to keep you from the party,' she said, but she moved to the sofa as she said it.

'Aren't you going?'

That was when she told him she was a *persona* considerably *non grata* to the Porters.

'I wouldn't worry too much about it. Hallie kept you on. And Amos has always appreciated talent.'

She took one of the drinks he held out to her. 'Tell me, what was it like to edit Amos Porter?'

Quentin sat beside her. 'Sheer hell.'

'I'd sell my soul for it.'

Her legs were close to his, and he put a hand on her knee. 'That's one of the ways you get to hell, my dear.'

'It would be so exciting.'

'To edit "the greatest American writer working today"?'

'What a challenge!' she breathed.

'If you'd ever worked with Amos, you'd know that's an understatement.' He took a swallow of his drink. 'But it would make your reputation.'

Quentin put his drink on the table. 'Is that why you dropped in tonight? To ask me to put in a word for you with Amos?'

She put down her own drink. 'That's one of the reasons. But only one.'

She stood, walked to the door to the outer office, closed it, and turned the lock. Then she came back and stood in front of him.

'Let's get one thing straight,' she said.

He dropped his head back on the sofa and looked up at her. 'By all means.'

'I sleep with you because I want to.'

'But we've never slept together, Olivia. We've never even lain together, as the phrase goes. If I remember correctly, and I think I do, that morning in my library we were in a chair.' He sat up and reached up under her skirt. This time she wasn't even wearing bikinis. And this time he wasn't surprised. 'If you want to be Amos Porter's editor, you must be precise about language.'

She stood there for a moment, smiling down at him. Gradually, she stopped smiling and closed her eyes. It wasn't an act. Quentin's fingers had an astonishing effect on her. She came suddenly, without warning.

When she opened her eyes, he was watching her. She moved away from him, leaned against the desk, and began to unbutton her blouse. In his library they hadn't even taken off their clothes. Olivia was very good at taking off her clothes. She unbuttoned, unzipped, slid things to the floor slowly, never taking her eyes from his face. When she was completely naked and could see that the muscles of his jaw had tightened, she moved back to the couch. Then she went to work on that proper gray flannel suit.

They managed to lie down together this time. The leather sofa stuck to her flesh. Above her in the softly lit room, Quentin's skin was a pale, blue-veined marble. His tongue was a red flame. She writhed in the fire it ignited. A book dug into her spine. Quentin eased her over on her stomach. The book slid to the floor. Olivia's overactive mind noticed the title.

Mailer's *Advertisements for Myself*. She laughed, then moaned in pleasure as he entered her.

There was a rattling of the doorknob. Olivia held her breath. Quentin stopped moving. His hands held her hips steady against him. The doorknob rattled again. They recognized the indistinct slavic mumblings of the cleaning woman.

'I'm working,' Quentin called. 'I don't want to be disturbed.'

The mumbling grew louder, then receded down the hall. Olivia began to laugh. The sound turned into a moan.

Hallie had meant to go straight to the party, but she'd run into Bob Sherwood in front of the elevators. Bob told her a dirty joke about two lesbians, then reminded her she'd never got back to him about the second printing of that thriller that was nibbling at the bottom of the bestseller lists. It was because of the thriller that Hallie went back to her office, then the phone rang and, as usual, she'd been incapable of not picking it up.

'Can you get out here next week?' Jonathan Graham asked. It wasn't really a question. 'Monday if possible. Tuesday at the latest. I want you to take a meeting with some of our people at World. I'm thinking tie-ins.'

Hallie began thinking of the half-dozen appointments and a couple of lunches and dinners she'd have to cancel. She told Jonathan she'd be there.

She was just leaving a note for her secretary to

make a plane reservation when the cleaning woman plodded in.

'Too late,' the woman chided her as she always did. 'Work too late.'

Hallie just smiled. She'd long before given up trying to bridge the language gap with anything more than a good night. Besides, what kind of publisher – not to mention a woman who's had her face on the cover of *Time* – tries to justify herself to the cleaning woman?

'You and boss.'

Hallie was still scribbling about the return flight and didn't pay much attention.

'Work late. Lock door. Crazy.'

Hallie looked up from the note. 'Mr Styles locked his door?'

'I try it. My job clean. No open.'

'Are you sure he was inside?'

'Sure. Go away, he yell. Work, he yell.'

Hallie left the note for her secretary in her out box, said good night to the cleaning woman, and headed down the hall to Quentin's office. She told herself there were any number of reasons he might lock his door, but only one came to mind. Quentin was sick and didn't want anyone to know. She thought of Amos signing the limited edition. All these aging men and their secret vanities. She swore, as only the young can, that she was going to grow old gracefully.

Hallie raised her hand to knock. That was when she heard a muffled voice on the other side of the door. She recognized it, even though it wasn't so much speaking as moaning.

'Oh,' Olivia cried, and 'Yes,' and 'Oh,' again.

Hallie began backing away from Quentin's office, then turned and hurried down the hall. The image of Quentin and Olivia followed her. She'd wondered that day at lunch. Now she was sure. Olivia was chipping away at her foundations, all right.

She should have known. First Jake had betrayed her. Now Quentin had let her down. She was no judge of men.

Outside the building, full and off-duty cabs sped by her. She felt invisible. The panic began to mount. She was already late for the party, Amos's party. She was letting down the one man she could trust.

XXI

Quentin sat on the locker-room bench, his elbows resting on his knees, and watched Amos Porter coming toward him from the showers. Amos's body had thickened over the years but not gone to fat. The shoulders were still massive, the chest a proud barrel, the arms and legs strong and muscular. When they'd been younger, Quentin had always felt like a skinny kid compared to Amos. It had been partly the difference between physical types and partly the brash self-confidence Amos radiated, as palpable as sweat when they were under German fire. At that time Quentin had had the insecurity of a man who'd been handed everything, Amos the boldness that is the only thing that comes easily to a self-made man.

War had been the first leveler. It had taught Quentin there were no heroes. They were only circumstances. Every man could be brave. All of them were capable of cowardice. Women had been the second. Crawling through the cafes and bistros of a newly liberated Paris, fighting their way across France and Germany, they'd found they were equals. The discovery had come as something of a shock to Quentin. Some women had preferred Amos, others him.

He smiled at the memories going down the years. They'd kept count of some things. Forty-four years; thirteen books, fourteen as of yesterday's publication; four marriages; three divorces; one christening. But what of the moments you didn't keep count of? How many games of squash had they played, how many nights had they got drunk together, how many women had they picked up? There was that night in Bastogne they'd been able to find two girls but only one room. That weekend after V-E Day when they'd rented an entire whorehouse. Whenever Amos told the story, Quentin always added that it was a very small town with a very tiny whorehouse. And after that, the first successes in New York and the heady trips to the coast. That was the time, the tenuous moment in both their lives, when their stars were still rising and their powers hadn't yet begun to decline.

Amos sat beside him on the bench. 'Don't look so bleak. You'll take me next time.'

'I wasn't thinking about the game,' Quentin said. 'I was thinking . . .' He hesitated. He didn't want to get maudlin. He'd said something to Cecelia about a new lease on life, and she'd laughed at him and quoted Scott Fitzgerald.

'I was thinking of that screenwriter. The one who told you she'd never go to bed with anyone who was a better writer than she was.'

Amos started to laugh. 'And I told her she was doomed to a life of celibacy.'

'We had some good times.'

Amos stood, moved to his locker, and pulled on a pair of jockey shorts. Quentin took a pair of sea island cotton boxers from his own locker. The old class differences, Quentin thought, lingered just beneath the surface.

Amos pulled on his trousers. 'I don't suppose you've reconsidered. About editing the next one, I mean.'

Quentin straightened from tying his shoes. 'You need a fresh eye. Mine is jaded.'

'I've never complained.'

Quentin let out a bark of laughter. 'Let's just say you're not complaining at the moment.'

Amos took a shirt from his locker. 'There's something undignified about being edited by your own daughter. It makes me feel like a doddering old fool.'

'There are other editors at R and S.'

'Schneider? He's a social butterfly, not an editor. Never done anything but celebrity biographies. Sally Worth? You think I want my next book to be brought out as a New Wave novel?' Amos continued down the roster of R and S editors. 'No, Hallie's the only one.'

'What about Olivia Collins?'

Amos shrugged into his jacket. 'I take it you're being facetious.'

They started for the bar.

'She's a good editor,' Quentin said. 'And she's doing more and more fiction. Serious fiction.'

'I'd feel like a worse heel than Jake.'

They took their usual table. The waiter brought their drinks without asking.

'She'd bring a fresh eye.'

Amos sipped his drink and remembered Olivia's comments about the heroine of *A Woman's Story*. 'She's perceptive. I'll give you that.'

'Look, Amos, don't do anything now. Let it ride. In fact, now that this one is out, why don't you take a vacation? Cecelia could use one, even if you couldn't.'

Amos leaned back in his chair and stared at Quentin as if, after all these years, he ought to know better.

'You're already well into the next one,' Quentin said.

'*A Woman's Story* may be just out for you, but it was over more than a year ago for me.'

'Don't you ever take a rest?'

'I'm like a shark, old buddy. If I stop, I die.'

Quentin shook his head and finished his drink. 'Okay, but still, you can't be that far along. Let the problem ride. For all we know, by the time you finish this one, Hallie and Jake may be back together. After one working session with you, Hallie will be glad to turn you over to Olivia. It'll be a kind of divine retribution.'

Amos's study was the most spartan room in the house. There was a desk, a chair, a table where notes and papers and manuscripts lay in messy but organised piles, and an IBM PC that Amos, who prided himself on his forward thinking, had taught himself to use. Three walls were covered with shelves of books, a fourth had two windows that overlooked the garden in back of the house. He'd never bothered to hang any art in the room, because in that room he never saw his surroundings. Sometimes he sat for hours staring into the garden and seeing nothing. His eyes might be turned out, but his gaze was always focused inward.

He was sitting that way now. Outside his window, the oak was a blaze of gold, and the stone patio beneath it a carpet of the same color. It was one of those late-October days that usually made him ache with pleasure. Today it only made him ache.

He stood, walked to the far wall, and took down an Italian-leather-bound book from a shelf full of identical books. They were Amos's diaries. He kept them for posterity, but he wrote them for himself, too.

When, as a young man hailed as a genius for his first novel, Amos had begun work on his second book, he, like many young geniuses in his position, had panicked. He'd never be able to rival the brilliance of that first novel. He didn't have another story like that in him. He'd blustered around town, pretending to enjoy the celebrity, pretending to accept the accolades, but behind the mask of confidence he was terrified. Gradually the fear gave way to certainty. He knew the truth. Amos Porter was a one-book author. Amos Porter was a has-been. A twenty-six-year-old has-been.

Finally one day, after a three-month dry spell and a three-martini lunch, he'd confessed to Quentin. By that time Quentin was a successful editor. Amos Porter was his star author, but he wasn't his only author.

'There comes a point in every book,' Quentin had told him, 'for every writer, when he begins to hate the book. It's the point of despair. The trick is to push beyond it. Because that's where the great books lie, old buddy. Beyond despair.'

Quentin had taught Amos something at that boozy expense-account lunch, and after that Amos had taught himself something else. His diaries were, among other things, logs of his work. They documented the points of despair in each of his novels. They celebrated the passages beyond it. The theory was that whenever Amos reached that terrifying point, he could take an old diary down from the shelf, as he was doing now, read about old trials and how he'd overcome them, and find solace. It wasn't a bad theory. The only problem was that, like most theories, it didn't have a lot to do with reality.

In the past he'd had another way of getting beyond the despair. Quentin. Quentin was the best editor Amos had ever known. His touch was light but sure. Amos trusted Quentin so completely that he'd given him unfinished chapters, early drafts, manuscripts bogged down in hopelessness. Quentin never came back and said, here's the problem or there's the flaw. He never suggested that Amos do this or change that. He simply asked an occasional question or murmured a few speculative words over some character development or plot twist or structural problem. And somehow those few words or occasional questions always got Amos back on the right track.

Amos returned the journal to the shelf and went back to his desk. The shadows in the garden had lengthened. Soon the sun would disappear behind the limestone apartment buildings of Fifth Avenue and the garden would be in premature darkness. Like Amos.

He needed another opinion, a fresh eye. He was too close to the manuscript to see anything. He couldn't even read the pages. Every time he tried to he ended up reciting them from memory. You couldn't tell what was wrong that way.

He supposed he ought to give it to Hallie. The idea was worse than undignified. It was silly. Like falling in love with Galatea. After all, he was the one who'd shaped Hallie's tastes, honed her critical abilities, taught her the facts of literary life.

Amos knew the reference to Galatea hadn't come out of the blue. He'd just read it in an old journal of his. 'C. was annoyed. I told her not to be foolish. I was no Pygmalion.'

Hallie had never felt so helpless. At least she'd never felt so helpless professionally. She was supposed to be a good editor. She had a stable full of successful authors who swore to the fact. She had dozens of dedications and acknowledgments and inscriptions that attested to the fact. But she'd read through Amos's pages for the second time and she still felt more like a daughter than an editor. She knew there were flaws – you couldn't miss the flaws – but she couldn't for the life of her put them together into a coherent problem that could be fixed.

She dialed Amos's study. The machine answered, but Amos picked up the phone when he heard her voice.

'There are some problems,' she said.

'I know there are problems. Why the hell do you think I gave you the manuscript?'

So that was the way it was going to be.

'Why don't you come in and we'll talk about them?'

'Come up here. Quentin always came here.'

It was absurd, Hallie thought, to be jockeying with her own father this way, but she knew she had to. If she went to his study, she'd be his daughter. If he came to her office, she might stand a chance of becoming his editor.

'For the past few years Quentin's had only one writer. I've got a tight schedule today.'

'You mean you're sandwiching me in?'

'They told me you were difficult to work with, they just didn't say how difficult.'

Amos was genuinely offended. 'Who said I was difficult? I'm a reasonable man.'

'Fine. Then why don't you come down here at around four?'

As it turned out Amos was reasonable. He never told Hallie she'd failed him. But Hallie knew without being told.

'I can't put my finger on it,' she said.

Neither of them mentioned that it was her job as an editor to put her finger on it.

They talked endlessly. Hallie made suggestions, Amos rejected most of them. She rejected the rest on second thought.

'Maybe I'm just too close to it,' she admitted. 'I'm supposed to see characters, but all I can see are parts of people I know. I'm supposed to hear their voices, but all I hear is yours.'

'Maybe we ought to give it time.' Amos took the manuscript from the conference table and stood.

Hallie got up too and put her hand on his arm. 'At least we didn't fight.'

Amos smiled down at her. 'That ought to surprise them.'

She walked him to the door to her office. 'You could ask Quentin to take a look at it. He isn't your editor anymore, but he's still your friend.'

'No!'

Hallie looked at him in surprise. Then it came to her. Amos knew the stories as well as she did. They were whispered at lunch, laughed at behind closed office doors, speculated about in conference rooms. They were the stories of authors whose books were so heavily reworked by their editors that they might have been written by their editors, stories of writers who couldn't write on their own. Amos was afraid of becoming known as one of those authors. Worse still, he was afraid of believing he was one of those authors.

Hallie knew the truth. Quentin hadn't written Amos's books. If Amos wasn't the greatest American writer working today, he was still a great writer. He didn't need an editor to write his books. But he did need one to edit them.

She'd seen him go into Hallie's office. She'd heard him come out. Amos's deep bass carried over half the sixteenth floor. Olivia cut off a writer in midsentence, hung up the phone, and started down the hall. She caught up with Amos in front of the elevators. She didn't have her coat, but that was okay. She could be going to the lobby for cigarettes – no, she didn't smoke anymore – newspapers, Lifesavers, if necessary. Amos nodded when he saw her, then waited for her to precede him into the elevator, but he didn't smile or speak.

'How does it feel to be back on the bestseller list?' she asked.

He just looked at her from under those diabolical black brows.

'Like coming home, I bet.'

He smiled, finally. 'A little,' he admitted.

'I guess you don't even worry about things like bestseller lists anymore.'

The doors opened. They stepped off the elevator together. 'You always worry about a book's reception.'

She indicated the box he was carrying. 'Is that the next one?'

He barely nodded.

'How's it coming?'

'Practice doesn't make perfect. Every one's a new one. And sometimes the first is the easiest. The real trouble is when the first is the best.'

Stop it, he warned himself. Stop babbling and whining and laying out your fears like an old fool. But he couldn't stop, even though he knew she was the last person he ought to be confiding in.

'You don't have to worry about that.'

'Not about that . . .' He didn't finish the thought. Amos didn't have to fear being a one-book genius. He'd gone far beyond that. All he had to worry about now was his diminishing powers. The irony struck him. At his age, some men feared their bodies would betray them, He was terrified his talent would.

'Not about anything,' Olivia said. 'I reread *A Woman's Story* over the weekend.'

'That makes three times now.'

'Four. Carrie is still the best character you've ever created. The best female character ever written by a man, as far as I'm concerned. I can hardly wait to read this one. In fact –' She stopped and looked up at him from under thick lashes, then went on. 'Carrie seems as if she sprang full blown from your imagination, but I know that a book like *A Woman's Story* doesn't just happen. I guess what I'm trying to say is I'd give anything to see how it does happen.' She hesitated again. 'I'd give anything to read an Amos Porter work in progress.'

Why not, Amos thought. Quentin said she was a good editor. Hallie used to say she was a terrific editor. And she'd certainly been on target about Carrie. Another reading wouldn't hurt. An intelligent reading by a stranger might help. And Hallie never had to know.

*　　*　　*

Quentin had to laugh. How many times had he sent flowers in his life? To how many women? His mind skipped back over the years. The formal arrangements to hostesses on the morning of a dinner party. The dozen red roses to a woman the morning after the night before. The camellia or gardenia or orchid to the girl he was taking to the party. He'd been sending flowers to women all his life. Dozens and dozens of flowers. Thousands and thousands of dollars. But never in his life had anyone sent him flowers.

He looked at the card again.

'In thanks for a crack at an Amos Porter manuscript – and much more.

'Love, O.'

He knew it wasn't extraordinary. Women did things like that now. Times had changed. The nice thing about the flowers – about the gesture, really – was that it made Quentin feel he was changing with them. He was grateful to Olivia. Again.

There was a limo waiting for Hallie at the L.A. airport, compliments of Jonathan Graham. There was a large, impersonal spray of fresh flowers in her suite at the Beverly Wilshire, compliments of Jonathan Graham. Hallie took it all in. You didn't go to all this trouble for a woman you were about to force out or fire. For the second time since the takeover, she dared to believe that Graham hadn't bought Rutherford and Styles to change it.

Hallie spent the next day in meetings. They made plans, opened lines of communication, set projects in motion. At one o'clock, platters of meager but artfully arranged steamed vegetables appeared in the conference room as if by magic. As Will Sawyer said, the trouble with Hollywood was that the bastards were always trying to undereat each other.

A man with a weak, handsome face that screamed of an easy youth followed by a groveling middle age produced a mirror and a little silver case. Jonathan Graham frowned at him. The man hesitated for a split second. The mirror and silver case disappeared. Hallie thought of the many rumors that circulated around Jonathan Graham. Her venture-capital friend had reported that he was a man entirely without vices. 'Scratch a man without vices,' Hallie had answered, 'and you find a celebrity with a good PR firm.'

Hallie was slated to take the red-eye back to New York. She knew that by tomorrow night she'd feel awful and look worse. Of course, tomorrow night there'd be no one waiting at home to notice how she looked.

Jonathan Graham walked her to the limo waiting in front of his office.

'Good meeting,' he said.

She agreed that it had been.

He held out his hand. 'Nice to have you on the team, Hallie.'

She took his hand. Two could play this game. 'Nice to be on the team, Jonathan.'

He still held her hand in his. 'You could have fooled me.'

211

'I admit I was wary at first.' She decided to go for candor 'You have quite a reputation, you know.'

He was still smiling. 'As a smart operator?'

'Among other things.'

He went on smiling. 'But not so smart that I knew about the return policy of my own publishing house. You and Quentin must have had a good laugh at that.'

She took her hand from his. 'Quentin and I never discussed it.'

'Are you telling me you didn't notice that clause in the contract?'

'Are you asking me to choose between incompetence and loyalty?'

For a moment the grin turned almost genuine. 'You're right. I couldn't forgive incompetence, but I have a sneaking admiration for loyalty.' He opened the door to the limo for her. 'Just remember one thing. You don't work for Quentin anymore.' As if she could forget it.

She was about to board the plane when it hit her. She was amazed she hadn't thought of it before. Olivia had come out to the coast to see a few authors and development people. Hallie had asked if she'd seen Jonathan Graham.

'Are you kidding? The CEO of Allied Entertainment doesn't have time for a lowly visiting editor from the east,' Olivia had said, and Hallie had believed her.

At least this time Hallie hadn't taken three months to catch on. She'd needed less than an hour.

Hallie decided it was time to put the contingency plan into action. She didn't even wait until she got back to New York. She called from the plane. Martha, her friend in venture capital, said she was free for lunch the following Thursday.

XXII

Olivia hurled the last page across the bed. How had she got herself into this? The manuscript read more like a college senior's idea of serious fiction than a novel by the greatest American writer working today.

That wasn't entirely true. The writing was okay. The writing was superb. The writing, in fact, called attention to itself, then stood up and took a bow. But there was nothing behind it. The characters were thin as the paper they were written on. The story rang false.

She could picture Amos's face if she told him that. But she didn't know what she could tell him. So much for being the editor of the greatest American writer working today.

The phone on the night table rang. She recognized Quentin's voice immediately.

'No one ever sent me flowers before. How can I thank you?'

'I can think of a few ways.'

Eight months before Quentin would have found the answer vulgar. Now he was merely flattered.

He asked if she was free for dinner the following night. She was supposed to go to a party with Jake, not one of those free-for-alls that any secretary could wrangle an invitation to but a small dinner at Lutèce. There'd be a lot of power at Lutèce tomorrow night.

She looked at the pages on her lap. That was when the idea came to her. She told Quentin she'd love to have dinner with him.

Olivia had told Quentin she'd meet him at the restaurant. On her way out of her apartment, she gave the rooms a once-over. Everything was in order. She walked back to the bedroom door. Amos's pages lay on the night table. Everything was in place.

They went to 21. It wasn't that Olivia had never been there before, only that she'd never been there with a member of the club. The food was still pedestrian, but the treatment was terrific.

Quentin's car and driver were waiting when they came out onto Fifty-second Street. The vintage Bentley stood out like a piece of sculpture against all those ungainly stretch limos. Olivia climbed into the back seat. It still reminded her of a cathedral, only now she felt like a convert rather than an infidel.

Quentin suggested a nightcap at his apartment, as she'd known he would. She'd been looking forward to that apartment. She'd never seen the second floor of a Fifth Avenue duplex. And she wasn't going to tonight. She had other priorities tonight.

'There's brandy at my place,' Olivia said. 'Probably

not as good as yours, but not exactly rotgut. And I think it's time you saw how the other half lives.'

The salacious doorman was on duty. He practically swooned when the Bentley pulled up and Olivia and Quentin got out. He was so bowled over he couldn't even manage his usual knowing wink.

'Pretty awful, isn't it?' Olivia said when they were in the elevator that some misguided landlord had painted bilious green.

'I've been in worse,' was all Quentin said.

Inside the apartment, she closed the door and switched on one lamp.

'And this is how the other half lives.'

He looked around. The living room was a white box filled with unremarkable furniture and a great many books. Through an open door, he could see the bedroom, another small white box. He thought of the Park Avenue penthouse where the politician's widow lived, when she wasn't in Marrakesh or Gstaad. The rooms full of impeccable antiques had reminded him of a museum. And he'd been one more dry and dusty exhibit.

He turned to Olivia and began unbuttoning her coat. At least – he thought but didn't say – the other half is alive.

They never did get to the brandy that night. Olivia didn't really like it. Quentin didn't want it. He was old enough to know when alcohol stopped enhancing his mood and began hindering his performance. They went into the bedroom.

She turned on a single lamp. He didn't look around the room. That was all right. She had plenty of time.

She began to undress. His eyes never left her.

That morning in his library she'd thought Quentin had taught her something about patience. Now she found out she hadn't begun to understand the meaning of the word. It wasn't that things moved slowly. It was just that he was determined to give her as much pleasure as he could.

She came and she came and she came, until finally, when he entered her, she felt as if she didn't have a single orgasm left in her. As it turned out, she was wrong.

'Do you mind if I stay the night?' he asked. They were still tangled together.

She laughed. 'You have what my mother used to call lovely manners.'

'You mean most men just assume?'

She didn't answer. She wasn't being demure. It was a little late for that. She just didn't think the question required an answer.

They lay in silence for a moment. He bet Jake Fox assumed. The thought didn't even rankle, not anymore. Quentin had realized something tonight. He'd known from the beginning that there were things Olivia wanted from him, practical things that Jake couldn't give her. Quentin didn't mind. He had no illusions about being loved for himself. Besides, his money and power and connections were himself, or at least extensions of him. But there was something else he knew now as well. Whatever was going on between Olivia and Jake, if in fact anything was still going on – Quentin hadn't asked, and no one had volunteered any information – it wasn't enough for Olivia.

She stirred against him now. 'I think I'm going to sleep for a week,' she murmured. She settled in, molding her body against his. 'You turn off the light.'

He reached for the lamp on the night table. That was when he noticed it. *Portrait of a Marriage.* 'Amos Porter' was printed just beneath the words.

'So this is Amos's new book.'

'Do you want to look at it?' Her breath was a warm mist against his shoulder.

'Not now.' He turned out the light.

Olivia cursed herself. She should have got up and gone into the bathroom. Then he'd have noticed the pages and picked them up automatically. The trouble was she didn't feel like getting out of bed. The idea made her smile. Imagine her, of all people, undone by sex.

She went on smiling. It was okay. She still had tomorrow morning.

Luck was with Olivia, as usual. It was a long time since Quentin had slept in a strange bed with a strange woman. He was up before six. He looked at Olivia, curled beside him in a fetal position, her hand childlike beneath her cheek. He touched her face. She didn't move. Her lashes didn't even flutter. She slept the sleep not of the innocent – that was for sure – but of the young.

He turned on the light. Again she didn't stir. He picked up Amos's manuscript.

*   *   *

Quentin had just about finished the pages when Olivia opened her eyes.

'What do you think of them?' she asked. Her voice didn't even sound sleepy. It sounded as if she'd been up for hours.

He put the pages on the night table and turned toward her. He put a hand on her breast. My God, she was warm.

'Do you really want to know now?'

Her only answer was her own hand on him.

'What do you think of it?' Olivia asked again. She'd got up and made coffee and brought a tray with two mugs back to bed. If Quentin missed the silver pot and the bone-china cups, he didn't say so.

'I think it needs work.'

'To put it mildly.'

'Amos isn't a great writer. He's a great rewriter. I used to tell him that all the time.' Quentin sipped his coffee. 'Mainly because he used to forget it all the time.'

'But it's not unpolished.'

'That's never been Amos's problem. The words are always perfect. It's the rest of it he has to rework.'

'Such as?'

He told her about the various drafts of *A Woman's Story*. He began to talk about the book before that one. Olivia was afraid he was going to work his way all the way back to the first novel.

'But what's wrong with this one?' She could barely keep the impatience out of her voice.

Quentin thought about it for a moment. 'For one thing, he's holding back.'

'Holding back?'

'This is a novel about a marriage, right? We both know whose marriage. And the book isn't working because Amos isn't telling the truth.'

XXIII

Cecelia could always tell when Amos was lying. Well, not always, but after a while she'd learned to. It had to do with his eyes. Some people couldn't look you in the eye when they lied. Amos couldn't look away. It was as if he dared her not to believe him.

She was more curious than worried. It was a long time since she'd worried about Amos's lies. A lifetime, it seemed. And she wasn't worried now. Still, she was curious. It was too early for Christmas – Amos never thought ahead – and too late for her birthday.

Amos was furious with himself. He hadn't lied to Cecelia in years, unless you counted the white lies like the day last December he'd said he was going to his club to use the library and he and Hallie had gone to Bergdorf's to look at sables for Christmas. But he'd lied to Cecelia this afternoon. What else could he do after Olivia called? He'd been in his study working, and as soon as he picked up the phone, he heard the catch of excitement in her voice.

'I can't wait to talk to you about it,' Olivia said.

'I think I figured out why you're having trouble,' she added when he said he couldn't possibly meet her that evening. That was the hook, of course. And Amos knew he was caught.

He'd come down from his study and told Cecelia, who was reading in the library, that he'd forgotten he had a squash date with Quentin.

'Didn't you play yesterday?'

'Quentin's on a fitness kick. I suspect a woman, a young woman, in the background.' The excuse had come to Amos out of the blue, but knowing Quentin, he knew it wasn't entirely out of the blue.

Cecelia had offered to call a car for him, but he'd said he'd pick up a cab on the street, and now he was standing on Fifth Avenue during rush hour, trying to find a cab and not to feel guilty.

He hated lying to Cecelia. Years before, he'd sworn he'd never lie to her again. But he'd had to lie now, because he knew what her reaction would have been if he'd told her he was going to meet Olivia. It didn't matter why he was going. There were no extenuating circumstances. If anything, Cecelia would have been furious that he'd given Olivia the manuscript in the first place. Funny how Cecelia was so eager to forgive Jake and so ready to blame Olivia.

Amos spotted an empty cab and hailed wildly. There was nothing to feel guilty about. Cecelia went on seeing Jake. He was just going to have a talk with Olivia. There was no difference. Except that Cecelia wasn't hiding anything. And he seemed to think he had to.

*　　*　　*

Hallie had known her venture-capital friend since their undergraduate years at Harvard. In those days Martha had wandered Nepal with a knapsack on her back and smoked any substance she could get her hands on. Now she belonged to several frequent-flyer programs and discussed the wineries of California and France with the sommelier. The sommelier suggested a 1974 Chardonnay. Martha insisted on 1975. She and Hallie got down to business.

Hallie laid out her plan. Martha said it wouldn't be a piece of cake but it shouldn't be too difficult to get backing.

'You've got a good track record. You've got a lot of visibility, thanks to that piece in *Time*. And from what you tell me, you're going to leave R and S the way the Pied Piper left Hamlin.'

Hallie hoped so. She decided to start with Will.

'I was going to phone you,' he said when she called him later that afternoon. 'I have those changes you wanted in *America at the Crossroads*.'

She suggested dinner.

'The first time you did that I had hope. Now I know you're just leading me on.'

Hallie let it go. She wanted to talk to Will about business. She had no intention of muddying the waters with sex. She could go to bed with Will for pleasure, though she hadn't that night, but not for gain. Misplaced scruples, Olivia used to tell her in the old days when they were sharing that railroad flat on Avenue A. Once or twice, Hallie had thought Olivia might be right. But then Henry Grainer had dropped Olivia, and Hallie had helped get Olivia a job and married Jake and decided there was some justice in the world after all. That showed how much she'd known.

She and Will got out their calendars. Will was even more booked than she was. He didn't have a free evening for two weeks. Hallie thought again of the revolving door to his bedroom. She forced her mind back to business. She didn't want to wait that long. They made a date for lunch.

The phone rang again as soon as she hung up. It went on ringing several times before she realized her secretary had left for the day.

At the other end of the line Jake asked how she was. She lied and said she was fine. He came back with something inane about the weather.

'Did you want something?' she asked.

'Do I have to want something to call?'

'Let's just say you usually have an agenda.'

'Damnit, Hallie –' He caught himself. 'All right. Sure. I have an agenda. I thought it would be nice to see you.'

'When?'

'Anytime you say. Is five minutes okay with you?'

It came to her then. She'd overheard Olivia leaving the office. Bob Sherman had made a crack about leaving promptly at five. Like a secretary he'd said, but Olivia had just smiled and said she was having drinks with an author. 'Major league,' she'd added.

'While Olivia's working, you mean.'

He slammed down the phone.

She sat staring at it. Cecelia told her she was

unforgiving, but then Cecelia had never had to play second fiddle to Olivia.

The phone rang again. She picked it up. 'I'm sorry,' Jake said, but he didn't sound sorry. He sounded angry.

'Apparently I hit a nerve.'

'Let's not start that again.'

'I'm not starting anything. You said you wanted to see me, and I asked if that was because Olivia was working. I mean, I know you have a busy schedule, and it can't easy fitting us all in. Like that night we had dinner –' She stopped abruptly.

'What about that night we had dinner?'

'Nothing.'

He wondered how she'd found out. Then it came to him. That second phone call, the one who'd hung up when he'd said hello. He never should have answered the phone. He never should have gone there that night. He wouldn't have if Hallie hadn't been so intransigent at dinner.

'You can't have it both ways, Hallie. You can't throw me out and then blame me for –'

She didn't slam down the phone. She just placed it in the cradle gently. She didn't want to hear what she could or could not blame him for.

She sat staring at the phone, waiting for it to ring again. The office was silent. The only sound came from far down the hall, where Sheila Dent was trying to book an author on Oprah Winfrey. There was a time when Sheila, forty-three and twice divorced, used to quote statistics proving that she had a better chance at remarriage than younger single women did at marriage. Sheila no longer quoted statistics. She just worked late and eked out the rest of her nights going to movies and dinners and publishing parties with women in the same position. Hallie had a feeling she was joining the club.

Olivia raced around the apartment, straightening cushions, shelving books and magazines, checking for traces of Quentin. She didn't want Amos to walk in and stumble over something that belonged to Quentin, or to Jake, for that matter.

Amos had suggested they meet at his club or a restaurant, but she'd pointed out that it might be better if he came to her place.

'I don't care if anyone sees us,' she said, 'but you might.'

He'd agreed to come to her apartment.

Not that Olivia had anything more than an editorial conference in mind. She had enough men in her bed at the moment. What she needed was a star writer on her list. What she wanted was the greatest American writer working today on her list. She just thought she stood a better chance of getting him on her own turf.

The doorbell rang. On her way to answer it, Olivia picked up her glasses and slid them on. She didn't need them for anything but the longest distances, but she wanted Amos to take her seriously.

Amos didn't so much enter the apartment as invade it. Olivia felt as if she were the visitor. She tried to right the balance by offering him a drink. He brushed aside the suggestion and sat in the wing chair. She sat across from him on the sofa. She thought of various openings, then decided to simply go for it.

'You're holding back,' she said.

The criticism was not what Amos had expected. He'd thought she'd talk about character or plot or structure. He was afraid she'd be too specific. He hated that. But she sounded just like Quentin. It was uncanny.

'What do you mean?'

'I mean you're not telling the truth.'

Now Amos was annoyed. 'I'm writing fiction.'

Olivia pushed her glasses back onto the bridge of her nose. They had a tendency to slip. 'I didn't mean you weren't telling a particular story the way it actually happened. I mean the story doesn't ring true.'

Of course it didn't ring true. Because he was holding back, because he wasn't telling it the way these things happen but the way society says they're supposed to happen. Olivia had heard the false note.

They discussed the problem. She made some general comments. He didn't ask her to be more specific. The entire conversation took about twenty. minutes. Amos knew he could have worked for a year and not seen things as clearly.

'How did you know?' he asked finally.

She shrugged, as if it were nothing. 'Any careful reader would have spotted it.' Any careful reader would have, but Hallie obviously hadn't.

Olivia took off her glasses and rubbed her eyes, though they didn't hurt.

'Now can I offer you a drink?'

Amos glanced at his watch.

'Just a short one?' she suggested. 'In celebration?'

She was right. He wanted to celebrate. He deserved to celebrate. He was back on track.

'Just a short one,' he agreed.

Olivia went into the kitchen to fill the ice bucket. Don't push it, she warned herself. You've got his confidence. In spades. She'd never forget his face when she'd said he wasn't telling the truth. Don't blow it by asking for his commitment. She wouldn't mention the word 'editor.' She'd just talk about his book. For now.

She carried the ice bucket back into the living room, mixed two drinks, and handed him one.

'To the new book,' she said.

He lifted his glass in salute.

'I can't wait to read the next instalment,' she said.

The idea came to him with sudden force and clarity. It was so simple. And no one would have to know. Besides, he was entitled. In some cultures, men had more than one wife. Since the beginning of time, men had had wives and mistresses. All he was asking for was two editors. Hallie would hold the official title and save face. Olivia would have the thrill and honor of working with a great writer. And he'd have the kind of editorial give-and-take he needed. He wasn't betraying Hallie. He was merely saving himself — his gift, really. She couldn't blame him for that. Not that she was ever going to find out.

He lifted his glass to Olivia again. 'I'm looking forward to having you read it.'

XXIV

The restaurant where Hallie had taken Will for dinner was trendy but without clout. For lunch she had her secretary make a reservation at the Four Seasons. Dinner had been for pleasure. This lunch was about power.

Will scented it immediately. He ambled into the Grill Room, a natural patrician in democrat's clothing.

'Jonathan Graham must be getting to you,' he said as he slid onto the banquette. 'If I'd thought about it, I'd have worn my power tie.' He kissed her on the cheek.

'You don't own a power tie,' she said. She saw Will's agent bearing down on them. Now, there was a man who knew about power dressing. Harrison Fist was a walking ad for Patek Philippe, Bijan, and Peal shoes. Hallie had never much liked Harrison, maybe because he always made her feel underdressed. Since her marriage to Jake, Harrison had detested her. The mutual antipathy, however, had never prevented them from cutting deals.

Fist's greeting was only a fraction of a degree

warmer than usual. He might be glad she'd separated from Jake, but he wasn't about to forgive her for marrying him in the first place.

Fist leaned close to Will's ear. 'I know that look in her eyes,' he said in a stage whisper. 'She's got designs on your foreign rights.'

Hallie forced a smile. 'My intentions are strictly honorable, Harry.'

Fist patted Hallie on the shoulder, pounded Will on the arm, and moved to his own booth across the room. Grace Robbins, the editor in chief of the house that published Will in paperback, joined him. They all smiled, nodded, and made an elaborate pretense of turning back to their respective lunch partners.

'This place gives me the creeps,' Will said. 'I get the feeling the martinis are bugged.'

'It's good for your image. Lets everyone know how important your publisher thinks you are.'

Will waited until the waiter had put down the drinks they'd ordered, then turned to her on the banquette. 'How important do you think I am, Hallie?'

That was her opening, and she went for it. 'Very. Harry's right. I do have designs on you.'

'You know, Hallie, if I didn't know you better, I'd think you were turning into a tease.'

But she was single-minded now. 'Remember the talk we had when Allied took over R and S? What would you say if I told you I was thinking of leaving?'

'I'd say we ought to get Harry over here right now and start him working on a deal that lets me buy back this book and go with you right away.'

232

'Even if it's not to an established publisher? Even if I'm thinking of starting my own house?'

He hesitated for a moment. She held her breath. Another moment went by. She resisted the urge to sell herself. Partly because she wanted him to make the decision freely, without pressure; mostly because she knew it would be a mistake. This was no time to look hungry.

'What are you going to call it?'

'I hadn't thought . . .' She hesitated. 'Maybe Unicorn Books.'

'Where does that come from?'

'I don't know. It's just an idea. Why? Does it matter?'

'Sure it matters. I want to be able to tell people the name of my new house.'

The news spread through her body like alcohol and relaxed every muscle. She hadn't realized just how scared she'd been.

'I'm happy for you, Hallie, really happy.' Then he did something that surprised her. He leaned over and kissed her on the mouth. It was light and proper. After all, they were in the Grill Room of The Four Seasons. But it was on target.

She put her hand over his on the table. 'You are one incredible friend.'

He looked at her for a moment, and a rueful smile crept across his face. 'Let's not start that again.'

At three o'clock on a weekday afternoon the streets of midtown Manhattan between Twenty-first and Fifty-seventh streets are crawling with editors and agents staggering back from lunch. That day Hallie ran into no fewer than four of them. An agent stopped her on the corner of Fifty-second and Park and asked how she liked the manuscript she'd messengered over the day before. At Madison and Forty-ninth, the sub-rights director of another house tried to get some information about the auction of Amos's latest book. Two blocks farther south, one editor told her another's wife had just left him for the midwife who'd delivered their last child. A block later she ran into Will's paperback editor again. Grace Robbins was a small woman with a brush-cut and gimlet eyes.

'How's our star liberal?' she asked Hallie.

'Writing his heart out.' She held up the manuscript box Will had given her as they'd left the restaurant. 'He just finished the revisions on the next one.'

'I can't wait to see it.'

'Neither can I. It was good before. I'm willing to bet it's great now.'

The gimlet eyes went on staring at her. 'You two are pretty tight.'

Hallie decided to ignore the innuendo. 'It's a good working relationship.'

'I guess he'd follow you anywhere.'

Hallie couldn't help herself. She had to smile. 'Is that what Harrison Fist said?'

The gimlet eyes blinked. 'You know Harry. He says a lot of things. You just have to figure out which to believe.'

Hallie spent the next day in meetings. By the time

she got back to her desk there was a pile of pink phone slips. She rifled through them. Jake had called again. She wondered what he was up to now, then remembered there was a problem with a contract for one of his clients.

She dialed his number. Her hand wasn't quite steady. She reminded herself she was calling about a simple contract problem. She wondered if she'd ever get to the point where she could call Jake and do business without thinking of other things. People talked about time healing wounds. Hallie didn't think there'd be enough, no matter how long she lived.

His secretary put her through right away. 'I have to see you,' he said.

'Can't we do it over the phone? It's not even six figures.'

'What are you talking about?'

'The contract on that hijacking thriller. What are you?'

'Something more important.'

'Okay, are we going to play twenty questions?'

'I'd rather not talk about it over the phone.'

'Come on, Jake. 'Were negotiating a thriller, not living one.'

'Does the name Unicorn Books mean anything to you?'

'How do you know about that?'

'That's what I want to talk to you about. Are you free tonight?'

'I can be.'

'I'll meet you at the apartment. Around eight.'

Hallie was so surprised she didn't even argue.

*   *   *

Hallie heard the bell to the apartment. The concierge hadn't announced Mr Fox from downstairs. Though he hadn't seen Mr Fox for a while, he hadn't forgotten that Mr Fox was the one who handed out the discreet white envelopes stuffed with crisp green bills every Christmas and July.

She opened the door. Jake was standing with his back to it, staring at the wall across from the elevator. 'What happened to the lithograph we had there?' he asked without turning to her.

Trust Jake. She was thinking about him and he was worrying about the Stella litho.

'I'm having it reframed. Tess knocked it down and broke the glass while she was dusting. Did you come to tell me something or to catalogue community property?'

He clenched and unclenched his fists. He wasn't even inside the apartment, and she was talking about divorce again. The only thing that surprised him was that he could still manage to be surprised by it.

He stepped into the apartment and took off his coat. She held out her hand for it.

'I know where it goes.'

He went to the closet and hung it up. He took off his jacket, too. She wished he hadn't. Some women went for tight jeans. Olivia couldn't go to the ballet without speculating which of the dancers had stuffed their leotards with socks. Hallie was a pushover for suspenders. She wondered if Jake remembered.

She asked if he wanted a drink.

'I know where that is, too. Unless you moved it.'

'It's in the same place.'

He crossed to the breakfront they used as a bar.
She'd filled the ice bucket. He asked if she wanted
one.

'Only if you promise it'll be Scotch and not
strychnine.'

She watched his movements at the bar. As he
reached for a decanter, his shoulders pulled against
his shirt. She turned away from the sight.

He crossed the room and handed her a drink. 'I
didn't put a twist in it,' he said. 'I know you don't
take a twist in your strychnine.'

'What a memory!'

'Truce?'

'Truce.'

They were standing in front of one of the sofas.
He sat. She debated her options. It seemed safer to
put a coffee table between them. She moved to the
other sofa. She noticed the tic pull at the corner of
his mouth.

'Okay,' she said. 'I swept the room. No bugs. Tell
me what's going on.'

'You tell me. What's Unicorn Books?'

She shrugged. 'Beats me.'

He looked at her from under those spiky lashes.
'Hallie, I'm on your side.'

'I doubt –' She stopped. 'I'm sorry. What did you
hear Unicorn Books was?'

'Your new house.'

'Where did you hear that?'

'Does it matter?'

'You know it does.'

'Some venture-capital type was asking around about you. People put two and two together.'

'And get five.'

'I don't think so in this case. Neither does anyone else. It makes sense. Graham takes over. You walk out. Some people expected you to go to another house. But I know you better. You don't like to answer to anyone.'

'I thought you said you were on my side.'

'I'm partisan, babe, not blind.'

'Thanks.'

'Anytime.'

'And that's what you couldn't tell me on the phone? That people are speculating about whether I'm going to leave R and S for another house or start my own?'

'It's a little more than that. This wasn't a ruse.'

She dropped her eyes. It was exactly what she'd been thinking. Hoping. She pulled herself up. She forced herself to remember Olivia.

'Do you want to tell me the rest, or do you want to make me beg?'

'You've never in your life –' This time it was his turn to stop. They'd declared a truce.

'When I heard about your plan,' he went on, 'I thought it was a good idea. You have the name – yours, not Amos's. You know how to run a house. And you've got a sweet stable to walk away with. I was figuring it out. Amos, certainly. Will Sawyer, definitely. Or so I thought.'

'What do you mean?'

'I had lunch with Grace Robbins today. Will's paperback editor.'

'I know who she is.'

He raised his hand, palm toward her. 'Hey, don't take it out on me. I'm just the messenger. It seems now that you're leaving, Will no longer feels any obligation to R and S. Grace has been wanting to start a hardcover line for years. Will told her that for a few million – she wouldn't say just how few – she can have the softcover rights to his next book.' Jake hesitated. 'And the hard.'

'He wouldn't do that!'

'He did.'

'But he promised –'

'That he'd go with you?'

She didn't answer, and he didn't press it. Jake had a good idea what Will had promised and why – he could damn well picture the scene – but he wasn't going to start that again.

She couldn't believe it. Not Will. Her old friend. Her almost lover. He'd sat there and sold her a bill of goods while his agent was sitting across the room and selling her down the river. When it came to men, she wasn't much of a judge of character.

'I just thought you'd want to know.'

'Thanks.'

'I'm sorry.'

She didn't say anything.

They sat in silence for a while. For the first time since they'd sat in this same room and she'd thrown that copy of *Time* at him, there was no edge between them.

'Can I freshen that for you?' He pointed to her drink. She didn't offer to do it herself. She'd almost forgotten it wasn't still his apartment, too. It was easy to slip into the old patterns.

When he brought the drink back, he sat beside her on the sofa. He noticed that she didn't move away, but then she didn't move closer, either.

'It's a nice idea,' he said. 'The name.'

'The name?'

'Unicorn Books.'

'It just came to me.'

He smiled, not the big smile, but a quieter one, turned vulnerable by that gentle tic in the corner of his mouth. 'I'm glad it did.'

'Why?'

'Do you need three guesses?'

'I don't know what you mean.'

'Don't you remember what Unicorn was?'

She looked at him blankly. 'The tapestries?'

He took a long swallow of his drink. Christ! Why did he bother.

It hit her then. No wonder the name had just come to her. *Unicorn* was the boat they'd chartered in Maine on their wedding trip. She felt like an idiot. He thought she was going to name her new publishing house after their broken marriage.

'I didn't choose it because of that . . . because of the boat . . . that week . . .' Her voice drifted off.

He finished his drink. 'No, you wouldn't be that sentimental.' He stood and went back to the bar. This time he didn't ask her if she wanted another.

'I mean . . .' she began.

'I know what you meant. You named it after the tapestries.' He came and sat across from her again.

'Hell, why don't you call it Gobelin House? Or Burgundian Sacraments Publishing? Now there's a catchy name. Who's your publisher? B.S.' He took another long swallow of his drink.

'You don't have to get nasty.'

'Why not? Why the hell not?'

'I wasn't the one who came in here asking what I'd done with the Stella litho. As if you were making up lists for the goddamn lawyers.

'You're the one who brought up community property sweetheart.'

'And don't call me "sweetheart"!'

'I was being sarcastic.'

'No kidding.'

They were both shouting now.

'You always did like terms of endearment,' she went on. 'Safer that way. No chance of slipping when were all "sweetheart" and "babe" and "dollface".'

He finished the drink in a single swallow. 'I never called you "dollface"!'

'Why? Did you save that one for Olivia?'

'Goddamnit' He stopped. They sat staring at each other. From somewhere down the hall a radiator clanked and banged. Outside a siren screamed down Park Avenue. The sounds of violence were all around them, but the room was silent. He put down the glass, stood, and left the room.

Hallie sat there staring into her own untouched drink. She heard the rattle of hangers in the hall closet, then the sound of the front door slamming.

She went on sitting there for a long time after Jake

had left. She was thinking about the last time he'd slammed a door on her. That had been the door to a taxi. He'd gone straight to Olivia. 'Dollface,' Hallie said aloud to the empty room.

Jake didn't go to Olivia's that night. He went to a bar on Third Avenue, the kind of dingy, no-nonsense bar where people go to get drunk.

XXV

Under ordinary circumstances, Hallie never would have gone to the party. It was sure to be one of those bashes where the guests were packed in like subway commuters at rush hour, the blaring music sounded as if it were made by jackhammers, and the Perrier flowed like champagne. But these were not ordinary circumstances. A woman about to start a house of her own couldn't afford to offend a coming literary agency celebrating its fifth anniversary. Especially if the woman about to start the house had just lost one of the star authors she'd been counting on.

The scene was every bit as bad as Hallie had expected. Someone spilled wine on her. At least it was white. She felt a hand on shoulder. She turned and came face to face with Will Sawyer.

'How's my publisher?' he shouted above the noise.

'Fine.'

Even in that din he picked up on the chill.

'You couldn't have hated the revisions that much,' he yelled.

'They're good.' Her voice was loud but flat.

'Try to keep your enthusiasm under control, Hallie.'

She didn't even smile.

He leaned closer as if trying to get a better look at her in the constantly flashing light. 'What's wrong?' he shouted above the noise.

'Nothing,' she yelled. 'I just wish you'd told me yourself.'

'Told you what?'

'I don't think this is the place to discuss it,' she shouted and started away.

He followed her. 'Do you mind telling me what you're talking about?'

She turned and faced him. 'Look, I don't blame you.'

'What did you say?'

'I said I don't blame you.'

Another couple jostled past and pushed her into him. Will grabbed her arm and began steering her toward the door.

The street was quiet except for an occasional car cruising past. He turned to face her, but he didn't let go of her arm.

'What don't you blame me for?'

'You've got your own career to worry about. I understand your not wanting to take a chance on a new house. I just wish you'd told me instead of giving me that song and dance about following me anywhere.'

'It wasn't a song and dance.'

'What about Grace Robbins?'

'What about Grace Robbins?'

She was getting tired of the game. She didn't blame him for taking the money and running – at least she was trying not to blame him – but she was tired of being lied to. By Jake. By him. By all the men in her life.

A cab came cruising toward them. She hailed it. 'The word is that you cut a seven-figure deal. For softcover rights' – she pulled open the cab door – 'and hard.' She climbed in. 'Congratulations.' She slammed the door before he could answer.

It was close to nine when the concierge called from downstairs. There was a Mr Sawyer to see her.

Hallie glanced at herself in the hall mirror. She'd taken off her makeup as soon as she'd got home. Her face looked pale and shiny as a kid's, a sick kid's. She was wearing an old Sulka robe that had found its way from Jake's closet to hers several years earlier. To hell with it. To hell with Will. She told the concierge to send him up.

He came into the apartment like a weather front. 'I just fired Harrison.'

'If you're looking for a new agent, Jake's not here.'

'I didn't know about that deal Harrison cut with Grace Robbins, Hallie. I swear it.'

She had no jokes for that. She just stood there staring at him. He stared back. She suddenly realized she wasn't wearing anything beneath the robe. She tucked one side under the other and pulled the sash tighter.

'Look, Hallie, you've known me for a long time. I'm not saying I'd never publish with anyone else.

I'm not that crazy. But I'd never sit there having lunch with you while my agent was across the room screwing you.' That good, clean, all-American face smiled. 'It's not the kind of task I'd delegate.'

She stared at him a moment longer, then made up her mind. 'I should have known it wasn't your style.'

He ran a hand through the unruly salt-and-pepper hair. 'Offer me a drink, and all is forgiven.' They went into the living room. 'In fact,' he went on, 'offer me a drink, and I'll give you some interesting news.'

She made drinks and asked him for the interesting news.

'Have you heard about the Max Perkins Prize?'

She said she hadn't.

'That's what you get for hanging around on the coast with all those movie people. You're losing touch. Some filthy-rich literary groupie died last year and left an endowment for a prize. Very prestigious. Very classy.'

'And you won it!'

'You aren't paying attention, Hallie. It's called the Maxwell Perkins Prize. What does that bring to mind?'

'It's an editorial award.'

'And they said you were slow. It's a prize for overall editorial excellence.' He hesitated. She sipped her drink and waited. 'And you've been nominated.'

'How do you know?'

'I'm on the board.'

'And you nominated me?'

'Me and about a dozen other of your authors. But

now I get to vote. You're looking at one of the five judges for the Max Perkins Prize. And I have every intention of beating the other four into submission. Not that I think it'll be necessary. The word is that you've as good as got the prize. It'll be a nice way to start the new house. First *Time*, then this, and finally Unicorn Books.'

It was exactly what she'd been thinking.

'I think this calls for another drink. In celebration.' He picked up both glasses and carried them to the bar.

'There's nothing to celebrate. I haven't won yet.' She wasn't exactly superstitious. She just didn't like tempting fate.

'You will. If I'd stopped to think, I would have brought champagne.' He returned with the fresh drinks and sat beside her on the sofa. 'But I was in too much of a hurry to stop to think.' He took a sip of his drink. 'I found something out tonight, Hallie. I found out I didn't like having you think I was a bastard.'

'That's funny.' She sipped her own drink. 'Because I didn't like thinking you were a bastard.'

He sat staring at her with those decadent Caribbean-blue eyes. 'I'm not speaking only professionally.'

She looked at him. She'd turned him down once. He was giving her another chance. She had a feeling it would be her last.

They went on staring at each other. He had such a straightforward face, all square jaw and clean features. Except for the mouth. She wanted to trace the outline of that full lower lip with her fingers, but she didn't move. She felt the shadows around her in the room. She waited for Jake's ghost to emerge from them. All she saw was Will's face getting bigger as she leaned toward it.

His mouth was warm. His tongue tasted of Scotch. It started all over again, slow and building. They stopped for a moment and looked at each other.

'What are you smiling about?' he asked.

'I was thinking that we're finally getting the timing right.'

He kissed her again. The touch of his hand beneath her silk robe was electric. She was suddenly aware of the hardness of his body against the softness of her own. She tugged at his tie, unbuttoned his shirt, felt the smoothness of his skin against hers.

His mouth traced a line down her neck to her breast. She ran her hands over his back. He was tight and hard and smooth as a statue. She felt herself falling on the sofa and him rising above her. He kissed her again, deeply and slowly, as if they had all the time in the world. Without taking his mouth from hers, he untied the robe and traced the line of her body, around one breast, then the other, down the long line of waist and hip, inching slowly, maddeningly down.

Her own hands moved as slowly. She reached for his belt.

The sound was harsh, more buzzer than bell. They froze but didn't move apart. They both waited for it to ring again.

'Is that the upstairs bell or the lobby?' he whispered.

'Upstairs.'

It rang again.

'Don't answer it,' he murmured.

That was when they heard the second sound. It was quiet, barely more than a few clicks, but she recognized it. So did Will. It was the sound of a key turning in a lock. They sprang apart. Hallie was tugging her robe back on, tying the belt. Will was buttoning furiously. They both knew who it was. At least, they guessed.

They couldn't see the door from the sofa, but they heard it open and close. Then Jake's voice came crashing into the room, calling Hallie's name.

She stood, smoothed her robe, and went into the hall. Jake smiled when he saw her. 'I didn't think you were – ' He stopped in midsentence. The smile drained from his face like blood. Hallie knew that Will had followed her into the foyer. '. . . home,' Jake finished.

The two men stood facing each other. Hallie looked from Jake to Will. For one crazy moment she thought they were going to shake hands. That was when she noticed it. Will had buttoned his shirt, but his belt buckle was still open.

She turned to Jake. His glance had followed hers. He was staring at Will's belt buckle.

She tugged her robe tighter. That was a mistake. Now Jake was staring at her. She wondered if he could tell she wasn't wearing anything beneath it. Of course, he could. He always used to tease her about that robe, his robe. He used to say the silk was like a second skin on her.

'You could have called,' she snapped.

'I did call. I also rang the bell.'

'We heard,' Will said.

Jake's eyes flickered to Will, then back to Hallie. 'But you didn't answer.'

'Is there a federal statute that says Hallie has to answer her door?' Will asked.

This time Jake didn't even look at him. 'I called and left a message with Tess,' he said to Hallie. 'I said I needed some papers I'd left in the file in the study and was going to stop by tonight.'

For a single moment Hallie considered murdering the housekeeper. Then she reconsidered and decided on suicide. Tess had left her a note on the kitchen counter, but Hallie hadn't read it. Decoding Tess's handwriting was as difficult as deciphering the Rosetta stone.

'If you don't mind, I'll get the papers and get out of here.' Jake started down the hall toward the study.

'There's a conspiracy against us,' Will said. 'Either that or he has the place bugged.'

Hallie didn't answer.

Jake came back down the hall toward them. He was carrying a manila envelope. He stopped and looked from one of them to the other.

'I'm sorry if I interrupted anything.' He didn't sound sorry.

'Maybe you ought to leave your key,' Hallie said.

Jake stared at her in silence for a moment. Then

he took a key ring from his pocket and yanked off two keys.

'Sure,' he said. 'No problem.' He slammed the keys down on the hall table, then caught himself and took a deep breath. It worked. He didn't even slam the door on his way out. And he waited until the elevator was halfway to the lobby before he drove his fist into the wall.

Hallie and Will went back into the living room. He made them another round of drinks. He sat beside her on the sofa. He took her hand in both of his. But it was no good. They'd finally banished Jake's ghost. Then Jake had come crashing into the apartment.

XXVI

Olivia didn't try to convince Jake to stay over often. She'd made a point of it that first time, the night he'd slammed into the apartment furious and they'd been on the floor in minutes. It had been a symbol, a power struggle, almost a point of honor to her. She'd had to get him to spend the night once. After that, after she'd won, she was perfectly content to lay naked and warm under the covers while he got up and dressed and went out into the cold New York night to hail a cab and find his way back to the Princeton Club.

Jake was better than most, but Olivia believed that there was a time and a place for men, and it wasn't between one and eight a.m. At worst, they snored and tossed and hogged the covers. At best, they wound themselves around her cloyingly and were there in the morning, expecting smiles and conversation while she worried about her makeup and the day ahead. Olivia usually preferred to go to bed with a man and to sleep alone, but sometimes there were extenuating circumstances. The night she'd wanted Quentin to read Amos's manuscript had been one. This was another.

It was Jake's own fault for being so secretive. If he'd just tell her the high bid in the auction, Olivia would top it by a few thousand and that would be that. But Jake was standing on professional ethics. Even while he was lying on top of her in her bed, he'd insisted in standing on professional ethics. He wouldn't tell her what the other publishers were offering. She bet he used to tell Hallie. The thought infuriated Olivia, but she wasn't going to let Jake see that.

'You can't go out in this,' she said and pulled the comforter up over their sweaty bodies. 'It's freezing.' She licked a bead of moisture off his chest. 'It's late.' She nibbled his ear. 'And there's no reason for it.'

Jake felt the pressure of her body all along his. She was right. He was exhausted, and it was late, and the radio and television and newspapers had screamed of record-breaking cold for November. Why should he bother to get up and shower and dress and go back to the Princeton Club? Why was he keeping up pretenses? He thought of Hallie when he'd walked into the apartment the week before. She hadn't been wearing anything under that damn robe. And Sawyer's belt had been open. But Jake would have known what was up even without the clothes. He thought of Hallie's mouth. It had had that soft, full, almost bruised look. It got that way from kissing and from . . . he thought of Sawyer's belt buckle. Goddamnit!

He told Olivia she was right. There was no point in going back to the Princeton Club.

He fell asleep holding her, but in minutes he'd rolled over to the other side of the bed. Thank God. Olivia couldn't sleep with anyone touching her. Besides, she wasn't ready for sleep. She hadn't convinced Jake to stay over so she could sleep beside him.

She got out of bed, crossed the room, and closed the door quietly behind her. He'd left his briefcase on the floor beside the sofa. It wasn't locked.

She began rifling through the folders and envelopes. She could hear her own shallow breathing.

She found the folder. Her eye raced over the memos and notes. She should have known Jake better. He wouldn't write down figures. He especially wouldn't write down figures and leave his briefcase unlocked. One point for the visiting team.

She was just about to close the briefcase when it caught her eye. The Max Perkins Prize, the letterhead said. She took the paper from the briefcase.

The letter described the award. Then it went on to say that any of his clients who had published at least three books of quality fiction or nonfiction was invited to nominate a candidate for the award. A board of five distinguished judges would then vote on the candidates. Her eye ran down the list of judges. Will Sawyer. Goddamnit! Carter Bolton. Hurrah! Adelaide Koenig. Gardiner Fairchild. Amos Porter.

Olivia read the last paragraph a second time to

make sure she was right. She had forty-eight hours to get herself nominated.

Olivia watched Jake's reflection in her bedroom mirror. He tied the discreet Hermes tie carefully, though he knew he was going to change it and the shirt as soon as he got to his office.

She sat up in bed so the sheets fell to her waist. Carter Bolton had once written a poem to her breasts. He'd already smoked several joints and polished off a bottle of wine when he'd done it, but still, he'd never written a poem to any of the others in the seminar. Carter would vote for her. She was sure of it.

'You never answered me last night. I asked you who your clients had nominated for the Max Perkins Prize, and you never answered.'

Jake's hands stopped moving for a minute, then yanked the knot into place. He had many flaws, but a faulty memory wasn't one of them. He reminded himself again to lock his briefcase if he had anything important in it.

'I don't know anything about it,' he said. 'I just passed on the information to my clients.'

'Come on, honey. I know you better than that. You're always tapped in.'

He turned away from the mirror and picked up his jacket. 'Just whom you'd expect.' He ran through a few predictable names.

'What about Hallie?'

He shrugged into his jacket. 'She's been nominated.'

'She's bound to get it.'

He was buttoning his jacket. 'She's up against some pretty impressive candidates.'

'And she's already got two judges. Will Sawyer and Amos. All she needs is one more vote.'

'I have a breakfast meeting.'

She got out of bed, crossed the room to him, and put her arms around his neck. 'You could suggest – discreetly, of course – to one or two of your authors that they nominate me.'

He laughed, but he put his arms around her. It was hard not to.

'Look, Olivia, I don't want to disillusion you, but I don't think you stand much of a chance. Even if you get yourself nominated, you'll be up against some of the biggest names in the business.'

She wanted to slap him for that. Instead she rubbed her thumb against his cheek.

'Don't you think I know that? I don't expect to win, honey. I just want to be nominated and taken seriously by the judges.'

Jake studied her. This wasn't like Olivia. Her aims were usually more concrete.

She moved away from him and put on a robe. She knew he was trying to figure out what she was up to. She sat on the end of the bed, and when she spoke again, she didn't look at him.

'I know what people say about me, Jake. Olivia Collins will do anything to get ahead. And they're right. Almost. But there's one thing they don't know.' She stopped and looked up at him from under the thick fringe of lashes. 'Why I'm so ambitious.'

'Does there have to be a reason?'

'Maybe not, but in this case there is.'

He sat beside her on the bed. Apparently his breakfast meeting could wait. 'Okay. What's the reason?'

'Do you promise you won't laugh?'

'I won't laugh.'

'My mother gave up her whole life for me. I mean that, literally. She broke her health on that damn sewing machine. I can still see her sitting there, her foot numb on the treadle and her nose practically resting on the machine because her eyes were shot by that time. And all so I could grow up with a few decent things and be able to take advantage of that college scholarship.'

'I've never heard you talk about your mother.'

'I never have.' Olivia dropped her eyes again. 'Since she died. Probably because I never trusted anyone enough to.'

He didn't say anything to that.

'Don't you see, Jake? That's why I'm so ambitious. For her. I have to make something of myself for her. Otherwise everything she did – all the work and the self-denial – would be for nothing. And that's why I want to be nominated – just nominated.' She looked at him and managed a weak smile. 'For her memory.'

He put his arm around her shoulders.

She rested her head against him. 'Now you know the one thing about me no one else does. Everyone thinks I'm such a bitch. Maybe I am. But now you know why.'

Jake looked down at the triangle of curls that

spread over his shoulder. Olivia was right. This was a side of her he'd never seen, never even imagined. He glanced at his watch. He tried not to think about the woman from development who was waiting for him in the dining room of the Regency Hotel. He went on holding Olivia and tried not to think about the fact that he was getting in deeper all the time.

'Sure I'll vote for you,' Carter Bolton said. 'For old time's sake.'

He was lying on his back in bed, holding a glass on his chest. She pushed his hand with the glass away and took its place on top of him.

'I don't call five minutes ago "old times".'

'I'll vote for you,' he repeated, 'but don't get your hopes up. The competition's pretty stiff.'

It was exactly what Jake had said, and she was sick of hearing it. 'So much for the competition, honey. Now what about you?'

XXVII

Hallie missed her weekly lunches with Quentin. She'd valued his opinions, relied on his guidance, enjoyed his company. A few months earlier she'd had so many allies. Jake, Olivia, Quentin. These days she was going it alone. She could do it, but that didn't mean she liked doing it. So she was pleased when Quentin called one morning and suggested lunch. It would be like old times. Almost.

'Incidentally,' Quentin said as she was about to hang up, 'Jonathan Graham wants to join us.'

So much for old times.

Quentin was already halfway through his first martini when Hallie arrived. Jonathan Graham showed up fifteen minutes later. In the keep-them-waiting game, he was the uncontested winner.

Jonathan was not a man for meaningless conversation. They got down to business. P and L's and projections, budgets and acquisitions. Hallie participated in all the planning as if she expected to be there to implement it. If Jonathan thought she might not be – if, like Jake, he'd got wind of Unicorn Books – he didn't let on. Of course, Jonathan wasn't exactly tapped into the publishing hot line. At least Hallie hadn't thought he was until coffee came.

'I guess congratulations are in order,' he said. 'Quentin tells me the award is very prestigious.' Jonathan smiled at her. The smile was boyish and disarming, and Hallie didn't trust it for a minute. 'Of course, Quentin also had to explain who Max Perkins was.'

'In that case I wouldn't think the prestige aspect would interest you much.'

'There are cases, Hallie – and I think this is one of them – where prestige translates into profit. An award like this attracts the right agents with the right clients. An award like this means better and, more important, bigger books.' Jonathan finished his coffee and put his napkin on the table with an air of finality. 'That's why I'm especially pleased that R and S has two candidates for the award.' He stood. 'Were the only house with both a publisher and an editor in chief in the running.'

Hallie sat in the cab, listening to the meter tick off the minutes and trying to relate her breathing. The traffic was impossible, and she was going to be late for her two-thirty meeting, but she wasn't thinking about the meeting.

She should have seen it coming. Olivia had stolen everything else from her. Why should this award be any different?

Only this was different. Hallie needed this award. It would start off Unicorn Books on exactly the right note. She even deserved this award. Olivia was a good editor, but Hallie was a better one. She was sure of it – she thought. And there was one more reason, one Olivia, of all people, would appreciate. Hallie wanted this award. Maybe she didn't want it for the right reasons. Maybe she wanted it for vindication or simply revenge. Maybe it wasn't high-minded of her, but to hell with high-mindedness. She was tired of losing things to Olivia. She wanted this award so much she could taste it. She wanted it enough to fight for it.

They ran into each other in the lobby in front of the elevators. There was a time when Hallie would have asked Olivia who she'd lunched with, and Olivia would have regaled her with stories of an agent's hand on her thigh under the table or a reviewer's heartfelt confession that his wife just didn't understand him. Then Hallie would have laughed and said she didn't get it. Those things never happened to her at lunch, and Olivia would have laughed along with her and said she guessed she was just lucky. Now they nodded and stood waiting in silence.

The elevator doors opened. They stepped into it. The doors closed. They were alone.

'I understand we're in competition,' Hallie said. 'For the award, I mean.'

Olivia dropped her eyes. The expression was supposed to be demure. Hallie wondered who she thought she was talking to. Jake? Quent? Carter Bolton? Then Olivia looked at Hallie with a small embarrassed smile. She was good, all right.

263

'Everyone knows I don't stand a chance,' Olivia said. 'Everyone knows you've got it all sewn up.'

Hallie went on staring at her for a moment. 'I'm not worried about what everyone knows,' she said finally. 'Only what you believe.'

It was a harmless practical joke. Well, perhaps a bit more than that, but nothing serious, nothing to feel guilty about, Hallie decided. She'd got the idea as she was coming out of Sheila Dent's office that morning. Sheila's office was next to Olivia's, and Hallie had heard Olivia call to her secretary. It was hard not to. When Olivia gave her secretary orders, it sounded more like a drill sergeant whipping the troops into shape than a woman telling her secretary to call a restaurant and book a table.

'And I don't want something in Siberia,' Olivia had shouted. 'I want a booth along the east wall. I don't care what you have to promise to get it – including your lithe white body. I'm lunching with Gardiner Fairchild, and you know what a snob he is.'

If the secretary didn't know, Hallie did. Gardiner Fairchild had made his reputation writing pseudo-morality tales about the old rich. In fact, he'd been writing about them for so long that most of the world believed he was one of them. Gardiner did nothing to dissuade the world. Few people, knew or remembered that he came from a small, dusty town in Idaho, but Hallie, thanks to Cecelia and Amos, was one of them. Hallie knew something else about Gardiner Fairchild. It wasn't a secret. Olivia knew it, too. Gardiner Fairchild was one of the judges for the Max Perkins Prize.

Hallie went back to her office. She told her secretary to call the Four Seasons and get Julian on the phone. Julian was a great admirer of Amos Porter and his work.

It took less than two minutes. She told Julian she was taking Amos to lunch, a working lunch. She wanted her usual booth. The implication was clear. They couldn't expect the greatest American writer working today to eat at anything less than a power table.

'One more thing,' she said. 'You know how Mr Porter is about work in progress. Very touchy and very private. I'd appreciate it if we weren't sitting near anyone in the business.'

Julian said he'd take care of it. Hallie said she'd be eternally grateful.

She called Amos next and told him she wanted to take him to lunch. Work must have been going badly, because she didn't have to plead. He accepted immediately.

Hallie hung up the phone. She knew she'd played dirty, and she wasn't a bit sorry.

Olivia usually liked to keep her lunch dates waiting just long enough to make them uncomfortable, but she was a few minutes early at the Four Seasons that day. There was no percentage in keeping Gardiner Fairchild waiting. He knew why she'd called and asked him to lunch, though neither of them had or would mention the award.

It was a little before one. Olivia came up the stairs from Fifty-second Street. Inside the door she checked her coat. That was another reason she was glad she was early. Gardiner Fairchild had probably never seen a woman in a cloth coat. Olivia could afford a fur coat if it came off the racks at one of those cut-rate places that ran television ads using her first name or the furrier's. 'Hi, Olivia, I'm Frank, and do I have a fox for you.' She was holding out for Revillon mink at least, sable she hoped.

She moved on to the dark wood reservations desk and greeted Julian by name. He didn't return the favor, though he was perfectly polite.

He began leading her across the Grill Room. She stopped to say hello to another editor and an agent. Julian kept going. When Olivia turned back, she saw he'd passed the booths and was heading for the stairs. The stairs, goddamnit!

Olivia caught up with him. 'Hey!' she said.

Julian turned at the strange sound.

Olivia dropped her voice to a whisper. She put on her best smile. 'There must be a mistake.'

Julian asked what the problem was.

Olivia was furious. He knew perfectly well what the problem was. She went on smiling. She explained that she'd had her secretary ask particularly for a booth downstairs. She added that she was lunching with Mr Fairchild. Mr Gardiner Fairchild, she added. Julian said he was terribly sorry, but all the booths downstairs were already booked. He even managed to look terribly sorry. He suggested that next time she call earlier. 'Perhaps a day or two in advance,' he said.

A day or two in advance! He was treating her like one of the bridge-and-tunnel crowd. Her high heels trembled in fury as she climbed the stairs to the balcony.

He led her to one of the back tables. This was too much. She might as well not have lunch with Gardiner Fairchild at all. She told Julian the table was impossible.

Julian hesitated, then led her to one of the front tables on the balcony. From there she could at least see the Grill Room below. Ten minutes before she would have been outraged. Now she was relieved, just as Julian had known she would be.

She ordered a drink and kept her eyes on the room below. The waiter had just brought a white wine when Olivia spotted her. Hallie was wearing a Chanel suit, but it wasn't the suit, which Olivia would have killed for, but the way Hallie carried it off. She might have been wearing an old pair of jeans. Olivia suddenly realized something. She'd learned about fashion. Hallie had been born with style.

It took Hallie some time to make her way across the room. It was more crowded now, and she stopped at several tables to say hello to people. Olivia charted her progress from the balcony above. She prayed Julian would lead Hallie to the stairs. She watched him sail across the room. She saw him come to a stop in front of an east-wall booth. Olivia wanted to throw something.

Amos arrived a few minutes later. He slid onto the

seat and kissed Hallie on the cheek. Olivia wanted
to cry.

Gardiner Fairchild was the next one into the room.
He took even longer to cross it than Hallie had. He
stopped at twice as many tables. Julian waited
patiently, inching him toward the stairs. Finally, they
reached the bottom step. Julian started climbing.
Gardiner Fairchild's face turned white with shock.
He might have just learned of a sudden death in the
family. Julian kept going. The blood rushed back into
Fairchild's cheeks to stain them crimson with shame.

'How's the book going?' Hallie asked her father,
though she was fairly sure that the answer was
badly. Very badly for him to turn off the machine
and come downtown for an impromptu lunch with
her.

He smiled at her over his martini glass. 'Is this going
to be a working lunch?'

'I don't know why you find that so amusing.'

He reached over and patted her hand. 'I'm not
amused. I'm delighted. It's not often I get to have
lunch with you. And in answer to your question, the
book is going well. Very well.'

'Now I know why you're in such a good mood. But
what happened? A couple of weeks ago you were
ready to burn it.' Hallie frowned into her glass. 'And
I didn't exactly help.'

He patted her hand again. He was in an
extraordinarily good mood.

'You helped a great deal. You let me talk.'

'That would be fine if I were a shrink, but I'm an

editor. I'm supposed to do more than listen.'

Amos signaled for menus. 'I'm back on track. The book's coming nicely. As an editor, that's all you have to worry about.'

Olivia was an intelligent woman. She could do more than one thing at a time. She could talk to Gardiner Fairchild and keep an eye on Hallie and Amos. Not that Gardiner had much to say. For a man who was known to dine out on his conversation, he was treating this lunch strictly as a fast-food experience. He answered Olivia's questions with monosyllables, raced through his meal, said he'd just remembered an appointment and didn't have time for coffee.

Olivia sat alone at the shameful table that Fairchild hadn't been able to get away from fast enough. She knew how he'd felt. She thought the check would never come.

She glanced down into the main room as if it were Eden. Hallie and Amos were still talking. They hadn't stopped for a minute. High-minded discussions about literature, Olivia was willing to bet. That was okay. That was just fine. Olivia was counting on Amos's high-mindedness. But first she had to line up the other judges.

XXVIII

Olivia sat cross-legged with the tiles and pictures spread out around her on the bed. For the first time since she'd hired her secretary, Olivia appreciated the girl. Debbie lived with a young man who worked at *Time*. Debbie had convinced him that her future at R and S depended on his pirating the magazine's file on Adelaide Koenig. Debbie hadn't been entirely wrong.

Olivia picked up one of the old newspaper clippings. It dated back to the early fifties. Adelaide Koenig had been even uglier when she was young. Olivia wondered how it must feel to go through life with a face like that. For a moment she almost felt sorry for Adelaide Koenig. Then she reminded herself that Adelaide Koenig wasn't going to feel sorry for Olivia when she cast her vote against her for the Max Perkins Prize. If she cast her vote against her for the Max Perkins Prize.

Olivia picked up another photograph. In this one Adelaide Koenig was standing on the steps of the Capitol Building with a man and another woman. The file identified the man, a left-wing magazine publisher, as Adelaide Koenig's 'longtime companion.' Gossip said she'd also had a fling with the woman, who was a painter. If you read between the lines in that file, you saw that for an ugly duckling, Adelaide Koenig had attracted a lot of swans.

Olivia went on staring at the two women. It wasn't that she was a prig. Hell, if she thought it would work, she'd try it. She'd try anything, once. But Adelaide Koenig had been living with another 'companion,' this one twenty years her junior, for ten years now. He was a minor-league writer who'd suddenly graduated to the majors by virtue of his in-progress authorized biography of Adelaide Koenig.

Sex was out, but there had to be another way. It didn't take a genius to see it. Half a dozen bold headlines screamed the solution. In the fifties Adelaide Koenig had been blacklisted. In the sixties and seventies she'd been arrested for refusing to pay the portion of her taxes that went to the military. She was currently head of half a dozen organizations to ban nuclear weapons and promote human rights and guard free speech. Olivia decided on the last. It made more sense for an editor.

The office furniture had been pushed against the walls to make room for the folding chairs. Two-thirds of them were already filled. More people milled around the edges of the room. Olivia recognized a few writers, one or two editors. The rest were strangers. She wondered why people with good intentions always dressed so badly. Half the women looked as if they were auditioning for parts in movies about salt-of-the-earth peasants who'd cornered the market on goodness and truth, if not beauty. The other half had never heard of natural fibers. Most of the men looked unkempt. A few were downright dirty. Olivia wouldn't have had a drink, let alone an affair, with any of them.

In one corner a desk had been turned into a makeshift bar. There were several bottles of wine, the kind with screw tops. A scribbled sign had the nerve to announce that the wine cost a dollar a glass. Bowls of greasy potato chips sat at each end of the desk. To Olivia's amazement, people were actually eating them.

At a long table in the front of the room, Adelaide Koenig sat with two men and two other women. Olivia recognized the poet she'd written her first college term paper on and a Pulitzer-prize winning journalist. She didn't know the other man and woman. The panel discussion started. Words flew. Tempers grew hot. They opened the debate to the audience. One man shouted. A woman booed him. Another woman hissed her. Olivia welcomed the histrionics. The topic itself wouldn't have kept her awake. She didn't give a damn about freedom of speech in Israeli-occupied Arab territories.

As soon as it was over, a crowd surrounded Adelaide Koenig. Olivia laid siege to it. It took her a few minutes to penetrate to the center. She introduced herself to Adelaide Koenig. She added that she was the editor in chief of Rutherford and Styles.

Adelaide Koenig's hard black eyes peered out from a puffy face that told of a lifetime of one or two or half a dozen drinks too many. 'I'm not here to do business.'

'Neither am I,' Olivia answered without missing a beat. 'I wanted to speak to you about that subcommittee to monitor censorship in the West Bank.'

'What about it?'

'I'm volunteering.'

Debbie was already at her desk when Olivia got to the office the next morning. 'Tell your boyfriend we need some files on censorship in the West Bank and get me my coffee,' Olivia said as she passed.

A few moments later, Debbie put a mug of coffee on Olivia's desk.

'About the files,' Debbie began.

'I need them ASAP.'

'I can't ask Gary to get me more files. He had to sneak the last one out.'

'Tell him we only need them overnight. Less than that. You can copy them on your lunch hour.'

'But he says if he gets caught, they'll fire him.'

Olivia looked up from the messages she was going through and stared at Debbie thoughtfully. Debbie hooked her hands in the back pockets of her jeans and shifted from one foot to another.

'Poor baby,' Olivia said. 'It must be a real drag living with a wimp.'

'Gary's not a wimp.'

Olivia went on staring at her as if she were trying

to figure something out. 'Oh, I get it, honey. He's the macho type. Screw your career, as long as he's getting ahead.'

When Olivia got back from lunch that afternoon the Xeroxed files were on her desk.

Adelaide Koenig hesitated when Olivia asked her to lunch. She was a busy woman who had no time for the editor in chief of a house that wasn't even her publisher. On the other hand, she could spare a couple of hours to fight censorship in the West Bank. It never occurred to Adelaide that Olivia had anything else in mind. Adelaide hadn't looked at the list of candidates for the Max Perkins Prize. In fact, Adelaide didn't believe in literary awards, though her scruples had never prevented her from accepting them. She certainly didn't believe in sitting on committees to present such awards, but her companion, who had other ideas, not to mention certain hopes about such awards, had convinced Adelaide she owed it to the cause of literature, not to mention the future of her biographer, to serve.

Unlike the fiasco with Gardiner Fairchild, everything about Olivia's lunch with Adelaide Koenig went perfectly, except for the fact that Olivia figured she'd have to live on tofu and steamed vegetables for the next week to undo the caloric damage. Adelaide had chosen the restaurant. It was an old-fashioned French bistro run by an ancient Frenchman who, Adelaide insisted, had fought in the Resistance. There wasn't a thing on the menu that didn't come swimming in a sea of sauce. The waiter actually tried to convince Olivia to have a profiterole for dessert. She almost did in celebration. By then she was sure she'd won Adelaide Koenig over.

At first Adelaide had been skeptical. She'd been fighting battles like this for a long time. When she'd testified back in the fifties, her name had become a household word. When she'd been blacklisted afterward, it had been almost entirely forgotten. She didn't trust this glib young woman who'd suddenly discovered a social conscience. But gradually Olivia convinced her. Perhaps it was the passion in Olivia's voice when she talked about censorship as crime against the human spirit. Maybe it was just Olivia's efficiency. She already had a functioning subcommittee. Adelaide was surprised at some of the members. An assistant at R and S, a young man at *Time* magazine, a few others.

'The young are so rarely political these days,' Adelaide said. Olivia insisted it was merely a matter of capturing their imaginations and firing them up. She left no doubt in Adelaide's mind about who had captured their imaginations and fired them up in this matter.

Adelaide asked Olivia how she'd got interested in the cause. 'I haven't noticed you at other meetings.'

That was Olivia's cue. She began to talk about books and writers, about society's need for a free exchange of ideas and man's, and woman's, need for self-expression. That, she explained, was why she'd become an editor in the first place. She segued into the editorial process – theory, practice, and, though she didn't want to sound immodest, her successes. And the best part about it was that Olivia wasn't after anything. They both knew Adelaide wasn't looking for a new publisher. And Olivia made it clear she wasn't trying to snare a new author. They were just two women, sitting over lunch, discussing matters of mutual interest, fostering a mutual respect.

Hallie stood on the threshold of the vast soaring lobby of the New York Public Library. The only thing worse than walking into a party alone was walking into a formal party alone. There was something about a long dress that cried out for a black tie to lean on.

She'd thought of calling Will and asking him to escort her, but she hadn't spoken to Will since that night Jake had interrupted them. Hallie had managed to get Jake out of the apartment that night, but it had been harder to get him out of her mind. She had the feeling Will had given up on her.

So she hadn't called Will, and she'd come to the benefit alone, and now she stood on the edge of a swirling mass of laughing, talking, drinking men and women. She straightened her shoulders, bared by the white crepe dress. She lifted the long narrow skirt an inch. She moved into the crowd.

It was like diving into icy water. The expectation was worse than the act. As soon as she got wet, she began to feel better. Several people said hello to her. A passing waiter held out a tray of champagne. A group opened like a door to let her in. Another publisher was telling an anecdote. Hallie had missed the beginning, and the publisher was using only first names but she got the jist, and by the time he reached the punchline she could laugh with the rest of them.

That was when she caught sight of Will. She wasn't surprised to see him. There weren't many benefits for good causes, literary or otherwise, that Will didn't receive an invitation to. But she was surprised to see the woman on his arm. Will didn't usually go in for society types, and Claudia Ellington had all the markings of a social butterfly. Her legs went on forever and, from what Hallie heard, so did her trust fund. But Claudia wasn't frivolous. She had a deep and abiding interest in the arts. A few years before her affair with Baryshnikov had made all the columns. After that she ran through a couple of actors, a cellist, and a rock star. But Claudia had tired of the performing arts. They were recreative rather than creative, she'd told one columnist who'd told the world. An affair with a sculptor had followed. And now she'd brought Will Sawyer to a five-hundred-dollar-a-plate dinner to promote literacy. Or maybe Will had brought her, but Hallie didn't think so. At least she hoped he hadn't.

Will caught Hallie's eye across the room. He smiled and raised his champagne glass in greeting, but he didn't break away from Claudia Ellington and her group to cross the room to Hallie.

She continued to watch him out of the corner of her eye as she pretended to follow another anecdote. She'd always thought of Will as a man made for rumpled tweeds and khakis. He shouldn't look this good in evening clothes. It wasn't fair.

The crowd began to take their seats at the pink-covered tables set for ten or twelve. Hallie found her place card. Gardiner Fairchild was on her right. Maybe her luck was changing.

By the end of dinner, she was grateful for Gardiner's formal manners. He followed the rules scrupulously and turned from one dinner partner to the other with each course. Hallie didn't think she could have listened to Gardiner through the quenelles and the veal and the salad and the dessert. It wasn't that he dropped names. It was that he dropped them and then proceeded to trace their pedigree to the fourth generation.

After dinner there were speeches. After the speeches there was dancing. Hallie had no intention of staying for that. It wouldn't be hard to slip away. People were milling about the room.

She saw Gardiner talking to Will. Celebrity made strange bedfellows. Socially and politically, Gardiner Fairchild and Will Sawyer could not have been further apart, but they went to the same parties and knew the same people and sat on the same literary-prize committee. Because they led the same kind of life, they had more in common with each other than with lesser mortals who held the same beliefs.

Hallie said good night to the others at her table, picked up her evening bag, and started toward the coat room. Will broke away from Gardiner and ambushed her halfway across the room.

'Hi,' was all he said, but one arm went around her

waist and the other took her hand, and before she knew it they were dancing.

He waited a beat before he spoke, though he didn't miss a beat. He was a good dancer. More important, Hallie noticed, he was a good leader. She knew, because she always had trouble following.

'Now you see what you've driven me to.'

'Charity balls?'

'Charity balls with the trust-fund trash. Do you know what they were discussing at my table during dinner? The price of private islands.'

'I guess Claudia Ellington hasn't read the chapter on inherited wealth in your last book.'

'Claudia doesn't read books. She buys books. And she wouldn't care if I were Karl Marx in drag, so long as the drag was black tie and I was on the bestseller list.'

'That's not a very nice way to talk about your hostess.'

His eyes crinkled. 'Yeah, but it's what you wanted to hear. Anyway,' he went on before she could protest, 'I'm glad to see your dinner was more productive. I just talked to Gardiner Fairchild.'

'Please! I talked to him through two out of four courses. Or, rather, he talked and I dozed. It's lucky his books aren't as dull as his conversation.'

'It's easy to see you haven't read one lately. They are. But tonight he had something interesting to say. At least to me. I don't suppose he mentioned the Max Perkins Prize to you.'

'We were too high-minded for that,' Hallie joked, but they both noticed that she stiffened in his arms.

'You've got his vote.'

Hallie missed a beat. Will laughed.

'Which means you've got the prize.'

'Don't,' she said. 'Don't tempt fate.'

'I'm not tempting fate, Hallie, I'm counting. There are five judges. You've got three of them in your pocket. Me. Amos. And Gardiner. We might as well hand the plaque over to you right now.'

Hallie didn't say anything. She couldn't fault his arithmetic, but she still thought he was tempting fate.

XXIX

When Olivia returned to her office that afternoon and found the message, she was furious with Quentin, so furious she didn't even have Debbie make the call for her. She picked up the phone and dialed Quentin's apartment, George answered. She told herself he was only a butler, but it didn't help. He managed to get a lot of disdain into 'I'll tell him you're calling.' Sometimes in her fantasies, the really wild ones in which she married Quentin, she imagined walking into the twelve-room duplex as mistress of the house. The first thing she'd do was fire George.

Quentin's voice replaced George's on the line. He felt dreadful, he said. And not just because he was letting her down. He'd been looking forward to tonight enormously. But he had to fly to North Carolina.

'North Carolina?' Olivia repeated. He couldn't be lying. If he were lying, he'd pick someplace more likely.

'Emergency meeting. Board of a small company I sit on. They're fighting a takeover.'

There was a moment's silence. Olivia didn't rush it. She was learning a lot about patience from Quentin.

'Look,' he said, 'they're sending the company plane for me, I'll be back by midnight.'

Now she was angry again. The board meeting was a cover. He'd just received a last-minute invitation to one of those A-list, blue-blood dinner parties. She wasn't good enough for the party, but she was good enough for a roll in the hay after it.

'Why don't you come along for the ride?' Quentin finished.

Olivia said she'd love to go along for the ride.

Walking across the tarmac at Newark Airport, she felt like Ingrid Bergman in *Casablanca*. Once aboard the small jet, she felt like the first lady on *Air Force One*. If her friends could see her now. More to the point, if her enemies could.

A steward took their coats and brought them drinks and asked if they were comfortable. When they said they were, he disappeared discreetly. There were, as she'd hoped, no other passengers.

The plane took off. She could feel it climbing. They were sitting in two barrel chairs facing each other. Quentin sipped his martini and looked at her. She held his eyes and smiled.

'Are you a member of the Five-Mile Club?' he asked.

It took her a minute to catch on. He wasn't talking about some frequent-flyer bonus or one of those private rooms where the airlines dispense free drinks and complimentary magazines to passengers waiting for delayed flights. He was talking about something more exclusive – and daring.

She slid off a shoe, put a foot between his legs, and moved her toes.

'What about the steward?'

'He won't come back unless we ring for him.'

'I think you have a thing about chairs. Only these aren't as big as the one in your library.'

He finished his martini and put the glass down on the table. 'I imagine we could manage, though there's no need to.' He stood and held his hand out to her. 'There are two staterooms. If I remember correctly, the aft one has the larger bed.'

She sat on the rumpled bed, watching Quentin knot the somber silk tie, button the dark gray vest, tuck the old-fashioned watch at the end of the long gold chain into the vest pocket. She remembered when she used to sit in meetings watching him and wondering what was going on beneath that proper veneer. She'd sensed something, but even in her best fantasies – and some of them had been pretty good; those meetings could get dull – she'd never expected Quentin to be like this.

'Life's unpredictable, Olivia Mae,' her mother used to tell her. It was one of the few truths her mother had ever spoken.

The meeting didn't run long. Olivia hadn't even got through the work she'd brought along when Quentin returned to the plane.

He sat on the arm of her chair, put his hand on her shoulder, and kissed the top of her head. His manner was so companionable, so affectionate it caught Olivia off guard. She wasn't accustomed to that kind of treatment.

'How did you get mixed up with Adelaide Koenig?' he asked.

Olivia glanced at the letter on her lap, slipped it into a folder, and put everything back into her briefcase. 'I'm on one of her political committees.'

Quentin moved to the chair across from hers. He was still watching her. 'Going to save the world?'

Olivia smiled and shrugged. 'Maybe just the Middle East.'

'This wouldn't have anything to do with the fact that Adelaide is one of the judges for the Max Perkins Prize, would it?'

Olivia's grin was wide now. That was one of the things he liked about her. She knew when to cut her losses. Cornered, she threw up her hands and said you got me.

'It has everything to do with that. You don't think I give a damn about who gets to publish what in some dusty strip of land I've never seen and can barely locate on the map.'

Quentin wasn't shocked. He wasn't even particularly offended. He had few, if any, illusions about Olivia. He liked to think he had few, if any, illusions about people in general, himself included. He wasn't in this for the high moral tone.

'No, I didn't think you cared about saving the world, but sometimes I wonder what you do care about. Besides climbing the ladder.'

She stood. 'Come inside, honey, and I'll show you.'

'You might be pushing your luck,' he joked. He'd actually come that far with her that he could joke. 'I'm not a young man, and I've just been through an ugly meeting, not to mention an arduous trip down here.'

Olivia sat on his lap and slipped her hand beneath his vest, then his belt. 'I'm not worried. But, just to be fair, this time I'll do the work.'

They went into the stateroom again. Olivia was as good as her word. She didn't mind. In fact, every now and then she liked taking the initiative.

It wasn't until later that Quentin told her she'd wasted her time. They were in the Bentley on the way back to town.

'What do you mean I wasted my time?' She'd been dozing on his shoulder, but now she sat up straight.

'Adelaide Koenig wouldn't have voted for Hallie, anyway.'

'How do you know?'

'Because Adelaide hasn't spoken to Amos in more than thirty years. They used to be great friends. We all were. But not anymore. I've seen her cut him dead at parties. I have no idea how they're going to sit on the same panel together.'

'What happened?'

'One of those falling outs, half literary, half political.'

Olivia didn't press it. That pirated file was full of similar vendettas. Adelaide Koenig was a woman of deep conviction and quick temper.

'But that doesn't mean she wouldn't vote for Hallie. Principle is Adelaide's middle name.'

Quentin reached an arm around Olivia's shoulders and pulled her to him again. Sometimes he forgot that she wasn't as worldly as she thought. 'You're right. Adelaide's a highly principled woman. And altruistic. She loves her fellow man. It's only individual men, and women, she hates. Take my word for it, Olivia. Adelaide Koenig will never do anything to help Amos Porter's daughter.'

He felt a stab of conscience as he said it. He hadn't minded helping Olivia with Hallie, but he'd never intended to help her against Hallie. A few months before he'd mourned the loss of sex. Now he remembered how it could skew things. At least he had nothing to do with this damn Perkins Prize. He knew where his allegiances lay, and it wasn't where his libido led. He was just glad he wasn't going to be tested.

Olivia put her head on his shoulder and closed her eyes for a moment. When she opened them again, they were coming down the ramp to the Lincoln Tunnel. Across the Hudson, the lights of the city traced an incandescent skyline in the black night.

'Quent,' she murmured.

'Yes?'

'How come you know so much about Adelaide Koenig?'

'I told you. We were all good friends at one time.'

Olivia lifted her eyes to him. 'That's what I mean, honey. Just how good friends were you?'

He started to laugh. 'I'm touched, Olivia.

Genuinely touched. If I didn't know you better, I'd think you were jealous.'

She laughed too, because it was a good joke. Olivia Collins didn't get jealous, at least not of past affairs. That was penny-ante emotion, the material of country-and-western songs. Her envy was headier stuff, the kind of all-consuming passion that made for great opera.

In the soft dark privacy of the Bentley she snuggled closer to Quentin and smiled at the analogy. She was ready for her big aria.

XXX

Jake couldn't put it off any longer. He had to face Amos. He had to give his father-in-law a chance to fire him.

He called Amos and suggested a drink.

'Business or personal?' Amos had asked.

'I don't think we can separate the two. That's what I want to talk to you about.'

They agreed to meet at the Century Club. It was neutral territory. True, Amos had been one of Jake's sponsors, but by that time Jake could have found a dozen other members to put him up.

They met in the small lounge on the second floor. Jake liked that room. It always made him feel as if he'd moved back in time to the era when publishing really was a gentleman's profession. He'd never told anyone but Hallie that. Hard-nosed agents who cut six-and seven-figure deals weren't supposed to long for softer times.

Amos came barreling into the room. They shook hands formally, ordered drinks, and waited in silence while the steward served them.

'I've been putting this off,' Jake began finally. 'I

guess I kept hoping it wouldn't be necessary. That this whole mess would blow over, and we could all go back to normal.'

Amos said nothing. He wasn't going to help him.

'But now I see it's not going to, so we have to face it. I have to face it.' He hesitated. It was the right thing to do, but it was a damn extravagant thing to do. Amos was worth big money. If he walked, Jake would have to rethink the plans for opening a branch office of the agency on the coast. He took a breath, then went on. 'I just want you to know that if you've decided to change agencies, if you want to fire me, I understand. There are no hard feelings.'

Amos stared at him. He took a swallow of his drink and went on staring at him for what felt to Jake like a long time. 'Why should I want to fire you? Did you screw up?'

'That's putting it mildly.'

'I said "screw up", not "screw around." That's between you and Hallie. Not that I'm not pissed. She's my daughter, and I don't like your walking all over her with your hobnail boots.'

Jake started to say something, but Amos went on before he could.

'But I don't fork over ten percent of everything I earn to have you take care of Hallie. I pay you to take care of the business end of the books. As long as you do that satisfactorily, I see no reason to change agents.'

Jake let out a long breath. He hadn't even known he'd been holding it.

'I'm grateful,' Jake said and held out his hand.

'Don't be. I'm not doing you a favor. This is pure business. You're a good agent. Besides, I'm used to you.'

But Jake didn't drop his hand, and after a moment's pause Amos reached out his own huge one and they shook.

They did business for the next half hour. Amos had to choose between movie offers. Jake had some suggestions. He brought Amos up to date on book-club figures and foreign rights. He said it looked as if this one was going to break all records. Amos better start talking to his accountant about tax shelters again.

They finished their drinks. Jake asked if Amos had time for another. Amos made a great show of looking at his watch. He said he didn't. Jake wasn't surprised.

He looked across the table at his father-in-law. 'I know you don't want gratitude. I know you said it has nothing to do with sentiment, but I just want to say I'm glad. And not just because of the money.' Jake managed a smile. 'Not that I have anything against the money, you understand.'

Amos rolled his shoulders beneath his jacket. The sentiment obviously made him uncomfortable. 'Why in hell should I change agents? It's bad enough I had to change editors.'

'How's that working out?'

'Fine.'

'And the new book?'

'Better than fine. Terrific.'

'When am I going to get a look at it? A couple of the magazines have been after me to run a chapter or two.'

'It's too early for that.'

'I'd still like to see it.'

Amos had been about to stand. Now he leaned back in his chair. Why not? It would be interesting to have Jake's opinion, a man's opinion, especially since he no longer had Quentin's.

'Sure,' Amos said. 'Send a messenger for it tomorrow.'

Jake closed the manuscript box. There was no doubt about it. This was Amos Porter writing at the top of his form. Amos had said it was about a third of the book. If he kept going like this, it would be the best thing Amos had ever written.

He picked up the phone and dialed his apartment. His former apartment, he corrected himself. It was close to midnight, but he knew he wouldn't be waking Hallie. She'd be in bed with that wall of manuscripts. Unless, of course, she was in bed with Will Sawyer. The thought didn't make Jake hang up.

Hallie picked up the phone on the first ring. If she was in bed with Will, he wasn't holding her attention.

'I just finished Amos's pages.'

Hallie rubbed her eyes with her thumb and forefinger. It was late. She was exhausted. She'd just come off an endless dinner with a hack writer who was beginning to believe her own publicity releases. It was bad enough she'd had to spend the night massaging another woman's ego. She was in no mood to have her own deflated.

'And?' she said.

'We're going to hold you up on this one. Highway robbery. And it'll be worth every penny of it.'

'What are you talking about?'

'Wake up, Hallie. Amos's next book. It's the best thing he's ever done.'

'It is?'

'Haven't you seen it?'

'I've seen a draft of it. I thought it was . . .' She hesitated. 'Well, a little rough.'

Jake couldn't believe it. He even had a sneaking admiration for her. Here it was, almost midnight. She was his wife. Okay, estranged wife. They were discussing her father's book. And she was negotiating. Wake her up in the middle of the night, and she'd probably come to muttering 'We get world rights or there's no deal.' Only that wasn't what she muttered when someone woke her up in the middle of the night. Jake remembered.

He forced his mind back to Amos's book. 'I thought Quentin was a tough negotiator. He's got nothing on you.'

Hallie supposed he thought he was complimenting her, and there was a time when he would have been. But somehow, sitting alone in bed at midnight and being called tough by your ex-husband was no longer her idea of a compliment.

XXXI

Olivia couldn't have asked for better timing. The coast was clear. Hallie was in Los Angeles. Jake was in London. Quentin was in Palm Beach. She would, have pitied herself for being left in New York if she weren't so busy congratulating herself on the idea. She wouldn't have to call Amos. She wouldn't have to cajole him into a meeting. All she'd have to do was plunk down three hundred dollars, which she'd write off on her expense account anyway, and turn up in the Rainbow Room to hear Amos Porter read from *A Woman's Story* for the benefit of Valhalla, America's oldest and most distinguished writers' colony. Afterward, there'd be a champagne supper. Olivia had no intention of waiting till afterward.

She arrived early and took the elevator up to the Rainbow Room. The doors opened. She felt as if she were stepping onto a movie set. It was all curved lines and sleek shiny surfaces. The only things missing were Fred and Ginger.

The waiters were still setting up. Olivia checked her coat. There were only a few garments in the checkroom. Olivia noticed a man's cashmere overcoat among them. It was large enough to fit Amos.

She walked to one of the tall windows and stood looking down for a moment. A million lights glowed in the cold winter night. There was something profoundly satisfying about looking down rather than up at the lights of New York.

She turned and crossed to the bar. The bartender said he was terribly sorry but it wasn't open. Olivia sat on one of the stools and leaned across the bar. She smiled. She said yes, she understood that, but she just wanted to get something for the guest of honor. The bartender wouldn't have to mix anything, just pour a little Scotch over some ice. She leaned closer. The smile turned conspiratorial. He wouldn't mind doing that for her, would he? Just pouring a couple of ounces of Scotch over some ice?

He made her two drinks and asked her if she wanted twists. She said they were fine as they were and asked where the guest of honor was. The bartender pointed to a closed door. Olivia slid off the stool, picked up both glasses, and headed for it. She had to take tiny steps. The long dress was that narrow.

As she reached the door, a scrawny young man materialized. Behind glasses thick as Coke bottles, he was doing his best to cultivate a James Joyce look. He put his arm across the door to block her way.

'Mr Porter is resting before his reading.'

'Whom do you work for?' She wasn't rude, merely authoritative.

'Valhalla.' She could tell from his tone that he took the name literally.

'I guess you're a little out of things way up there in Maine. I'm Amos's — excuse me, Mr Porter's — editor. And I think he'd appreciate this' — she held up one glass — 'before he begins his reading.'

She didn't take the time to enjoy the look of awe that flickered behind those thick glasses.

Amos looked up as she came into the room. Before he could say anything, she held out one of the glasses. 'I thought you might want to wet your throat before the reading.'

Amos sat staring at her for a moment as if he were debating something.

She dropped her head back and began to laugh. 'For God's sake, Amos. I'm not trying to slip you knock-out drops or anything. I was early, and when I heard you were in here, I thought you might like a drink.'

He started to laugh too, then took the drink from her. 'I always get a little jumpy before these damn things.' He took a sip of the drink.

'Is it okay?'

'Perfect,' he said. 'Exactly what I needed.'

'I remembered what you drank from that evening in my apartment. When we toasted the new book.'

Amos didn't say anything to that. She took the club chair across from his.

'How is it going?'

'Well.'

She leaned back in the chair and sipped her own

drink. 'It's nice to think I could make even the smallest contribution.'

'I'm grateful,' Amos said, but he didn't sound grateful. He sounded wary.

'Then I really did help a little?'

Amos lived by only a handful of rules. The cardinal one was that when it came to his work, he had to be straight. 'Actually, you helped quite a lot.'

She took another sip of her drink, then frowned at him. 'I hope you didn't tell Hallie that.'

'Why shouldn't I tell Hallie that?' He knew the answer but was hoping she didn't.

'Before any of this started – this business with Jake, I mean – Hallie was my friend. My closest friend.'

When Amos didn't say anything, she went on. 'Can I speak frankly?'

'I thought that's what you were doing.'

'I don't think it would make her feel any better if she knew I'd pulled off something she hadn't been able to handle.'

'She can handle it. She was just too close to spot that particular problem.'

Olivia smiled and shook her head. 'God, I wish I had a father like you.' She stood. 'Then we are agreed. Neither of us is going to mention that I'm the one who's done the real editorial work on the manuscript so far.'

She started for the door. Amos watched her go. He wondered why she'd thought the conversation necessary.

At the door, she stopped and turned back to him.

She stood leaning against it with her hands behind her. She knew how she looked, and it was a lot more self-possessed than she felt. She'd tried a lot of things in her life, but blackmail wasn't one of them.

'And, of course, I'd never in a million years expect you to vote for me for the Max Perkins Prize.'

Now he knew why she'd felt the conversation was necessary.

'I'm glad, Olivia, because I have no intention of voting for you or against Hallie.'

'It would kill Hallie.'

'Let's just say it would hurt her.'

Olivia hesitated for a moment. She wanted him to sweat it out.

'Yet you have to admit it's not exactly fair. I'm the superior editor, but Hallie gets the award.'

'Hallie's an excellent editor.'

This time her smile was indulgent and a little sad. 'As I said, Amos, I wish I had a father like you.'

'This has nothing to do with my paternal feelings.'

'Just your honest judgment?'

'Exactly.'

'The amazing thing is that everyone will believe that. With your reputation. Like that article you wrote a few years ago, condemning writers who reviewed books written by friends or enemies without stating their personal prejudices up front. You said that any honest writer should refuse to review the work of another writer he knows personally. The only honorable course, you insisted, was to disqualify yourself.'

'You've done your homework. I wrote that letter years ago.'

'But the point applies. Adelaide Koenig and I were discussing it just the other day at lunch. You know Adelaide, don't you, Amos?'

'We both know I know Adelaide and what she thinks of me, or you wouldn't be bringing this up now.'

'She obviously respects you as much as I do, because she said she was surprised that you didn't disqualify yourself as a judge after Hallie was nominated.'

'Why do I think this conversation smacks of blackmail?'

'Blackmail! Come on, Amos. How could I blackmail a man in your position? By telling Adelaide that I'd actually edited your book? After Hallie had given up? That isn't exactly front-page news. No one would even care – outside the business. And inside it, people would just say you were a loving father as well as a great writer. I suppose there'd be some nasty talk about Hallie. About how she never could have made it if she hadn't been your daughter. But then there's always been talk like that. Hallie will get over it. She has before. Though she may have a hard time understanding why you gave me the manuscript in the first place. After that business with Jake and all.'

Amos put his drink down on the end table. It was good Scotch, but it had left a bitter aftertaste. 'You'd do all this to win a prize?'

'But I'm not doing anything, Amos. Except talking reason.'

*   *   *

'Of course I understand,' Hallie said, though she didn't. All she'd known from the minute she'd come out of the boarding sleeve and found Amos waiting for her in the terminal was that something was wrong.

'Is Cecelia okay?' she'd asked immediately.

'Cecelia's fine.'

'Then it must be Jake. Is something wrong with Jake?'

'I just thought it would be nice to meet you and drive back into town together. You know a Sunday-afternoon drive, as if we were normal people.'

Hallie kept her face averted as she handed Amos her carry-on bag. She hadn't meant to burst out about Jake that way.

Amos had left the Jaguar in a no-parking zone. There was a ticket on it. He plucked it off the windshield and jammed it into his pocket without a word. Now she knew something was wrong.

On the drive into town he asked about the trip. He inquired about her flight. He even wanted to know what the movie had been.

Hallie took off her dark glasses and turned to Amos. His hawk's profile stood out against the grim Long Island landscape racing past the window.

'Why don't you just tell me what's wrong?'

He did.

She sat very still for a moment. The ugly buildings and gray afternoon continued to rush past the windows. On the radio, a well-modulated voice with a faint English accent told her she'd been listening to Mozart. Only she hadn't. She hadn't heard anything but Amos's words.

'It's exactly what I'd expect you to do.' Her voice was stretched as tight as the violin strings that had started up again on the radio.

'Let you down?'

'You're not letting me down. You're telling me to stand on my own two feet, and you're right. If I can't win the award on my own, I don't deserve it.'

Amos took his big hand off the steering wheel and reached over to pat hers. 'You deserve it, baby.'

It was the 'baby' that did it. That simple term of endearment, a legacy from childhood, convinced her that Amos was doing the right thing by disqualifying himself. It also made her twice as determined. She'd win that damn award. She'd show Amos and Quentin and Jake and all of them.

XXXII

'What in hell is going on up there?' Will asked as soon as Hallie picked up the phone.

'Up here? Where are you calling from now?'

'Washington.'

'Straightening out the president again?'

'Only a couple of senators. I just got a call from the Max Perkins people. Amos resigned.'

'I know.'

'Your old man is quite a guy.'

'He felt it was the only right thing to do.'

'It was a dumb thing to do. No one could fault him for voting for his own editor.'

Hallie said nothing to that.

'But it's too late to worry about that now. Did you hear whom they chose to replace him? Prudence Abbot.'

'I've never met her.'

'No one has. She's practically a recluse.'

'But fair. Everyone says she's fair.'

'That's what I'm counting on,' Will said.

'What do you mean?'

'She'll vote for the best editor. Which means you're still going to win.'

Hallie thought of Amos's manuscript again. 'I wish I had your confidence.'

Will hesitated for a moment. He'd been working with Hallie for a long time. They'd come of age together professionally. He knew her strengths. He also knew her failings.

'I wish you did too.'

'Listen,' she said, 'it's really nice of you. To take such an interest, I mean.'

He laughed. 'I'm not being nice, Hallie. I told you, I have ulterior motives. I figure once you win the award you'll be beholden to me. We're going to get that timing right if it kills us.'

Someone had once told Olivia that the only time her mind stopped clicking away was during sex. She'd never forgotten the words, though she no longer remembered the man who'd said them. Whoever it was, he'd been right. Up to a point. Sex was the one thing that could turn her mind off, but even sex didn't always work. It wasn't working now.

Jake was spread-eagled beneath her on the bed. His beautiful symmetrical features were twisted in something between pain and pleasure. His beautiful long arms and legs were wound around her. He was absolutely perfect, and if her mind insisted on clicking away, it ought to be clicking away about him. Instead, the name Prudence Abbot kept beating in her head. The name pounded in rhythm with their movements. Prudence Abbot herself would have been shocked.

Olivia closed her eyes and tried to concentrate on

feeling Jake inside her. It was no good.

She opened her eyes again and saw Jake watching her. She'd been faking it with her body. Now she tried to fake it with her face. But Jake was no fool. He eased her over until he was on top of her. His movements were slow and deliberate and agonizingly promising. She forgot Prudence Abbot. She forgot Jake. Her mind floated away. And only later did it regather in an explosion of her own internal fireworks. Olivia had been known to cry out a variety of words during orgasm. Occasionally the man's name. More often 'darling.' And frequently no words at all, merely sounds. But this was the first time a full name had ever gone off in her head. 'Prudence Abbot!' her mind howled, as her body convulsed. Fortunately her mouth was closed at the time.

'What do you know about Prudence Abbot?' Olivia asked Jake.

'Mmm,' he murmured. He was half asleep. She hadn't asked him to stay over. He'd just assumed she wanted him to. Now that she no longer begged and schemed to keep Jake from going back to the Princeton Club, he showed less and less inclination to go there.

'I asked what you knew about Prudence Abbot.'

'Just what everyone else does. Absolutely nothing.'

'Who's her agent?'

He'd been lying on his stomach. Now he turned over and looked up at her.

'Do we have to discuss this now?'

'When else do I get to talk to you?'

Jake remembered his father's words. He rubbed his eyes with his thumb and forefinger. 'She doesn't have an agent.'

'Her publisher?'

'Wigdons.'

'Then you know her.'

'I sold one of her books my first year out as a traveler, Olivia. I don't think that qualifies as knowing her.'

Jake closed his eyes again. Christ, didn't she ever stop? And what about him? There had to be something wrong with a man who kept ending up with these driven women. Then he remembered Olivia's story about her mother. He knew it was melodramatic. And he knew Olivia had milked it shamelessly. But that didn't make it any less moving.

He opened his eyes. Olivia was still sitting with her back against the headboard, her eyes focused blindly on the wall across the room.

'Give it up, Olivia.'

'What do you mean?'

'Prudence Abbot. There's no way to get to her.'

Olivia didn't say anything. She didn't even look down at him. She just sat there with her candy box of a face all scrunched up.

Jake pulled her down beside him and smoothed the hair back from her forehead. 'Look, you said you wanted to be nominated.'

She didn't answer. He figured she couldn't, with her face all contorted that way.

'Well, you were nominated. Why can't you be proud of that?'

She opened her mouth, but he went on before she could speak.

'Your mother would be.'

'You think so?'

'I'm sure of it.'

XXXIII

The grandfather of the man who'd endowed the Maxwell Perkins Prize had made a small fortune off a patent for a device used in threshing machines. The father had turned it into a large fortune by manufacturing farm machinery that he'd sold to the third world, then known as the colonies. The simple threshing device had grown into an international conglomerate with headquarters at Park Avenue and Fifty-eighth Street on that least agricultural of islands, Manhattan. It was in a conference room on the forty-second floor of that headquarters that the judges for the Maxwell Perkins Prize met on a wet Wednesday afternoon early in February.

Rain streaked the tinted-glass walls and smeared the red and green traffic lights of the city below, but inside the room was warm and convivial and smelled faintly of alcohol. Gardiner Fairchild had come straight from lunch at Côte Basque, where he and an impeccably dressed and pedigreed society matron had polished off a bottle of Chateau Margaux '66. Adelaide Koenig had consumed her share of Polish vodka at a meeting of Americans for

311

Solidarity. And Carter Bolton and Will Sawyer had gone down to Pete's Tavern — for old time's sake, they said — and had hamburgers and ale in the booth where Melville once sat to write 'Bartleby the Scrivener,' or so the story went. Of the five judges of the Maxwell Perkins Prize, only Prudence Abbot could have passed a Breathalyzer test that afternoon.

They took their seats around the conference table. It was like sitting around a pond, or at least a mirror. The mahogany surface was that highly polished. A beautiful young woman in a severely cut suit wheeled in a wooden trolley with a silver tea service on it. She poured and passed and served and, when everyone was taken care of, quietly disappeared, as beautiful young women in such offices are expected to. The committee got down to work.

Everyone had a favorite. Everyone, except Prudence Abbot. She sat and watched and listened. Occasionally she refilled her tea from the silver service the severely dressed secretary had left behind. Prudence Abbot took her tea black.

By the end of the first hour, the February dusk had begun closing in outside the windows and the field had been whittled down to Hallie Porter, Olivia Collins, and Hiram Sabatier. Hiram had been Adelaide Koenig's editor for the past twenty-three years. He had an impressive reputation. Everyone admired him. No one liked him. No one, that is, except Adelaide.

'This isn't a popularity contest,' she snapped at one point.

'True,' Will said, 'but it seems to me a good editor has to know about more than words. He, or she, has to know about people. Or at least writers.'

They debated the issue for a while. Adelaide told how Hiram had browbeaten her into a rewrite of the first book she'd ever published with him. 'I fought him every step of the way. And I ended up with a book that was twice as good as the one I'd started with.'

Will said that not everyone was tough enough to take it.

'If they can't stand the heat, let them get out of the kitchen.'

'Hell, Adelaide, I'm glad you write better than you talk,' Will said and proceeded to tell another story about a writer he knew. Young, talented, and fiercely ambitious, she'd driven a cab by day – this was no shrinking violet – and written at night. A year and a half after she'd come to the city, she'd sold her first novel to Hiram Sabatier. 'Needless to say, she was euphoric. Not only had she sold her novel, but she'd sold it to a star editor. I won't bore you with the details of the editorial process,' Will went on, 'but six months later the woman ended up in Bellevue with bandages on her wrists.'

'You're not going to tell me that was Hiram's fault.'

'I'm not going to,' Will said. 'Her suicide note did. If she wasn't a writer, she didn't want to live. And Hiram had convinced her she wasn't a writer.'

Adelaide suggested the young woman hadn't had the guts to be a writer in the first place, but she conceded that Hiram might be a controversial choice.

'As far as I can see, Hallie Porter's the only acceptable choice,' Gardiner said. 'Or at least the only one we're likely to agree on.'

'I'm not likely to agree on her,' Carter said.

'What do you have against her?' Gardiner asked.

Carter glanced at Will. They hadn't discussed the matter at lunch, but they knew they stood on different sides of this issue. That was okay. Over the years they'd stood on different sides of more substantial issues than who won a literary award.

'I don't have anything against Hallie,' Carter said. 'Except that she is – as you said, Gardiner – the *acceptable* choice. The establishment choice. Fine. Let her win all the old established awards. But I thought this prize was supposed to be given in a different spirit. The spirit of Max Perkins. He didn't publish the old established writers. He went out and found new ones. And he made literary history doing it. So I think we ought to give this award to a new face.'

Or body, Will thought but didn't say. For one thing, he wasn't exactly in a position to cast the first stone. For another, he knew Carter believed everything he'd just said. The fact that he occasionally went to bed with Olivia had nothing to do with it.

'But you can't seriously expect us to give this award to Olivia Collins,' Gardiner said. 'She's a newcomer.'

'Exactly my point,' Carter insisted.

'I'm willing to concede Olivia's published a couple of decent books,' Will broke in, 'but you can't point to a body of work. Unless you include potboilers and bodice-rippers and a whole lot of nonbooks.'

'But that's my point. We're supposed to be judging editorial expertise, not the reading taste of the American public. If people like to read that stuff, and if Olivia Collins turns out the best of that stuff, then she ought to get the award for editorial excellence.'

'I don't agree,' Will said.

Carter's eyes held Will's for a moment. 'I didn't expect you to.'

'I refuse to pander to the bad taste of the American public,' Gardiner insisted.

'We're judging editorial excellence,' Carter said, 'not electing the ten best-dressed minds of the year, Gardiner.'

'I think Carter has a point,' Adelaide said. 'I understand Olivia Collins has several serious political works on her upcoming list.'

'This is a prize for past achievement,' Will said, 'not a vote of encouragement for future development. And if you're looking for a body of work of consistent excellence, you have to give the prize to Hallie Porter.'

The hard black eyes stared out from the puffy face. 'We don't *have* to give the award to anyone, Will. We don't *have* to give the award at all.'

Will leaned back in his chair and smiled. He tried to make the smile as sincere and winning as possible. He'd seen Adelaide Koenig with her back up. 'It would be a damn shame not to,' he said. 'Give the award, I mean.'

'I think we ought to give it to Olivia Collins,' Carter said.

'As do I,' Adelaide added.

'I cast my vote for Hallie Porter,' Gardiner announced.

'So,' Will began, 'we're two and two.' Four heads turned to Prudence Abbot. 'You haven't said anything, Miss Abbot.' The term of address escaped before Will had a chance to think about it. He hadn't called anyone 'Miss' in years. 'Ms.' maybe, but not 'Miss.' Prudence Abbot, however, reminded him of his third-grade teacher. The resemblance to that tall, gaunt woman whose bra strap was continually sliding out of her blouse was uncanny. The 'Miss' had come out atavistically.

'I've been listening,' Prudence Abbot said. 'Carefully.'

They all waited for her to go on. She let them wait.

'And?' Will asked.

'I don't know either editor personally. I did know Hiram Sabatier at one tine. He used the word "presently" when he meant "currently".' Clearly, Hiram Sabatier wasn't going to win Prudence Abbot's vote for editorial excellence.

'We've already dropped Hiram,' Adelaide snapped. 'We've narrowed the field to these two women.'

Prudence held Adelaide's hard little eyes with her own clear ones. 'I understand that. I was merely making an observation.' She glanced from one to the other of the group. No one was going to rush Prudence Abbot. 'As I said, I haven't worked with either of the editors in question –'

'I have,' Carter began, but Prudence's look silenced him.

'But I have made inquiries among those who have. The question here isn't who's published the best books or the most books or' – she glanced at Adelaide again – 'the books that take the correct political stance. It isn't even a question of who knows the language, despite my anecdote about Mr Sabatier. For me, it's a question of which of these editors I, as a writer, would like to work with. Which of these editors would bring out the best book that is in me.'

She was silent again, but this time no one rushed to fill the void.

'After reading several books each of them has published,' she went on finally, 'and talking to several writers – something I'm usually loath to do – I have come to a decision.'

She stopped again, and Will realized she was enjoying this. The woman wasn't only a recluse, she was a sadist. But she was also smart. She'd asked the only valid question. He knew from the silence in the room that the others thought so too. And he knew one other thing. The answer to that question. He just hoped Prudence Abbot knew the same answer.

'Are you going to put us out of our misery and tell us your decision?' Gardiner asked. 'Or are we expected to read your mind?'

Prudence's eyes swept the table. 'You're all in such a rush. I only hope you gave the matter more consideration than you're giving it time.'

'For God's sake,' Adelaide said. 'We've been here for more than two hours. I have other things to do, even if you don't.'

'We're almost there,' Will said. 'Let's not turn on each other now.'

'Right, Adelaide.' Carter flashed her a smile. 'Just mellow out.'

That was when Will realized that Carter was thinking the same thing he was. There was only one answer to Prudence Abbot's question. Only Carter's one answer was different from Will's.

'If I were a young writer looking for an editor,' Prudence began. 'Or if I were looking for a new editor myself . . .'

Come on, Will thought. Stop milking this and spit it out.

'I would choose . . .'

Will leaned forward in his chair. He realized Carter was sitting the same way.

'Hallie Porter.'

The room was silent for a moment. When Will finally spoke, his voice was quiet, almost offhand. After all, this wasn't the Miss America Contest or the Oscars. This was a serious professional meeting.

'Then I guess that does it. Three of us are in favor of giving the Maxwell Perkins Prize for editorial excellence to Hallie Porter.'

'I trust,' Gardiner said, 'no one will divulge the balance of the vote. Now that we've made the decision, I think it should be announced as unanimous.'

They were all standing now. Everyone agreed the decision would be announced as unanimous.

'And of course,' Carter began and caught Will's eye with a wicked congratulatory smile, 'no one will reveal the result of the vote until it's officially announced.'

XXXIV

Will didn't wait till he got home. He called Hallie from a phone on the corner of Fifty-ninth and Park. As he waited for her secretary to connect him, he watched the crowd coming out of Christie's. The furs raised his environmental hackles, but the sleek, long-legged women wearing them only made him wish Hallie would hurry.

'You must be calling from a plane again,' Hallie said when she got on the line. 'I can barely hear you.'

'A street corner.'

'You're coming down in the world. A street corner where? A week ago you were leaving on a ten-city tour to promote the paperback of your last book.'

'It's the street corner across from Christies. I haven't seen so many dead animal skins since I was in Africa.'

'You still haven't told me why you aren't on the road, hawking your book.'

'I had to come back for a meeting.' He didn't say what kind of meeting, and Hallie didn't bother to ask. Will went to a lot of meetings. 'I don't suppose you're free tonight. Or let me put it another way.

321

I know you're tied up, but cancel it and have dinner with me. Please.'

'You convinced me. I think it was the "please" that did it. Where should I meet you?'

'I thought we could have dinner at my place.'

'I didn't know you could cook.'

'I'm a man of many talents.'

Will Sawyer couldn't cook, but he knew how to use a telephone. When Hallie arrived he took her into the kitchen, where he was making drinks. 'If you want to be helpful, you can get the onions for the gibsons.' She opened the refrigerator. It was overflowing with up-scale take-out containers.

'Your fridge looks like a Zagat's. An out-of-date Zagat's. I hope this isn't dinner. Everything's growing a beard.'

'Cultures, Hallie. It's a very cultured fridge. Nope, dinner's on the way. From Indochine.'

'I didn't know they delivered. I especially didn't know they delivered from Lafayette Street to the Upper West Side.'

Will shrugged and handed her a drink. 'They do for me.'

They went into the living room. It was, in its way, as bizarre as the refrigerator. The room was huge, with a sweeping view of Central Park. The achingly up-to-the-minute furniture was the kind any savvy young designer would choose. It didn't have much to do with Will, though he'd managed to leave his imprint. Books, magazines, compact discs, and odd articles of clothing covered every piece of furniture and half the floor. A laptop computer stood open on one table, a manuscript lay on the beautifully restored marble mantle, and yellow legal pads were scattered everywhere, just in case someone felt the need to make a note.

'Gee, you shouldn't have bothered cleaning up for me,' Hallie said.

Will swept a pile of books and two sweaters off the Memphis sofa. 'I wanted to put my best foot forward.'

She sat on the sofa. He sat beside her. 'Aren't you going to ask what kind of meeting I had to come back for?'

'Save the whales? Protect the ozone layer? Impeach the president?'

'You're not thinking, Hallie.'

But suddenly she was. 'I thought that didn't happen for another week.'

'The judges for the Maxwell Perkins Prize met at three o'clock this afternoon. They met. They argued. Boy, did they argue. And they made their decision.'

Hallie sat absolutely still. She was sure she could hear her heart beating. She wondered if Will could hear it too.

Will put his drink down and stared at her. 'I'm in a bit of a bind here.'

Her heart was no longer beating. It had stopped. She waited for the bad news. She wondered how bad it was. Had she merely lost, or had she lost to Olivia?

'As one of the judges, I'm sworn not to reveal the winner until she's officially announced at tomorrow's press conference.'

'It's all right, Will. I won't ask you.'

'But even judges are allowed to offer toasts.' He picked up his glass and held it out to her. 'To you.'

'You mean –'

'Hey!' He held up his hand. 'I'm a man of my word. Why don't you just accept my toast?'

She did. Then she spilled both their drinks getting to him.

He tasted like gin and euphoria. Or maybe she did.

'I hope this isn't just gratitude,' Will murmured, his mouth on hers.

She unbuttoned his shirt and slipped her hand inside. 'Do you care if it is?'

He pulled back and looked at her. The Caribbean-blue eyes were suddenly dark, as if something had been churned up from the bottom. 'The funny thing is I do.'

She put her fingers on his mouth, partly to silence him, but mostly because she had to touch that full lower lip. 'It's not just gratitude.' She brushed her lips over his. 'You said it yourself.' She kissed him. 'We've been working up to this for a long time.' She kissed him again. 'And now were finally getting the timing right.'

It shouldn't have happened again. The odds were against it. But it did. The bell rang. She groaned. He didn't let go of her.

'Unfortunately, Indochine seems to be on the same schedule,' she said.

His hand moved down her body. 'We don't have to answer.'

She nibbled his ear. 'You'll be sorry later. Or at least hungry.'

'Are you always this practical?' He climbed over her and started for the hall.

At the door, he took the bag from the delivery boy, dug into the pocket of his wrinkled khakis for money, handed over a fistful of bills without counting them, and kicked the door closed.

'Don't move,' he said as he started for the kitchen. 'And whatever you do, don't lose your place. I'll be right back.'

She didn't know where she got the idea. It wasn't the kind of thing she'd do. When she thought about it later, she realized it was the kind of thing Olivia would do. But Hallie did it. Maybe because of the look in Will's eyes when he'd asked if it was only gratitude. Maybe because she'd just won the Maxwell Perkins Prize for editorial excellence and was feeling pretty good about herself and everyone else.

She was off the sofa in a second. She unbuttoned her suit jacket and dropped it on the floor. Not that he'd be likely to notice it in the rest of the mess. She started down the hall. She'd never been in the apartment before, but the bedroom could be in only one direction. She kicked off her shoes on the hall floor. She pulled off her blouse and left it hanging on a doorknob. She unzipped her skirt and dropped it in the doorway to the bedroom. As she began tugging off her pantyhose, she thought of Olivia. She was sorry she didn't have stockings and a garter belt to mark the trail.

She heard Will's voice in the living room, calling

her name. She didn't answer. She unhooked her bra and dropped it on the floor. Her bikinis fell at the foot of the bed. She was just about to slip under the covers when she heard Will's voice behind her.

'Are we playing Hansel and Gret – ' His voice died when he saw her.

She turned. They stood staring at each other. For a split second she was the old Hallie again. Her hands started up to cover her nakedness. Then they fell back to her sides.

They went on staring at each other for a moment. Then he crossed the room to her. He put his fingers on either side of her neck and lightly, as if he were barely touching her, traced the line out to her shoulders.

'Hallie,' he said again, but this time it was a kind of sigh. Hallie learned something that night. Not a new position or practice or anything that mundane, but a new truth. She'd always hated the discussions about sex. 'Is he a good lover?' Olivia used to ask in the old days on Avenue A. Olivia had graded her own experiences on either alphabetical or numerical scales, the latter having the advantages of decimal points. But Hallie hadn't believed sex could be rated like an Olympic event. She'd thought whether people cared for each other was more important than what they did to each other. She still thought that, but now she knew something else. If expertise wasn't as good as love, it had its advantages. Will was a wonderful lover. In fact, he was such a wonderful lover that she never even thought about how he'd got that way until it was all over. And he was such a wonderful lover that it wasn't over for a long time. Only then did she think about Jake, and then she thought about him for only a moment. She didn't compare him to Will. She didn't rate them. She just thought of Jake. Then she turned over and fell asleep in Will's arms.

They slept curled together, her back warmed by his chest. When one of them turned in sleep, the other did too. Somewhere toward dawn, Hallie opened her eyes. Her cheek was against his shoulder. He smelled of some spicy aftershave and sex. She rubbed her face against his skin. He turned and moaned quietly and put his arms around her, but he didn't wake.

She lay there absorbing his warmth and luxuriating in his scent and thinking about the night. Her mind crept back through it, through the passion that had left them sweating and tangled together on this bed, back to the moment when they'd sat in that impossible living room. That was when it came to her. He hadn't said anything.

Even in his sleep, he felt her stiffen in his arms. He opened his eyes. Her own were wide open only inches away.

'Will?'

'Mmmm?' His voice was thick with sleep.

'I know we said we weren't going to talk about it.'

His arms tightened around her. 'Hell, Hallie, do you still need the words? After this?'

She didn't say anything but went on staring at him in the darkness.

'All right. I love you. I'm not sure what it means.' He yawned fighting to stay awake for this. 'It

327

probably doesn't mean the same thing to me as it does to you. But for what it's worth, I love you.'

'I didn't mean that. I meant . . .' Her voice drifted off.

He opened his eyes wider. Then he started to laugh. 'I should have known.' He was awake now, and he knew he wasn't going back to sleep, at least not for a while. 'You didn't misunderstand.' His hand cupped her breast. 'I love you.' He kissed her. 'Gardiner Fairchild loves you.' His mouth burrowed into her neck. 'The whole damn judges panel loves you.' He moved on top of her. 'Now are you happy?'

She smiled up at him in the darkness. 'I was happy before.' She wound her arms and legs around him. 'Now I'm ecstatic.'

XXXV

Jake turned the collar of his Burberry up against the March night. The wind slapped him in the face. He had to stop kidding himself. Tonight had been proof of that, as if he needed more proof. For months Hallie had been telling him it was over. Tonight she'd practically drawn him a diagram.

It was bad enough that Sawyer had presented the award. And he'd done a lousy job of it, if you asked Jake, though nobody was asking Jake anything about Hallie these days. Will hadn't been able to resist the personal asides about how he'd worked with Hallie and knew firsthand what a terrific editor she was. And he hadn't been able to resist the in-jokes about the writer-editor relationship. He might as well have worn a button: 'I'm sleeping with Hallie Porter.' And in case anyone hadn't got the message during the presentation, Sawyer hadn't left her side for the rest of the party. Every time Jake had spotted Hallie in the crowded, noisy ballroom of the Yale Club, goddamn Will Sawyer had been at her side. Once Jake had looked over and seen them standing in the center of an admiring group. Admiring, hell!

Fawning. Hallie was saying something and everyone was laughing. Sawyer was laughing harder than any of them, and the bastard had his hand on Hallie's shoulder. She was wearing that Chanel suit Jake used to love because it was so damn ladylike, and every time he saw her in it all he could think of was taking it off her.

But he wasn't going to think about Hallie, and he especially wasn't going to think about Hallie with Will Sawyer. As he walked up Madison Avenue in the frigid night, putting distance between him and that ballroom, his hands balled into fists in his pockets at the thought of what he wasn't going to think about. He told himself to forget it. He unclenched his hands. The light of a cruising cab caught his eye. He raised his arm to hail it.

'Take it easy, man,' the diver said when Jake slammed the door. He gave the driver Olivia's address.

Olivia had been right not to go to the party, though Jake hadn't thought so at first. 'You were nominated,' he'd insisted. 'You'll look like a sore loser if you don't show at the presentation.'

'If I don't show,' she said, and even though they were on the phone, Jake could tell from her voice that her jaw was clenched, 'no one will remember that I was nominated. If I go, they'll all remember I lost.'

'Listen,' he said, because the clenched jaw sounded as if it might give way to tears, 'you didn't really expect to win.'

'Sure.'

'You said you only wanted to be nominated.'

Now she didn't say anything at all.

'And you were.'

'Bully for me.'

'Your mother would be proud.'

There was a moment's silence. 'I suppose you're right,' she said finally.

Now Jake was sure she was going to cry. That was when he suggested they have their own celebration that night. He'd slip away from the party early.

She told him not to worry about the time. She had to take a writer for drinks. She'd leave her keys with the doorman, in case Jake got there before her.

Olivia sat in the lobby of the Algonquin, watching the woman's mouth move. It was like watching a silent movie. Olivia had tuned her out that completely. God, she hated authors. They took themselves so seriously. Did this dumpy psychologist really think her book would teach women how to put exciting sex back into their drab little marriages?

The woman's mouth was still moving. Olivia caught the word 'orgasm.' She wondered if Quentin had gone to the party. She hadn't seen him since that night they'd flown to North Carolina on the private plane. He'd left for Hong Kong the next day. Something about Allied Entertainment distribution agreements But he'd said he'd call her as soon as he got back. Only he hadn't. Olivia knew, because she'd heard Hallie's secretary telling her that Mr Styles was on the phone. Of course, Quentin had gone to the party. Hallie wasn't only the publisher of an Allied Entertainment company. She was Quentin's goddaughter. Olivia wondered how she'd been so dumb. She'd actually expected solace from Quentin. She'd actually expected him to care that she hadn't won the award. Obviously, the sex had got to her. But not to him.

The woman was still talking. She didn't even seem to notice that Olivia hadn't answered her for some time. Egomaniacs. Writers were all egomaniacs. If only you could publish books without them. The woman went on talking. Olivia went on brooding. She'd lost the Max Perkins Prize, and from the look of things, she wasn't doing too well with Quentin either. Her mother's voice came creeping into the venerable wood-paneled lounge. 'A bird in the hand, Olivia Mae . . .'

Jake had gone to the party, but he'd promised to leave early. For her. She made up her mind. Screw the award. And screw Quentin. Only she wasn't going to anymore. She'd lost sight of the original plan – that was Quentin's fault – but now she was back on track. She remembered the picture of Hallie and Jake. Couple clout. Hallie could have the award. Olivia had Jake.

She rang the small bell attached to the cocktail table. The waiter appeared immediately. She asked for the check. The woman who was going to tell the women of America how to put sex back into their marriages looked surprised and more than a little offended. Well, screw her too. Olivia had more important work to do that night. It was time Jake started thinking about divorce. And marriage.

*   *   *

Jake was sitting on the sofa. There was a drink on the table beside him, but there was no manuscript in sight, no contract, not even a magazine. He was just sitting there, staring at the door.

'Are you okay?' Olivia asked as she closed it behind her.

'Fine.'

'You didn't have any trouble getting in?'

'Evidently not.'

She dropped her briefcase and coat, sat beside him on the sofa, kissed him, apologized for being late, and kissed him again. He might as well have been made of stone.

She went into the kitchen to make a drink for herself. She needed time to figure it out. He'd gone to the party, which meant he'd seen Hallie. She remembered the times when he'd been angry at Hallie. The night she hadn't come back from London and they'd ended up on the sofa of Hallie's living room. The night he'd had a fight with Hallie and they'd ended up on the floor of Olivia's. His anger had worked like an aphrodisiac then. She went back into the living room, hiked up her straight skirt, and sat on his lap facing him. She brushed her lips against his. Still no response. If he was angry at Hallie, it sure wasn't working like an aphrodisiac tonight.

Damn men! She was the one who'd lost the award. She was the one who deserved to be comforted. And here he was, sitting like a great stoneface while she tried to jolly him out of whatever funk he was in.

'Either it was the worst party of the century,' she said, 'or you just lost your top ten clients.'

'The party was okay.'

'Try to control your enthusiasm, honey.'

'How can I be enthusiastic? You didn't win.'

Olivia stopped squirming around on his lap. 'You mean that all this gloom and doom is for me?'

He looked at her for what felt to Olivia like a long time. 'In a way.'

She'd made the right decision. Jake really did care about her. She held his eyes with her own. 'You don't have to feel sorry for me.' She kissed him again. 'Hallie has the award.' She began loosening his tie. 'But I have you.'

'What about your mother?'

'You said it on the phone, honey. I wanted to be nominated for her memory. And I was.'

'To give her life meaning.'

'Yes.'

'And her death.'

Olivia concentrated on opening his shirt and didn't say anything.

'Isn't that the way you put it? That she'd sacrificed her life for you. Broken her health on that damn sewing machine, I think you said, so you could have a few advantages.'

'It's true.'

'I know it is.'

Olivia had finished with the buttons on his shirt. Now she stopped, with her hand on his belt. 'Why are you looking at me like that?'

'You got a call while I was here. I answered the phone. I hope you don't mind.'

'Of course I don't mind, honey.'

Damn, that's why he was in such a rotten mood. Quentin had called. Well, she'd talked herself out of worse jams.

'Quentin probably has those figures for me.'

He recognized that wary look in her eyes. He knew that tight smile. He'd never even thought of Quentin. Well, so what? It was a good joke on him. Another good joke on him. 'Quentin?'

'As long as he was going to be in the Far East, I asked him to look into production costs. You know, for art books and stuff.' She smiled at him. 'It never hurts to let top management know you're thinking about cutting costs.'

'It wasn't Quentin on the phone.'

She was silent for a moment. 'Who was it? Or are we going to play twenty questions?'

He pushed her off his lap and stood. 'It was your brother. Bobby, he said his name was.'

'You're kidding. I haven't heard from him in years.'

'So he said. Of course, it isn't easy to hear from people when you don't tell them where you live and your phone number is unlisted. It took him four days to track you down. By then it was too late.'

'Too late for what?'

'Too late to make your mother's funeral. She died last Sunday. He didn't say whether she died knowing you'd been nominated for the Maxwell Perkins Prize or not.' Jake picked his coat up off the chair where he'd thrown it. 'I don't suppose you called to tell her.'

She sat staring at him. Her body was still, but her

mind was racing. What was that dumb line about the best defense? She stood and crossed the room to him. When she looked up at him, she was smiling.

'Spare me the holier-than-thou act, honey. I'm not the first person who hid her family because she was ashamed of them. I don't see you trucking your sweet old mama up from Miami Beach to attend publishing parties.'

'You don't see me telling people she's dead, either.'

'You want a medal for heroism?'

He'd taken a step toward the door, but now he stopped and stood there with his hand on the knob. 'I always liked you, Olivia. I don't mean just the sex. I always admired your guts. And in a funny way your honesty. I thought because you owned up to some pretty dirty tricks—'

'Like screwing my best friend's husband.'

He winced. 'You had some help on that one. But I always thought that because you admitted to some pretty bad stuff, I knew the worst stuff. I was wrong.'

'And you're shocked?'

'Disappointed.'

She turned away from him. 'Forgive me if I don't buy your high moral tone, honey. It was just one more luxury I couldn't afford back there in Smithsburg.'

'You've come a long way from Smithsburg. You can afford all kinds of things now.'

'That's right, I can. But maybe a high moral tone is like caviar. Expensive as hell and something I've never acquired a taste for.'

*   *   *

Olivia didn't bother to go back to Smithsburg. There was no point. She'd already missed the funeral. And she was too late for anything else.

Still, she didn't shirk her responsibilities. 'Someone's gotta pay the undertaker,' Bobby said.

'The undertaker or your dealer?' Olivia asked, but as soon as she got off the phone she wrote a check to Bobby Collins. Then she closed her checkbook with a feeling of relief. That chapter of her life was over.

The next morning she called Jake as soon as she got to the office. There was no point in playing waiting games. Her only hope was a full and abject apology. I know it was an awful thing to do, honey, absolutely unspeakable, but . . . Then she'd paint a picture of her mother coming to visit with her tacky clothes and fractured grammar and racist epithets.

Why hadn't she thought of that before? Jake, good knee-jerk liberal that he was, would be horrified. She smiled as she told Jake's secretary it was Olivia Collins calling.

'He's in a meeting,' the secretary announced in that crisp tone reserved for bald-faced lies. So he'd given the order. No calls from Olivia Collins.

Olivia hung up the phone and sat staring at the pile of manuscripts on her desk. That was it. She'd write to Jake and tell him the whole story. She went on staring at the manuscripts. The one on top was by a woman who'd been abused as a child. The second brainstorm hit. She wouldn't overdo it. No serious violence, just a few swattings around, the kind a cruel narrow-minded mother would be likely to visit on an innocent but right-thinking daughter. That's why she'd made up the story of an idealized dead mother. Because she couldn't face the reality of a vicious living one. Let Jake try to pull moral rank on that.

She swiveled her chair around to face her word processor and flipped on the switch. If only half her fiction writers had a quarter of her imagination.

XXXVI

As Hallie's venture-capital friend, Martha, had predicted, she was leaving Rutherford and Styles the way the Pied Piper had left Hamlin. She was taking Amos, Will, half a dozen other leading authors, and the publicity and sales directors. She'd expected Jonathan Graham to be furious. He was philosophical.

They were in her office, which she still thought of as Quentin's. They'd been in meetings all day, and at the end of the last, Hallie had asked Jonathan if he had a minute.

'I'm not exactly surprised,' he said when she told him she was leaving. 'Sorry, but not surprised.'

They talked for a few more minutes. They agreed there were no hard feelings. He told her he'd enjoyed working with her. She said it hadn't been as bad working for him as she'd expected.

'I told you I wasn't going to interfere,' he said.

She had to admit he hadn't, much.

'Do you mind if I tell you something?' he asked.

She said she welcomed his advice. She wasn't being polite. He was a smart businessman.

'You're making a mistake.'

She started to laugh, though she found the warning anything but funny. 'Because you think I'm bound to fail?'

'Because I think you stand a good chance of succeeding.'

'Then why am I making a mistake?'

'Once you do, once you have a sweet little house turning out best sellers and turning a profit, some guy like me is going to come along and buy you up.'

'In which case I'll be right back where I started.'

'In which case you might be in worse shape than you are now. Like you said, I left you pretty much alone. The next guy might play by different rules.

'One more question,' Jonathan said as they stood waiting for the elevator. 'Do you have any suggestions for your successor?' Hallie thought about it for a moment. 'You have a good group of editors.'

'That's not what I asked.' She decided she could afford to be magnanimous. 'The editor in chief would be the logical choice.'

'If there's one thing I've learned, Hallie, it's that the logical choice isn't necessarily the smart choice. I know Olivia's a good editor. The question is, would she make a good publisher? Can she handle the big picture as well as the books?'

They stepped into the elevator. Hallie debated her answer. She could tell the truth. Or she could get a little of her own back.

'I take it from your silence that you don't think she can handle it.'

'I'm not exactly Olivia's biggest fan.'

'So I've heard,' Jonathan said.

'And you still asked my opinion?'

'I'm still waiting for it.'

The doors opened and they stepped out of the elevator. Hallie was still thinking about the answer. She'd already got some of her own back with the Max Perkins Prize. And she was never going to get Jake back, at least not the old Jake. Besides, years before she'd told Olivia you didn't have to be a bitch to get ahead.

'She can handle it,' Hallie answered.

Jonathan Graham wasn't surprised by Hallie's decision to leave and start her own house. Neither was Olivia. The rumors had been flying for weeks. She'd had the feeling Hallie was just waiting till she won the Max Perkins Prize to make the announcement. Now she had the damn award and she'd made the announcement. The headline ran across four columns at the top of the book-review page. 'PORTER LEAVES R & S TO FOUND NEW HOUSE.' Olivia's eyes raced through the article. 'According to a spokesperson for Mr Graham, a new publisher has not yet been appointed.' Olivia jammed the paper into her briefcase and told the cabbie she'd changed her mind. She didn't want to go to the R and S building after all. She gave him the address of the East Coast office of Allied Entertainment and told him to hurry.

Olivia was an authority on the relationship between physical work space and professional power. Even if she hadn't known who Jonathan Graham was, she would have placed him from that office.

The room was huge. The furniture was early English – not reproductions, but the real thing. The windows commanded a view of a wide stretch of the winter-black Hudson and half of northern New Jersey. What a waste. Jonathan used the office fewer than thirty days a year. She thought of Quentin's office that had become Hallie's office. The view wasn't as spectacular as this, but it was pretty good. She decided she'd redecorate. She wanted a high-tech look, stark and expensive. She glanced around Jonathan's once again. On second thought, the English country-house look might send a more subtle power message.

Olivia took the chair on the other side of Jonathan's desk. 'I appreciate your seeing me,' she said. 'And I know you're busy, so I'll get right to the point.'

'You want to be publisher.'

'You have no other choice.'

He raised his eyebrows.

'If you want R and S to continue growing.'

'You know how to grow it?'

'I told you some of my ideas that night we had drinks on the coast. Audios. Videos. Computer software.'

'Fine, but do you know anything about audios and videos and computer software?'

'I'm a quick study.'

He smiled. It was so boyish and genuine that if Olivia had been more gullible she would have thought she'd pulled it off. 'I'm sure you are, but I'm not sure I want to pay for your education. There are people out there who already know.'

She stared at him and debated. It was a big risk. If only he'd give some sign. Like Quentin that morning in the library. Nervous as she'd been, she'd felt Quentin's eyes on her as she'd crossed the room to him and known what he was thinking. Behind those prim rimless glasses his eyes had been undressing her. Across the desk from her now, Jonathan Graham's merely stared at her.

She took a deep breath, then she leaned forward and crossed her arms on the edge of the desk so that her breasts were resting on them. It was close to an offering. 'Take a chance on me, Jonathan. You won't be sorry.'

He leaned back in the swivel chair and went on staring at her. 'I assume you're speaking about the job.'

'Did you have something else in mind?'

The smile wasn't boyish now. It was amused and not particularly kind. He shook his head slowly. 'No, Olivia. I didn't. I really didn't.'

She forced herself to go on smiling at him. She'd lost a round, but she hadn't been knocked out of the ring.

'I still say I'd make the best damn publisher you're likely to find.'

'Maybe. Maybe not. But I'll tell you one thing. You're in the running.'

The editorial meeting was already in session when

Olivia arrived. She slid into her seat on Hallie's right. The position encouraged her. It was such a short distance from her chair to Hallie's. And Jonathan had said she was in the running.

She glanced around the table, tallying the heads that would roll. The mystery editor had been around forever, bringing in those polite English whodunits with little-old-lady sleuths. Olivia decided she'd force her to take early retirement and hire a young guy who could handle the drugs, sex, and violence genre. She'd have to keep Schneider on. He brought in all those celeb biographies. If Hallie weren't taking Sheila Dent with her, Olivia would fire her. Sheila knew her job, but Olivia wanted an up-scale publicity director, maybe a trust-fund baby, not a dumpy, disgruntled middle-aged divorcée.

She was still working her way around the table, firing here, promoting there, when Hallie's secretary came into the conference room. She said Mr Graham was on the phone. Hallie left the meeting. She didn't even have to tell Olivia to take over. It was accepted procedure.

Olivia took over, but she no longer felt secure about it. She didn't know why she hadn't thought of it before. Jonathan Graham would ask Hallie's opinion on her successor. Olivia knew what Hallie would say.

Her only hope was Quentin. Olivia put in a call to the coast as soon as she got back to her office.

Quentin's secretary answered the phone. She said Mr Styles was out of the office. Olivia asked if he was in New York. The secretary said he wasn't, but she didn't say where he was. Olivia hung up and tried the house in Malibu. The housekeeper was more forthcoming than the secretary but, since Olivia didn't speak Spanish, less helpful.

Olivia hung up the phone. Quentin wasn't in Los Angeles. He wasn't in New York. That left only a couple of dozen other places he might be. Palm Beach. Palm Springs. London. Paris. He'd joked about taking her to Paris on the plane that night. At the time she'd been dumb enough to think it might not be a joke. Only it was, and it was on her.

They were all having a good laugh. Quentin, who'd given her the oldest line in the world, 'I'll call you when I get back.' Hallie clutching her Max Perkins Prize and warning Jonathan Graham against her. Even Jake. He must have got her letter by now, and she still hadn't heard from him.

Olivia picked up the phone again. Hell, what else did she have to lose. Jake's secretary said she thought he was in a meeting, but she'd check. Olivia listened to the dead sound at the other end of the line. After a while she began to think the secretary had forgotten her.

'He said he'll get back to you,' the secretary said.

Fat chance, Olivia thought. 'Thanks,' she said.

Olivia began thinking the day had nowhere to go but up. She was wrong. At lunch Jackie Kay, of the skyrocketing Jackie Kay Agency, confided that to be perfectly truthful she was a little reluctant to submit anything to Olivia at the moment. 'There's a lot of upheaval at R and S. With Hallie leaving and all.'

'I'm still here,' Olivia said.

'For how long?'

The words had more kick than her drink. Olivia put her Bloody Mary down with a sickening feeling. At that morning's editorial meeting, she'd made a mental hit list. It hadn't occurred to her that another publisher would have a hit list of his or her own.

'If things don't go the way you want them to,' Jackie went on, 'you might walk, too.' The words made Olivia feel a little better but not much. 'I can't take that chance. I have a responsibility to the authors I represent.'

Back in Olivia's office there was a message from Norman Silver, the editor in chief of her old house, Apogee. A feeler perhaps? An outright job offer? She returned Norman's call immediately.

'I want to pick your brain, Olivia. About R and S. What's going on over there?'

'Hallie's leaving.'

'I know that. I was hoping for a little more in the way of inside dope.'

'Why?'

'Jonathan Graham called me this morning. He suggested lunch.'

They both knew what that meant. Norman was in the running for publisher.

'It'd be fun working with you again,' he said.

'Fun, honey? It'd be terrific.' The words tasted bitter in Olivia's mouth, but she managed to sugarcoat them. She even managed to replace the phone in the cradle rather than slam it down.

It rang immediately. Olivia picked it up. Jake was on the other end. Maybe her luck was changing after all. Then he started to talk, and she knew it wasn't. He sounded like a stranger. He said something about first and second serial rights of a contract they had under negotiation. She said sure. This was no time to argue. He said good-bye.

'Wait!'

From the silence on the other end of the phone, she gathered Jake was waiting.

'Didn't you get my letter?'

'I got it.'

'And?'

'You've got to be kidding, Olivia.'

'But it's all true.'

He started to hum. For once Olivia could recognize the tune. 'It Seems to Me I've Heard This Song Before.'

'It's true. I swear it.'

There was another silence, and when Jake spoke again, he didn't sound angry, only tired. 'I don't think you know what the truth is anymore, Olivia. But that's not the point. I've had it.'

'Listen,' she pleaded, 'I know you don't love me. But you said last week you've always liked me. You said we were friends.' She stopped for a minute, and it wasn't for dramatic effect. She was having a hard time getting the words out. She wasn't used to this kind of thing. 'And we were friends. For a long time. So why don't you give an old friend another chance?'

She wound the telephone cord around her finger

347

and closed her eyes. The silence seemed to go on forever.

'Because,' Jake said finally, 'I realized something when I left your place the other night. I may have liked you, but ever since this thing started, ever since that night Hallie didn't come home from London, I haven't liked myself much.'

'That's guilt talking.'

'Guilt is a perfectly normal human emotion, Olivia. You ought to try it some time.'

'Listen, honey –'

'I've got to run.'

'But –'

Then Jake did something no one had ever done to Olivia. He simply hung up the phone.

The office seemed unusually quiet. The sound of other phones ringing and people talking came to Olivia as if from a great distance. Gradually she recognized one voice. Amos's deep bass rolled down the hall into her office. Olivia listened to it. Another lighter sound mingled with it. Olivia recognized Hallie's laughter. The two voices wound around each other in a sweet, smug duet that grew louder and louder until it filled Olivia's office, almost crowding her out of it.

She made up her mind then. She might be going down in flames, but she wasn't going down alone.

Sheila Dent was packing the top drawer of her desk when Olivia entered her office.

'It's not going to be the same around here without you.'

Sheila's head snapped up. She wasn't sure Olivia was speaking to her, but there was no one else in the room. Not that they didn't get along. When Olivia was pushing for a big review or a major talk show for one of her authors, she couldn't have been nicer to Sheila. For the rest of the time, she merely ignored her. Now Sheila was leaving R and S. There was nothing more she could do for Olivia. And here was Olivia, standing in Sheila's office, talking about how she was going to miss her. It didn't make sense. In fact, it made Sheila nervous.

'We'll have to do lunch sometime,' Olivia went on. 'Or a drink.'

'Sure.' Sheila knew the formula. 'Let's do lunch,' people promised each other. 'Have your girl call mine,' they added, and then you knew for sure. That was one lunch that would never happen. She took her calendar from the top of her desk and started to put it in the carton.

'Wait!' Olivia put her hand over Sheila's. 'Let's make a date right now.'

Sheila was too surprised to object.

XXXVII

The offices of Unicorn Books, Inc., Hallie Porter
president and publisher, were on the ground floor
of a well-kept, unremarkable brownstone on East
Thirty-seventh Street. In the front hall, a dark wood
receptionist's desk and a couple of leather chairs
looked as if they'd wandered in from an English
men's club. In the small back room overlooking the
garden, the room that served as Hallie's office, a
Chinese rug, a Georgian desk, and a couple of Queen
Ann chairs gave the same impression. Both rooms
were lined with bookshelves waiting to be filled with
Unicorn Books. The large area between, divided into
cubicles for the rest of the staff, was regulation
metal and plastic. It resembled half the offices across
America and might have handled the paperwork for
shoes or basketballs or widgets. But the reception
area and back room set the tone. They told you
something lofty and possibly discomforting was
going on, though it was going on in a comfortable
setting.

Unicorn Books had been in residence for less than
a month when Sheila came into Hallie's office one

morning and announced she was having lunch with
Olivia. 'Any advice?'

'Keep your back to the wall at all times and you
may survive.' Hallie stopped thinking about the
manuscript she'd been skimming and considered the
question again. 'How come you two are having
lunch? You weren't exactly a team at R and S.'

'I've been trying to figure it out myself.'

'She's after something.'

'What?'

'What do you have she might want?' Only after the
words were out did Hallie realize they were the same
ones Quentin had used about Jake years earlier.
Quentin had been right. And now she was sure she
was on to something too.

'Maybe she just wants to find out what's going on
over here,' Sheila said. 'What you're signing. Stuff
like that.'

It was the obvious answer. The only problem was
that if Olivia's style was obvious, her motives were
anything but. 'Just be careful,' Hallie warned.

'Don't worry,' Sheila said on her way out of
Hallie's office. 'I won't give away any state secrets.'

'I'm not worried,' Hallie called after her. 'We don't
have any state secrets. Yet.'

Olivia didn't ask for any. She talked about R and
S over white-wine spritzers. Jonathan still hadn't
appointed a publisher. She talked about her personal
life over their salads. It was finished with Jake. She
asked how things were going at the new house over
coffee. She said she supposed they were pretty
busy.

'Everyone else is,' Sheila said. 'But you can't do publicity if you don't have any books to publicize. Our first pub date isn't until next fall.'

'You managed to get a lot of press on the house itself. I haven't been able to pick up a newspaper or magazine without reading about Unicorn Books. I hope Hallie realizes what a dynamite job you've done.'

'Hallie's fair,' Sheila admitted.

Olivia laughed. 'You're quoting me, honey. That's exactly what I told the interviewer from *Time*. Remember when that piece ran? "Hallie Porter is demanding but fair." It's the party line.'

'It's true.' Sheila believed in loyalty. She also didn't trust Olivia. Whatever Sheila said would be used against her. Besides, Hallie was fair. The fact that she was also demanding, sometimes impossibly so, had nothing to do with it.

'Still . . .' Olivia sipped her espresso. 'You've got to keep the name in the spotlight until the books begin coming out. You can't let agents and writers and reviewers forget there is a Unicorn Books.'

'I'm not worried. Hallie's got a terrific reputation. She's a terrific editor.'

Olivia put down her coffee cup and looked at Sheila with wide eyes. 'That's it!'

'What's it?'

'You know those articles they run in the *Times* magazine section on the creative process?'

'Sure.'

'What about one on Amos and Hallie? A piece on the dual creative process. Writing and editing.'

'It's not a bad idea.'

'It's a great idea. I wish I'd thought of it.'

Sheila's round shiny face broke into a smile. Did Olivia think she was an idiot? 'You did think of it, Olivia. And don't worry. I won't forget. I owe you one.'

Sheila didn't bother mentioning the article to Hallie. There was no point promising something she couldn't deliver. As soon as she got back to the office, she called one of her contacts at the *Times*. The contact said it was an interesting idea. He'd get back to Sheila.

He didn't. Like most journalists, he distrusted public-relations flacks. He called Hallie.

'Everyone over here thinks its a great idea,' he said. 'The collaborative creative process.'

'It's not collaborative. Amos Porter is the writer. All do is publish him.'

'Are you saying you don't touch his manuscripts? They go straight from his word processor to production?'

Hallie heard another article building in the man's mind. Why Editors Don't Edit. 'I'm saying that the creative process is his. I just make a few suggestions here and there.'

'You don't win the Max Perkins Prize for making a few suggestions.'

'Amos Porter doesn't like publicity.'

The man just laughed.

'All right,' Hallie agreed. 'I'll talk to him about the idea, but I can't promise anything.'

'I have a better idea. I'll talk to him. I'm sure I can persuade him.'

The man from the *Times* didn't waste any time. Amos was back on the phone to Hallie in minutes.

'What do you want to do about this article?' he asked.

'Get out of it.'

'It's good publicity.'

'You don't need the publicity.'

'That's true, but you do.'

'I'd feel like such a hypocrite. I haven't done a thing to that manuscript. I haven't even seen this draft.'

'There's no point until I'm finished.'

'You showed it to Jake.'

'Only because the magazine and movie people were breathing down his neck.'

'Sure,' Hallie said, but she wasn't going to argue. She'd let Amos down once. She didn't blame him for not turning to her now. 'But that's one of the reasons I think we ought to cool this article.'

Amos said she was right to take the high moral ground.

Hallie didn't explain that she had no choice. If she gave that interview, she'd not only feel like a hypocrite, she'd look like a fool. How could she talk about editing Amos Porter when she'd never even moved a comma, let alone helped shape a novel?

'I'll promise him an interview when the book is out,' Hallie said.

* * *

The second time Olivia called and suggested lunch, Sheila wasn't even surprised. She'd told Olivia that first time that she owed her one. Sheila suspected Olivia wanted to collect. The only question was what she wanted to collect.

If Olivia wanted a favor, she didn't ask it at lunch. They talked business. They talked books. They gossiped about agents and editors and writers. By the time coffee came, Sheila was beginning to believe that Olivia just wanted a friend. Olivia had said the last time that it was all over with Jake. Sheila watched Olivia stir a piece of lemon peel in her espresso. Olivia was still gorgeous, but as Sheila knew, there was a whole new crop of gorgeous young women coming up. Sheila didn't consider herself vindictive, but she found a certain satisfaction in the idea of Olivia Collins's loneliness.

'Did you ever do anything about that article we discussed?' Olivia asked as she signaled the waiter for the check. 'The one on Hallie and Amos?'

Sheila said she'd pitched the idea but hadn't heard any more about it.

Olivia asked whom Sheila had talked to. Sheila told her.

'Do you know him?' Sheila asked.

Fortunately for Olivia, she did.

The man from the *Times* would say only that Hallie and Amos Porter had refused to be interviewed until the book came out. Even when Olivia ordered a third round of drinks, he wouldn't say more than that.

'I wonder why they're being so secretive,' Olivia said.

'They're not being secretive. They just want to milk it. You know the reasoning as well as I do. All the attention in the world won't sell books unless the books are in the stores. And his next one won't be in the stores for a while.'

'Normally I'd agree with you. But were hawking more than a book here. Hallie could use the publicity. Unicorn Books could.'

'I hear she's doing pretty well.'

'Not so well that she couldn't do better. No, I think there's a reason she's refusing to talk.'

The man had finished his third drink and leaned forward in his chair as if he were about to get up. Now he settled back again. 'Such as?'

'Did you ever wonder why Amos Porter disqualified himself as a Max Perkins judge?'

'Because he was the father of one of the candidates.'

'That's what he said. But that candidate also happens to be his editor. No one was going to object to his voting for his own editor. If she is his editor.'

'What are you getting at?'

Now Olivia was the one who leaned forward as if she were about to stand. 'I really don't think I ought to say any more. I used to work with Hallie. With both of them, really.' She hesitated, to let that one sink in. 'I mean, it would be like telling tales out of school.'

'Are you saying Hallie Porter's just the front? She doesn't edit the old man's work?'

357

Olivia didn't bother to answer that one. She knew she didn't have to. The world at large didn't give a damn about who edited Amos Porter's novels or whether they were edited at all. The paper of record that printed all the news that was fit to print didn't deem innuendo news fit to print. But the publishing industry was another story. It had taken only a few drinks and a couple of well-placed words to start the rumors. It would take a lot more than that to kill them.

The first mention appeared in a column. Three brief lines about the real editor behind Amos Porter.

Olivia called the columnist. 'How did you get that?' she demanded.

The columnist said she never divulged her sources.

'I hope you realize you're wrecking a career.' Olivia sounded as if she were close to tears.

'Hallie Porter's career isn't that fragile.'

'I wasn't talking about Hallie Porter's career.' Now it was a wail. 'I was talking about mine. No one in the business will ever trust me again.'

The second item ran a few days later. It was no more than a question. Was it true that Hallie Porter took the credit while her assistants did the work? No particular assistant was mentioned.

Olivia called the columnist again. 'For God's sake!' she screamed. 'Why didn't you just mention me by name? Everyone knows whom you're talking about anyway.'

The third item ran two days later. 'The publishing biz is wondering if the prestigious Maxwell Perkins

Prize shouldn't have gone to Olivia Collins. Amos Porter, who ought to know, is keeping mum.'

Amos was the only one who was. At lunches and dinners, in offices and conference rooms, people were speculating.

'I always said Hallie Porter got where she is on her father's coattails.'

'Better than getting there on her back,' a woman who didn't particularly like Hallie but hated Olivia said.

'Quentin Styles was the brains of R and S. Hallie Porter was nothing more than a figurehead.'

'And when Quentin left, Olivia Collins took over the real work while Hallie Porter kept getting the glory.'

The voices of dissent grew fewer and fainter. Most editors and agents and writers and reviewers adhered to an age-old law of nature. Where there's smoke, there must be a fire.

XXXVIII

When Olivia heard Quentin's voice on the phone, she surprised herself. She knew the smart thing to do. You didn't hold a man's interest by sulking. You didn't convince him to put in a word for you by whining. But she couldn't help herself. It wasn't the first time Quentin had had that effect on her. The words were out before she realized it.

'I thought you were going to call me when you got back.'

He listed a series of trips that had followed the one to Hong Kong. She let it go. It was bad enough she'd slipped once. She wasn't going to turn into a nag.

'Well, wherever you were, I'm glad you're back,' she said with the old brashness. 'I missed you, honey.'

'Me or my influence? I understand Jonathan still hasn't appointed a publisher.'

'Both.'

He laughed. 'At least no one can accuse you of hypocrisy. It might interest you to know that Jonathan is flying east tomorrow. He wants to see you.'

She closed her eyes and pressed her lips together in prayer. 'Has he made up his mind?'

'Not quite, but he's getting close.'

'Is that all you're going to tell me?'

'He's impressed, but he's not convinced. It's up to you to convince him.'

She was silent. He could hear the wheels spinning.

'Not the way you convinced me, Olivia. I don't think Jonathan's interested.'

'I wasn't –'

'It's all right,' he went on before she could finish. 'Or, rather, it's not all right, but I don't want to talk about that now. Just play it straight with Jonathan and you'll be fine.

'Anything else?'

'Yes. He's flying east tomorrow. I'll be there the day after.'

She said she'd be waiting.

When Quentin got off the phone, he sat in his corner office of the Century City headquarters of Allied Entertainment thinking about his conversation with Olivia. 'It's all right,' he'd told her when she'd mistaken his meaning about her and Jonathan Graham. 'Or, rather, it's not all right, but I don't want to talk about that now.'

He told himself he was a fool. There was no point in talking about it now or ever. Men and women who went around trying to reform each other were asking for disappointment. Worse than that, they were asking for humiliation. Every instinct told him it was impossible. Then he thought of a recent evening and knew he had no choice.

Quentin hadn't lied to Olivia entirely. He had been traveling a lot for the past eight weeks. But he'd also been in New York several times. Each time he'd thought of calling her, then changed his mind. He was grateful to Olivia. But that didn't mean he had to make her a permanent part of his new life. Or so he'd thought until a week before.

He'd gone to a dinner party in Beverly Hills. An actress who'd just finished shooting a movie for World Pictures had been seated on his right. There was nothing unusual about that. The problem wasn't that the party had been similar to hundreds of others he'd gone to over the years. The problem was that it had been exactly like the one he'd gone to at the house of that politician's widow. How long ago was that now? Since he'd met Olivia he'd stopped counting. Since that night in Beverly Hills he'd begun calculating from a new date.

He didn't want to make too much of it. Olivia wasn't the only woman in the world who aroused him. She just happened to be the only one he'd gone to bed with in the last two years.

This time the sun was a garish orange ball over the Hudson beyond Jonathan Graham's window. From where Olivia sat facing him, it almost blinded her.

They'd been talking for half an hour. She'd answered questions, solved theoretical problems, sidestepped traps, and showed her smarts as she never had in her life. If Jonathan didn't want her, he was crazy. If Jonathan didn't choose her, she'd be devastated.

'Well . . .' He leaned back in his tall swivel chair and made a steeple of his long fingers. 'You make some interesting points.'

Interesting! She'd given him stuff he wouldn't hear outside the Harvard B. School.

'I'm impressed.'

She listened carefully. Was there a but in his voice?

'Others are, too. Quentin thinks you're the woman for the job.'

She fought to keep her face impassive.

'Hallie said you could handle it.'

'I bet.'

He stopped tapping the tips of his fingers together. 'What?'

Olivia regrouped. 'I meant, of course I can handle it.'

He went on staring at her for a minute. To Olivia it felt like the better part of a decade.

'I'm not so sure,' he said finally.

The breath Olivia had been holding went out of her in exhaustion.

'But I'm going to give you a chance.'

Air came rushing back into her lungs and sent her sky high.

George let her into the duplex. He said Mr Styles's plane was late, but Mr Styles had telephoned and said that she was to make herself comfortable. He asked if she'd like a drink.

You bet I would, buster, she thought. 'I'd like that

very much,' she said. 'Vodka,' she added.

There was a hard glint in George's eyes. What had he expected her to ask for. A boilermaker?

He asked if she'd rather wait in the living room or the library. She chose the library. It held some nice memories.

When Quentin arrived, she was still sitting in the chair they'd been in that first morning.

'I spoke to Jonathan from the car on the way in,' Quentin said. 'I understand congratulations are in order.'

She stood, crossed the room, and put her arms around his neck. 'How can I ever thank you?'

His hands ran down her body. 'I imagine we'll think of a way. We usually do.'

That was how Olivia finally got to see the second floor of a twelve-room Fifth Avenue duplex.

The article in the *Times* announcing Olivia's appointment was shorter than the one that had reported Hallie's departure. It said that Olivia Collins was the new publisher of Rutherford and Styles, mentioned where she'd worked before, and listed a few of her authors. Olivia had given all the information in a phone interview. When the reporter had asked for the names of some of her leading writers, Olivia had mentioned Carter Bolton and several others. Then she'd hesitated a moment. Jonathan Graham had said he wasn't certain she could do the job, but he was going to give her a chance. He'd named her publisher. Now she had to prove she was one. She had to woo the superauthors and win the megabooks. For that she'd be up against publishers with bigger reputations and better connections. Publishers like Hallie. Olivia thought of the other thing Jonathan had said. She didn't for a minute believe that Hallie had recommended her for the job. She didn't owe Hallie anything.

Olivia went back to listing some of her more important authors. 'And Am – no, forget I said that.' Unfortunately the reporter had.

The woman from *Publishers Weekly*, the trade magazine, was more persistent. 'Do you mean Amos Porter?' she asked when Olivia hesitated after the first syllable again. This interview was taking place in Olivia's new office, which had been Hallie's and before that Quentin's.

'I really can't discuss that,' Olivia said.

'But you must be aware of the rumors. About how you do the editorial work and Hallie Porter takes the credit.'

'Hallie Porter is an old and dear friend. She's also an excellent editor.'

'Then you're saying there's no truth to the rumors?'

'No comment.'

'Would you like to edit Amos Porter?'

'What editor in her right mind wouldn't?' Olivia launched into a discussion of Amos Porter's greatness. *A Woman's Story* was brilliant, she said, but this new one, *Portrait of a Marriage*, was even better. She talked about the character development, the structure, the power and poetry of the story.

'Obviously you're familiar with the manuscript.'

Olivia shifted in her chair as if she were uncomfortable. 'Of course, everything I've just said is strictly off the record.'

The woman went back to her office and called Hallie. She said she was doing an article on works in progress. Could Hallie tell her something about what the greatest American writer working today was actually working on?

Hallie said she couldn't.

'You mean you don't know?'

'I mean Mr Porter doesn't like to discuss work in progress.'

The article in *Publishers Weekly* on the new publisher of Rutherford and Styles was much longer than the one in the *Times*. It discussed Olivia's philosophy of publishing. It talked about her plans for R and S. It mentioned some of her star authors. Amos Porter fell into that category. The article never actually came out and said she was his editor. It just mentioned her enthusiasm for his next book, which was peculiar, since his next book would be published not by Rutherford and Styles but by Unicorn Books. The last line reported that Hallie Porter, Amos Porter's editor, refused to comment on the book. It was a simple statement absolutely libel proof. But everyone in the business knew what it meant.

XXXIX

Most people in the industry read *Publishers Weekly* to keep up with their profession. Cecelia Porter read it for the same reason, only her profession was her husband and her daughter.

She closed the latest issue, picked up the phone, and dialed Hallie's number. The secretary said Hallie was on another line. Cecelia said she'd wait. While she did, she flipped open the magazine and read the last paragraph of the article again. She fought the urge to throw it against the wall. Hallie hurled magazines. Amos threw typewriters. Someone in the family had to remain in control.

'How bad is it?' Cecelia asked when Hallie got on the line.

'The article drew blood. Now the sharks are circling.'

'I think Amos ought to make a statement. He thinks we ought to ignore the whole thing.'

Hallie looked at the lights flashing on her phone. 'Easy for him to say, locked away in his study.'

'My point exactly. Stop by for a drink tonight. We'll hash this thing out.' When danger threatened, Cecelia circled the wagons.

After she hung up the phone, she stared at it for a moment, then picked it up again. She dialed Jake's number. Hallie couldn't object. After all, Jake was Amos's agent.

Hallie stopped in the doorway to the library. Her mother sat at one end of the long leather sofa, Jake at the other. They were both beautifully dressed, Cecelia in trousers and an oversized silk shirt, Jake in impeccably cut pin stripe. They were both lightly tanned. They looked like an ad for clothing or vodka or *Money* magazine.

'I didn't know it was a party,' Hallie said.

'I thought Jake might be able to help,' Cecelia explained.

Hallie moved to the bar and began making herself a drink. 'I don't think I can afford any more help from Jake.'

'What's that supposed to mean?' he asked.

Hallie took her drink and sat in one of the club chairs opposite them. 'You're the smart agent. You figure it out.'

'You don't think I had anything to do with that piece?' Jake was incredulous.

'How else did Olivia find out about Amos's next book?'

Jake put his drink down. 'Let me get this straight. You think I gave Amos's manuscript to Olivia?'

'I don't think Amos did. And you are his agent.'

'Which means I saw it. But I didn't pass it on. Amos said he didn't want anyone to see it yet. Hell, I didn't even send it to you, Hallie. Why would I give it to Olivia?'

'You don't really want me to answer that.'

'I did not give her the manuscript.' He spaced the words as if he were taking aim with gun shots. She knew he was furious. That made two of them.

'You're not being fair,' Cecelia said, then caught herself. That was the terrible thing about being a mother. Sometimes you wanted to protect them, others to shake some sense into them. It was too late for either.

'All right,' Hallie conceded. 'Maybe you didn't give her the manuscript. Maybe you just left it in your briefcase or' – she paused for emphasis – 'on the night table.'

'I haven't seen Olivia in a couple of months.' He watched it sink in.

That was what Olivia had told Sheila. Hallie hadn't believe Olivia. She was afraid to believe Jake.

'All that proves is that she read it a while ago.'

'Damnit, Hallie –' He took a deep breath. 'Listen, I didn't give Olivia Amos's manuscript. I didn't leave it around for her to find. And I didn't come here to fight.'

'What did you come here for?'

'To help.'

'Aw, shucks. And I didn't bring any Brownie points to pass out.'

'Hallie!' Cecelia couldn't help it. 'You're not being fair.'

Hallie's face swiveled to her mother. 'The world isn't fair. Out there, beyond these beautifully paneled walls, the world is unfair as hell. But then that's something you wouldn't know about.'

Cecelia didn't answer, and the three of them sat in silence for a moment. Hallie picked up her drink. The ice rattled noisily. 'I'm sorry. I didn't mean to take it out on you.'

'I'm sure you didn't mean to take it out on either of us,' Cecelia said.

'The point is,' Jake began, 'there's a simple way out of all this. As long as there was nothing more than those plants in the columns, we couldn't fight back.'

'*We* don't have to fight back. *I* do.'

He stopped and looked at her for a moment. 'Let's not start that again.'

Hallie didn't answer.

'The point is, now that there's been something in *PW*, Amos can clarify things. All he has to do is make a statement.'

'Does someone want to tell me what kind of a statement I'm supposed to make?' Amos stepped into the room. He seemed to take up a lot of space.

'You know what kind of statement you're supposed to make. I told you at lunch.' Cecelia softened her voice. She knew her husband and the best way to deal with him. 'There's a pitcher of martinis on the bar, darling.'

Amos moved to the bar and poured himself a drink. 'And I told you at lunch, Cecelia. I refuse to dignify that article or the rumors by replying to them.' He carried his drink to the other chair and arranged his large frame in it. 'If we just sit tight and ignore the whole incident, it'll blow over in a couple of day's or a week.'

'That's easy for you to say, sitting up there in your study, locked away from all the mess.' Jake's words cut a small chink in Hallie's armor. They made her remember the times when she and Jake had thought alike. 'Hallie has to go out and face people.'

'Jake's right, darling,' Cecelia said.

'Hallie can fight her own battles. She always has.'

'Maybe this time she could use some help.'

Amos turned to Jake. 'I think it's a little late for you to play the protector. In fact, I think it's damn peculiar for you to be here at all.'

'He's your agent,' Cecelia said.

'I'm not aware of any contracts that need negotiating at the moment.'

'I thought that if you didn't want to make a statement yourself, you could issue it through Jake.'

'You thought wrong, Cecelia.'

Cecelia stared at her husband. She knew him when he got like this, and she usually let it go. But then it usually didn't concern Hallie.

'Just tell me one thing, Amos. Why do you refuse to make a simple statement that would clear Hallie's reputation?'

'I have my reasons.'

'In other words, you refuse to answer on the grounds that it might incriminate you.'

'You'll just have to trust me.'

'Not this time.'

That was when it came to Jake. At first he pushed the thought away. It didn't make sense. Why would

Amos give his manuscript to Olivia? He thought of the reason men usually did things for Olivia. Jake knew it was possible, but he didn't think it was likely. He wasn't saying Amos had never been unfaithful. Jake had seen pictures of him as a young man. Sun glinted off a smile that had been shiny and dangerous as a knife, and there was the hint of a swagger even in the still photographs. The pictures suggested a man intensely aware of women and his effect on them. But that had been a long time ago. It wasn't that Jake thought his father-in-law was too old for lust or even passion. It was just that Jake had never picked up any of the signs, and Jake was sensitive to the signs, especially these days. He was pretty sure Amos hadn't slept with Olivia. As sure as he was that Amos had given her his manuscript. And he knew one more thing. Olivia had edited it. There was truth to the rumors.

Jake felt a flash of pleasure. He hated himself for it, but he couldn't help it. Hallie wasn't perfect. She was flawed and human and – the thought almost propelled him off the sofa and across the room to her – in need.

Jake turned from Hallie to Amos. 'You gave Olivia your manuscript, didn't you?'

Amos's eyes slid to Jake.

'You did, didn't you?'

'I don't see how this concerns you.'

'Did you?' Cecelia asked.

Amos still didn't answer. By that time, he didn't have to.

'But why?' Cecelia's voice was shrill with disbelief.

'I had my reasons.'

'Your reasons!' she began, but Hallie cut her off.

'He gave it to Olivia because he needed an editor, and I couldn't handle it. I couldn't hack it. I was a bust. A failure. Incompetent. The winner of the Max Perkins Prize for editorial excellence can't edit.'

'Stop it,' Cecelia said.

'Sorry.' Hallie stood. 'I forgot.' She took a step toward the door. 'In this family, we maintain our dignity at all costs.' She saw them staring up at her. The outlines of their faces shimmered and waved. Damnit! She'd sworn she wasn't going to cry. The blur that was Jake was coming toward her. She turned and started down the hall.

'Hallie,' she heard and 'wait,' and other meaningless sounds of superiority. Poor Hallie. Pathetic Hallie. Don't we all feel sorry for her.

She kept going. He caught up with her and put a hand on her shoulder. She wrenched away.

'I don't want your pity.'

'It's not pity.'

She turned back to him. His image was still wavy. 'The hell it's not!' She grabbed her briefcase and wrenched open the front door.

'Hallie,' he pleaded.

She slammed the door on the sound.

Cecelia sat staring at her husband. Amos sat staring at the wall of books with his name on them. He didn't dare meet her eyes.

'You could still make a statement,' Cecelia said.

'It would be dishonest.'

'It would save Hallie.'

'Women have no sense of morality.' He spoke quietly, as if he were taking to himself, but he wasn't talking to himself. He was trying to reestablish his position.

'I suppose you're right,' Cecelia said. 'If morality means breaking your daughter's heart.'

XL

Amos was right. The gossip flared for a week or so, then died down. By Memorial Day weekend when the book business traditionally gathers to clinch deals, hawk next season's blockbusters, overindulge appetites, and commit indiscretions – in other words, hold a convention – people had stopped talking about the scandal surrounding Hallie Porter. Of course, by that time, people had pretty much stopped talking about Hallie Porter. What was there to say? The first releases from Unicorn Books were still in the future. The Max Perkins Prize was in the past. People who came to Hallie's office admired the bronze plaque hanging over the mantle, but fewer people were coming to Hallie's office these days. She was no longer at the heart of the industry. She admitted she no longer had the money to bid against the big houses like Rutherford and Styles for the major books. Others whispered she no longer had the nerve.

Hallie knew what they were saying. She managed to ignore the rumors in New York. She knew she'd have to confront them at the convention in San Francisco.

377

For years she'd been grumbling that she hated the American Booksellers Association Convention. Everyone grumbled. The complaints were as much a part of the convention as the garish publishers' booths, the wandering booksellers with bags full of handouts, and the smell of hot dogs and orange drinks that, like everything else about the ABA, smacked more of a circus than a literary gathering. Even the swankier events, the intimate lunches in overpriced restaurants and the exclusive parties in buildings of local historic interest, had the aura of a carnival. Hype was the language, excess the style. Normally moderate men and women stayed up too late, drank too much, and said and did things they'd later deny or at least regret. Like everyone else in the business, Hallie had always complained about ABA conventions. But she'd never dreaded one.

As soon as she checked into the hotel, she knew her fear wasn't unfounded. Olivia had taken a suite at the Four Seasons. The rest of her entourage took up most of the rest of the eighth floor. Jake was staying at the Campton Place, which was less well known and even more exclusive. There was nothing wrong with Hallie's hotel, except the two threadbare towels in the ancient bathroom, the tiny overfurnished bedroom that she couldn't cross without stubbing her toe or hitting her shin, and the other guests who all wore the same shamed look of having been caught there. The hotel reminded her of the first ABA she'd ever attended, but then Jake and Olivia had been staying at the same seedy place, and they'd raced up ad down the halls to each other's airless rooms sharing gossip and expense accounts and word of the best parties.

Hallie overtipped the elderly stooped bellboy who'd needed three attempts to get her hanging bag into the closet bar. So much for Unicorn Books's austerity program. Then she took a cab to the convention center.

It wasn't a carnival, it was bedlam. People queued up to get name tags, and collect handouts, and meet famous authors, and buy cold hot dogs and warm soda. Thousands came for the fun of it, a handful to do deals. Hallie recognized the faces. She also sensed the change. At one time the power brokers – editors and agents, sub-rights directors and foreign publishers – would have gravitated to her as if she were a magnetic force. 'Lunch,' they would have murmured. 'A drink?' they would have asked. 'I've got something you've got to see,' they would have promised. 'What's the chance my getting an early look at that property?' they would have pleaded. Now they merely smiled and nodded. A year before they would have left lesser mortals hanging in midsentence to speak to her. Now she wasn't worth crossing a few feet of convention floor to meet.

She made her way past the elaborate display booths of the major houses. Apogee Books had set up a miniature ice rink to promote the memoirs of an Olympic gold-medal winner. Slater House had installed a small kitchen where a four-star chef turned out wild mushroom and truffle canapés. Rutherford and Styles had settled for a plastic jungle where the last of the Great White Hunters autographed copies of his memoirs. Off in a corner Olivia was talking to Jonathan Graham. Neither of them noticed Hallie as she hurried past.

Unicorn Books's booth, if you could call it that, was crowded into the area reserved for small, independent publishers, otherwise known as Siberia. There was a long table covered with galleys and jackets of books Hallie would publish next fall, a backdrop with the Unicorn logo, and pictures of Amos Porter and Will Sawyer. Her two star authors, Hallie explained to conventioneers who stopped at the booth. Her father and lover, those who didn't stop snickered.

A few of the power brokers drifted over out of curiosity, one or two out of loyalty, a handful out of prudence. They weren't putting any money on Hallie Porter, but they weren't writing her off either.

Jackie Kay belonged to the last group. Her agency was getting hotter by the minute. She represented Will Sawyer now and a handful of other established names as well as the stable she'd built herself. Jackie was a leggy woman given to wild black hair, flamboyant clothes, and awkward accidents. The first time Hallie had taken her to lunch, Jackie had spilled her drink on Hallie's suit. The second time, Jackie had caught the tablecloth in her wide hand-tooled leather belt and practically overturned the table when she'd stood. But Jackie was no ditz. She had an unerring eye for promising young writers. She had an uncanny ability to put the right authors and editors together. And she was a mean negotiator. Hallie respected Jackie Kay. She also liked Jackie

Kay. And that afternoon, standing in her meager little booth with sore feet and an aching smile, she was overjoyed to see Jackie Kay.

They made the usual comments about the ice rink and the kitchen and the jungle. They lamented the death of art and the triumph of commerce. They swapped stories of editors changing houses as if they were playing musical chairs. Hallie was just beginning to feel like a publisher again, or at least a person, when an editor from Campbell and Grainer swept down on them and carried Jackie off.

Hallie had one other visitor from the old guard that day. Two if you counted Jake, but she wasn't counting Jake.

'You okay?' he asked as he stood looking at the tiny booth.

Hallie suddenly saw the dream of her own publishing house for the childish fantasy it was.

'Why shouldn't I be okay?'

'No reason. You just look a little tired.'

What he meant, of course, was that she looked like hell. She'd planned to have her linen suit pressed, but the hotel didn't have a valet service. And she'd been so rattled this morning she'd forgotten to put a lipstick in her purse.

'I'm fine,' she snapped. 'Never better.'

His eyes slid from her to the picture of Will Sawyer on the wall behind her. 'Glad to hear it,' he answered in the same tone, then turned and walked away.

Quentin showed up about an hour later. Hallie was surprised. Quentin hadn't come to an ABA in years. It wasn't that they were in questionable taste, he used to say. They were in execrable taste. But then as Hallie knew from the night she'd stood outside the closed door of Quentin's office and a rumor she'd heard recently, Quentin's tastes were coming more eclectic.

'What on earth are you doing here?' she asked.

'I happened to be in town, so I thought I'd stop by. How're you holding up?'

She didn't have the energy to lie to him. 'Now I know how the ancient Christians felt in the Coliseum.'

'Come on. Close up shop and I'll buy you a drink.'

She was just about to accept when he glanced at his watch. 'Unless you have to get back to your hotel to change. I understand that black-tie dinner at the Campton Place starts early.'

'I wasn't invited.'

Quentin didn't miss a beat. 'Terrific,' he said, though they both knew it wasn't at all terrific. 'Then we have time for a drink.'

They went to the Top of the Mark. 'Are we playing tourist?' Hallie asked.

'We're waxing nostalgic,' Quentin said as he held her chair out for her. They ordered drinks.

'Amos and I came here the night before we shipped out for the Pacific.'

'But you never fought in the Pacific.'

'That's right, but we didn't know we wouldn't have to the night we came here. We were that sure we were going to buy it over there. Can you imagine what it felt like? We'd been in the war in Europe. We'd survived the Battle of the Bulge. We thought we were safe. Then the generals decided they had another job for us. You haven't got kids, they said. You haven't even got wives. Just a couple of girls waiting for you to come home. You're the men for the job.'

'So the two of you came here and got drunk.'

'To put it as ineloquently as possible, we got fried. We sat here from four in the afternoon until closing time. We watched the fog lift and the bridge come creeping out of it and another fog settle and the sky grow dark and we just kept drinking. But the funny thing was, Hallie, it never went away. We drank and we drank and we drank, but the fear and the misery and the anger never went away. At least not until we got the news aboard ship. The war in the Pacific was over, and we were going home after all.'

'It must have been like a reprieve.'

He looked past her to the Golden Gate Bridge that was beginning to emerge from the fog, just as Quentin said it had that night when he and Amos had sat there looking out into infinity, or may it was only death.

'It was more than a reprieve. It was a second chance at life.' Quentin finished his drink and signaled the waiter for another round. 'I suppose you think I'm maudlin.'

'There's nothing maudlin about wanting to live. I'm glad you told me the story.'

'It wasn't just the aimless musings of a doddering old man.'

She leaned over and patted his hand. 'I know it wasn't.'

'I mean, I told you the story for a reason.'

Hallie had a feeling she knew the reason. Quentin was running interference. He was telling her she oughtn't be so hard on Amos. She ought to give him a second chance.

'I wanted to speak to you, Hallie. To make you understand.'

'I understand,' she said, though she wasn't sure she did. No matter which way she looked at it, Amos's act still seemed like betrayal.

'It's rare enough for a man to get a second chance at life. It's practically unheard of for him to get a third.'

'Let's not be melodramatic, Quent.' He really was making too much of it. She'd been furious at her father, and now she was trying to forgive him. It wasn't what she'd call another chance at life.

He shook his head. 'You're right. I'd better watch it, or I really will turn into a sentimental old ass. The kind I've always laughed at. You know what I've started doing? I've started clipping things from the paper.'

'You always clipped news articles and columns and stuff. You're the one who taught me to. Sometimes they lead to good book ideas.'

'That's not the kind of clipping I'm talking about.' He reached into his pocket and pulled out a scrap of paper. 'This is the kind of thing I'm clipping now. And the worst part of it is, I'm not even ashamed.' He handed it to her.

The room was growing darker, and she had to lean toward the candle in the center of the table to read it. It was one of those fillers newspapers run. What happened in history on this day. Sports records. Household hints. This one was headlined 'Proverb for the Day.' Underneath it were two lines. 'An old man in love is like a flower in winter.'

The words swam before her eyes, but everything else fell into focus. That night she'd stood outside the closed door to Quentin's office. The rumor she'd heard back in New York. The new chance at life.

She dropped the paper. It fluttered into the candle, flamed briefly, and shriveled.

Quentin looked from the charred scrap of paper to Hallie. 'I guess you don't understand after all.'

'Let me get this straight. You're telling me you're in love, in love' – her voice climbed so that the couple at the next table glanced over, then quickly away – 'with Olivia.'

'I know it sounds ridiculous.'

'Ridiculous! It sounds a hell of a lot worse than that. It sounds stupid. Dumb. Senile, for God's sake.'

'Why? Because she's too young?'

'Not because she's too young. She could be in diapers for all I care, if I thought you really loved her. Or that she was capable of loving you. Face it, Quent, you're screwing her. I understand that's quite an experience. But you're the one who's going to get screwed in the end.'

'Are you finished?'

'Not by a long shot, but I can see it isn't going to do any good.'

'You're right. It's not. I know what you're saying,

Hallie. I even know some of it's true. Olivia's done some pretty awful things.'

'Aw, come on, Quent, don't damn with faint praise. Olivia is an unmitigated bitch.'

'Was.'

'You're telling me she's changed?'

'I'm telling you she's beginning to. At least around me.'

Hallie stood. He started to get out of his chair, but she put her hand on his shoulder. She remained that way for a moment, staring down at him with her hand on his shoulder.

'I knew you were having an affair with Olivia. I suspected it that day at your club when you told me not to fire her.'

'I did that for you, not her,' he insisted.

'Maybe. And I was sure of it the night of Amos's party, when I went to your office to get you.'

At least he had the good grace to drop his eyes at that.

'I was furious at you then. I felt you'd betrayed me and gone over to the enemy. But I'm not angry at you anymore. I couldn't be.'

He put his hand over hers on his shoulder and met her eyes again. 'I knew you'd understand.'

'I might as well be angry at a child.' She patted his shoulder. 'Or a mental defective.'

Hallie told herself she was glad she didn't have a dinner appointment. She wasn't up to putting on an act, and the last thing she wanted was food. What she wanted was another drink. She thought of her father and Quentin sitting at the Top of the Mark all those years ago, looking out over their uncertain future. What she wanted was a lot of drinks.

There was a small lounge off the lobby of her hotel. She took a chair in the corner. The upholstery was torn. Stuffing spilled out of it like guts. The cheap wood table was pitted and scarred. Hallie ordered a drink.

'Do you come here a lot?'

She looked up before she realized it was a mistake. A beefy face with a sweat-glistened forehead and a droopy black handlebar mustache grinned over at her. She stared back in amazement. He couldn't really be talking to her.

'I said, do you come here a lot.' The grin grew wider. He seemed to think he'd said something clever.

'Not bloody likely. It's a long commute from New York.'

A simple no would have been more effective. The beefy face took the information as a come-on. The soft, fat body picked up a can of beer and slid into the chair opposite Hallie. He held out a meaty hand. The fingernails were black. 'Name's Ron.'

She looked from the hand to the face. 'I'm going to count to three,' she said. 'If you're not out of that chair by then, I'm going to scream.'

'Hey, I was just –'

'One.'

'Okay.'

'Two.'

He picked up his beer and carried it across the room to a table in the far corner.

It should have been funny. It should have been one of those stories she and Olivia used to laugh at. Only it wasn't funny. It was pathetic. It was worse than that. It was scary.

Olivia was at a black-tie dinner at the Campton Place. Quentin was back at Olivia's suite at the Four Seasons. God only knew where Jake was or with whom. All over the city people were eating and drinking, cutting deals and making love. If she closed her eyes she could hear the clink of ice in glasses and hear the words of promise, she could smell the enchantment and taste the success. But her eyes were open, and she was sitting alone in the tacky bar of a seedy second-rate hotel, easy prey for any on-the-make tourist. She signaled the waitress for another drink. She was all those things, and what was worse, no one in the world gave a damn. She wasn't even sure she did anymore.

Hallie was taking the red-eye home on Tuesday night. So, judging from the mob of familiar faces crowding around the boarding gate, was half the publishing industry. She took the early edition of the next morning's *San Francisco Chronicle* from her briefcase and opened it wide instead of folding it into a more manageable shape as she usually did when she read a paper in a crowd. That way she could hide behind it. There was no one she wanted to see. More important, she didn't want anyone to see her. She'd had enough humiliation. She was glad now that Will hadn't come to San Francisco with her. As his publisher, she didn't want to lose his confidence. As his lover, she didn't want to lose his respect.

A disembodied voice announced that TWA Flight 143 would be boarding in a few minutes. Over the top of the paper, Hallie spotted Jackie Kay. What was worse, Jackie spotted her. It was too late to hide. Jackie collapsed into the seat beside her. She managed to overturn her handbag as she did.

'Don't worry,' Jackie said. 'I feel as tired as you look. I don't want to talk. I just wanted to tell you that I was thinking of you last night. I'm going to send you a manuscript as soon as we get back. It's a first novel, and I think it's perfect for you.'

Hallie read the subtext. It's a minor book. I'll never get the big, established houses to go for it, but maybe Hallie Porter will pay a few thou. God knows, she needs a list.

'Thanks,' Hallie said. 'I'll keep an eye out for it.'

The disembodied voice floated over them again, announcing the boarding of the old, the infirm, and the first class.

'Here we go,' Jackie said.

'There you go.' Hallie managed a laugh. 'Unicorn Books is a frugal operation. Just remember that when we start negotiating.'

A few minutes later they announced the boarding of rows H through N. Hallie picked up her carry-on bag and briefcase. They felt as if she'd packed rocks. She trudged toward the gate. The attendant took her boarding pass, gave her a slick plastic smile, and told her to have a good flight. There wasn't much chance of that.

The line crept down the boarding sleeve. The woman behind her stepped on Hallie's heel. The man in front swung his briefcase. It hit Hallie's knee. He didn't even bother to apologize. Another attendant, this one with a sneer that was more genuine than the smile, looked at Hallie's ticket. 'Through the curtains to the next compartment,' he ordered.

Hallie fought the urge to tell him she knew the way. She wasn't going to start taking her frustration out on strangers.

She inched down the aisle between the first-class seats. Those passengers were already settled. A few eyed the newcomers as if they were a marauding band. Most ignored them.

The handle of her hanging bag caught on an arm rest. Hallie stopped to free it. She felt someone watching her. She looked up and saw Olivia in the window seat. Her chair was tipped back, and she'd kicked off her shoes and tucked her legs beneath her. There was a pillow under her head and a blanket over her. Only it wasn't a blanket. It was a coat. It was the most beautiful sable coat Hallie had ever seen.

Olivia followed Hallie's eyes to the coat. She reached one arm outside it and stroked the soft pelt as if it were a much-loved kitten. 'I know, honey,' she said. 'It's vulgar this time of year, not to mention absurd. But Quent and I went shopping one afternoon, and he told me that old saying. 'The coldest winter I ever spent was summer in San Francisco.'

'Mark Twain.'

Olivia shrugged. 'I don't know who said it, honey, but I'm sure glad he did.'

Even under the best of circumstances, Hallie had a hard time sleeping on planes, and this wasn't the best of circumstances. She felt ashamed. There was no other way to put it. Her intellect told her she had nothing to be ashamed of. She hadn't committed any major or minor sins. She hadn't lied, cheated, or stolen anything. She hadn't even committed any gaffes. But her heart told her she'd committed the greatest sin of all, at least according to the world she inhabited. She'd failed.

The man in front of her pushed his chair as far back as it would go. His head was practically in her lap. She couldn't even cross her legs. She had the middle seat in the center row of five. The diminutive woman on her right snored mightily. The bodybuilding giant on her left spilled over his seat into hers. Behind her a man and a woman were doing a postmortem of the convention. Hallie tried to tune them out, but it was no good. Their voices carried over the vibrating drone of the engines. The author of the biggest-selling health and fitness book in history had turned up drunk for her press conference. A widely respected editor had been removed, bodily, from one of the gay bars. At a formal dinner celebrating thirty years of that much-loved, multimillion-dollar juvenile series, 'Benny the Bunny,' Benny's creator had hurled a drink at his editor.

Hallie wished she'd taken the earphones. Even

canned music would be better than this rehash. She closed her eyes. She tried to close her mind. But the conversation crept through.

'The parties were a little lean this year,' the woman said. 'Crummy hors d'oeuvre. Tacky jug wine.'

'You didn't hit the right ones.' Her companion listed a handful of the more elaborate celebrations. 'And R and S threw a real bash. If there's one thing Olivia Collins knows, it's how to spend money.'

'The question is, does she know how to make it? She's in over her head in that job.'

Hallie wasn't trying to shut out the words now.

'I don't know. I hear she's doing pretty well.'

'She's made some big buys. Only time will tell if they were smart buys.'

'She's no dope. Wasn't there some talk a while ago about her and Amos Porter? If you ask me, Olivia Collins was always the brains in the R and S operation.'

'What about Hallie Porter?' the woman asked.

'I almost forgot about her. What's she doing now, anyway?'

'Wasn't she going to start her own house?'

'Did she?'

'Beats me.'

Life, unlike fiction, is not punctuated by epiphanies. Few people can pinpoint the moment at which they suddenly saw the light, made a choice, started down a road. But Hallie Porter would always remember that at 1:37 a.m. Pacific Standard Time, 4:37 a.m. Eastern Standard Time, thirty-five thousand feet above the surface of the earth, crushed between two sleeping strangers, her eyes flew open to a fact of life. If you didn't have to be a bitch to get ahead in the world, you did have to be a fighter, and not necessarily one who adhered to the marquess of Queensberry's rules.

XLI

Hallie closed the manuscript box. It was a good novel, not a great novel, but a perfectly good one. More important, it was right for her purposes. She called to her secretary in the outer office to get Jackie Kay on the phone. Hallie played phone games rarely — never with Jackie — but this was important. She wanted to go into this with all flags flying. Hallie waited until her secretary said Jackie was on the phone to pick up her own.

'About that first novel you sent me,' Hallie said. 'It's a nice little book. I like it.'

'I knew you would.'

'Will the author take direction?'

'Are you kidding? She'd been working on this for six years. She'll do anything to get it published, short of selling her body on Forty-second Street. For all I know, she'll even do that. She's a nice kid but she's a little intense about her art.'

'That's what I'm afraid of. I want to know if she'll make changes including major cuts.'

'I think so.'

'Find out.'

Jackie was back on the phone in eight minutes.

'She'll write it in Sanskrit if you want.'

'English will be okay, though she's going to have to work on her dialogue. She doesn't have much of a flair for the colloquial.'

'I hate to sound crass, Hallie, but before you start editing, you could mention an advance.'

'Three thousand.'

'You've got to be kidding. Nobody pays less than ten anymore. Even for first novels.'

'I do.'

'I can get eight from Slater House.'

'I thought you said no one pays less than ten anymore.'

'I exaggerated. Hell, I'm her agent.'

'The book will get lost at Slater. I'll make it the lead on my spring list.'

'I thought you said it's a nice little book.'

'I can make it a sensational big book. Listen, Jackie, let's be honest. I know you're not bluffing. You probably can get eight from Slater or someone else. They'll print seven thousand copies, it'll get reviewed in Dubuque, the paperback rights will go for twelve thousand, and that'll be the end of it. I want to make this book. I want to build this author. Use me to make her reputation, and let me use her to get the word out that Unicorn is the kind of house that can turn serious first novels into commercial blockbusters.'

'I have to talk to the author. Five thousand dollars may be peanuts to us, but she's been waiting tables for the past six years.'

'Then she won't mind doing it for one more until the book comes out. Tell her you got me up to four thousand. Talk to her, Jackie. She'll listen to you.'

The author did.

Hallie had the book. Now she had to make good on her promise. She sat in her office with her chair turned to face the garden behind it and ran down the list of powerful paperback editors in her mind. Grace Robbins was the logical choice.

Hallie drafted a careful letter. The first paragraph was a discussion of Will's next book. That would lend credibility. The second paragraph was the one that counted:

'As for that first novel we talked about at the ABA – *Women's Rites*, by Leslie Random – I'm afraid I have to go back on my word. I know in San Francisco I promised you an early peek at it, but since then I've had so much interest I feel I owe it to the author to keep it absolutely under wraps until the auction. I'm not breaking my promise entirely, though. At auction time, I'll give you a chance to set the floor – providing you come in for six figures.'

'What's a floor?' Hallie's secretary asked when she brought in the typed letter. This was Maude's first job, but from the way she caught on to things, Hallie knew it wouldn't be her permanent job. Maude wanted to know how things worked. She wanted to know how people got things done. Sometimes Hallie felt Maude studying her as if she were a textbook.

'It's an amount a paperback house agrees to pay for the reprint rights to a book. When the book is auctioned off, the house with the floor gets to top the highest offer.'

Hallie went on reading the letter.

'Perfect. Now, I want two more copies. Not Xeroxes. Run two more copies out of your printer. When you send out those three letters I gave you this morning, I want you to put one of these in each envelope.'

'But those letters are to two other paperback editors and a book club.'

'You got it.'

'Then shouldn't I put cc at the bottom of this one and the three other names?'

'God, no! just fold this letter in with the other one intended for that particular editor. You know, as if the two pages stuck together and you put them in the same envelope by mistake.'

'Then what do I send Grace Robbins?'

'Nothing.'

Maude stood in front of the desk, staring at Hallie. Slowly a grin tugged at her full mouth. Understanding illuminated her dark almond-shaped eyes. Maude had more than intelligence going for her. When Hallie had hired her, Bob Sherwood had pronounced her a knockout.

'Oh,' she said finally. 'I get it.'

'Let's just pray no one else does.'

Sheila Dent was unwrapping the croissant she bought on her way to the office each morning when Hallie came into her cubicle. A manuscript sat on Sheila's desk beside the mug of coffee.

'How'd you like *Women's Rites*?' Hallie asked.

'It's a nice little book.'

Hallie stood over Sheila's desk. 'Don't ever call it "little" again. It's the lead book on our spring list.'

'My mistake. It's sensational.'

'It will be when I'm finished with it.'

Hallie picked up the manuscript to take it back to her office. 'Remember that editor at the *Times* who wanted to do the piece on Amos and me? The collaborative creative process.'

Sheila said she did.

'Set up a lunch for the three of us.'

'You, Mr Porter, and him?'

'You, me, and him.'

'I thought you said you didn't want to be interviewed till Mr Porter's next book came out.'

'Just do it, Sheila,' Hallie said on her way out of the cubicle.

Hallie was halfway to her office when she thought of it. She retraced her steps back to Sheila's cubicle.

Sheila had the croissant in one hand and was flipping through her Rolodex with the other.

'Please,' Hallie said.

Sheila looked up from the Rolodex. 'Please what?'

'Please set up the lunch, Sheila.'

Just because Hallie was playing hardball didn't mean she had to be a bitch.

Four days after Hallie's secretary sent out the letters, Kevin Barrington, the publisher of Apogee's paperback division, called.

'I just thought I ought to tell you, Hallie, somebody down there at Unicorn screwed up.'

Hallie's mind began calculating the odds. Her voice was innocent as a child's. 'What do you mean?'

'I got a letter from you the other day.'

'It's nice to know the mails are working.'

'Grace Robbins didn't.'

'Grace Robbins didn't what?'

'Get a letter from you. Your secretary made a mistake and put Grace's letter in the one for me.'

'Oh, God!' Hallie wailed. 'Is my face red!'

'You guys better get your act together.'

'Thanks for telling me, Kevin. I'll straighten it out. It was good talking to –'

'Wait!'

Hallie waited. Her heart pounded.

'About this novel. *Women's Rites*. I'd like a look at it.'

'You know I can't do that. You read that letter to Grace.'

'Grace's house isn't the right place for that book.'

'How do you know? You haven't even read it.'

'I know how they do things over there. Perfectly okay for Will Sawyer and for thrillers, but not for a book like this.'

'And what's this book like?'

'*Women's Rites*. That says it all, doesn't it?'

'You like the title?'

'Like it? Christ, Hallie, I could sell a couple of hundred thousand copies on the title alone. Come on, sneak me a look.'

'I'd like to, Kevin. I really would. But I can't.'

'How long have we known each other, Hal?'

'A couple of hundred years.'

'Since the old days at Slater. Remember that sales conference? The one on Long Boat Key? There was a party in someone's suite.'

'There were several parties in several suites.'

'And who was the guy who pried old Tom Templeton off you?' He started to laugh. 'If I hadn't come along, he would have had at you right there under the palms.'

She started to laugh with him. 'I suppose you're right.'

'So for old time's sake, Hal. For the old pal who saved you from the fate worse than death. Come on, let me take a look and give you a floor.'

'You read my letter to Grace. It's going to have to be a big one.'

'Have I ever let you down, Hallie? Ever since that night on Long Boat Key?'

'Not that I can think of.'

'Right. So how soon can I see the manuscript?'

She said she'd messenger it over that afternoon.

By July Fourth weekend Hallie had a quarter-of-a-million-dollar floor from Apogee Books.

'I guess I don't have to wait tables this weekend,' Leslie Random said. 'I guess I can go to the beach.'

'You can buy the beach,' Hallie said. 'Or at least a small house on it.'

The following week Hallie had lunch with Sheila and her contact at the *Times*. He said he was still interested in the piece on Hallie and Amos. Hallie said she had a better idea. There were dozens of articles on Amos, hundreds. She had to force out the next line.

'And it isn't as if a writer of Amos's stature needs a lot of editorial guidance.'

'I don't know,' the man said. 'I still like the idea of the collaborative creative process.'

'So do I. That's why I wanted to talk to you. You know where the real excitement is? In discovering new talent. In bringing it along. In taking all that raw intensity and pain and perception and helping shape it into a polished work of art.' Hallie didn't have to fake the breathlessness in her voice. The words were politic. She also believed they were true.

'I see what you mean.'

Hallie told him about working with Leslie Random on *Women's Rites*.

'It's interesting, certainly.'

Hallie heard the 'but' that was coming.

'But an unknown writer with an untested novel. That's a slim reed to hang a major piece on.'

Hallie shot Sheila a look. Sheila went into her song and dance. A major book. A new voice that spoke for her generation. She managed to sound as if she really believed all those shopworn phrases. Like Hallie, she was a professional. Or maybe, like Hallie, she was a believer.

But the man from the *Times* had little patience with professional PR hacks. 'I have a better idea.' He cut Sheila off in midhype. 'We'll do a piece on you and your stable of young, promising writers.

Didn't you win the Max Perkins Prize a couple of years ago?'

'Last winter.'

'And then you started your own house.'

'To publish the unknown writers the big houses won't take a chance on. To discover new talent. To nurture it.' If Hallie had looked down and seen that her linen suit had turned into a Girl Scout uniform, she wouldn't have been surprised.

'I like it,' the man said. 'I like it a lot. Unicorn Books, a literary David against the bottom-line-oriented Goliaths of publishing. I can see the picture now. No Amos Porter. No big names. Just you, the publisher, surrounded by a bunch of your new authors.'

'I hate to mention this,' Sheila said when she and Hallie were alone in the cab on the way back to the office, 'but we don't have a bunch of new authors. We have Amos Porter and Will Sawyer and several other big names you brought over from R and S. We have Leslie Random. But we do not have a bunch of new writers.'

'The interviews for this article aren't going to start till the fall. By then we will.'

It didn't take that long. The word was out. Hallie Porter wasn't interested in the stars. She already had enough of those. She wanted to discover new talent. That summer every agent who had a serious book by a promising unknown sent it to Unicorn Books first.

Will took a house in Nantucket for the summer. He

403

said he had to get away to start thinking seriously about his next book.

He tried to convince Hallie to go with him, but she said she couldn't take time off. Will didn't argue. He knew you couldn't walk away from an infant publishing house any more than you could from an infant.

Hallie did manage to fly up for two weekends. Will said he worried about that. Those little puddle jumpers weren't made to carry a couple of hundred pounds of manuscripts.

During the day they lay on the beach and read. In the evening they sat on the deck sipping vodka tonics and watching the sky turn from pink to mauve to violet. At night they went to bed in the big corner room swept by breezes that smelled of the sea and made slow, familiar love. One weekend, when a full moon hung so close outside the window they thought they could touch it, the untanned parts of their bodies glowed like white beacons in the night.

They talked a lot during those weekends. They brought each other up to date on what had happened while they were apart. They discussed books and business and politics and people. They even reminisced. But they never so much as mentioned the future.

Hallie didn't want to go to Sag Harbor for Labor Day weekend. Her idea of getting away wasn't sitting in traffic for three hours to see the same people you saw all week in front of a different backdrop. But Jackie Kay and the writer she lived with had invited

Hallie and Will, and Hallie didn't want to offend Jackie. Will came down from Nantucket. He and Hallie drove out to Sag Harbor.

There was a small dinner of eight, all in publishing, on Friday night. There was volleyball on the beach – agents and editors against writers – on Saturday afternoon. There was a party in Easthampton on Saturday night. It was in one of those bleached wood houses that are supposed to look like pieces of driftwood washed up on the beach. This one had washed up with a pool, tennis court, and a hot tub. The party was as big and glitzy as the house, so Hallie wasn't surprised when she walked into the living room on Saturday night and saw Jake out on the deck. In fact, if she was going to be honest about it – to herself if no one else – she'd been thinking that he might be there while she'd dressed. She supposed that was why she'd worn the white halter top with the white linen trousers. She'd had a halter top that summer they'd been married, and every time she'd worn it, Jake had said she had sexy shoulders. Until then, she'd thought they were just wide and bony.

He was talking to a woman Hallie didn't know. Her cheekbones could have shaved wood. The arrogant tilt of her chin said she knew just how good they and every other part of her were. When Jake noticed Hallie, he nodded in her direction, then turned back to the woman.

The party escalated. Ashtrays began to overflow. Plates of half-finished food and glasses of unfinished drinks collected on tables. Music blared. People raised their voices to be heard above it. Tanned faces glistened with sweat. Hallie had a feeling her own face had the same unappealing glow. She wandered out onto the deck. On one of the chaises, a couple talked quietly. In another a man was either asleep or dead. She walked to the railing and stood looking out into the night. The sand was a pale carpet in the moonlight. It rolled down to a black sea that broke in foamy ribbons of white. Inside the house someone had changed the compact disc. Behind her she heard Susannah McCorkle singing 'Thanks for the Memories.'

'The night you worked and then came home with lipstick on your tie,' she sang.

Stairs led from the deck down to the beach. At the bottom of them, Hallie stopped and took off her shoes. The sand shifted beneath her feet as she started toward the water. The sound of the breaking waves drowned out Susannah McCorkle.

When she reached the water, she rolled up her trousers, then took another step. The waves rushed around her ankles. After a while, she backed up out of reach of the water and sat in the sand, hugging her knees to her chest. The waves went on whispering. The black night gathered around her.

'Looks a lot like Maine, doesn't it?'

Jake sat beside her and rested his elbows on his knees. Their four bare tanned feet made parallel marks in the sand.

'Different landscape,' she said.

'But the sea's the same. The sea's always the same.'

She didn't answer.

'How're things going?' he asked.

'Okay.'

They sat in silence for another moment, looking out to sea rather than at each other.

'Every place I go I hear good things about Unicorn Books.'

She leaned back on her elbows. He did too. She glanced at him out of the corner of her eye. The skin of his neck and face was almost black against the pale blue shirt. His profile chiseled a piece out of the night. 'I guess it all depends on where you go,' she said.

'Beginning of the summer I went to lunch with two editors. Two different days. Two different editors.'

'Isn't that what agents do?'

'The funny thing was these two different editors told me the same story. It was about you. People always think I want to hear the latest about you.'

'I'm sorry.'

'Not your fault. Anyway, they're right.' He waited for her to say something. When she didn't, he went on. 'So this was the beginning of the summer, maybe a little earlier. Before people started talking about how well you were doing. In fact, both these editors –'

'I don't suppose you want to tell me who they were.'

'Don't be so impatient. You'll know when I finish the story. Both of them said you must be running a hell of an operation down there. You couldn't even manage the mail without a screw-up.'

She turned to him. He met her eyes. His smile was impossibly white in his tanned face.

'It seems both these editors got letters intended for another editor.'

'I have a new secretary. She's enthusiastic but erratic.'

'Yeah, that's what I figured. At first. Then they told me the rest of the story. It seems both of them got letters intended for Grace Robbins.'

She went on staring at him but didn't say anything.

'It didn't occur to me until a few days later. If each of them had got a letter for a different editor, it would have made sense. Given this erratic secretary of yours. But what were two identical letters to Grace doing on her desk to begin with?'

'A copy for the file?'

'Possibly. But it still seems unlikely that she'd make the same mistake twice. I mean, even a cretin would notice that there wasn't anything left to put in an envelope to Grace, let alone file.'

They went on staring at each other.

'Did you point that out to either of them?' Hallie asked.

'None of my business.'

'Thanks.'

'It's nothing.' He laughed quietly. 'Besides, why would I want to spoil things? It was a genius stroke.'

Now she was smiling too. 'Let's just say it was a good idea that worked.'

What he said next startled her, though by now she

should have known better. They'd never been able to stick to business.

'I miss you, babe.' He reached out and ran a finger over her bare shoulder. 'I miss you a lot.'

She shivered. It would be so easy. Like floating. All you had to do was give yourself up to the force – water or Jake or maybe just the attraction – and before you knew it you were suspended in happiness. But floating was a dangerous endeavor. It left you vulnerable to any stray current or rogue wind or sudden storm. Then before you knew it you were out of your depth and fighting for your life.

Suddenly she could hear the music from the house again. Nobody had bothered to change the CD.

'The night you worked and then came home with lipstick on your tie,' Susannah McCorkle sang.

'Isn't that something about Olivia and Quentin?' Hallie asked.

'Did you hear what I said?'

'Did *you* hear what *I* said?'

She stood and brushed the sand off her trousers. 'I have to get back to the party. Will's waiting.'

Will was on the deck when Hallie returned to the house. He didn't ask her where she'd been or whether she'd been there alone, but later, back in the guest room of Jackie Kay's house, he did ask one question.

'It's none of my business, Hallie, but are you doing anything about a divorce? I mean, do you have a legal separation or anything? I was just wondering.'

She kept her back to him while she took off her earrings and bracelet. 'I keep meaning to, but I haven't had a chance. You know, with the new house and everything.'

'Sure,' he said. 'I know.'

XLII

If Hallie had used dirty tricks to get a floor for *Women's Rites*, the auction itself was completely above board. Apogee had offered a floor of two hundred and fifty thousand dollars. The book, heavily edited and restructured by Hallie, came out. The reviews came in. Apogee ended up paying 1.2 million for the privilege of publishing in paperback.

The author, Leslie Random, bought a word processor, a loft in Soho, and a half interest in the trendy restaurant where she used to wait tables. The agent, Jackie Kay, was so inundated with unsolicited manuscripts that she had to begin charging a fee for first readings, an unfortunate agents' practice she'd once sworn she'd never adopt. And just a little less than two years after her picture had appeared on the cover of *Time* magazine, Hallie Porter was once again the hottest publisher in town. When the press did an article on the state of the book industry, Hallie Porter was the first person they quoted. The piece on the collaborative creative process had featured a full-page color photo of Hallie surrounded by her stable of promising young writers. And every few

411

weeks the trade news announced that another established author had gone over to Unicorn Books. 'Carter Bolton Bolts R and S for Unicorn' ran one headline. In the brief article that followed, Olivia Collins, publisher of Rutherford and Styles, said that though she was sorry she couldn't publish Carter Bolton's next book, especially since she'd done so well with the last, R and S was a large house with a long history. 'We don't depend on one or two big-name authors.'

That particular scrimmage hit the papers, but usually the battle was played out in privacy. Though neither Hallie nor Olivia would admit it, they both kept a running tally of who won in the big auctions. When Olivia walked off with a potential best seller by a surrogate mother, Hallie cursed herself for coming in with a low bid. But the next night when she ran into Olivia at a party, Hallie actually crossed the room to tell her she'd done a good job. A month later, Hallie walked off with the memoirs of a politician who'd been at the heart of the last administration, and Olivia called to congratulate her. Neither of them had forgiven or even forgotten anything, but both of them were determined to keep up appearances. As Hallie had screamed at her mother under different circumstances, the Porters valued dignity. Olivia had more practical reasons. A few weeks after she'd become publisher of R and S, she'd had a meeting with Jonathan Graham. The rumors about Amos and Hallie and Olivia were just beginning to die down.

'One more thing,' Jonathan said as Olivia was

about to leave his office in Century City.

Olivia stopped at the door and turned back to him.

'Leave the columns to the movie division of Allied. I expect you to go tooth and nail against Hallie Porter and every other publisher for books and authors. I don't expect personal vendettas and back-stabbing. I especially don't expect them to be carried on in the newspapers.'

The comment had surprised Olivia, but then in those days Olivia was still trying to figure Jonathan out. That was before Quentin explained everything, or at least the part Olivia couldn't figure.

At first she'd tried all the logical sources. She'd spent a endless evening with Allied's top attorney, a man who'd know Jonathan ever since they'd been assigned to the same barrackslike room on the campus of that cow college in Montana. By the end of the evening, all she'd learned was that Jonathan had finished the cow college in two and a half years with the highest academic average in its history and that the attorney was still pining for a would-be actor who'd thrown him over five months earlier for a porn star.

'Were you and Jonathan ever an item?' she asked the attorney.

He laughed. By that point in the evening, he was close to tears and the sound came out as a hiccup. 'Are you kidding? Old homophobic Johnny? Once — it was right after we won the battle to take over World — I put my arm around him to congratulate him. You would have thought I put my hand on his fly. You should have seen the bastard jump.'

Olivia worked her way through a few more executives. They'd come to the company later and knew even less than the attorney.

Olivia had just about given up when Quentin solved the problem for her.

'How do you know?' she asked.

'Rumors.'

'But I haven't heard any.'

'Jonathan Graham is a powerful man. Most people are afraid to talk about him.'

'Then how did you hear these rumors?'

'Because there are some people who are even more powerful than Jonathan.'

She moved closer to Quentin in bed. Not only had Olivia now seen the second floor of a twelve-room Fifth Avenue duplex. When Quentin was in town, she lived there. 'And you're one of them?'

'I'm not, but I have friends who are.'

'And he's really impotent?'

Quentin closed his eyes for a moment. He was an old-time publisher, a man who believed in the power of the word. That particular word still terrified him.

'That's not what I said. He's uninterested.'

'But no one's uninterested in sex.'

He traced the smooth curve of her breast. 'Impossible as you may find it, Olivia, some people are.'

'I can't believe it.'

'Think about it for a moment. Sex is time consuming – if you do it right. It also takes a lot of energy.'

'She pressed the length of her body against his. 'If you do it right.'

'And what are the rewards? I'm not talking about using sex to get something else. I mean, what are the rewards of sex?'

'Pleasure.'

'Not a commodity Jonathan Graham values. He believes in power. He believes in profit. Anything that doesn't result in one or the other is just a waste of time and energy to him.'

'But why?'

'You mean what makes a man that way? I have no idea. He obviously doesn't have much of a sexual drive. Some people don't, but I'm sure you can't imagine that either. Maybe he was traumatized as a child. I knew a boy in boarding school who'd been raised by a strict German nanny. Bathed under a rubber sheet. Had to sleep with his hands tied to the bedposts. But despite her best efforts, he till managed to get the occasional uninvited erection. Each time he did, he was punished accordingly.'

'What do you mean, punished accordingly?'

'Use your imagination, Olivia. It's a highly erotic organ. The point is by the time the boy reached boarding school, he was more than a little screwed up.'

'You think something like that happened to Jonathan Graham?'

'I have no idea what happened to Jonathan. I'm not much for psychological explanations. All I know is that he's entirely immune to sex.' He pulled her on top of him. 'And given the fact that you're working for him, I can't say I'm particularly sorry.'

Hallie sat at her desk staring at the phone. She didn't have to look up Jonathan Graham's number. She remembered it from the old days. But she still hadn't made up her mind to call him.

She wished she could discuss it with someone. She could call Will, but it was after eleven in London. Besides, she didn't like taking her troubles to him. She didn't like taking her troubles to anyone, Cecelia insisted, but it was more than that. Affairs don't stand still, Olivia used to say. They either get better or worse. Olivia, Hallie had decided, was as misguided about that as she was about everything else. Things hadn't changed between her and Will. The sex was still terrific. The friendship was still strong. They liked each other's bodies and respected each other's minds and enjoyed each other's company. They rarely fought when they were together, and they were both too busy to miss each other excessively when they were apart. The relationship had started out good, and it had remained exactly the same way. Hallie forced her mind back to the problem at hand. There was no one she could call for advice. She decided not to call Jonathan Graham for help. She'd let things ride for a while.

Hallie hadn't even thought of calling Quentin or Jake. It never occurred to her that Quentin or Jake would call her. Quentin suggested lunch. He suggested it casually, as if they were still meeting every Tuesday, though they hadn't done that in a few years.

Hallie said her schedule was tight these days. Quentin pressed. 'There're a few things I want to talk to you about.'

'Are you going to tell me war stories again?'

'Do stories about a takeover war interest you?'

She agreed to meet him at his club the following Tuesday.

Quentin was waiting at his usual table when Hallie arrived. From across the room, it all looked the same. He sat erect but easy in his austere gray suit with his proper vest and dull gold watch chain. His long fingers toyed with the stem of his martini glass. He wasn't even particularly tanned. The coast hadn't changed Quentin.

Hallie crossed the room to his table. He stood and leaned across it as if to kiss her. She held out her hand. That was when she realized it. The coast hadn't changed Quentin, but Olivia had. Olivia or a plastic surgeon, and Hallie was fairly sure it wasn't the latter. Quentin looked, as the saying went, ten years younger.

'Olivia agrees with you.' The words were out before Hallie had a chance to think about them.

'She does. And it's nice of you to say so.'

The waiter pulled out the massive chair that was too heavy for Hallie to move. She slid into it. Quentin watched her.

'But don't worry. I didn't ask you to lunch to talk about my life. Or at least not only my life.'

'Why did you ask me to lunch?'

'Because I feel I owe you something. Not because of Olivia, but because of that business with Jonathan Graham.'

'That worked out all right. I didn't have to leave. I chose to leave.'

'Still, I should have given you more warning. I didn't do it then, but I want to now.'

'Warning of what?' she asked, though she was fairly sure she knew. The only surprise was that Quentin did, too. If word was getting around, this was more serious than she'd thought.

'What do you know about Sebastian Fitch?'

'Only that he owns half the media in the UK and makes Jonathan Graham look like a pussy cat.'

'Fitch makes Rupert Murdoch look like a pussy cat. And half is a bit of an exaggeration, though the UK is an underestimation. He's powerful in Australia and Canada, too. And he's been trying to buy an American publishing house for some time now.'

'I'm too small for him,' Hallie said, because she was still hoping that was so.

'A year ago you were too small for him. Now you're a foothold. He's been talking to your backers.'

'From what I hear, Fitch talks to everyone.'

'You can't afford to be an ostrich about this, Hallie.'

'I'm not being an ostrich. I've heard the rumors too. Though thanks for telling me. The point is, I don't have a lot of options.'

'You have one. I've been talking to Amos. We figure it'll take about eleven million to buy out your

418

original backers. I'm willing to put up three, Amos says he'll come up with two, and we'll finance the other six.'

'Absolution doesn't come cheap.'

The waiter handed them menus. Hallie studied hers. When she looked up, Quentin was watching her.

'Well?' he said.

'I'll have the salmon.'

Quentin started to say something, then changed his mind. He took the pad and pencil from the table, wrote down their orders, and handed them to the waiter.

'Don't be proud about this, Hallie. More to the point, don't be stupid.'

'In other words, I should let you and Amos bail me out.'

'It wouldn't be bailing you out. It would be helping you out.'

'Then you and Amos could run Unicorn Books.'

'You know better than that. It's your house. We'd let you go on doing things the way you want.'

'Isn't that what Fitch says when he takes over a company?'

'You're not telling me you trust him to keep his word?'

'I'm not telling you I trust him. I'm telling you I don't trust you and Amos. Not anymore. So, thank you for the offer, Quent. I know you mean well. That's not irony. I think you do. But I can't afford to rely on you and Amos anymore.'

*   *   *

419

'How is Amos's book coming?' Quentin asked over coffee. They were going through the motions of a normal lunch.

'He says he's going to deliver it any day now. Swears it's the best thing he's ever done.'

'He told me the same thing. I knew it would be – once he decided to tell the truth. In fact, that's what I said to Olivia when I read that early draft.'

'You told Olivia what was wrong with that early draft?'

'I made a few suggestions. Nothing major. I didn't want Amos to know. He was pretty sensitive at the time.'

He wasn't the only one.

Hallie told herself it didn't matter. Olivia's failure didn't turn her own into a success. Still, she couldn't help feeling better. At least for a few moments.

'I told you I didn't invite you to lunch to discuss my personal life,' Quentin said as he signaled for the bill, 'but there is one thing I want to say. I've already told Cecelia and Amos.'

Hallie stopped with her napkin halfway to her mouth. She didn't know why she was surprised. If she had any sense, she would have stopped being surprised by Olivia a long time ago.

'Don't tell me. Let me guess. You're going to marry her.'

'Yes.'

She put her napkin on the table and stood. She'd had enough.

'Give Olivia my congratulations. I know you're not supposed to congratulate the bride. After all, I'm

Cecelia's daughter. You're supposed to say congratulations to the groom and good luck to the bride. But I don't think the etiquette rules apply in this case. I think Olivia deserves congratulations. And I think you're going to need all the luck you can get.'

Only when Hallie was back in her office did she think of the practical ramifications, and then she found she didn't give a damn. Losing Quentin's inheritance didn't hurt. Losing Quentin finally and completely – losing him to Olivia did.

Jake called a few days later. He suggested dinner. She said she didn't have a free night for weeks. He tried lunch. She said she was just as heavily booked. He mentioned Sebastian Fitch. She agreed to meet him for a drink. He probably knew no more than she did, but she couldn't take the chance that he might.

Hallie was only a few minutes late, but Jake was waiting. Though it was early June, his face was already bronze from the sun. She waited for the big shark's smile to light up the tan. He just nodded and asked her what she was drinking these days.

The conversation was remarkably similar to the one she'd had with Quentin, even down to the offer of money. He too had been talking to Amos.

'Just sitting around over lunch, kicking helpless Hallie and her problems around.'

'You're anything but helpless,' he said. 'And just for the record, as Amos's agent, I think it would be a good investment for him.'

'What about you? 'Where does your contribution come in?'

'Amos would have to put up the lion's share. You know that. But I'd be willing to sell the house in the country, and if you wanted to sell the apartment, I wouldn't object. We ought to be able to realize about four million on both properties. You'd get half outright, and I'd invest my half –'

'Oh, I get it. This is equitable distribution time.'

'That's not what I mean. I was just trying to come up with some cash.'

'I appreciate it.'

'Don't be so damn sarcastic.'

'Don't you be so damn patronizing.'

'I was just trying to help.'

He was just trying to help. He and Amos and Quentin. They had peculiar ways of doing it. He'd gone to bed with Olivia, and Amos had given his manuscript to Olivia, and Quentin had sold the company out from under her and was going to marry Olivia. Each of them had betrayed her, and now they were all coming to her and saying she could rely on them.

To hell with that. To hell with them.

'You have helped,' she said. 'You've made me see things more clearly. I've got to do something about Fitch.' She picked up her glass and drained it. 'And about us. This has dragged on for too long. It's time we settled things. It's time we made a clean break.'

The words fell between them. Jake could hear them clatter on the small table like broken glass. They were the only sound in the room. It didn't make sense. There was conversation all around them. But all he could hear were the words she'd just spoken. And he knew with a sickening feeling somewhere in his gut that she was right. It had dragged on for too long. It was over.

XLIII

'I've been waiting for your call,' Jonathan Graham said.

'Does that mean you're going to say I told you so?'

He laughed. She could tell he was pleased to hear from her. 'I don't have to. You've already said it for me.'

'I'd like to talk to you. I can get out to the coast the end of this week.'

'No need to. I'll be in New York tomorrow.'

They agreed it would be better if neither of them went to the other's office. They wanted to keep the preliminary talks secret. Jonathan suggested he stop by Hallie's apartment the following evening.

'I'll be in disguise,' he said. 'But you'll be able to recognise me. By my white horse and armor.'

Hallie couldn't help laughing. When she'd first met Jonathan Graham, she'd seen him as the enemy. During the time she'd worked for him she'd modified her opinion. But it taken Sebastian Fitch to make her see Jonathan Graham as a white knight.

Hallie opened the door to her apartment to find

Jonathan Graham studying the Stella litho in the hallway. She wondered if he was admiring the art or calculating the value.

He turned from the picture to her, and they shook hands.

'I left my white horse, and my battery of lawyers, downstairs. I thought this ought to be an informal discussion.'

She agreed, led him into the living room, and poured him a Perrier.

For half an hour they discussed financial arrangements. That was the easy part, or at least the cut-and-dried part. They agreed the lawyers would meet next week to begin hammering out the details.

Jonathan put his glass down on the table and leaned forward with his elbows on his knees. A shock of cornsilk hair fell across his forehead.

'I just want to repeat something I said a few years ago, Hallie. I told you then I didn't take R and S over to change it. And I want to reassure you now. I'm not buying out your backers to take over Unicorn Books. You're a good publisher. Hell, you're an extraordinary publisher. I'm paying sixteen million for Unicorn Books. But you and I know Unicorn Books is nothing more than you.'

'I've got a good list of authors.'

'A third of whom you discovered. The rest came over because of you. All I'm saying, Hallie, is that this time I wish you'd believe me. I'll rap your knuckles if I think you're getting out of line financially. Otherwise, like I said a few years ago, just keep doing what you've been doing.'

Hallie sat across from him in one of the two deep sofas. Her legs were crossed and her hands were in her lap. She knew how she looked. Proper but relaxed. And she knew how she felt, which was anything but relaxed, because there was still one thing they had to discuss, and it was critical.

'That was a nice speech.'

'If you don't believe it, why did you call me in?'

'I called you in, as you predicted some time ago, because Sebastian Fitch makes you look like the National Endowment for the Arts. And I do believe it. Up to a point.'

'Olivia Collins?'

'Unicorn Books is a small house. R and S is a big operation. I don't want to be eaten up.'

Jonathan was still hunched forward over his knees. Now he leaned back and spread his arms out along the top of the sofa.

'I was wondering when we'd get to that.'

'It's the crucial issue.'

'It's an important issue for me. It's the crucial one for you. All right, Hallie, I'll spell it out. We'd be crazy not to have R and S distribute for you. You'll use their sales force. Beyond that, you remain independent. You see, I like the idea of having two houses. It'll keep both of you on your toes.' He stood and smiled down at her. 'Not that I think you or Olivia need any more incentive.'

The lawyers met for three days. On the third Jonathan Graham and Hallie joined them. She went straight from the signing to the restaurant where Will

427

Sawyer was waiting. He'd got in from England less than an hour earlier. She'd said he'd be too jet lagged for dinner, but Will had a theory. The minute he got on a plane, which he did often enough to make the theory necessary, he set his watch to wherever he was going. Then he proceeded to will his body clock to conform to it.

'Does it work?' Hallie had asked once.

'About seventy-five percent of the time.'

It seemed to be working now. His clothes looked rumpled, but his clothes always looked rumpled. The rest of him looked terrific. Or maybe it was only the way his face creased into a grin when he saw her crossing the room toward him that was terrific.

He stood and kissed her. He'd been away for three weeks. She had a feeling from his response and her own that the kiss could have gone on for that long.

He let her go and stood looking at her for a moment. 'Why did I suggest meeting in a restaurant?'

'I was just wondering the same thing.'

They sat and ordered drinks. He took her hand.

'I missed you,' he said.

'I missed you too.' It wasn't entirely a lie. She'd been so busy she hadn't had a chance to think about him much, but when she'd thought about him, she'd missed him.

She asked him about England. His lectures had gone well. The project with the BBC was going even better.

He asked her what had gone on here. She told him about Sebastian Fitch.

'Why didn't you say something when I called?'

She shrugged. 'You had enough on your mind. With the BBC and all.'

'What are you going to do?'

She told him what she'd already done. She laid out all the details. He agreed she was taking a chance, but her chances were better with Jonathan Graham than with Sebastian Fitch. She hadn't mentioned Quentin's offer or Jake's.

'I took care of another legal matter while you were away.'

He put his drink down and stared at her.

'I saw a divorce lawyer.'

The waiter was approaching with the menus. Will waved him away.

'You know,' he said, 'all of a sudden, I don't feel hungry.'

'Maybe the jet lag's finally getting to you.'

'Maybe.' He took her hand again and rubbed his thumb back and forth across the palm of her hand. 'All I know is that if I don't get to bed right away, I may die.'

They left Will's apartment only twice that weekend. On Sunday morning he went out for the paper. On Sunday night there was a party where she had to show her face. She promised they'd stay only an hour. As it turned out, they stayed for less than that. When Hallie came out of the bathroom where she'd gone to escape an enraged novelist whose book she'd rejected, she found Will standing at the door.

'Let's get out of here,' he said.

'We just got here.'

'Okay, if you won't leave . . .' He began edging her back into the bathroom. His hand went under her sweater.

'Okay, we'll leave.'

There was an empty cab in front of the building. They were back in bed in seven minutes.

Quentin had told Hallie he was planning to marry Olivia. He'd also told Cecelia and Amos. He just hadn't mentioned it to Olivia. The decision wasn't as final as Quentin had made it sound. He hadn't needed Amos to tell him there was no fool like an old fool. He hadn't needed Hallie's ironic congratulations. He hadn't even needed the pitying look that Cecelia had given him in place of any comment at all. He knew what he was getting into, and it was more than the bad graces of the people to whom he'd once been closest.

He'd gone through it a hundred times in his head. He knew all about Olivia, more than she'd ever admitted to him, certainly. He knew about the ambition that would stop at nothing. But as the publisher of R and S and the wife of Quentin Styles, she didn't have a lot left to be ambitious for. And he knew about the sexual opportunism. That bothered him, but it didn't unhinge him. For one thing, though he'd never say as much to anyone else – he didn't want to give them any more reason to laugh at him – he had a feeling Olivia was being faithful these days. For another, he was a reasonable man. Quentin had always believed that people made too much of sex. At least he'd believed it till he'd been unable to make anything of it at all.

Quentin wasn't, as Amos had said, an old fool. He was just an aging man with a common, if devastating, problem who'd stumbled across a solution. He'd be an idiot not to hold on to that solution and try to make her as happy as possible.

The week after Hallie told Will she'd seen a divorce lawyer, Herbert Shine, a bluff-voiced man who specialized in matrimonial law, called and told Hallie the meeting was set for the following Tuesday at eleven.

'What meeting?'

'With Mr Fox and his attorney.'

'Why do I have to meet with him?'

'To hammer out a few points.'

'But we've already agreed on everything. It's equitable distribution.'

Shine sighed. It was a very theatrical sigh. 'If only it was that easy.'

'Can't you do it without me?'

'Listen, Mrs Fox –'

'Ms Porter,' she snapped.

'You don't have to be afraid of him. I'll be there.'

'Afraid to see him! I'm not afraid to see him.'

Shine didn't point out that he'd said afraid of him, not afraid to see him.

'I'm sorry. I just meant that some women . . . you know, if they've had a bad time or the husband's been rough on them . . . not necessarily physically, but, you know, emotionally intimidating –'

'I'll be there at eleven.'

Shine hung up the phone. This was one of those cases where he was going to have to watch himself. Professionally, he represented the wife. Personally, after that conversation, he couldn't help feeling sorry for the husband. When Hallie Porter had first come to his office, he'd thought she was a cool cookie. Efficient, businesslike, unemotional. But she'd sat across from his desk with her legs crossed while he'd taken down the pertinent information, and her leg had kept swinging in a quick staccato beat. She had good legs, and he'd found himself wondering what it would be like to get behind that cool exterior. It was probably what Jake Fox had thought, and look where it had landed him. After this morning's conversation, Shine knew instinctively what it had probably taken that poor bastard Fox years to learn. Behind that cool exterior was an even colder interior.

The nights Olivia spent in the Fifth Avenue duplex had taught her one thing about life at the top. It was as soft and easy and delicious as she'd always imagined. But it wasn't quiet. In her old postwar one-bedroom with the paper-thin walls, crying babies had disturbed her days and acrobatic lovers her nights. The sounds of Fifth Avenue were more anonymous but no more pleasant. The apartment was across from a transverse through the park, and at least once a week between midnight and four in the morning a mind-piercing screech of brakes was followed by a catastrophic crash. On Tuesday and Friday mornings the gears of sanitation trucks gnashed and ground like the teeth of huge prehistoric monsters. And the sound of doormen's whistles and taxicab brakes was a constant. Olivia didn't understand how life nineteen floors above the city could be so noisy.

'Sound rises,' Quentin explained.

But that Friday morning for one astonishing moment the grinding gears of sanitation trucks and the whistles of doormen and the screeching brakes of taxis all stopped. The bedroom nineteen floors above the city was absolutely silent. Olivia couldn't hear a sound in the world except the echo of Quentin's words.

She stopped on her way to one of the two master baths and turned back to him. She was naked, but for once in her life she wasn't aware that it was an advantage. 'What did you say?'

Quentin was sitting up in bed, watching her over the top of the *Wall Street Journal*. 'I said, would you like to get married?'

She went on staring at him. Her mouth was pressed closed and her eyes narrowed, as if she were trying to fathom a language she didn't understand. He almost laughed, but he didn't.

'Perhaps I should rephrase that. Make it more specific. Would you like to marry me?'

She walked back to the bed and around it to his side, but she didn't sit. She just stood there, staring down at him. 'Are you teasing me, Quentin? Because if you are I'll kill you.'

He took her hand. 'I'm perfectly serious. I'd like to marry you.' He cleared his throat then and repeated the sentence he'd spoken three times before in his life. 'Will you marry me?'

Olivia didn't answer him. She sat on the side of the bed, and then she did something no one had ever seen Olivia Collins do, at least not as an adult. She began to sob. Not clever, controlled tears, or a useful watering of the eyes that made them look even more melting, but big, messy-sounding sobs. Quentin put his arms around her and she put her head on his chest and they stayed that way until she stopped crying and for some time after that.

XLIV

Herbert Shine was a big man with a penchant for suits a size too small. He thought they camouflaged his weight. They merely outlined it. He came out to the reception area to meet Hallie. Shine divided his clients into two classes – those his secretary came out to meet and those he did.

He took Hallie's outstretched hand in his meaty one and said it was a nice morning. Then he saw the look on her face. 'I mean the weather's pleasant, but I'm sure this is very difficult for you.'

'Not in the least.'

He led her down the hall to the conference room. He offered her coffee; the facilities, as he called them; anything. She looked at her watch and said she had an appointment at twelve-thirty. That was when the receptionist buzzed to say that Mr Fox and Mr Coyle had arrived.

Herbert Shine was an old hand at these meetings. He liked to say he'd seen it all. He'd seen husbands and wives who refused to look at each other, and husbands and wives who addressed each other in terms that would scandalize the average sailor, and one husband and wife who'd embraced in the conference room – not greeted each other with one of those antiseptic cheek-against-cheek maneuvers but actually gone into a clinch in the conference room. Shine could have sworn the guy had his tongue in his estranged wife's mouth. But these two were something else. It wasn't that they were different from the chilly ones, only more perfect. They said good morning. They shook hands. Damned if they didn't tell each other they were looking well. His back was ramrod straight. Her chin was lifted. You would have thought two crowned heads of Europe were meeting.

Hallie and Shine sat on one side of the conference table, Jake and his lawyer on the other. Coyle took a sheaf of papers from his briefcase. A pile about an inch high was already in front of Shine.

'Papers, papers,' Shine chuckled as he straightened them with his big hands. 'You'd think we were finalizing the SALT agreement.'

Jake grimaced. Hallie didn't move a muscle. Shine and Coyle exchanged glances. There'd be no jokes at this one. They got down to business.

When they'd first met in the conference room, Shine had thought he'd never seen anything like it. As the negotiations progressed, he was sure. He was accustomed to disagreements about property, but not disagreements like this.

'About the Stella litho . . .' Coyle began.

'Mr Fox can have it,' Hallie said.

'But it's in the apartment, which you get in the settlement,' Shine pointed out.

'He can have it.'

'As for the first editions of Hemingway and Fitzgerald and Joyce . . .' Shine began.

'She can have them,' Jake said.

'But according to our schedules, you collected those,' Coyle pointed out.

'They mean more to her.'

'Mr Fox can have the piano,' Hallie said.

Shine consulted one of the papers in front of him. This was getting to be too much. 'The piano belonged to the Porter family.'

'I don't play,' Hallie said. 'He does.'

Shine glanced across the table at Jake. 'I think my client is being more than generous, Mr Fox.'

'Ms Porter,' Jake said, and the first word came out as a hiss, 'isn't being generous. She's simply taking the high moral ground. It's her favorite stand.'

The lawyers glanced at each other. This was more like it. It was a shame that the meeting was over.

Olivia crumpled the newspaper and threw it across her office. It hit the wall and sailed to the floor without damage. Even her rage was impotent.

She should have seen it coming. Quentin should have warned her. Surely Quentin had known.

She told her secretary to get Mr Styles on the phone.

'But it's ten after six in California.'

'I know what time it is,' Olivia screamed. 'Just get him!'

The secretary was back in a minute. 'There's no answer at the house in Malibu.'

437

'Try again,' Olivia barked. 'And keep trying till you find him.'

A fear winged past her consciousness. The only reason a man would be out at six o'clock in the morning was because he hadn't come home the night before.

'Wonderful,' she muttered to the empty office. 'Terrific.' Everything was falling apart at once.

A moment later her secretary said she had Mr Styles on the phone.

'Was that you a couple of minutes ago?' Quentin asked. 'I was in the shower.'

'I was beginning to think you hadn't come home last night.'

'Are you going to be a jealous wife?'

'Me? Are you kidding?' Olivia said, but her laugh had a tinny ring. Then she remembered she had more important things on her mind.

'Did you know about Jonathan's latest acquisition?'

'Excell?'

'That record company's yesterday's news. Allied just bought Unicorn Books.'

'No!'

Olivia could hear the incredulity three thousand miles away. Quentin hadn't known. Things weren't all right, but they were better.

'Yes. What I can't figure is why he'd do it behind your back.'

'The Graham style. I'd be the logical one to make the deal. Given my connection with R and S and with Hallie. So instead of bringing me in on it, he keeps me completely in the dark. Just to prove it's a one-man operation. We all work for Allied Entertainment. Jonathan Graham is Allied Entertainment.'

'The paper says he's not going to merge the two houses.' She waited for Quentin to say something, but he was still turning the information over in his mind. 'Do you think he means it?'

'I don't know?'

'Can you find out?'

'I can try.'

'Congratulations,' Quentin said when he walked into Jonathan Graham's office later that morning. 'I hear you just picked up another publishing house.'

Jonathan smiled his vintage Huck Finn smile. 'It was in the New York papers this morning. I hope Olivia didn't wake you too early.'

'A little after six, and I was up.'

'You can tell her I mean what I say. It makes sense to keep the two houses separate. For one thing, they've got different styles. They're good at different kinds of books.'

'And for another?'

'You've known Hallie longer than I have, and you know Olivia better. You tell me.'

'Each of them is going to be fighting tooth and nail to build a better house.

'You got it.'

Jonathan Graham was as good as his word. There was only one new rule, and it applied to both houses.

R and S and Unicorn were not permitted to bid against each other in auctions. The rule had repercussions. Since Hallie and Olivia couldn't compete for the same books, they ended up casting a wider net. And the confrontations between them, if not the competition, subsided slightly.

In September Olivia married Quentin in a small ceremony in the Fifth Avenue duplex. The wedding was scheduled to take place several days before the Frankfurt Book Fair. As soon as Hallie received her invitation, she told her secretary to rebook her flight to Germany. She'd decided to leave a few days early and make a stop in London. Then she wrote a note – a perfectly nice note, really – saying how sorry she was that she'd have to miss the wedding but she'd be in London at the time.

Olivia and Quentin stopped in Frankfurt on their wedding trip. Hallie ran into them one afternoon on the floor of the exhibition hall. Quentin looked even better than he had when Hallie had last seen him. Olivia looked sensational. She carried herself differently, too. Her head was high and her shoulders were squared, but there was no chip on them.

Hallie congratulated them both. Then she went back to her hotel room and called Will.

'What's up?' he asked, because they'd spoken only the night before, and they didn't usually speak daily when they were on opposite sides of an ocean.

'Nothing,' Hallie said. 'I just wanted to hear your voice.'

Two weeks later, on one of those blindingly bright

October days when the air is as clear and sharp as a Hopper painting, Frank Coyle called Jake and told him the divorce was final.

'You're a free man you lucky s.o.b.'

Jake wondered if the lawyer really envied him or was just making the appropriate noises. At one of their meetings, Coyle had spoken proudly of 'the missus,' but at another he'd gone off on a tangent about the number and diversity of available women in the world. 'You must be drowning in them,' he'd said, and there was actually a thin thread of spittle at the side of his mouth. The lawyer was salivating.

He had reason to. In the last decade of the twentieth century, Jake Fox was an endangered species – a single heterosexual male. Moreover, he had power, money, few bad habits, no addictions, a clean bill of health, and a strong sex drive. As if that weren't enough, he didn't even have another woman's children turning up every weekend. He was, as more than one woman had told him, too good to be true.

Jake thought of the lawyer's words as he crossed the backyard of the farm that night on the way to the woodshed. He bent and began putting logs in the canvas carrier. He was a free man. He straightened and lifted the carrier. And the world was full available women. He started back toward the house. It was his house now. His shoes made crackling sounds in the dead leaves. And one of those available women was inside it.

He stopped a few feet from the back porch. The light was on in the kitchen, and he could see her moving around as she put away the things they'd brought from town. She was young. Twenty-five or -six, or may -three. He never could remember. He stood in the dark yard watching her in the warm, brightly lit kitchen. She bent her head to do something at the table. A curtain of silky copper-colored hair fell forward over her face. She straightened and tossed the hair over her shoulder. Her profile was as pale and perfect as a Greek statue. She lifted a finger to her mouth. Her tongue darted out to lick it. The gesture was all the more erotic for its privacy. She didn't know she was being watched. He waited for a response. A flickering of tenderness. A flash of desire. A surge of lust. There was nothing. His mind didn't want her. His body didn't react.

He took a few more steps toward the house. His shoes crackled in the leaves. A chill wind whipped around his head.

He told himself to hurry. It was cold out here. He had the logs for the fire. The fire would warm him. So would she.

He stopped at the back porch. The carrier full of logs was suddenly too heavy to hold. He put it down on the steps. Then he sat beside it with his elbows on his knees and his head in his hands. He couldn't do it. He couldn't go back in the house.

He was still sitting that way when the woman with the curtain of copper-colored hair came out to look for him twenty minutes later.

When Herbert Shine called Hallie on that Friday afternoon he didn't tell her she was a free woman or a lucky one or even congratulate her. He simply told her the divorce was final.

She saw Will that night. He was leaving for Africa the next day. He had a lot on his mind. Letters to people he had to see. Books about them. Notes he'd made. Inoculations he'd had. Hallie never got around to mentioning the call from her attorney.

The next morning there was a limo waiting in front of Will's apartment. Hallie was going to drop him at the airport, then on to Connecticut. It had seemed like a good idea when they'd thought of it, but the last thing Hallie wanted this morning was to take a limo to the airport. The timing was terrible. She could barely bring herself to climb into the back seat. She kept thinking about that night so many years before, when Jake had picked her up at the airport. Then she'd remember that other night when he'd hired another limo and tried to surprise her again, and she hadn't been on the plane.

They said good-bye in front of the terminal. For a minute Will thought she was going to cry. For a minute she thought so too.

'I told you you should have come with me,' he said.

Hallie surprised him. He'd been expecting the usual reasons for not being able to accompany him on a trip. 'You were right,' was all she said.

They kissed good-bye quickly, the way people in airports do, and a little more desperately than they ever had. Then Will turned and walked into the terminal, and Hallie got back in the limo. It wasn't any better being alone in the back seat, but it wasn't any worse.

*   *   *

When Hallie had told her parents she'd come up for the weekend, she hadn't known the divorce was going to become final that Friday. She'd simply thought she'd like to get away for a weekend. Now she knew she needed to get away. She also knew it wouldn't work. Her loss and failure would follow her to Connecticut or Africa or wherever she ran. But still the image of that big white farmhouse of her youth kept coming back to her as a kind of solace. Hallie knew you couldn't go home again, but that weekend she couldn't help wanting to.

The limo pulled into the long drive leading up to the house. In the diamond-hard October sunlight, it glowed big and white and safe. Cecelia and Amos came down the steps from the porch to greet her. Amos hugged her. It was like leaning against a sturdy oak. Cecelia took her arm and led her into the living room. The asylum turned into a haunted house. Everywhere Hallie looked she saw pictures of herself with Jake.

'I can't believe it!'

'What can't you believe?' Cecelia asked.

'That you still have all these around.' Hallie reached out to indicate a framed photograph of her and Jake, but the movement was so abrupt she knocked it over. It fell to the floor and the glass inside the walnut frame shattered. They all stood staring down at it. Hallie didn't apologize.

'I agree with Hallie,' Amos said. 'I think it's time you cleaned house.'

'I guess I just keep hoping,' Cecelia said.

'Hoping! Hoping for what?'

'There's no reason to shout,' Amos told his daughter.

'There's every reason to shout. The man had an affair with my best friend. We've been separated for almost three years. Now we're divorced.'

'It came through?' Cecelia asked.

'It came through yesterday. And you tell me you keep hoping. Well, you can stop hoping. It's over. Finished. Dead.'

Hallie felt her parents eyes on her like spotlights revealing every flaw. She knew they were sorry for her, but she didn't want their pity.

She stooped, picked up the broken frame, and took the photograph out of it. Slowly, methodically, she began tearing it into pieces. They fluttered to the floor. The picture was nothing more than confetti. It lay at her feet on the wide floorboards that had endured two centuries of family use.

'Nothing in life is that final,' Cecelia said.

'God! Not again!' Hallie's voice was a screech, but this time Amos didn't tell her there was no need to shout. 'Another of St Cecelia's lectures on forgiveness. Tell us again how you forgave that typewriter against the wall. Tell us how the long-suffering wife had the room replastered and repainted. It must have been hell.'

The last word died and the sun-flooded room fell into an unnatural silence. Amos put his hands in his pockets and gazed at the floor. Cecelia's and Hallie's eyes locked together across the room. In the harsh midday glare they both looked painfully pale.

Without a word, Cecelia crossed the room, past the agonizingly tasteful early American furniture, past her husband, past her daughter. Her rubber-soled country shoes made soft-squeaking sounds on the floorboards of the big square front hall. A door opened and closed. Her footsteps crossed the porch and died away down the front steps.

Amos finally lifted his eyes from the floor. He and Hallie stared at each other. She was shocked. It wasn't like her mother to storm out of an argument. The gesture was too melodramatic.

'I'm sorry,' Hallie mumbled.

Amos just stood with his hands in his pockets and went on rocking back and forth. Unlike his daughter, he knew Cecelia hadn't stormed out. She'd just gone down to the pumphouse they'd converted into a study for him. She'd be back in a moment. She'd be back with the goods.

They heard Cecelia's step again on the porch, then the soft squeaking sounds across the front hall. She came into the room and faced Hallie. She was holding a manuscript to her breast, clutching it, really, the way an adolescent girl clutches her books.

'What's that?' Hallie asked.

'St Cecelia's canonization.' She dropped the manuscript on the long oak library table. It made a heavy thud in the silent room and knocked over another framed photograph. This one was of Amos and Cecelia.

'It's your father's manuscript,' Cecelia went on. 'I think it's time you read it.'

XLV

Cecilia looked up from the book she was trying to read as soon as Hallie appeared in the doorway to the sunporch. A stream of late-afternoon sun spilled across the floor. Hallie blinked into the slanting brilliance. She was still holding the manuscript.

'He's writing about your marriage, isn't he?'

Cecelia nodded.

'I never guessed.'

Cecelia closed her book. 'No, I made sure of that.'

Hallie crossed the room, sat at the other end of the wicker sofa, and put the manuscript on the table.

'But why?'

'Why did I want to keep it from you?'

'Why did you want to live a lie?'

'If you read that line in a novel you'd turn the manuscript down.'

'How can you joke about it?'

'I didn't joke about it then. I promise you that.' Cecelia thought for a moment. 'You know what I did when I found out? I got in the car. Amos had just bought me a Buick convertible for our anniversary. It was cream colored with red-leather upholstery and an automatic shift. In those days that was really something. I can see that car as clearly as I can remember that night. I got in the car and drove up to the hills. I kept driving for most of the night. Except when I stopped for drinks. Until that night, I'd never in my life walked into a bar alone. Nice women didn't in those days. But I walked into quite a few that night. Roadhouses, really. I remember in one a man tried to pick me up. I was terrified, but I was flattered too. I didn't think anyone would ever want me again.'

'You!'

'Yes, me, baby. Look what I was up against. Amos Porter wouldn't cheat on his wife with just anyone. He had to choose America's sex symbol. Half the men in the country were in love with Lily Hart. Amos Porter was sleeping with her. I let that man buy me a drink. Then I got back in the car and drove some more.'

'That was smart.'

'I wasn't feeling very smart that night.'

'And the next morning?'

'Amos came and got me. The state troopers called him. I did a pretty thorough job on the car.'

'You wrecked it?'

'It would have been hard not to in my condition. But I was lucky. I walked away with a few bruises and some glass from the windshield in my forehead. I had a scar for a while. Then it faded.'

'And you stayed with Amos.'

'I didn't have much of a choice.'

'But you did! You were still young. You'd worked before you'd married him. You'd even sold those short stories. You didn't need him to live.'

Cecelia smiled. 'But I did, baby. I did need him to live. Or at least I thought so at the time. It was a different era. Single women with jobs weren't career women. They were old maids.'

Hallie started to say something, but Cecelia went on before she could. 'Oh, I know there were exceptions. Women with the drive or talent or passion to be more. But I wasn't one of them. I wanted to be a wife and mother. It was what I was brought up to be. And I was never a rebel.'

Hallie wasn't sure whether she heard a touch of regret in her mother's voice.

They sat in silence for a while. The puddles of sunlight on the floor had faded, and the room was disappearing into the shadows, but neither of them moved to turn on a light.

'Are you ever sorry?' Hallie asked finally.

Cecelia didn't hesitate. She'd known the question was coming. It was the reason she'd told Hallie the story in the first place. She leaned over and took her daughter's hand.

'I'm not sorry I chose to stay with Amos. God knows he has his weaknesses. But every time I get angry, I think of all the things about me that bother him. Maybe that's the real secret to making a marriage work. just remembering you're as impossible as your mate.'

'I have a feeling we're not talking about you and Amos anymore.'

'A minute ago you asked me if I ever regretted going back to Amos. I wasn't sorry about that, but when you started to grow up, I began to see things a little differently. Of course, I wasn't exactly alone. The women's movement was in full swing. I wasn't part of it. You know that. And I never felt I was inferior to Amos or discriminated against or anything like that. It's pretty hard to feel sorry for yourself when you have a brilliant and successful husband and a child who gives you a great deal of pleasure and every material comfort. But every now and then, I did get a little tired of being introduced as "and his lovely wife".' Cecelia reached out and turned on a lamp. The room flared into light. They blinked at each other. 'I made up my mind that would never happen to you.'

'Thank you.'

'I wasn't asking for gratitude, baby. I didn't do it alone. Amos felt the same way. And God knows you have a mind of your own. But sometimes I wonder if we didn't all do too good a job.'

'You mean I would have been better off if I hadn't had a choice? If I'd had to go on with Jake? I don't believe that.'

'Neither do I, but that's not what I meant. A long time ago, I guessed that Jake's affair with Olivia had started when you were in London, and you got angry at me.'

'I'm sorry.'

'I'm not asking for apologies. Any more than I am for gratitude. I was right about the timing. Jake told me the whole story about going out to the airport to meet you. You weren't on that plane, but you hadn't bothered to let him know.'

450

'Didn't Amos ever forget to tell you he wasn't coming home for dinner or something like that?'

'Good Lord, does the fact that they do it make it all right?'

Hallie didn't answer.

'I'm going to make another guess about that night, Hallie. You didn't let Jake know you weren't coming home, but I bet you telexed your office.'

'How did you know?'

'Because I know Olivia. She didn't turn up at your apartment that night by accident. She went hunting.'

Hallie jammed her hands into the pockets of her trousers and stretched her legs out in front of her. She was no longer angry at Cecelia, but she was still angry.

'So what's the moral of this story? If you aren't going to telex your husband, don't telex your office?'

'I said I know Olivia. I also know you. We aren't talking about one night. We're talking about a way of life. I didn't want you to be totally dependent, but I did hope you'd find someone to share your life with. That takes work. As much as any career. Jake let you down. There's no question about it. But you let him down, too. There's only one difference. Jake betrayed you with sex, so the world condemns him. You betrayed him with work, so everyone admires you.'

'I never thought of it that way.'

'It's about time you did.'

There was another silence. Cecelia knew the pauses were as important as the words. She was giving things time to sink in.

'Even if you're right,' Hallie said finally, 'it's too late to make any difference.' She took her hands out of her pockets and stood. 'The divorce is final.'

Cecelia looked up at her daughter. The skin seemed to be pulled too tight over Hallie's cheekbones, and there were faint smudges under her eyes. 'I told you this afternoon. Nothing in life is final.'

'This is. Take my word for it. Jake doesn't care anymore.'

'How do you know?'

Hallie looked at Cecelia, then away. 'Jake has someone else.'

'Jake always has someone else. It's his nature. That doesn't mean he cares about her.'

'He does about this one. I heard the other day at lunch. She's been telling people she and Jake are looking for an apartment together.'

When Amos came up from the pumphouse around five, he was uneasy. He knew how Hallie had spent the afternoon, though he didn't ask her about it. He didn't even meet her eyes. He wasn't going to justify himself. He wrote what he had to. He stayed true to his art. If people wanted to see analogies with real life, that was their problem.

By the time the dinner guests began arriving, he'd managed a few tentative words and sidelong glances. By the time they'd left, he'd slipped back into his old persona. His wife had forgiven him a long time before. He saw no reason why his daughter shouldn't now. Hallie lived up to his expectations, as usual. Disappointment, even anger, didn't put an end to love, as she well knew. The next morning, before breakfast, Amos asked her if she'd like to drive into the village with him to get the Sunday papers. She knew he was holding out an olive branch. She grabbed it.

It was only a little after ten, but the village was already alive. Weekend visitors up from the city strolled Main Street, carrying bulky Sunday papers and grease-stained bags smelling of freshly baked bread and muffins. Locals cut back and forth across the town square to the First Congregational Church on one side and St Joseph's on the other.

Amos pulled up in front of the luncheonette. He said there was no point in parking the car. Hallie said she'd pick up the paper.

'Make sure it has all the sections,' Amos called after her. Hallie called back to him that she hadn't brought him an incomplete paper since she was twelve.

She passed from the bright October morning into the dim luncheonette. The old wooden screen door banged shut behind her. It took a minute for her eyes to adjust to the gloom. Fred, who'd worked behind the counter longer than Hallie had been buying papers, said that it was a nice morning and he hadn't seen her for a while. Hallie said he was right on both counts and handed him money for the paper.

She picked up a Sunday from the stack piled near the door. It must have weighed ten pounds. They were close enough to the city to get most of the ads. She rested the paper on one of the red leatherette stools and leafed through it. She had to go through it a second time to find the sports section. Amos rarely looked at it, but he liked to know it was there.

She picked up the paper and started for the door. Through the screen she could make out shadows on the other side. Just as she lifted her hand to pull the door open, someone pushed it from the other side. Hallie stood face to face with Jake and a woman with a mane of silky reddish-blond hair.

Hallie had two immediate thoughts. The first was that she should have known. She and Jake always used to come into the village to pick up the paper before breakfast on Sundays. The second was that sun glanced off the woman's hair as if it were polished copper. Hallie stood in the darkness feeling drab.

It took Jake's eyes a moment to adjust to the gloom. When they did, his arm dropped from the woman's shoulders. A familiar tic pulled at his lower lip.

They stood there for a moment. Hallie was looking up at him, he was looking down at her, and the woman was looking from one to the other of them, as if she were watching a slow-motion tennis match.

Hallie said good morning. Jake said hello. Or maybe it was the other way around. The woman looked from Jake to Hallie and back to Jake again. When she moved her head, her hair swung like a silk curtain.

All Hallie wanted to do was get out of there, but they were blocking the door. She moved to one side. In trying to get of her way, Jake managed to get back in it.

He tried to smile. It came out as a grimace. He made a strangled sound that was supposed to be a laugh. For some reason, he seemed to think introductions would help.

'This is . . . uh . . . Hallie Porter,' he said to the woman.

Hallie held out her hand.

'And this is . . . uh . . .' This time he hesitated for longer.

'Katherine Wales,' the woman said. It wasn't that she was composed, only less unhinged than the two of them.

Then Hallie said something about Amos waiting in the car, and Katherine Wales said something else about its having been nice meeting her, and Jake stepped aside. Hallie pushed out of the dim luncheonette into the blinding October morning. The sun made her face feel as if it were on fire.

'I hear you ran into Jake in the village,' Cecelia said that afternoon. Amos had gone down to the pumphouse to work, and she and Hallie were alone on the porch. The sun poured down, turning the afternoon back into summer. Hallie was in the hammock with one section of the paper, Cecelia in an Adirondack chair with another. Hallie didn't answer at first. The only sound was the squeak of the hammock and some mourning doves that had nested behind the house.

'Jake and Katherine Wales,' Hallie said finally.

'Is that the woman he's supposed to be moving in with?'

'Unless he's started cheating on this one early.'

'I thought we agreed it wasn't entirely Jake's fault. He had a little help from you. Or rather he didn't have enough.'

'All right. I admitted I made a mistake. Now can we leave it alone?'

'You still don't get it, do you?'

'Get what?'

'That conversation we had yesterday. It's those telexes, or a lack of one, all over again. When it comes to your work, you're not afraid to fight. Olivia or anyone else. And you're not afraid to fight dirty. Like those letters about *Women's Rites* that went out "accidentally." You'll fight tooth and nail for books and awards and success. But you won't lift a finger to hold on to Jake.'

Hallie caught hold of the railing and stopped the hammock. 'What if I lose?' she asked finally in a voice Cecelia hadn't heard in years. 'What if he tells me it really is too late? She was gorgeous. And young.'

'I admit it's a possibility. You wouldn't believe me if I said it wasn't.

Hallie let go of the railing and the hammock began to swing again. 'Exactly.'

'It was a possibility with the Max Perkins Prize and the new house, too.'

'That was different.'

'How?'

Hallie didn't answer.

'You're right, baby. You could lose.' Cecelia's head turned. Her eyes focused on the hills in the distance.

'But if you don't even try, you're sure to.'

They went back to reading the paper then. At least Hallie pretended to read it. But she returned to the subject once more that afternoon. She stopped in the middle of an article and looked up suddenly.

'I just thought of something! What about Will?'

Cecelia looked up from the 'Book Review' and met her daughter's eyes. 'I like Will.'

'So do I.'

'Exactly. You like him. But if you just thought of him this minute, you don't need me to tell you the answer.'

XLVI

In the old days in the railroad flat on Avenue A when faced with certain kinds of problems, Hallie used to ask herself what Olivia would do in the circumstances. Then she'd resolve to do the same and invariably end up doing the opposite. Hallie hadn't asked herself the question in years, but after her talk with Cecelia, she began asking it again. She also wasted a great deal of time concocting elaborate scenarios that answered it. When she heard through an editor that Jake was in Russia making a contribution to literary *glasnost*, she figured she had ten days of respite. She was wrong. Her mind kept writing those scenarios.

The practical aspects were the easy part. She and Jake still used the same travel agency they'd used when they were together. It was a piece of cake to find out when Jake was due home. They also still used the same limo service.

'Is the car taking anyone out to the airport?' Hallie asked the woman who booked reservations for the Executive Limo Service.

The woman said she'd check. Hallie's fingers beat a nervous tattoo on the desk.

'Nope. Just a one-way trip,' the woman said.

That took care of the physical problem of Katherine Wales. The emotional ramifications of Katherine Wales were more problematic, but Hallie wasn't going to let herself think about that. Olivia wouldn't have.

Jake's plane was due in on Sunday night. In some ways the day was a replay of that afternoon she'd picked up the phone and overheard Jake telling Olivia he was going to be late. Hallie's stomach roiled. At one point she was sure she was going to throw up the eggs benedict she'd toyed with during brunch. Jonathan Graham was in town, and brunch was the only meal he had free. Hallie was still Hallie. She agreed to meet him even though she'd already arranged to have the limo pick her up at four and knew she'd be in no condition to talk business from one to three. She didn't throw up the eggs benedict, but she must have picked up the phone half a dozen times between three and four to call Executive Limo and tell them to forget it. Each time, she asked herself what Olivia would do under the circumstances. Then she reminded herself what Olivia *had* done and hung up the phone.

She must have changed clothes a dozen times during that hour. She put on a suit, decided it was too formal, took it off. She tried trousers and a sweater. No, not trousers. The heap of clothes on her floor mounted. She reminded herself again of Olivia. For a moment she remembered the old days on Avenue A and the campaigns they'd waged for jobs and men. It would have been nice to have someone there cheering her on. Hallie settled on an unmatched skirt and jacket. The unmatched pieces were supposed to make it look as if this were a last-minute inspiration.

On the way out of the bedroom she caught a glimpse of herself in the full-length mirror. She would have gone back to change again, if the concierge hadn't already called from downstairs to say a car was waiting. Her skirt was too short, her jacket too boxy, her face gray as the afternoon.

It had started to drizzle. She knew she should have taken her Burberry. The doorman held an umbrella over her head as he escorted her in the shelter of the canopy from the building to the limo. He held the door open, then closed her into the deeply upholstered vault. The limo purred away from the curb.

Hallie sat in the back seat and stared through the rain-streaked windows. The smoked glass turned the afternoon even bleaker. The humidity would make her hair go limp. The few bites of brunch rioted in her stomach again. She was making a big mistake.

The traffic was heavy. The limo inched its way along the Van Wyck Expressway. Hallie wondered where all these people were going on a gloomy Sunday afternoon in late October. Every one of them probably had a more legitimate destination than hers.

Signs for particular airlines began to drift by the windows. How had she ever thought she could go through with this? She was no Olivia.

There was a small bar in the limo. She'd always laughed at that. Limo bars were for the dipsomaniacal or the pretentious. At least she'd thought they were till now. She reached for one of the fake cut-crystal decanters – she didn't even care which one – and poured half a glass. She thought of all the clichés about fool's courage and liquid courage. That was okay. She'd take any kind of courage she could get.

The limo pulled up in front of the terminal. The driver got out, came around, and held the door open for her.

That was when she knew she couldn't go through with it. She wondered again how she'd ever thought she could.

'You meet Mr Fox,' she said. 'I prefer to wait here.'

The driver had to open the front door to get out a piece of cardboard. Hallie pictured him standing at the gate with one of those handlettered signs. Fox.

It was raining harder now. Water sluiced down the tinted windows. She couldn't see a thing beyond the back seat. It would be hell getting a taxi, but she could do it. She still had time. She could get out of the limo, slip through the terminal, and come out at the taxi stand. She could be back in her apartment within the hour, safe and warm. Well, safe anyway.

She tried thinking of Olivia. It didn't help. Jake had left Olivia in the end. And now he was with Katherine Wales. An image the two of them on that Sunday morning flashed through Hallie's mind. Jake had had his arm around Katherine Wales's shoulders. Until he'd seen Hallie. She'd embarrassed him then. She was going to embarrass him now. And herself.

She'd been crazy to think she could pull this off.

She put the drink down. She reached for the door handle. It opened from the outside. From where she sat all she could see was a headless body. She would have known it anywhere. Even without the beautifully tailored pin-stripe suit. Especially without the pin-stripe suit.

He bent to get into the car. That was when he saw her. He stopped in midmovement. No. He didn't stop. He recoiled. She was sure of it. Then he climbed into the back seat. She retreated to the far corner.

'This is a coincidence,' he said. 'They usually drop off one customer before they pick up another.'

She started to laugh. She didn't think it was funny, but she was so nervous she couldn't help herself. It had never occurred to her he'd misunderstand her being there.

She stopped laughing as abruptly as she'd started. 'I'm not going anywhere. I mean, I was only coming out here. I mean, I thought I'd come out to meet you.'

He thought about that for a minute. 'Why?'

She hesitated for another minute. It felt like an hour. She thought of all the reasons she might give. She thought of what he might say to them. She thought of Katherine Wales with her silky copper-colored hair and her youth. Then she thought of Olivia and what she'd do in the circumstances.

'Because I owe you one. Two, really. I owe you for that first time you met me at the airport. And I owe you for the second time when I wasn't on the plane. I especially owe you for that one.'

The limo was back on the highway and moving quickly now, but in the back seat it was absolutely still. He sat staring at her. She sat staring back at him. Again, she asked herself what Olivia would do in the circumstances. The answer was unequivocal.

She started to move across the seat. A miraculous thing happened. Jake met her halfway.

Epilogue

Hallie knew she was taking a chance. Given the dispositions and drinking habits of writers and editors, publication parties provided enough opportunities for disaster indoors. If you held one outdoors, you were asking for trouble. It might rain. In New York in June it was likely to be too hot or too cold. Only one factor mitigated against these possibilities. Amos wouldn't allow them. He'd no more permit the weather to ruin the party to celebrate the publication of his fifteenth novel than he would a guest to disrupt it.

On a soft mauve evening early in June, three hundred of Amos's dearest friends gathered in the garden of the old Carnegie mansion to congratulate Amos on his most recent and stunning achievement. Across Fifth Avenue, Central Park lay like a green carpet rolling south and west toward the glittering skyline of the city. Outside the tall iron fence, ordinary mortals stopped and gawked at the well-dressed guests. Inside the beautifully manicured garden, waiters in immaculate white jackets circulated with trays of champagne and smoked salmon and caviar.

465

Sheila Dent had been planning the party for months. People had been calling for weeks to try to wheedle their way onto the guest list. Regrets only, the invitation had said. No one had regretted.

The names milling around the garden glowed as brightly as the lights that were just going on all over the city. The guest of honor, Amos Porter. His lovely wife, Cecelia Porter. Legendary corporate raider Jonathan Graham. Quentin Styles, publisher, sportsman, old rich. Olivia Collins, publisher, beauty, new rich. Will Sawyer, best-selling author and political activist just back from Nicaragua with a magnificent dark-skinned woman no one recognized but the photographers kept snapping because they knew how those cheekbones would look in the pictures. Carter Bolton, seven-figure novelist. Jake Fox, literary agent for presidents, celebrities, and even real writers. Hallie Porter, head of the fastest-growing publishing house in town.

The columnists jotted down names. The photographers jockeyed for position. One of them managed to get a shot of Jonathan Graham standing on the steps of the massive graystone mansion with the women who ran his two publishing houses. None of the three knew the picture was being taken. Jonathan Graham was squinting into the setting sun. Olivia Collins's eyes were focused over Graham's shoulder. And Hallie Porter stood with her hands crossed in front of her stomach in the classic pose of a pregnant woman.

Jonathan excused himself from his two publishers. The sky began to fade from mauve to pink. Hallie and Olivia stood looking down at the guests swirling around the garden.

Anyone who knew them would have assumed they were talking about books or business or personalities. A few years before they would have been. Now they had other things on their minds.

'When are you due?' Olivia asked.

'July.' Hallie was sure she could figure the time to the minute. 'The end of July.'

'How does it feel?'

'At the moment heavy. In the physical, not the spiritual, sense. And absolutely wonderful.'

'Does Jake think so, too?'

'Jake thinks so even more.'

They stood in silence for a moment, still watching the guests. They hadn't spoken in a long time, not long enough for Hallie to forget – she didn't have enough years left for that – but long enough for things to have changed again.

'How have you been?' Hallie asked finally.

'Happy. Unbelievably, unexpectedly, and' – Olivia laughed – 'many would say undeservedly happy.'

'You always said you'd run a house someday.'

'We both did. And now we are.'

'And you always said you'd live on Fifth Avenue. Not to mention Malibu, Palm Beach, Palm Springs, and . . . did I leave any out?'

'It's not just that, you know.' Olivia saw the smile that played around Hallie's mouth. 'Oh, I admit that doesn't hurt. I hated being poor. And I hated all the rest of it. White trash. Hick. Not our kind of people dear. Now I'm Olivia Collins, publisher of Rutherford and Styles and Mrs Quentin Styles, and if people think I'm not their kind of people, they don't say so. I love all that. I admit it. But the funniest part is . . .' Olivia hesitated. The word 'love' had always come easily to her, until she'd begun to mean it. Her eyes drifted from Hallie's face to the guests below them. Hallie's followed. Quentin Styles was the kind of man who stood out in a crowd. For one thing, he was tall. For another, he carried himself well. Even now, with his head inclined forward to catch the words of the woman he was talking to, he made an erect and impressive column of distinction.

A waiter passed a few inches from him. Quentin put the glass he was holding on the tray, took two fresh ones, and handed one to the woman without taking his eyes from her.

'Who's that?' Olivia asked.

'Her name is Maude Atherton.'

Olivia went on staring. 'She's very attractive.'

'Only if you think perfect features and a body that looks like an ad for a health club are attractive.'

'Anyway, as I was saying . . .' Olivia started again, then stopped as Maude Atherton put her hand on Quentin's arm and went up on her toes. She didn't exactly whisper in his ear, but even at this distance you could tell that she'd dropped her voice to tell him something confidential. He looked down at her and laughed.

'What's she doing here anyway?' Olivia asked. 'There are never any secretaries at Amos's parties.'

'You're only partly right. She used to be my secretary, but I had to make her an editor. It was either that or lose her to another house.'

'I take it she's ambitious.'

'Lends a new dimension to the word. Smart, too. In some ways she reminds me of you. When we were young.'

Over Olivia's shoulder Hallie saw Jake crossing the garden toward them. Even before he reached them, she knew what he was up to. He was going to tell her she should get off her feet. He was going to suggest they slip away. The hell with couple clout, he'd said the other night as they lay side by side in bed reading. They did that a lot these days. Hallie used her stomach as a bookrest, and when the baby kicked, the pages of her manuscript danced. The baby had been kicking for months now – editorial comment, Jake said – but they still stopped reading every time it did. They had to watch and marvel. The other night Jake had started to talk about names again.

'Executive,' he'd said. 'It's a good strong name.'

Hallie had laughed. 'Why don't we just call him CEO?'

'Sexist pig. I want to call *her* Executive. After the limo service. If it's a boy, I like Van Wyck.'

'Van Wyck Fox. How pretentious can you get?'

'I see nothing pretentious in naming the kid after the parkway where he was conceived.'

Now Hallie turned back to Olivia. 'Anyway, you were saying, the funniest part is . . .'

Olivia forced her eyes away from her husband and Maude Atherton and back to Hallie. Her attention seemed to drag behind. 'Oh, yes. The funniest part is, honey, it isn't just the trappings. It's Quentin. I love him. I really do. Who'd've thunk it?'

The two women went on staring at each other. Pregnancy had smoothed the angles of Hallie's face into curves of temporary contentment. Olivia's expression had a beautiful animal watchfulness. Hallie smiled. There was only the faintest touch of triumph in it.

'Now you know, Olivia honey. Now you finally understand. Because now you've got something to lose.'

More Compelling Fiction from Headline:

THE COURT

ELIZABETH WALKER

Vast, crumbling and magnificent, The Court has been the Yorkshire home of the Hellyns for centuries – it is part of them, part of their lives. But when the fifteenth earl dies, his four children are shocked to find themselves suddenly penniless and saddled with debt. Theirs is an awesome heritage – and it is one they doubt they can retain.

Mara, beautiful and sensuous, goes wildly off the rails. Men are attracted to her like bees to honey, but Mara falls for the one man she cannot have. The Hellyns may lose their home – now they face family disgrace. The younger sister, Lisa, forges an unlikely alliance with an Australian millionaire in a desperate bid to keep the family solvent. It isn't enough, for her or for The Court. Marcus, the heir, has his own demons to fight, and his twin, Angus, is forced to sacrifice his hopes to shoulder his brother's burdens.

The Hellyns are drawn back again and again to The Court. Through birth and death, triumph and tragedy, it shelters its children, but only one of those children loves it enough to save it . . .

'Earthy, exciting and well written . . . I was immediately hooked' *She*

Also by Elizabeth Walker from Headline
VOYAGE – 'Once you start reading you won't be able to stop' *Woman's World* – and ROWAN'S MILL – 'Whips along at a cracking pace – ideal' *Prima*

FICTION/SAGA   0 7472 3238 5   £4.50

More Compelling Fiction from Headline:

THE DIETER

A Delicious New Novel By

SUSAN SUSSMAN

'*The Dieter* is about gaining and losing: pounds, husbands, habits, and friends. It is a delightful novel, intelligent, witty and very moving.' Susan Isaacs

One little bite won't hurt . . . Chocolate doughnuts, fudge icing, deep-dish pizza with loads of extra cheese . . . the enemy pursues Barbara everywhere, invading her nostrils and seducing her taste buds.

It all begins when Barbara, as a gesture when her best friend dies of cancer, gives up smoking – overnight. At first it's hardly noticeable that she's gaining a little weight – after all, she always was on the thin side. The next few pounds, she reasons to herself, are just temporary. The next *few?* That's when it starts getting hard. And Barbara's husband, her children, her friends – all are behaving quite differently towards her.

Driven into the clutches of Weight Watchers, Nutrisystems and Nautilus, Barbara finds her problems grow with her waistline. Until she goes back to work and meets Mae, a sexy, rumpled crime reporter who helps her view of the world expand, too. So maybe thin isn't perfect . . . maybe size 8 doesn't equal happiness . . . after all, life does have riches to be savoured . . . delicious, spicy, sweet, scrumptious life . . .

The Dieter – the best no-calorie treat of the year!

'For every women who's ever wanted to whittle down her waistline, *The Dieter* is a funny, moving, thoughtful tale . . . It's a delicious novel' *Woman's World*

'Poignant, brave, and so very real' *She*

'Merciless in her appraisal of how women use weight problems to disguise deeper emotional traumas. Susan Sussman's novel is funny, feisty and compulsive' *Time Out*

FICTION/GENERAL   0 7472 3315 2   £3.99

A selection of bestsellers from Headline

FICTION

THE COURT	Elizabeth Walker	£4.50 ☐
LANDSCAPE OF LIES	Peter Watson	£3.99 ☐
RAGTIME GIRL	Elizabeth Warne	£4.50 ☐
THE GLITTER AND THE GOLD	Fred Mustard Stewart	£4.50 ☐
THE PLUNDERED LAND	Fiona Kendall	£4.50 ☐
BALKENNA	Gary Shearston & Michael Thomas	£4.99 ☐
VOYAGE	Elizabeth Walker	£4.50 ☐

NON-FICTION

THE GOLDEN SCREEN	Dilys Powell	£6.99 ☐
SMOKEY: INSIDE MY LIFE	Smokey Robinson with David Ritz	£4.99 ☐
MICROWAVE GOURMET	Barbara Kafka	£5.99 ☐

SCIENCE FICTION AND FANTASY

INTO NARSINDAL Chronicles of Hawklan 4	Roger Taylor	£4.99 ☐
THE NEXUS	Mike McQuay	£4.50 ☐

All Headline books are available at your local bookshop or newsagent, or can be ordered direct from the publisher. Just tick the titles you want and fill in the form below. Prices and availability subject to change without notice.

Headline Book Publishing PLC, Cash Sales Department, PO Box 11, Falmouth, Cornwall, TR10 9EN, England.

Please enclose a cheque or postal order to the value of the cover price and allow the following for postage and packing:
UK: 80p for the first book and 20p for each additional book ordered up to a maximum charge of £2.00
BFPO: 80p for the first book and 20p for each additional book
OVERSEAS & EIRE: £1.50 for the first book, £1.00 for the second book and 30p for each subsequent book.

Name ....

Address ....

....

....